And about the envious brain cold poison clings and doubles all the pain life brings him. His own woundings he must nurse, and feels another's gladness like a curse.

—AESCHYLUS, *AGAMEMNON*

ALSO BY SAV R. MILLER

MONSTERS & MUSES

Promises and Pomegranates
(includes the novella "Sweet Sin")
Vipers and Virtuosos
Oaths and Omissions
Arrows and Apologies
Souls and Sorrows
Liars and Liaisons

MONSTERS WITHIN

Endless Anger

Jealous Rage

San xoxo

Jealous Rage

SAV R. MILLER

sourcebooks
casablanca

Published by Sourcebooks Casablanca, an imprint of Sourcebooks
1935 Brookdale RD, Naperville, IL 60563-2773
(630) 961-3900
sourcebooks.com

Cataloging-in-Publication Data is on file with the Library of Congress.

The authorized representative in the EEA is Dorling Kindersley
Verlag GmbH. Arnulfstr. 124, 80636 Munich, Germany

Printed and bound in the UK and distributed
by Dorling Kindersley Limited, London
001-356664-Jan/26
CPI 10 9 8 7 6 5 4 3 2 1

For those who found solace in
pretending to be someone else.

Content Note

Jealous Rage is a dark academia romance containing material that may not be suitable for all audiences, including: explicit sexual scenes, graphic violence, graphic depictions of rape, sexual assault, sexual violence, gore, sex cults, ritualistic sacrifices, and murder.

For a full list of content warnings, please visit savrmiller.com.

Jealous Rage is the second book in the Monsters Within series, which is a second-generation spin-off of the Monsters & Muses series. For the best reading experience, *Jealous Rage* should be read after completing *Endless Anger*.

In addition to US academic institutions, Avernia College (and Fury Hill) was heavily inspired by ancient Greece and Rome, as well as their mythologies. Some words, phrases, and spellings may have been altered to fit within the context of the story.

Secret Societies

Secret societies move in the shadows and write their histories in blood. Can you follow their trail through Avernia College?

The
Curators

Death's
Teeth

Daughters of
Persephone

Visio
Aternae

Playlist

"Risk"-Gracie Abrams

"Granite"-Sleep Token

"Gethsemane"-Sleep Token

"Fable"-Gigi Perez

"Not Strong Enough"-boygenius

"Medicate Me"-Rain City Drive x Dayseeker

"In My Room"-Julia Wolf

"Exit Music (For a Film)"-Radiohead

"Los Angeles"-St. Vincent

"Talk"-Hozier

"i'll remember tonight"-sombr

Chapter 1

Elle

FURY HILL, NEW HAMPSHIRE, IS A DEAD TOWN.

Even if it wanted to come to life, I suspect resuscitation would be difficult given the only two places open past ten on the weekend are Lethe's, a little brick bar the local college kids frequent, and a tiny gas station off the highway that smells like old doughnuts and wet floors.

Or maybe I'm just bitter. Coming from a massive city like LA to some Podunk with a gloomy film clinging to the air will do that to a person.

I scan the plethora of trinkets and travel-size items available to purchase at the convenience store attached to the gas station. The one thing I stopped in to find, though, is the only thing they seem to be out of.

There's ChapStick in every color and flavor, wet wipes, solar-powered dash decorations that fidget while you drive. They even have a variety of birth control products—from condoms to sponges and spermicides, if you've got a late-night, last-minute need, the Fury Hill Stop N Go has you covered.

Which makes sense, I guess, considering the biggest draw to the town *is* Avernia College, and statistically speaking, one in every four college students gets an STI. Options for prevention are smart.

But there are no lighters.

Not the cheap BICs you can grab in a five-pack. Not the kitchen ones with the handles. Not even a Zippo or box of matches.

Sighing, I lean forward and press my forehead into the top shelf.

This is so pathetic.

Ten months ago, I was waking up at my beachfront apartment with a heart full of dreams.

Nine months ago, someone went out of their way to crush them.

It's a strange feeling, watching everything you've ever wanted go up in flames before you've even managed to grab on to it. Grieving something that didn't really belong to you is both pointless and unending.

What's worse, I wonder—the actual end of your life or a metaphorical death you relive every time you open your eyes?

I wouldn't be in Fury Hill at all if my parents hadn't expressed grave concern over my mental state when I moved back in with them. They had relatives over daily, subtly checking my wrists and keeping me from the internet as if I was one sleazy tabloid article away from ending it all myself.

As if I'd let a man have that satisfaction.

A throat clears beside me, and I jump. My jacket sleeve gets caught on the shelf corner, and it pulls away from the stand it's attached to, sending the contraception flying.

I let out a squeal, grabbing for the metal at the same time a large, veiny hand appears, catching it before it can collapse. Warmth seeps into my side as a second hand joins, fitting the hooks back into place with a satisfying *click*.

Breathing hard, I glance at the stranger, my chest constricting as I scan his profile: a smooth, chiseled jaw that could easily be on display in some art museum right now, medium brown hair that's tousled from the wind, or maybe his fingers, and soft lips with the slightest bow in the center that I could fit the tip of my pinkie in.

He turns to me, and my breathing stalls entirely as I meet his eyes. Soft and guarded, the color of raw jade, they rove over my face as if inspecting me for injury.

I want to cut myself on any of the sharp angles of his face, but it's the eyes I can't look away from.

The man clears his throat again. I blink, waiting for one of us to speak, though my tongue won't unstick from the roof of my mouth to do so.

This is what movie stars wish they looked like. Adonis in a modern body. A man the ancient Greeks would write epic poems about. Michelangelo would have killed to immortalize such perfection in stone.

Silently, he offers me a black box. I swivel my gaze down, taking in the dark red sweater he has on, the umber chinos, pausing to admire the hands again as my stomach cramps.

Whether it's from the visceral attraction I'm feeling or PMS, I can't be sure. Not that I'm paying much attention to my body other than the heat radiating through me.

"I didn't mean to startle you," he says, averting his eyes. "Here's your…"

Pink stains his lightly tanned features as he trails off, flushing his entire face.

Finally, I look down at the box he's attempting to offer.

A vibrator.

Of course.

Of *course* they sell them here and that's the item he happened to pick up.

I shake my head. "Oh, no, that's not mine."

"Well, not yet. You haven't paid for it, presumably."

Yep, PMS cramps. Definitely not getting fluttery feelings from this guy. "I wasn't *going* to pay for it."

"I'm not sure this is worth a theft charge," he says, turning the box in his hands. The text on the side says Personal Massager; Thirteen Different Pulsating Modes to Satisfy. "Despite the messaging here, nothing at the Stop N Go lasts terribly long."

"Maybe I don't need longevity."

Jesus *Christ*, what am I even saying? I don't have a hair-trigger clit, and it's not like this man asked.

He stares at me for a beat, an unreadable expression on his face. The flush from before seems to dissipate a little, the natural color of his skin returning slowly.

I sway on my feet. "Um, besides, like I said, I wasn't getting that."

Both our gazes slide to the condoms dangling at eye level, some still swinging from the earlier commotion. His brows quirk as if in understanding, and I groan internally.

"Wait, no—"

"Hey." He places the box on a lower shelf, where I somehow missed an entire row of personal massagers. "I'm not judging."

Before I can say anything more, he moves down the aisle toward the ready-made deli food.

My throat feels funny as I watch him crouch down, peering at the individual pizzas.

"Staring is impolite," he notes without glancing at me.

"I…" My palms are sweaty, and I have no idea why I'm getting so tongue-tied. I've been performing onstage for audiences for as long as I can remember; talking to strangers has never been a hardship. "So is judging."

"But I said I wasn't judging."

"With judgment in your eyes."

His nostrils twitch as if in amusement. "Sounds like projection to me."

"Projection? You think I'm judging myself?"

He doesn't reply, instead reaching for a box of pizza, lifting it to read the ingredients.

Irritated, I turn away and pick up the items that have fallen to the ground. When I straighten, I hit my head on the shelf, displacing it once more. The man catches it again before the heavy piece can fall on top of me.

The edges are sharp, and he grabs it right as the corner scrapes my cheek, hauling it out of the way.

"You're quite clumsy," he says, holding the pizza in one hand and the shelf in the other. "Get what you needed this time? I think they cost a little less if you buy in bulk."

I hold up my fists, which are clutching a dozen single-packs of condoms. They fall to the ground when I open my fingers. "There's that nonjudgment again."

"What you do in your free time is none of my business," he says, shrugging.

"There's nothing wrong with casual sex."

Something flashes in his eyes for the briefest moment, an eclipse that's gone by the time I blink. "Never said there was."

"In fact," I continue, my nerves jumbling up the longer I'm

in his presence, "a woman should always take precautions into her own hands. You can't solely rely on a man to be prepared or safe."

He doesn't say anything.

For some reason, I keep talking. "Besides, birth control is pro-feminist, even if some of the methods aren't."

"Is that so?"

"Yes. Like the IUD? Novel invention, barbaric insertion practices. Most doctors don't even *offer* pain medicine before the procedure, and they try to downplay the horrors. I've heard stories, you know? My aunts, my friends, my cousin—"

"Not personal experience?"

A shiver skates down my spine. "No. I take the pill religiously. Have since I was fifteen. Although back then, it was for these really awful periods I'd get, where the cramping was so bad I'd vomit, and there was no other way to alleviate my suffering. It cut into my rehearsals for community productions, kept me from going out with friends. Turned out to be endometriosis, which explained a lot."

He continues staring at me, his expression blank, and I scream inside.

Someone shoot me in the face. Please.

For some reason, I can't seem to stop myself.

"But back to the casual sex—"

An employee in a gray uniform comes out, their blue eyes wide as they approach the aisle. They say something to the man in a different language, and he replies easily, setting the shelf on the ground.

The employee exhales, offering a timid smile before heading to the front of the store again to continue counting lottery tickets.

"Was that French?" I ask, peering up at the man. He's got at least eight inches on me, nearly as tall as my father, which feels sort of rare. The men in my family have always felt like giants compared to the average people I stumbled upon growing up or even in LA.

"Oui," he replies, abandoning me once more to peruse the other end of the aisle. "My maternal grandmother was originally from France. She taught it to us to keep us connected to our heritage."

Huh. I wonder what that feels like.

"Are you from around here?"

"Born and raised." He still doesn't refocus on me. "Am I correct to assume you're not?"

"What would make you think that?"

"Grandeur Playhouse jacket." His gaze flickers to me for a split second, and he nods at the insignia embroidered on the breast of my hoodie. "Not many people from Fury Hill know about LA community theater. Especially not enough to have its merch."

"Then how do *you* know about it?"

He says nothing, which I find infuriating. Here I've already spilled half my life story, and all I know about him is that he has French ancestry and is from Fury Hill, which I could have guessed.

A man who looks like that doesn't show up in a place like this by choice. He must have deep family ties or financial obligations.

I squint at his handsome face as he scans the nutrition label of a Pop-Tart. He tucks a brown sugar and cinnamon one beneath his arm with the pizza, then circles around the end of the aisle, heading for a display case against the far wall with bottled drinks.

A part of me expects him to grab a box of cheap wine from the alcohol section—the haphazard, late-night meal and disheveled appearance make me think he's single, living alone, and probably prepping for the new semester that starts soon—but he goes for green tea instead.

Shaking off the encounter, I try to compartmentalize my embarrassment and get back to the task at hand. If I'm late to meet Quincy and Asher, they'll never let me live it down, and I'm not trying to spend the next sixteen weeks as their mutual punching bag.

I got enough of that as a kid. My sister and brother were quiet and preferred their alone time, where I was outgoing and the life of the party. I wanted to be surrounded by people and the center of attention, which is how I got into acting in the first place.

Lot of good that interest did me over the last seven years, but I digress.

Not everything works out the way you hoped. That doesn't mean it's the end of the world.

At least that's what I'm trying to convince myself.

After spending a solid five minutes scouring the shelves for a lighter of some sort, my shoulders slump in defeat. As I turn the corner of a display case empty-handed, patting my jacket for my phone, the toe of my shoe catches on the heel of someone else's.

I grit my teeth, pinching my eyes shut as a solid wall of muscle grunts ahead of me. My nose bends, colliding with his back, and for the first time, I get a short whiff of his cologne: something soft, masculine, and woodsy with a touch of citrus.

His exhale is loud in the small store, and I feel it in my chest somehow.

"You should really look where you're going," he says, turning with a white plastic bag in hand. "Leaving without a purchase?"

"Ah, yeah. I've got someplace to be, and I can't find what I was looking for."

"So not condoms then?"

I clench my teeth, my eyes narrowing. "No."

"Right. Because you're on the pill." He pauses but starts again before I can reply. "You know that does nothing to protect against STIs, right? Most healthcare professionals recommend two methods of contraception."

"To prevent pregnancy."

"Doesn't sound like a bad habit either way."

"You sound like my *dad*," I say. "Or a teacher."

"I'm trying to be helpful."

"By mansplaining contraception to a grown woman."

"Public education sometimes fails people."

I let out a groan, slapping my hands over my eyes. "This is such a weird conversation to be having with a stranger."

"Or perhaps it's a perfectly civil conversation to be having," he suggests with a shrug. "As I said—no judgment."

"Which was a lie." My hands fall to my sides. "I was looking for a lighter or some fire-starting equivalent."

"What for?"

"Um…" I clasp my hands behind my back, posturing as I push my chest out.

The stranger glances briefly at my offered cleavage, his face blossoming a bright pink once more. My insides flutter, warmth spreading through my limbs like liquid honey, but then he returns his gaze to my face.

Waiting.

"I have a meeting," I say finally.

"A meeting where a lighter is required?"

"Is *that* your business?"

"Well, I don't know. You seemed to think your menstrual history was my business, so I'm not exactly sure where lines are being drawn at the moment."

Heat scorches my face, and I imagine my skin matches his as he reaches into his pants pocket, pulling out a gold Zippo lighter. There's a symbol etched onto the front of the lid, though it's difficult to fully make out what it is since it's worn, likely from years of use.

"Here." He reaches forward, the plastic bag jostling as he overturns my wrist, placing the lighter in my palm without skin-to-skin contact.

"I can't take this."

"You're not going to find a lighter or matches anywhere in Fury Hill," he says. "An incident a few years back at the town's favorite watering hole left city officials uneasy, and they've all but outright banned the sale. You could drive to Concord, but I'd hate to see you miss your *meeting*."

It's clear he thinks the meeting is code for sex, but I don't care. Better he believe that than be privy to what I'm actually up to.

I close my fingers around the lighter as he withdraws. "But it looks expensive. Or important at least. Is it a family heirloom? Memorabilia from your veteran great-grandfather's estate?"

The man chuckles, and I find the sound intoxicating. My lips part as if to ask to hear it again, but I bite down on the urge.

"Nothing like that," he says. "Just consider it a loan."

"But loans are given with the intent of being returned." I frown. "I don't know anything about you really. How am I supposed to find you to give it back?"

A smirk tilts his face. "Should something catch fire tonight in Fury Hill, *temptress*, perhaps it'll be I who finds you."

Chapter 2

Sutton

MOONLIGHT FILTERS THROUGH THE SKYLIGHT OF A SECLUDED stairwell in the Apollodorus, the second-largest library on Avernia College's campus. Its basement is a spiraling labyrinth, used for storage and sealing off depravity from the general public.

The celestial glow is the only illumination afforded me as I knock on a door marked STAFF, though it's technically mislabeled.

More than staff come through here. Just not everyone is welcome.

You need an invite. A stamp or brand.

And a mask.

I flash the gold-embossed invitation at the door, and a slot opens, snatching it from me. Within seconds, I'm welcomed into an expansive underground territory of antiquated luxury.

I'm still reeling a bit from the encounter at the Stop N Go earlier, my fingers tingling where they'd voluntarily touched another person, even if through the sleeve of their jacket. But there'd been something about that woman that drew me in from the instant I saw her glaring at the gas station's selection of condoms.

Normally, I resist such interactions, but her face had flushed a deep red, and I found myself unable to stay away. She'd smelled delightful too, like freshly ground vanilla beans and warm honey.

Which makes her bad news, but that's all right. It was clear she was a tourist of some sort, so I have no expectation of seeing her again.

Dvorak's Romance in F Minor caresses my ears as I step inside the underground ballroom, its elegance almost enough to obscure the reality that we're tucked away where many have met their untimely demise over the centuries.

It's one of the school's better-kept secrets, but you can still feel it in the air. That volume of blood doesn't leave the walls it's shed upon, no matter how many coats of dark green paint or what polished hardwood floors you place over it.

Nearly every building on campus has a similar story though. Death is as much a part of the fabric of our university as the intricate network of references and stellar academics needed to apply.

An ache flares behind my temple, splitting my skull in half. I should've taken a pill to ward off the migraine before I came, but I suppose there's no time now.

One doesn't leave a Death's Teeth function until they've fulfilled their duties.

Mors neminem manet.

Death waits for no man.

Two large black marble fireplaces flank the immediate area, their warmth seeping beneath the mask I've donned for the occasion. Discomfort radiates over my skin as I'm guided into a tall ebony chair with red wine–colored cushions at the center of the room, then handed a short glass of amber liquid and instructed to relax.

A masked man and woman in velvet gold cloaks kneel at my feet as I spare a quick glance around the room; three halls are blocked off by similarly costumed guards, who remain expressionless even as the atmosphere ripples with lust.

The grand piano in the corner next to a harpist dilutes the sounds of moaning and slick flesh being manipulated, but I'm aware of the acts happening around me nonetheless.

Shiny gold candle sconces and floor candelabras light the room, shrouding my fellow patrons in flickering tenebrosity. Only their silhouettes are revealed as folks grind and writhe against one another, seeking pleasure down here like they somehow deserve it.

Debussy's Estampes replaces the sonata from before, and for a moment, I'm not participating in this space at all. I'm eleven years old, watching my twin sister twirl around in a ballerina's tutu while our mother enchants us with tunes from her favorite French composers.

It would be only a few short years before arthritis would rob her of the ability to play the piano at all.

The man at my feet slides his large, brown hand up my thigh, pinching the material of my slacks, and I'm pulled from my rumination. Suddenly, I'm back in the basement, where Avernia's most depraved can exploit my weaknesses.

My body tenses up of its own accord. A conditioned response.

I ignore it. Or try to at least.

The woman beside him leans in as well, gliding her flushed-pink fingers along my forearm. Over the faint scarring on the back of my left hand.

I grit my teeth, reaching down to rub the mangled skin.

She perks up, the mask covering all but her mouth. It shifts slightly as she moves to take my thumb between her lips.

"Your hands are cold, Elder," she coos. "Would you like our assistance in warming up?"

It's not quite that simple, but I don't feel like explaining Raynaud's to strangers.

Next to her, the man slinks closer, grabbing hold of me. His mask stays perfectly in place, his short, curly hair askew from where the material's a bit too large for his face.

He presses a kiss to my wrist, tangling his tongue with hers as she retreats from my thumb. Their saliva coats my skin as they kiss over me, around me, like I'm not a person and merely an object for their mutual sexual gratification.

An organization ruled by death only knows how to satisfy their carnality. They seek sin that gives purpose to their lives, making the cycle worthy of its inevitable end.

I never wanted to be a part of it, but once they decide they want you, there's no way to decline.

You're *in* it. Forever.

Til death do you part.

Anticipation or unease sluices through my veins. Without withdrawing from the woman, the masked man finds my lap. He presses, searching, and expertly frees the button and fly of my pants with just one hand.

I swallow when hers joins. They fish me out together, and my nostrils flare as I gaze around the room again. My bones itch to crawl out of my skin, but I force myself to stay put, looking for any signs of note.

A stolen glance that lingers far too long. The lopsided tugging of a mouth as its owner enjoys my misery. Something that hints they know I'm not fully invested.

This is part of the role. The *main* part. At least at these parties.

Things change outside the Apollodorus. Aboveground, within the wrought iron gates separating us from the Primordial Forest and Fury Hill beyond, expectations are different.

Destruction scrapes at the fringes of this university, so we feign ignorance. Bind ourselves to secrecy and anonymity. But the fabric is being torn, even as tradition aims to keep it whole.

And beyond the fence… That's where deterioration awaits.

Death to those who refuse to fear it.

My sister paid that price, so the story goes.

Not that it matters. I remain out of obligation—and because no one's ever left the organization and lived to tell about it.

One of the masked figures takes my cock in their mouth, but I don't bother looking down to see who. It doesn't make a difference—I stay soft. Flaccid. Underwhelmed by their attempts.

I close my eyes and let my hips rock forward a bit. My jaw clenches so tight that stars burst behind my eyelids.

Nausea spreads in me like a violent maelstrom, threatening everything in its path.

A flash of pain rips through my limbs.

My lungs expand as if they intend to explode.

A dream—no, a memory. The sensation of suspension—of being helpless—tears through me, shredding my insides on contact. Hands everywhere, all at once, despite pleas to cease.

My breathing hitches. Two tongues find my slit, lapping lazily.

I grip the arms of my chair until my fingers are numb.

Terror slides into my esophagus, blocking my airway.

"What's the matter, Elder?" the woman rasps, rubbing her face against my leg. "You seem pent-up. We can fix that."

"Yeah," the man agrees, the word vibrating against me. A deep gagging noise drowns out the sound of the piano for a moment, and I realize it's him sucking me down. "Relax and use us. We're here to serve you, Elder Dupont."

Part of me wants to note that those are opposing forces—I can hardly let loose and use them at the same time.

I will myself to unclench, but nothing happens. It never does.

The breath stalls in my chest. I count to ten and then twenty, waiting for my dick to cooperate, but all I can do is focus on my breathing. It comes in short, angry bursts, choked by my own fear.

A migraine pounds behind my eyes, fueling the nausea roiling around my gut.

I flinch when one of them—the woman, I see when I open my eyes—presses her lips to mine.

That's it. The final straw.

Gasping silently, I tear myself from the chair, stumbling over the masked pair when I get to my feet. My fingers tremble as I refasten my pants and slide them casually into my pockets, clearing my throat.

Other partygoers look over, pausing mid-fuck to stare at the commotion. A figure in a dark crimson cloak watches from the shadows. Her mask—gold and oblong, with two snakes slithering up the sides like horns—hides her face, but her pale skin is exposed when she lifts a hand as if to stop the party altogether.

The Director. Mainly responsible for throwing these soirees—ornamental and not much else. She holds no real power over the Death's Teeth organization, especially if I'm around, despite my objections to claiming responsibility.

Once you do that, the line between selling your soul and giving it away for free is erased. There's no way to differentiate: You're just as awful as the rest of them.

She looks at me for several beats, as does the rest of the party. After a moment, though, she flicks her wrist and turns away, sending a shiver down my spine.

The party resumes. Moans fill the air again, drowning me in their noise.

I should stay, if only to keep up appearances. The more I leave early, the more they pay attention to what I'm doing—or rather, *not* doing.

But I don't want to focus on that at the moment, so I duck out instead.

Again.

The Director's voice is a sensual caress as I pass by on my way to the exit. "There's always next time, Professor."

Yes, I think as I extract myself from the crowd, keeping my face down. *That's precisely the problem.*

I make my way through Avernia's overlapping quadrants, past the Lyceum—the main academic building, a large castle-like structure with its courtyard bordered by various sculptures—and toward the Elysian Dorms, a section of campus home to the four main student housing buildings.

A bright orange haze cuts against the starry night sky, filling me with the heavy dread that's been a perpetual nuisance since an incident in the caves last semester ended with the deaths of several students.

Only a few made it out alive. My younger brother, Beckett, was one of them—though not a hero by any definition.

He was the match who incited the slaughter, and he nearly paid for it with his life.

I don't want to imagine the catatonic state Mother would've been pushed into had she lost a second child. Bellamy's death is still a sore subject eight years later.

For all of us.

The clock tower in front of the Obeliskos chimes midnight, and I cut to my left, heading for the light.

At the edge of campus property, where a wrought iron fence cuts off the Primordial Forest, a house is engulfed in angry flames.

It's the dean's. The double-paned windows on the second floor are lit up as a fire ravages the lower level, snaking through the wrap-around porch to cut off access inside and out.

A shadow passes by an upstairs doorway, frantic. Searching, likely, for a way out.

Someone different might spring into action and assist him.

Not me though.

Dean Bauer's a fraud, and given his affiliation with the Curators—the shady organization my brother *was* president of—I'm inclined to believe he had more to do with those students' deaths than he lets on.

He probably has more to do with the unsavory things that happen at Avernia than he'll ever admit.

Three figures walk in my direction, away from the scene as the fire rages on. Smoke fills the night air, casting a sickly buzz across the cobblestone pathways and surrounding buildings.

It's clear they set the fire. Or at least one of them did. The Fury

Hill Fire Department should be showing up soon and will have questions—even if they ultimately end up with little to report.

That's how Avernia operates. Mystery and intrigue are the reason it remains open, and the board has first responders in its pocket.

My gut churns as the hooded group passes by, though I get a sudden whiff of something as they do—a sweet scent, just barely discernible in the night air.

Vanilla and honey.

I stumble to a stop. The shorter figure turns slightly, pausing as well, but it's impossible to fully make out their identity because of the ski masks they have on.

There's no way it's her. *The universe cannot be that cruel.*

All I did was lend her a lighter. Surely the implications aren't *that* far-reaching.

My mouth parts, but no words escape. I'm not sure what I'd say either way. I don't exactly come off looking good here considering I wasn't going to help the dean out.

Neither of us moves for the briefest moment, and then the figure carries on, scurrying away to catch up with the others. That vanilla and honey scent lingers, but the longer I stare at the space they were just occupying, the easier it becomes to convince myself that I'm imagining things.

I learned long ago not to believe in coincidence. If she were here for something as big as *this*, I'd know.

Right?

Instead of pursuing the thought further, I continue on to my apartment without a word.

Chapter 3

Elle

"DOES EVERYONE FEEL BETTER NOW THAT THEY'VE TORCHED the dean's house?"

Aurora swings her golden blond ponytail from side to side as she stabs the lone olive swimming in her martini glass. No one else at the booth says anything, and she exhales, shaking her head.

My brother leans his forehead on his girlfriend Lucy's shoulder, practically smothering her in the corner. Quincy sits on the other side of him, wiping the lenses of her cat-eye glasses with a cloth from her cross-body purse.

Both their midnight-colored locks have gotten longer since I saw them last, with Asher's falling into his eyes and Quincy's bangs sweeping into her brows.

It's a little disturbing how much they resemble our father, stoic expressions and all. Considering they just made me an accomplice to arson at the school where I *just* enrolled, you'd think they could stand to look a little guilty.

"No one feels better at all?" Aurora repeats.

"I don't feel worse," Lucy says.

"You also had nothing to do with it," I point out.

"So…what now? Vengeance didn't work, so are you just destined to be traumatized by the shit that happened last semester for the rest of your lives?" Aurora groans, bouncing in the seat next to me. A cousin by proximity, not blood, but as much a part of our family as anyone else considering how close all our parents are.

"Shut *up*, Ror," Asher grumbles, closing his eyes. "Some of us are trying to sleep here."

"We're in a public bar," she snaps at him. "Maybe you should go home and be a dud there."

He threads his fingers through one of the crimson streaks in Lucy's raven locks. "If I leave, I'm taking my girlfriend with me."

Aurora frowns, then returns her attention to Lucy. "Come *on*, Luce. This is the spring semester of our senior year. It's supposed to be fun."

Lucy's blue eyes dance as she tosses her cousin—by blood, since their dads are brothers—a look. Her fingers tap a constant rhythm on the table, always in motion. "You've been using that line since we were freshmen."

"And for almost four years, I've suffered through your endless rejections." Aurora leans against me, throwing a hand against her forehead. "Nelly, drink with me. *Please*."

I make a face. "Not sure you're helping your case with that atrocious nickname."

"No one invited *me* to set anything on fire," she says, pouting. "Haven't I earned the right to regression here?"

"Jesus, all right, *fine*." I slide from the booth and grab Quincy's arm, dragging her out with me. "A round of Kamikazes coming up."

We make our way to the bar at the other side of the room,

which is not nearly as packed as I'd expect a college dive to be right before the start of the semester. Maybe it's the bitter cold outside, though, keeping students away tonight.

Lethe's is practically a ghost town, so I put in our order and lean my elbows against the counter, aware of my sister's sharp stare boring holes into the back of my head.

"You okay?" she mutters eventually, the sound barely audible over the tawdry country tune playing through the loud speakers. "I know you weren't exactly on board with what went down tonight."

"Setting fire to the dean's house before I've officially started school didn't seem like a great idea is all."

Two hours ago, we watched the dean's house go up in flames while he was trapped on the second floor.

We didn't stay to see if he got out. Instead, I changed into a slinky dress and coat, then came here with them.

Quincy folds her forearms on the counter beside me. "If we waited any longer, we risked him not getting the message."

The message being that my siblings are aware of the role he played in the deaths of several students last semester. Not to mention Lucy and our cousin Foxe's near-death experiences at the same time.

Lucy and Foxe were kidnapped and dragged to the caves with their friend, who was killed in front of them. Foxe was tortured, and the only reason Lucy got out with some minor injuries was because one of the kidnappers had a last-minute change of heart.

Those events were stoked by a conspiracy steeped in traditions, founding families, and a supposed curse alleging that the Anderson bloodline will eventually cause the downfall of the university and, by extension, Fury Hill itself.

But the bloodshed and agony only shook the community for

a few days before the dean and the school's board of trustees had swept everything under the rug again.

Somehow my siblings convinced our parents they'd be okay at Avernia for one more semester, even though it's clear the town does not want us here. They put our family on a pedestal and fear us at the same time, a dichotomy I'm now being forced to endure alongside them.

"School will be a good change of scenery for you," my mother had said.

I'd only floated the idea to get her off my back when I was living at home again. It was a way to get my parents to believe I wasn't completely caving to my depressive state, though it was obvious the drastic shift in my life was taking its toll.

Still, considering what happened the last time I visited, I was surprised either of my parents were on board.

They trust Quincy, though, and feel we're stronger as a unified front. The power of three or whatever.

I wonder if they realize that's the exact principle that makes us a target.

Casting a sideways glance at my sister, I watch as she adjusts the gold rings stacked along her fingers.

"Arson just feels like a pretty robust statement," I tell her.

"If you're worried about being found out, don't be."

"Because we covered our tracks?"

Asher appears at my other side, signaling for a water. There's an indentation in his nostril from where his nose ring was pressed against it. "Because the dean isn't going to say anything. He's a spineless fucking jellyfish."

"How does that translate to him not reporting a crime?"

"He answers to the school's board of trustees, and they don't want to hear about unrest. They work so hard to make this seem like a luxurious, serene place. After that fucking shit show in the caves, they're going out of their way to avoid any bad press. Scares donors and shit. Avernia is only as powerful as its treasure trove of secrets."

"Dean Bauer even personally asked me to ramp up my campus beautification efforts," Quincy adds. "The Daughters of Persephone have a *long* history of clashing with him, so the request just proves how far Avernia is willing to go to maintain a facade of order. I'd bet they had funding threatened or worse."

I'm not sure what would be worse for a private university than losing its endowment funds, but I don't question it. If it's enough to involve the student organization that Quincy cofounded, which typically struggles for administrative support, then I guess it doesn't really matter.

"Okay, but… It was still wild. You don't think the dean will report it at *all*?"

"Would I have asked you to do this if I thought it would worsen the target on your back?" Quincy asks.

"I don't know," I admit. "You didn't use to set buildings on fire. That's always been Ash's thing."

He grins. "Felt good though, didn't it?"

"If you're a destructive psychopath, I guess."

"You're a theater major, right? Dramatic flair is your thing, so this should make perfect sense to you."

I open my mouth to protest but shut it just as quickly. "Damn it. I do love the symbolism."

His brown eyes crinkle up at the corners. As close to a smile as anyone besides Lucy ever gets. "Exactly. You understand."

"I'm not sure I'd go that far," I say. "But if you guys really don't think it'll be a problem, then I guess I can stop obsessing."

"*Nelly*!" Aurora slings her arms around my neck, shoving me into the lip of the bar as she hugs me tight. "A very nice gentleman gave me some tequila shots on my way back from the bathroom. Where are the Kamikazes?"

Asher's face screws up as she slurs her words. "I don't think you need any more liquor."

"You're not my dad," she says, smushing her cheek into mine. "You're *barely* my friend, Ash-tree, and you're responsible for Foxe being the way he is now, so maybe mind your damn business."

He blinks, and for a moment, I think I see a blip of emotion in his expression. His eyes stay clear and focused, but there's the slightest twitch, a muscle thumping beneath his pale skin as if he's bothered by her words.

Foxe is back in Aplana Island recovering from extensive injuries and surgery, but there's no denying the change his experience in Fury Hill had on him. Can't blame him really. According to the bits and pieces I overheard when my dad and Uncle Alistair were talking, they'd violated his body over and over.

Violations like that don't leave you. They haunt your body and soul forever.

Even when you're not the one they did it directly to.

Asher steps back without reacting, and Lucy appears. She slips her arm around Aurora's waist, prying her off me.

"That's probably our cue to go home," she says, propping the blond up.

"And why you don't accept drinks from men you don't know," I say.

Aurora sighs, rolling her blue eyes. "I *know* him. I've seen him at school before. He's sitting right there."

She points in the general direction of the end of the bar, where a sole patron sits with his head down, chatting on his phone with a glass of red wine in front of him. It's untouched, and he rubs at his temple with his free hand.

A hand I swear *I've* seen somewhere, but he keeps his face tilted, obscuring his identity.

"You coming?" Quincy asks as she slides off the barstool.

I shake my head. "You guys go on. I can make it back to campus on my own."

She hesitates, gnawing on her bottom lip as the other three head to the entrance. We watch as Lucy stumbles beneath Aurora's weight, and Asher lets out an irritated noise, bending to toss the blond over his shoulder.

As he does, Lucy leans in and gives him a kiss on the cheek. I can't see his blush from here, but the way he lingers, staring at her like she's the only thing in the world that matters to him, tells me enough.

"If you want to talk about LA—" Quincy says.

"I don't," I answer sharply.

Not with anyone, but especially not with her.

"Noelle, honestly."

Shaking my head, I give her a look. "It's fine, Q. Don't worry about it. Everything is in the past. Hollywood was never gonna work out for me, right? You always said so."

Disappointment lines her brown irises behind her glasses, but she relents, apparently not actually interested in unearthing old wounds. "All right. Text me if you need someone to pick you up, and please don't drink a lot."

"Okay, *Mom*."

She frowns. "I just don't want to have to tell our parents you got murdered in a creepy bar weeks after they barely got their nephew back. Sue me."

I remain silent as she walks out, and the bartender comes back, asking if I still want the shots.

Shaking my head, I decline. Drinking alone is only fun if you're an alcoholic hermit lamenting the loss of your beloved wife or career.

Oof. I push that last thought away, spinning on the barstool. My gaze catches on the only other patron currently in this part of the building, still chatting away on his phone. The bartender—a beautiful woman with short curly dyed-blond hair and warm brown skin—stops in front of him, saying something I can't hear.

He glances up, nodding at her, and she replaces the wine with a fresh glass.

The breath stalls in my throat as his chin lifts, revealing familiar bone structure and electric green eyes.

I slip my hand into my coat pocket, wrapping my fingers around cool metal and one of the condoms I accidentally managed to leave the Stop N Go with.

"Just consider it a loan," he'd said.

Maybe repayment could benefit us both.

Chapter 4

Sutton

"Heard a fire broke out on campus and wanted to check on you," Beckett says over the phone.

I ignore the burst of giggling that comes from a table across Lethe's main room, ducking my head as another migraine threatens the edges of my skull. It's been a couple of hours since I left the Death's Teeth party, but the filth still clings to my skin.

Normally, I'd have taken my meds by now, but after the incident at the dean's house, I decided not to stay on school property in case board members showed.

"I'm fine," I tell Beckett. "It had nothing to do with me."

"Ah, right." His exhale makes me cringe. "You know, Sutty, your life is pretty boring. You could stand to live a little."

"And setting fires at my place of employment is the way to do that?"

"If that's what you're into."

"I think one homicidal sociopath is enough in this family. Don't you?"

The silence that ensues is deafening. I drag a hand over my face, considering the wine Angelica—Lethe's owner—slid in front of me half an hour ago. For once, I'm tempted to down its contents.

Eight years. That's how long it's been since I had a drop of the stuff. Eight years I've spent lamenting my sister's death and questioning whether things would be different had I not drank at that party.

Not that I can remember much. Just the general sense of violation and the stripping of free will. Broken memories that don't leave, even if your brain shields the details.

The body remembers.

"I'm not homicidal," Beckett says.

"Tell that to the three bodies they dragged out of Tenarus Cave a few weeks ago."

"Three of *five*. Besides, it's not like I was the fucking mastermind. The Curators had their personal vendetta against the Andersons, the whole town believes in that curse, and Dad's always saying—"

"Father's business is his own. I've tried telling you that for years. Doing his bidding only gets you into trouble."

"Yeah, well. Someone has to carry on the Dupont legacy. You're certainly not interested."

With good reason, but Beckett's at a point in his life still where he thinks the Fury Hill founding families are gods. Even with the bullshit they've dragged him through, he believes their word is law and their superstitions are truth.

It's an easier pill to swallow when you've only touched the surface of depravity. When you believe their legacy is just wealth and prestige instead of sin.

Death's Teeth would eat him alive, so I use my membership to keep him off their radar. As long as they're trying to recruit me for leadership, they'll ignore his existence.

"Enough," I tell him. "There's no point in trying to justify yourself to me. You can take it up with the board when you contest your expulsion."

He groans. "Can't you wave a wand and make the charges disappear?"

"How would I do that?"

"I don't know. Tell them I've been good. That I've been giving back by volunteering for your student group and behaving under the watchful eye of my big bro?"

"No."

"What?" he huffs. "Why not? Visio Aternae is the only organization open to all Avernia enrollees, so how hard could it be to fudge the membership forms and put me down for a canned-food drive or something?"

"That you find the philanthropic efforts of my students to be so frivolous they can be forged is enough of a reason," I reply. "But I'm also not going to lie for you."

"A good brother would."

"Perhaps I'd be willing to do more had you not made a complete mockery of my production last semester."

"Oh, for fuck's sake. Are you talking about that stupid play again? I *told* you, I was only in your class—"

"To terrorize the students who actually wanted to be there," I finish, gritting my teeth. "But you realize many of my students end up as Visio Aternae members or vice versa, right? Who in turn help with the productions my classes put on as their finals. Your antics caused delays in set design and performances. Some students *barely* scraped by."

He quiets for a couple of seconds. "It was *Hamlet*, Sutty. How much assistance did the class need?"

"Whether *Hamlet* or Susan Glaspell's *Trifles,* a play deserves the same amount of effort and respect by the people putting it on. Actions have consequences, and I'm not sure you fully understand what sort of position you've put me in here. I want to help you, but I have an obligation to look after my classes."

"Don't you have an obligation to look after your little brother? Or was Bellamy the only sibling you actually cared about?"

Fire sears my throat. "I'll put out some feelers. See if I can get a read on the board members and how they're leaning in terms of keeping you expelled or not."

His sigh makes the line crackle, and I move the phone away briefly.

Angelica sweeps past again, asking if I'd like a refill on my wine. I nod, even though I have no intention of drinking this one either, and watch as she swaps the glasses.

As soon as her hand disappears, another takes its place—this one pale and smooth where Angelica's is warm brown and calloused from years of tending bar.

The pale hand holds a blue tinfoil square and the lighter I lent to a stranger mere hours ago.

My chin lifts, and I don't hear my brother's reply—something about *Trifles* being Bellamy's favorite play and if I brought it up to guilt-trip him. Like he didn't just pull the same shit.

Two hazel eyes blink at me, their hue a glassy mix of brown tourmaline and citrine, volatile and curious in their perusal. They're framed by elegant brows and long, midnight lashes that strike her porcelain skin as she slowly blinks.

I stare for several beats longer than necessary, the flecks of gold and rust in her irises mesmerizing, like shattered crystal.

That gas station lighting did *not* do her justice.

Luscious umber hair spills down slender shoulders and purposeful cleavage, peeking through the deep neckline of the short navy dress she has on beneath a long, heavy overcoat.

The dress clings to her like the scales of a tempting viper, emphasizing the delicate curves of her figure. Her legs seem to stretch without end, tapering down to a pair of designer heels, the aurous straps of which wind up her ankles.

As I look at her, the only thoughts spinning in my mind are… well, *of* her. She's a drop of watercolor paint on an otherwise lackluster canvas. The fine disruption of a lifetime.

The earlier events at the Apollodorus aren't just a distant memory; they're ancient history, and she's the victor who made them so.

In truth, she exudes a level of sophistication that doesn't fit in with Fury Hill at all. She'd blended well enough when we first met at the Stop N Go, but this is a different woman entirely.

A star. Très magnifique.

My mind flashes to earlier in the evening. Someone who recently committed a crime wouldn't be standing just down the road from the scene of it, interacting with locals. Not in such a showstopping outfit. From the corner of my eye, I catch a flash of blond hair and pale skin when Angelica's husband, Zane, does a double take on his way to the back offices.

If she'd been the one to set the dean's house on fire, surely she'd be in hiding now.

The stranger's lips, heart-shaped and gently moistened, part as she waits for my reply, but I'm suddenly at a loss for words. She stares at me, and my insides liquefy.

I hang up on my brother without telling him goodbye.

"Well, well. Looks like you found me after all."

The woman smirks, leaving the lighter and condom on the counter in front of me. "Sometimes fate works in a girl's favor."

"Fate?"

"Maybe." Her smirk widens, and she shrugs. "But it's not like there were many places you could've been. In a town as small as this, I'm surprised we aren't constantly running into one another."

"Spoken like a tourist. There are hiding places in Fury Hill you could probably only dream about."

She shifts, leaning an elbow on the bar. "Is that an invitation?"

"An invitation?"

"Are you suggesting we visit these hiding places together?"

I glance at the lighter and foil packet, then again at her. "What, you think you deserve a reward for bringing this back?"

"Don't I?" She flutters her lashes, and my chest tightens.

"Not for doing something you were supposed to, no. Perhaps if you surprised me, I'd be willing to consider it. Given your schedule for the evening is clear, that is." With one finger, I slide the foil packet back to her and turn my attention to my wineglass, taking the stem. "I'd hate to get in the way of any—what did you call it?"

"Casual sex."

"Ah, yes. *That*."

"You say it like it's something I invented," she says. "Hookup culture is older than me, you know."

Turning my head, I meet her stare. "I wouldn't, actually. I prefer to get to know my partners before engaging in lasciviousness."

There haven't *been* real partners in years, but I don't mention that. Just at Death's Teeth parties, and even then, it's not like my equipment exactly works. Nor do I reciprocate, though they wish I would.

Being touched at all makes me want to crawl out of my skin, but especially when I'm wearing one of those fucking masks.

"Ooh, a Boy Scout." She cocks her head to the side. "How old are you?"

"How old are *you*?"

"Twenty-five." When I don't respond immediately, her eyebrows knit together. "What, you don't believe me?"

"I've no reason not to."

"Can I guess your age?"

"Something tells me you'd do it even if I tried to stop you."

"A quick learner." She grins. "I like that."

My throat constricts, heat blazing at its base. "Still not interested in casual sex."

"Yet you keep bringing it up. I never even said that's what my *meeting* was for."

"Yes, but I'm afraid if I let you steer the conversation, you'll go back to talking about the forms of contraception."

"Why, does it make you uncomfortable?" Pink stains her cheeks. "You didn't try to stop me before."

"I didn't say I *minded*. You have a lovely voice. I'd likely spend the rest of my evening listening to whatever topic you picked."

The bar lights cause her irises to glitter, and I feel my tongue in my throat.

"But," I continue, "you seemed embarrassed by the oversharing, so I merely sought to keep things a tad less personal."

"By asking indirectly about my plans."

My fingers curl around the wineglass stem. "Admittedly, I'm not terribly well-versed in flirting."

"*That* was flirting?"

Heat fans my face as she barks out a laugh, tipping her head back. My eyes lock on the expanse of her neck, all smooth and unblemished, practically begging me to sink my teeth into.

Jesus, Sutton. Where did that *come from?*

Shifting on my stool, I lift a shoulder. "As I said, I'm not well-versed in it."

"Then... How do you get to know people well enough to fuck them?"

I glance at her mouth as it curves around the word *fuck*, my heartbeat ratcheting inside my chest. There's something alluring about the way she says it, like it's loaded with a thousand different meanings, all of them lewd.

But I'm not sure what to say to her. The short answer is that I don't really, and that feels a bit too personal to divulge.

The long answer is even more personal, and I'm certain a stranger doesn't care about the traumatic past I can barely recall.

My head throbs, sending a wave of nausea through me.

"Work keeps me busy," I eventually relent. It's true enough. "I don't normally have the time for dating, casual or otherwise."

"You're a director, right?"

I cock an eyebrow, and she slides onto the stool next to me, tucking a strand of hair behind her ear.

"Yes, I was eavesdropping. Rude, maybe, but now we have something else to talk about."

I smother a grin. "Clever."

"One of my many shining qualities." She reaches up, toying with the snake charm on her choker necklace. "'It was an awful thing that was done in this house that night, Mrs. Hale. Killing a man while he slept, slipping a rope around his neck that choked the life out of him.'"

Silence pulses between us, confusion wrapping around my thoughts.

"Ugh, how can you invoke the great Susan Glaspell to make a point and not even know her work when someone recites it to you?"

"I'm more surprised that *you* know it," I admit, wincing slightly at how elitist it sounds.

"Well, I've been acting since I was old enough to walk and studying plays since I could read. I memorized my favorites and have a tendency to interject when I hear someone talk about them. My mom used to get on me for it, even though it was her fault I fell in love with the medium in the first place. I mean, she and my dad would drag me and my siblings to theaters every chance they got, and—"

"Seems like you have a habit of rambling too," I note. As if I'm trying to form a barrier against the instant attraction—something to keep the bad decisions at bay.

I can't recall the last time anyone caused such a disturbance within my being. Certainly not since my undergrad years, when I stopped letting myself get caught up in romance or its relatives.

My body could no longer handle it. Not after that night.

"That's true, I do ramble. I come from a pretty quiet family, and as the only extrovert, filling the silence is a superpower of mine."

"Silence isn't a bad thing though. It's good to ruminate on thoughts before speaking them."

She ignores that. "The point is I'm a Susan Glaspell fan. Well, less specifically her fan and more interested in a lot of the female-written works from her time. I've starred in a couple community productions of her plays. I always think it's interesting how so very little has changed for women in society, even decades later."

"What a terribly bleak analysis."

"Do you disagree?"

"Well, women can vote now. You can own property, get divorced, and the protections for actors have definitely improved since Glaspell wrote the play."

"Ah, yes, you're right. Equality achieved. Alert the community aid workers. They'll be so pleased to know their jobs are done."

Warmth flushes my skin, and I push the wineglass away. "I didn't say things were *equal*. Just better. Maybe. For some."

"Yet here I sit—drinkless."

"Is that a hint?"

"The polite thing to do when approached by a woman at a bar is to offer her something."

"Doesn't chivalry go against the whole equality thing you were just talking about?"

She grins, placing both forearms on the counter. As she does, her tits press obscenely against the neckline of her dress, and I have the distinct desire to shove my face between them.

I'll bet they're soft, her skin smooth as butter and just as supple.

"I'm thirsty and forgot my wallet," she says, reaching out with her index finger. She places it beneath my chin, pushing up so my eyes meet hers once again. "I'd appreciate it if you helped me out."

"With what?"

"A drink. Pay attention."

The command in her tone makes me swallow. Hard. "Are you flirting with me?"

"If you have to ask, I must not be doing a very good job."

"As I stated before, I'm not familiar with the concept."

"Which I find odd, by the way. A guy that looks like you doesn't even *need* to flirt. You could pick up anyone in this bar just by sliding a drink and condom their way."

My eyes flicker to the counter as she drops her hand, her pinkie brushing the edge of the foil packet from before. "Are you really twenty-five?"

"Why, are you thinking about what I look like naked already?"

Self-consciousness flares deep within me, and I wonder if she can smell the depravity from earlier on my skin. No matter how many times I try to scrub it off, it never feels like I come all the way clean.

I must look skeptical, because she gives me a two-fingered salute, then crosses them over her heart. "Scout's honor, I promise."

"You weren't a Girl Scout."

That makes her laugh. She rests her chin in her palm, fluttering her lashes at me. "What else?"

"Huh?"

"What else can you tell about me from just looking?" She straightens her spine a little, giving me an expectant nod. "Go on."

"You've already revealed an awful lot of information."

"Yeah, but I want to know what you see. From the director's eye or whatever. So come on. *Do me.*"

The demand makes my chest tighten, the double entendre not lost as she leans in, angling her cleavage so her tits are practically falling from her dress.

They'd rest nice and heavy in my palms. Not that I intend to take things that far, but goddamn if my dick doesn't have other ideas. After a near decade of struggling to get it up without panicking or disgust, its sudden throbbing interest is alarming.

And intriguing.

Still, the woman waits.

"Ah…" I cough, facing forward. "All right. If I had to guess, you're not from Fury Hill?"

She shakes her head.

I fold my icy fingers together. They tingle as I rack my brain for something else. "You like theater and have been in plays, so clearly you're an actress. Career or hobby?"

"Sore spot," she says, her mouth twisting.

Ah. Okay, redirect. "Do you prefer lead or ensemble?"

"Preference? Lead. But all roles are important."

"Okay, so a rising starlet perhaps." Pursing my lips, I scan the shelves of alcohol across from the bar. "I'd guess middle child? Intrinsic need to be noticed by everyone to make up for feeling invisible to family?"

One of her eyebrows arches.

My stomach feels like it's in knots. "And…you came into a stuffy dive bar wearing a skintight dress and fuck-me heels, so I'd be willing to bet you're running from some kind of heartbreak. Maybe looking for a distraction."

"Wow." She snorts. "That's a terrifying skill you have."

"Directors are trained to observe. I happen to pay more attention than most."

"To everyone?"

I peek at her from the corner of my eye. Her lips purse, and I wonder what the strawberry color of her lipstick would look like smeared onto her skin.

Swallowing, I meet her stare. "To those I find interesting."

There's a strange glint in her eyes though. Something distant and detached, but she seems to shake herself out of it seconds later, fixing her gaze on me once again.

She lets it dip all the way down to my feet, hooked on the bottom rung of my stool, and slowly drags her focus up the entire length of me. I feel each covered inch like a zap of electricity in my spine, and it takes every ounce of willpower I possess not to make a noise of desperation.

The way my body aches for this woman I just met should be a crime.

"Do you act?" she asks, tilting her head.

"Not recently, but yes. My entire childhood. I was a theater major in college."

"An educated man."

"I make an effort. Knowledge is important."

She nods, pinching the foil packet between two fingers, then slides it my way. Without lifting her finger from it, she holds my stare. A fire blazes in hers, unyielding and wanton, and I wonder if mine reflects the same carnality.

Raw desire—something I'm not accustomed to. Normally, tearing myself away from obvious advances is a simple enough task, but for some reason, I can't make myself do it right now.

Her beauty is ethereal. Transcendent. I want to bite into it directly.

"Say there was a role up for grabs," she says, looking at me from her lashes. "One that a handsome green-eyed man with theater experience would be perfect for."

I don't reply.

Don't breathe.

"So perfect," she continues, sliding forward on her stool until I can smell that lush vanilla and honey scent, "that he wouldn't even need to audition."

Sweat breaks out along my hairline. "Lead?"

"No, no. That's mine."

Maybe it's the fact that the two masked figures left me unsatisfied earlier, and now this girl is offering herself without so much as an exchange of first names. No thoughts or feelings, just pure lust. The opportunity to expel some pent-up energy with a stranger.

Or maybe I'm losing it.

Either way, I find that I don't mind all that much.

"What part would you like me to play?" I ask, my voice hoarse.

Her tongue darts out to wet her lips, and I'm glued to the movement, my body alight with need as she answers. "*Under*study."

Chapter 5

Elle

"FIRST RULE AS AN UNDERSTUDY: *LEARN YOUR LEAD*."

The stranger's car is cramped, and I realize too late that it probably isn't the best place for a hookup. But seated next to this six-three Adonis with messy, dark brown hair and eyes like soft green moss, I don't really care.

"Isn't the first rule usually something like *be positive*, or *take the role seriously*?"

I lean over the console, pressing my index finger to his lips. "Shh. Understudies don't question the director's authority."

"But I thought you were the lead."

"There you go again."

His swallow is audible. "Okay. I'll be good."

"You say that, but it doesn't really feel like you're trying."

"What else can I do?"

"Well, for starters, we're still *so* far apart."

He glances between us, then at my hand still against my mouth. Seeming to come to some sort of conclusion, he reaches around his side, sliding the seat back a couple of inches with the yank of a lever. The chair reclines, freeing up space on his lap.

"Climb over," he says softly, spreading his thighs a bit. Strong, powerful thighs that strain beneath the fabric of brown slacks, bunching up at his groin so the outline of him is obscured.

My breath hitches anyway.

"Are you sure?" I ask, peering closer.

Discomfort lines the edges of his face, and he sweeps his large hands over his legs as if trying to psych himself up.

"Just do it, temptress."

Something about his no-nonsense tone has me scrambling, losing my tenuous grasp on control of the situation. For a moment, as I'm shimmying over the console, I wonder if it's possible he's tricked me into thinking he doesn't do this kind of thing.

It wouldn't be the first time a man lied to get me into a vulnerable position, but I'd thought I'd gotten better at detecting their bullshit.

My throat burns as I crawl into his lap. I half expect him to paw at me the moment I'm in his vicinity, but instead he keeps his hands dutifully low, watching every move I make with the eyes of a hawk.

I brace myself on the headrest and plant my knees at his hips. Though he doesn't touch me, there's a heat blazing in his gaze, caught in the moonlight spilling in through the sunroof.

"Temptress?" I probe in a low voice. He called me that earlier too. At the gas station.

"Siren, vixen, dragueuse. Whichever label you prefer."

"Dragueuse?"

"It's French."

"What does it mean?"

His breath skates across my collarbone. "*Flirt.*"

My pulse scatters. "I see. So you were lying when you said you weren't familiar with the gesture."

"No. I meant what I said. Flirting is not my forte." Shifting, he rests his head against the seat, letting his eyes dip to my lips briefly.

"Then I just bring it out in you?"

"If this conversation qualifies, I suppose so."

This feels so different from every other hookup I've had. No matter what gender, a quick fuck is usually just that—quick. Fleeting. Over once you've climaxed—or, in a lot of cases with my masculine partners, *pretended* to—and moved on to the next thing.

In LA, *everyone* in my adult community theater troupe was fucking. It was like its own little commune, the place where jealousy, lust, and moral support thrived.

But it was easy enough not to get attached, especially when I ventured outside the group.

Maybe this just feels different because it's the first time I've sought any external gratification since my dreams went up in flames.

Or maybe it's the soft glint in those mossy eyes that warms me from the inside out.

"So…" He fills the silence, drawing me back in. "Where are you from?"

My shoulders slump. "And you ruined it."

"What?" He frowns. "Did you not just tell me to get to know my lead?"

"I meant like"—I grab one of his hands, placing it high on my thigh where my dress has ridden up—"*this*."

His swallow reverberates in my stomach, and his touch is ice cold. "Ah."

"Well?"

"Well…what?"

"What do you think?"

A fire licks up my spine as he pauses, then curls his fingers against me, leaving indentations where he grips. The pressure is delightful, and my throat contracts around nothing, desire searing the inside.

"I think you're dangerous."

Covering his hand with mine, I slide it even higher, over my side and up to the curve of my breast. Without my coat, the outline is perfectly visible, and my muscles cinch tight with the contact.

He doesn't resist, just lets me do what I want, and I find that oddly fascinating.

"Dangerous," I mutter, letting my palm fall to his chest. I fan my fingers out, waiting to see what he does next. If he's an actor who takes stage direction into his own hands or one that needs guidance all the way through. "Is that another one of your theories?"

"You ask a lot of questions."

"No more than you." I slip my pinkie beneath a gap in his neckline, touching bare skin. "Besides, you seem like someone with answers."

"That's where you're wrong," he replies, his words barely audible as his thumb grazes the underside of my breast ever so gently. "I know very little, actually. Everything inside was a lucky guess."

His featherlight touch makes me dizzy. "So you're not omnipotent?"

"Pattern recognition and heightened observation skills. Nothing terribly fancy, I'm afraid."

My eyes narrow. "You're deflecting."

"Yes." He glances at my lips, licking his. "I am."

"Why?"

"You make me nervous."

"Oh."

"Not in a *bad* way," he adds quickly. "In a *you could probably ruin my life and I wouldn't stop you* way."

Heat flares in my abdomen, radiating downward. "Are you always so honest?"

"No," he whispers.

I hum, leaning forward so our noses brush. "I'm not sure I believe you."

He smells like apricots and trees, cedar or pine. Like danger and bad decisions.

"What would I get for lying? If anything, I'm the vulnerable one here."

"You could overpower me if you wanted."

There's a long pause, but eventually his free hand comes up, his thumb plucking lazily at my bottom lip. Again, his touch is icy, and I wonder if it's because of how warm my skin feels.

"Not the kind of vulnerability I'm talking about there, temptress."

My heart hammers in my throat. "I have a name."

A dark glint flashes in his gaze. He swallows, allowing that same hand to fall before sliding it around my waist. My dress hikes up my thighs, leaving just his pants and the thin fabric of my underwear between us.

Slowly, he leans in, disturbing the snake charm choker fastened at my throat and skimming his nose along my collarbone. Inhaling me. "What is it?"

I can barely hear him. "What is what?"

His chuckle sends goose bumps spraying down my arms. "Your name."

My stomach twists, and I sit back a little, meeting his electric gaze. A heaviness fills the air, and I wonder if he feels it too—if it's just performance anxiety or the Fury Hill atmosphere that's so suffocating.

"I'm sorry," I tell the stranger, withdrawing. "I really wasn't looking for anything serious."

"And a name changes that?"

"Obviously."

"Why don't we test that theory?"

"What do you mean?"

Before I can disentangle myself, his palms slide beneath the straps of my dress, lifting them from my shoulders in one smooth move. He keeps his eyes on mine as he slips the straps off, waiting for me to protest, but I don't.

Now my chest is totally bare, and as he drinks me in, embarrassment fans across my face.

I don't know *why*. I've never been uncomfortable in my body before. But something about this moment makes me crave his approval.

The man's nostrils flare, as if he likes what he sees, and the knots my stomach tied itself into unravel a bit.

I'm not expecting it when he glides a thumb over one puckered nipple, so the gasp that escapes me disappears into the air between us.

"This okay?"

My chin dips in a nod.

"Give me a name," he demands softly, breathlessly, "and I'll prove it doesn't have to mean anything."

"Aren't I supposed to be teaching you how to touch me?"

"I thought you were showing me how to flirt."

"Clearly, I've overestimated your need for assistance."

The next words out of his mouth are gentle. Shy almost. "Have I done something wrong?"

"No," I grumble, my back arching, seeking more from him in a way I find terrifying and overwhelming.

The loss of control is disconcerting. I want to lash out, shift the dynamic, but for some reason, the words die on my tongue.

He brings his free hand to the opposite breast, cupping me so firmly that my spine bows.

Introductions are messy and unnecessary when all you're chasing is a little satisfaction. I know better than to get involved with anyone past a few short hours.

But it's almost like he needs more. The way his eyes rove over my skin before his touch grazes me. Is he *actually* nervous?

I open my mouth to say we can stop or to give a *fake* name or insist he say his first, but instead, just one syllable comes out. "Elle."

It's almost a whisper, murmured as I bury my face in his neck.

His soft laughter brushes my hair. "See? That wasn't so hard."

"Easy for you to say."

"*Elle*."

Tension threads through my limbs. It sounds a lot different coming from him.

"You're right," he mutters. "That was very easy to say."

Annoyed with everything, I sink my teeth gently into his jugular, earning a surprised grunt from deep in his chest.

He continues kneading and rolling, winding me up, but doesn't move otherwise.

Almost like he isn't sure what to do next.

For some reason, the hesitation is endearing. Sitting up, I meet his hungry stare. Something forlorn and needy unfurls in my chest. In my soul.

"Kiss me."

His throat bobs. "Are you sure?"

"Learn by doing."

"I know how to kiss," he replies.

"Prove it." I slide my hands along his jaw, threading the tips of my fingers behind his ears, and seal our mouths together.

The world tilts on its axis as our lips collide. Adrenaline and arousal shoot through my abdomen, setting me ablaze. My nipples scrape the fabric of his sweater as I lean forward, curling against him, and grind my hips downward.

He's *big*. I can tell that much through the layers separating us, and suddenly I want nothing more than to have him inside me.

His tongue slips tentatively past my teeth, flicking against mine as one of his palms finds my spine, pressing me tighter into him. Once more, I'm taken aback by the chill of his touch, and I make a noise of surprise that he swallows.

I feel trapped, unable to move within the compact space of his embrace, but it doesn't particularly bother me.

If anything, the restriction heightens my senses. The scent of his cologne envelops me, and his frigid fingers relieve my heated flesh.

"You're cold," I mutter against his mouth.

"You're hot," he sends back.

"Very astute observations there."

He pulls away, just an inch or so, wiping a bit of saliva from the corner of my mouth. "Is it bothersome? The temperature? It's not something I can…turn off, but…"

A blush stains his cheeks, and my heart hammers behind my rib cage.

"No." I shake my head, leaning into his grasp. "It feels amazing."

He kisses me again, abandoning my breast to cup my cheeks. This time, it steals my breath, throwing me completely off-kilter as he maneuvers me, deepening the gesture, seeking more.

More, more, more.

My brain chants that single word over and over, craving everything all at once.

Chest heaving, I lift my ass to grant him better access, but he keeps me flush with his lap.

When I reach for the fly of his pants, he pulls away on a staggered grunt. He watches as I work the button free with shaky fingers, then leans in, sweeping the hair from my shoulders.

"Is this part of the role?" he whispers, lips grazing my collarbone.

Nodding, I lean over the console, patting my coat pockets for the condom tucked inside. I straighten and slide back on his thighs a bit, tearing the foil with my teeth.

"Opening night," I manage.

"We skipped some rehearsal." He pushes my dress up, exposing my lace panties. Black with a little red bow on the front.

"Haven't you ever done a cold read?"

He shifts, dragging the flat of his thumb over my pubic bone, down the center. His eyes stay on mine as he brushes my clit, the friction of the lace coupled with his deliberate stare making my stomach cramp.

It's a little unnerving how he slips between scandalized Boy Scout and experienced sex god with just the flip of his hands. Like a mask he can take off whenever he pleases.

A part of me wonders if we have that in common. The compartmentalization that keeps us sane.

"Of course I have. But are you sure you want to do this with a stranger?"

I undo his zipper, our breaths ratcheting with each *clink* of its teeth parting. His abs contract as I slide my hand beneath the elastic waist of his boxers, gripping him in my fist.

Yep, *big*. Heavy. My mouth waters at the weight in my palm as he stiffens beneath my touch.

"It helps to think of it as a part, *understudy*," I say. "We're just two people taking on important roles."

"With no audience."

"Would you like one?"

He seems to consider this, then swipes his tongue over a diamond-hard nipple while his thumb presses *just so* between my thighs. "No," he admits, his breath warm on my skin. "I don't think I want anyone else to see you like this."

My throat dries up. "Good, you're getting into character."

"You're wet," he notes.

"Everyone's different, but that tends to happen when a good-looking person has their hands all over me." My face heats, and I fish the condom from its wrapper. "Doubly so when they're a good kisser."

His smirk incinerates something inside me. "Good-looking *and* a good kisser. Hm. Quite the package you have beneath you."

No kidding. "I'm afraid I'll require a bit more proof."

"Huh?"

I give him a squeeze, and he jolts, his thumb making me see stars. It's a single rush of force against my pulse point, and it scatters my nerve endings. Pinching the tip of the rubber, I position it at the head of him, but he quickly brushes my hands aside, lifting his hips so he can pull his pants down more.

"Let me," he says.

My heart throbs once his cock is fully out, and he fists it in one palm, taking the condom. His fingers tremble as he slowly unrolls it on himself and releases an unsteady breath.

I inch forward while he holds it straight, positioning myself. His chest heaves with each passing second, rising and falling as sweat slicks across his forehead. I lean in, licking a droplet before it can fall into his eyebrow, then continue a path with my tongue down the side of his face, pausing to taste his bottom lip.

Our eyes lock when his tip bumps against me. I reach under my ass, tugging my panties aside, and slowly sink down.

His free hand tangles in my hair, grounding me in place as he dives in for another kiss. I'm unsteady, unpracticed, and this car is small, so the bite of painful resistance between my legs is not entirely unexpected.

Frustration bleeds into me when I can't glide him right in, and I pull back, glaring at where we're connected.

"Are you okay?" he asks, swallowing loudly.

I nod. "Fine, just—can I—"

My hand hovers close to his, and after a long, weighted pause, he relents. I wrap my fingers around him and angle my hips to take him better.

"What do you need?"

"Nothing," I grit out, annoyed and on the verge of tears when it *still* isn't working. God, what an embarrassing time for my body to fail. "It's just—"

I suck in a startled gasp when he presses two wet fingers to my clit, swirling gently. Pressure coils in my abdomen, and I nearly collapse with the euphoria that races through me.

His cock sinks in an inch.

"There's no point if you're not enjoying it," he says, and I blink up at this stranger, wondering why he's so thoughtful and attentive when he barely knows me.

Not even the people I've known my entire life have ever cared this much about my feelings or comfort, no matter the situation.

Asher always thought I was a brat. Quincy thought I was too emotional. My parents, I think, often didn't know *what* to do with me if I wasn't acting. Eventually, I learned to keep the mask on, playing whatever role made them most comfortable.

When I went to LA, the mask was so embedded within me that I'd forgotten there was pain and fear I'd stuffed somewhere. I lost sight of myself, my passions, and let them be exploited.

Sitting here now, all the reminders come rushing back just with this man's acknowledgment, and I let out a strangled noise, overwhelmed by everything.

"It helps if you come, right?" he asks. "Can you do it like this?"

I swallow over the knot in my throat and nod again. "I-if you put them inside me, it goes much faster. Usually."

His eyes glaze over as he lifts me off his cock, replacing it with one finger while his thumb remains on my clit. He watches me as if cataloging my reactions and storing them to redouble his efforts.

My mouth falls open, and I press my forehead to his as he creates a heady longing in my stomach. He curls forward, stroking languidly, and when he manages to slip a second finger in, my composure falters.

"I didn't think you'd be good at this," I pant.

He chuckles. "I'm a quick learner, remember? And I suppose it helps that I've been thinking about doing exactly this from the moment I handed you that vibrator."

I place one hand on his thigh behind me, leaning back, and cock an eyebrow. "Really? I thought I'd messed everything up."

"On the contrary, *temptress*," he replies, covering the point of my breast with his mouth. He teases the tip of my nipple, his fingers working in and out of me, and I can't concentrate on any one thing as electricity sparks at my spine, spiraling upward. "I didn't think you were messy enough. Allow me to remedy that though."

My mouth opens to reply, but I'm cut off by a spasm, my inner muscles clenching tighter and tighter.

"There it is. You look so hot taking my fingers like this," he praises, making my stomach flip violently as the lewd squelching sounds grow incredibly loud in the car. "Tell me what you want, Elle."

"Don't say my name like that," I whine.

"Why? Do you like how it sounds?"

I nod, my insides swirling. Euphoria singes every cell in my body, lighting me aflame.

"Elle, Elle, Elle," he taunts, his lips vibrating against my sensitive, puckered flesh. "Jesus. You're soaking my lap, temptress. How long has it been since someone made you come?"

"I–I don't—"

"Of course you don't remember. No one's ever felt this good inside you, have they?" His tongue lashes at my skin, and then he's curling his fingers, brushing a spot that sends a wave of delicious pressure through me.

"*Fuck*," I pant, squeezing around him, losing my hold on the situation as he continues.

Normally, I'd push back. Regain control.

But right now, I don't want to.

It happens quickly, my orgasm rising and chasing out all other thought as he continues stretching and filling me. I feel him in my chest, in my throat, wherever nerve receptors exist in my body.

They explode on impact, stealing my vision for the briefest of moments. I come hard, gasping for clarity, for air, for this stranger making me see stars.

He's right. It's *never* felt this way before.

I flood his hand as I crest the edge of oblivion, an animalistic noise shrieking out of me. Sweat beads on my forehead, and I struggle to catch my breath, even as he keeps stroking me.

"Beautiful," he notes quietly, finally lifting his head. "Feel better?"

My breasts are heavy, slick, and swollen, matching my pussy. I nod and let out a little laugh, then reach for him once more. He eases out of me, raising his hand to his mouth and sucking my juices off each finger, one by one.

"Are you just getting out of a serious relationship or something? I find it hard to believe a guy who doesn't know how to flirt can—"

"Make you come with his fingers?"

"Well, I wouldn't say you *made* me."

"Right, I just coaxed it out of you."

I frown. "Just answer my question."

"Well, flirting and finger fucking are two separate skill sets—" He grunts when I poke his jugular, chuckling. "I'm not just getting out of a relationship, no. Don't worry. There are no jealous ex-partners waiting to accost you once you leave here."

Cocking my head, I give him another once-over, trying to determine whether he's telling the truth. He *did* say he isn't always honest, but I'm not sure he stands to gain anything other than a quick fuck. It's the same thing I'm gaining; there's no power imbalance here. Nothing he can lord over me at a later date.

Besides, none of this will matter in the morning anyway. I won't be seeing him again.

He takes his cock in hand, adjusting the condom around the rigid length, and I wonder how he's managed to stay hard this entire time. But before I can voice my question, he's tugging me forward and lining us back up.

The tip slips through my glistening flesh before he presses in, and I grab his biceps as he eases me down with his hands on my hips.

There's a slight pinch as I adjust to his size, but *nothing* like before.

Fuck, the stretch is a beautiful thing. I release a moan, tilting my pelvis at the same time he huffs a pathetic little noise.

"*God*, you feel so good—"

A buzzing sound splits the air, loud and obnoxious as it cuts off his words. His phone slides across the dash, lighting up with a name I can't make out from my vantage.

"Shit." He shifts forward, lodging more of himself inside me, and I bite down on my lip to keep from coming again so soon. A ragged breath escapes him as he pauses, fisting the sides of my dress to keep me in place.

"Ignore it," I suggest.

"All right," he agrees instantly, no question.

"Just like that?"

He nods, leaning back so the veins in his throat are exposed. They ripple as he swallows, and I tighten around him involuntarily, swiveling my hips slightly. "Just like that, temptress."

The buzzing doesn't cease, though, and after a few moments where the air is so heavy it feels like it could collapse right on top of us, he curses under his breath and snatches the phone from the dash.

Silently, I watch as he scans the screen, his green eyes darkening.

"Is…everything okay?"

"Family stuff."

"You have a family?"

"Most people do." He glances at me, cringing. "Not…not a *wife and kids* kind though."

I don't say anything.

"I'm serious." His jaw shifts as the phone buzzes again, and he tosses it to the back seat. "Sorry, Elle, but I'm afraid I need to go."

I blink. "You what?"

"I'm needed elsewhere."

"Your dick is currently *in* me."

"Oh, I'm aware. But family emergencies don't wait." He grips my hips in both hands, hauling me off, and I wince at the sudden loss of pressure and fullness, then shake my head to try and clear that sensation.

It's never felt like that before.

Like losing a limb.

Immediately, I'm annoyed, so when he tries to help resituate my dress straps, I shove his hands away and fix them myself.

This is so *humiliating*.

He sits back in his seat, wrenches off the condom, and sighs. "Elle, I didn't mean—"

Shoving open the passenger door, I shake my head, gathering my coat in my arms. "Save it, *Boy Scout*. You're not the first guy to use me, and you probably won't be the last, because evidently I can't learn a goddamn lesson."

I scramble out of the car before he can reply and slam the door shut, ignoring the fact that he didn't *actually* get anything out of the encounter, and watch him peel out of the parking lot without another word.

Wrapping my hair in a towel, I move down the hall, sliding a key into the lock of the door to let myself inside. After showering, exfoliating, and flossing, I feel like an entirely new person, able to *nearly* forget the embarrassment at Lethe's.

Aurora's sitting on her bed, her blond hair wrapped around heatless curlers as she paints her toenails pink. Her blue eyes find me as I discard my bathrobe and slippers, diving beneath the covers of my bed with my laptop.

I hadn't expected her to be awake when I got back tonight considering the state she left the bar in, but in truth, she rarely seems to leave campus at all these days. Most people at Avernia College go home for winter break, but Aurora transferred dorm rooms and claimed to have some online fashion show to work on, so she was still around when I got special permission to move in early.

Normally, the four dorms—Erebus, Cadmus, Rhadamanthus, and Blessed Hall, making up the aptly named Elysian Dorms—don't allow anyone new in when there are no RAs, but the dean was willing to make an exception.

Or rather, my parents didn't give him another option.

"How're we doing?" Aurora asks, eyeing me with a lifted brow. She seems to have sobered up quite a bit.

"I'll live," I tell her, sliding my heating pad out from my pillow and fitting it over my stomach.

Those earlier cramps *had* been PMS, as it turns out. Or rather, an endo flare-up triggered by the early stage of my cycle.

The thing about chronic conditions like endometriosis is that even when the symptoms are only moderate, the threat of pain looms over you forever. It consumes your life. Even a few years after my diagnosis with stage two, I still struggle to anticipate the days when the pain is tolerable, minimal, or excruciating.

And while I *do* think the idea of birth control is pro-feminist like I told that sexy stranger, it's also loaded with its own issues and not a real fix. It doesn't stop the disease from spreading, it just alleviates the symptoms.

There's no cure, so all I can do in the meantime is manage it.

Orgasms sometimes help, so pairing my earlier encounter with the heating pad and pain meds I just took, I'm hoping I'll be able to sleep tonight.

So long as I avoid dreaming about the Primordial Forest, that is.

"What'd you end up doing after we left?" Aurora continues.

"Oh. Um…nothing, really. Just drank a little and called an Uber. Fed a couple of wayward pigeons. I don't really remember much beyond that. Must've had more to drink than I realized."

"Ew. Birds are fucking terrifying." Her nose scrunches up. "Anyway, don't blame yourself. It's Lethe's, and why I avoid that place like the plague. No one ever seems to remember what they did once they leave."

"Are you saying my memories will magically disappear?"

"Depends. Did you drink the tap water?"

I shoot her a horrified look. "When have you ever known me to do that?"

She laughs. "Fair enough. You really didn't meet anyone when we left though? That seems so unlike the Noelle I remember."

A flash of that stranger's green gaze flickers in my mind, and panic seizes my chest at the thought of her knowing what I did. Of knowing he rejected me.

"Nah," I lie, rolling to face the cement wall. "Just thought it'd be nice to hang out in one of the few attractions available in Fury Hill."

She snorts. "Yeah. If Lucy hadn't roped me into coming here, I'd be at Pratt and going to *actual* fashion shows and five-star restaurants on the weekends—not stuck here pretending everyone doesn't wear the same polyester skirts and tweed jackets all the time."

"We're not *that* far from the city," I point out. "You could go on weekend trips if you wanted."

Aurora sighs. "Avernia might not be nearly as trendy and modern as Pratt, but the course loads are too intense. Why else do you think I stayed over break instead of back home visiting my mom and dad?"

Neither of us note that her parents—my aunt Lenny and uncle Jonas—made a special trip up to exchange Christmas presents or that we know the real reason she didn't go home has less to do with homework and everything to do with Foxe James.

Not that I have room to talk. I left LA because of my mistakes after all.

I curl into my heating pad, exhaling heavily. *Fuck*, that feels good. The lingering pain is soothed by the warmth seeping into my skin, and I pull my knees up, keeping it in place.

Propping my head on a pillow, I open my laptop and sift through my favorites folder on some streaming site. I swipe past dozens of classics and musicals, eventually cuing up *Casablanca*. My favorite.

Focusing on Humphrey Bogart, I lie there for a while, desperately trying to keep my mind off the green-eyed stranger from earlier and the pleasure he wrung from me.

And the fact that I didn't get his name at all.

Chapter 6

Sutton

For centuries, Dupont Manor has hidden away in the foothills of the White Mountains, overlooking Avernia College. It's a haunted shell of an estate, complete with massive sitting rooms, outdated floral wallpaper, and a swimming pool no one bothers to fill now that my youngest sister, Gigi, is at boarding school in London.

I don't enjoy coming here. Sometimes it still smells like Bellamy, like hope and mint chocolate, though before her death, she lived on campus like me.

Ice lines Beckett's blue eyes where he glares from across the main living room, like twin glaciers attempting to freeze me solid.

I glare back, because what appears to be an impromptu meeting between him, Mother, and Dean Bauer does *not* constitute a fucking emergency, yet he ended my night early by claiming there was trouble brewing.

A night of mistakes, maybe, but one I was looking forward to nonetheless.

The scent of latex still clings to my fingers as I enter, glancing past Beckett at Justin Bauer, who sits on one of the sofas gawking at my mother.

She's a stunning woman in her own right, but I imagine it's more the novelty of having Claire Dupont in his midst that's causing his rapture.

It's rare for the lech to get invited places because he's wildly unpopular among the founding families. But he's so gutless, they keep him around.

Hence, I imagine, his presence now.

Dean Bauer is also easily intimidated and seduced by severe women, so I find his impropriety unsurprising.

What I do find surprising is the fact that he's here at all, considering I watched his campus home go up in flames mere hours ago, and I was certain he'd been in it. Yet he's clean and polished, freshly showered and feigning nonchalance as if nothing happened at all.

Such is the way at Avernia. Without mystery and anonymity, the university doesn't function. I don't know why I'm ever shocked at the lengths city and school officials will go to to cover shit up.

Mother lifts her chin, her dark green gaze unyielding as it meets mine.

"What the hell is this?" I ask, breaking the silence when no one else tries to.

"An intervention," Mother replies, sipping from a porcelain mug. She pretends it's oolong tea, but I don't need to walk over to know it's spiked with something—an antidepressant or French wine, perhaps.

Between arthritis ending her career as a pianist early and losing a child, I wouldn't blame her for sedating herself more openly.

Beckett huffs at her answer. "Is an intervention a group therapy session where we talk about my faults and wonder out loud if I can be trusted in public anymore?"

"Sometimes yes," Mother says, patting the space on the love seat beside her, beckoning me. "Sutton, darling, come sit. This is important."

I walk over, perching on the cushion before she can ask again. "Where's Father?"

She rolls her eyes. "Jean-Louis is having one of his spells. You know how those go. Don't expect to see him outside his bedroom unless you're a Westwood or Blackwater."

"They are on the city council together," Dean Bauer notes, like he thinks any of the current patriarchs of Fury Hill's founding families might be able to hear him kissing their ass. "I'd find the will to face them no matter how bad I was feeling as well."

Mother's expression remains unimpressed. "Yes, you do enjoy bending over for them, don't you, Justin?"

Beckett snorts, earning a dirty look from her. He groans, dropping his head over the back of the couch and running a hand through his black locks.

"Can we get on with things?" I say, checking the ornate gold analog clock mounted above the ebony fireplace across the room. "Some of us have classes to prepare for."

"Right. Speaking of which, this concerns your brother's expulsion," the dean replies.

"I thought his board hearing wasn't for another few weeks."

"It was, but we had an emergency session tonight, and that's what brings us here."

My gaze snaps to Beckett's. *Did he know about this when he called?*

"Normally, I'd say no to allowing a…troubled pupil back on

campus so soon," Dean Bauer continues, glancing at my brother as he tugs on his tie. "But Avernia's board has reversed their initial decision."

My brows knit together, and I cross one ankle over the other. "How is that possible? They are aware of *why* he was expelled, right?"

"Thanks for having my back," Beckett mutters.

Dean Bauer clears his throat, taking a drink of the water on the polished end table next to him. "Indeed, the board is intimately familiar with the...*incident* that occurred in the Tenarus cave last semester. However, in the short time we've employed you as an adjunct, you've proven to be more than trustworthy. No codes of conduct have ever been broken—despite several students' attempts to sway you, that is."

He laughs as if it's some big joke. I roll my eyes.

Like I'd ever be so fickle as to be tempted by a *student*. I was one not long ago.

They do not interest me.

"So in respecting you as a professor at Avernia, not to mention your family's influence, the board is willing to release Beckett from his punishment. After all, I'm certain he's had time to learn his lesson, and we'd hate to lose such a bright young mind for good."

Beckett stretches out, hooking his long legs over the couch's arm as he stares up at the vaulted ceiling. His index finger taps a rhythm on the sleeve of the black Curator blazer he wears.

Being president of the most prestigious student organization on campus had been his greatest accomplishment. It was his pride and joy, which is why it pained me so much to watch him throw it away all for some bullshit curse our father convinced him to believe in.

"That's wonderful to hear," Mother says, offering a small smile to my brother. "Don't you think, darling?"

"I'm waiting for the catch."

"No catch. Though I do think it's important we set some ground rules." Bauer sweeps a hand over his forehead, wiping off the sweat collecting on his pale skin. "For instance, Beckett's previous residence in the Curator clubhouse will be revoked. He'll be expected to live in Cadmus Hall."

I nod. "Seems fair."

Beckett makes a noise of disapproval. "*Cadmus*? Why don't you just take me behind the Lyceum and shoot me?"

"Darling," Mother chides. "Dean Bauer is doing you a favor here."

"A favor," he repeats, laughing humorlessly. "Wait til Father finds out. Cadmus is the *worst*-kept dorm on campus. I'd rather be stuck in Erebus with the social rejects."

"Cadmus Hall is our newest dorm," Dean Bauer says. "The accommodations might be sparse compared to what you're used to at the clubhouse, but I assure you, each residence hall is safe and adequate as far as housing for college students goes."

The dean cuts me a quick look, as if to challenge that claim. We both know the dorms are frequent targets for trouble.

Of the four acknowledged student organizations, Death's Teeth and the Curators have the vilest histories, but only one of those is school-sponsored and on the books. After last semester, I imagine the Curator presence itself will be much less intense going forward.

At least until things die down enough that the group—which thrives on important networking opportunities to maintain their reputation—can operate without question again.

Avernia's attention span for controversy is low despite

supposedly being a university for the best and brightest. I guess not even intelligence can save you entirely from your personal biases and desires.

The Curators' platform has always been about exclusivity. They're usually the most sought-after organization, with membership being invite-only, so I'm sure the murders and curse talk will become ancient history in a short while.

On the other hand, Death's Teeth is the school's most *elusive* group. They operate in the shadows, in library basements and caves within the Primordial Forest. It's a fringe organization run by anonymous founding family members and Fury Hill officials. Their purpose is to emphasize the cyclical nature of life and the importance of tradition, and highlight how everyone must bend to death.

They exploit fear and anonymity to maintain order, recruiting anyone with Fury Hill blood, trying to keep the line of their leadership "pure."

Fledglings aren't privy to such information, but when you're the one they think was chosen by some made-up god to run the organization, you get more insight than you bargained for.

Even if you refuse to step into the role of Incarnate, knowing it's a far more complex situation—involving human sacrifice, blood oaths, and exhibitionist displays—than they say.

That's why I'm still just an Elder despite years of participation. If I go any higher, whatever freedom I have left disappears.

Not to mention if I'm not the target, that puts Beckett in their path.

I suspect that's what made Bellamy their sacrifice eight years ago, though there's no proof. No body was ever recovered, and my parents didn't look into it. Any journals logged by the campus parasite, Pythia—who runs the school's hyperbolic and invasive newsletter from a faceless account—were lost or destroyed.

When I offer no objection to the dean's claims, he goes on. "It's also imperative that we don't draw attention to your relationship. The two of you don't look *that* much alike, so it's possible the average student won't notice if we don't point it out…and if you don't spend too much time together in public."

My skin starts to itch as the migraine from before returns, pulsing around my nose.

Mother scoffs. "Avernia is much too small to get away with that, no? Everyone knows who the Duponts are."

"We have a record-high number of nonresidents of Fury Hill attending this year," he tells her. "I think it's a possibility. Or perhaps it would be more beneficial if we had Beckett reside in Sutton's faculty quarters instead? Lowers the risk of him running into people who know his last name."

"It would also be much easier to keep tabs on him," Mother says.

"Fine," I reply. "Otherwise, our interactions will remain at a minimum outside the apartment."

Beckett grits his teeth. "Sounds like another way for Mr. Goody Two-Shoes to exert his authority on campus by pretending I'm some troublemaker."

I level him with a look. "Need I remind you of the reason we're here at all and why you need looking after?"

"We're going to ignore the fact that I was attacked by another student?" he retorts. "Who, by the way, I notice is absent. What're the chances he's also being treated like a ticking time bomb?"

"Beckett, darling, you *kidnapped* a student." Mother pinches the bridge of her nose, turning her angular face away. "I'm not sure you have the grounds to be offended here."

"Officially, though, the school says nothing even happened. They've covered everything up, so why are we still acting like I'm a convicted criminal when the crime, *on paper*, doesn't exist?"

A fair question. His antics ended with kidnapping, breaking and entering, and the deaths of three other students. But since the Curators have the dean's personal approval and are so intricately woven into the fabric of the university, everything was covered up, and Beckett was merely deemed too unstable for leadership. They stripped his title while he bled outside the caves, having been beaten badly by one of the students who came to the kidnappee's rescue.

I'm still not entirely sure *why* he did it. The curse, some amorphous ramblings about how one founder's misdeeds will apparently bring destruction in the form of his descendants, needed three Andersons on campus at once to even be valid. Last semester, there were only two.

Though I suppose when you crave your father's approval the way he always has, you might do whatever you can to get it. Even if it means following ridiculous orders.

Jean-Louis's absence doesn't exactly bode well on that front.

Dean Bauer's face pales, and more sweat seems to accumulate on his forehead and beneath his beady eyes. "Despite the efforts Avernia College goes to in ensuring the safety of its students—"

Beckett snorts.

"—there are still examples to be had. There were too many whispers, especially on that damn school forum, about what happened for us to let you go unpunished. Frankly, Mr. Dupont, I think you're getting off easy."

"You're only letting me attend under the condition that my

brother be my babysitter," he replies. "I can't go to official Curator functions because I was kicked out, everyone will probably steer clear of me, and I have to report to *Sutton*. How is that easy?"

"Well, the alternative was that you didn't return, period. You should be grateful to be coming back at all. What would your ancestors, the co-founders of this great town, think of your actions?"

If they believed the curse, I imagine they'd be fine with them. All except one, at least.

"Dean Bauer," Mother interjects, sloshing her drink around. "I'd appreciate it if you didn't try to intimidate my sons. Lest I remind you of the other child I left in your care who did not return to me."

Her remark is the end of the discussion; a few moments later, the dean excuses himself. Mother walks him to the manor's foyer, silently bidding him adieu, and when she reenters the room, she reaches for Beckett's face, giving him two kisses on each cheek. She repeats the gesture with me, pinching my skin as she half drags me off the couch.

If she notices the way I flinch at her touch, she doesn't let on. She never has.

"I expect to hear nothing but *good* anecdotes about your semester," Mother says, eyeing both of us. "Beckett, darling, please understand the gift you've been given here. This kind of proximity to a prodigy like your brother is an opportunity some would kill for."

That makes my face screw up. It isn't true—I'm no *prodigy*. My love for the theater was just one of the few things my parents accepted growing up, so I poured all my time and energy into studying it. The only reason I'm teaching now is because Avernia offered a dual degree program in which a bachelor's and master's could be earned simultaneously, giving me the option to graduate with both in less time than my peers.

After that, I spent some time in London and LA working for different theater companies and studying, before a position opened up here. Since Jean-Louis is on the board of trustees, they hired me without an interview, and I've been killing myself to be *good* ever since.

Which translates into tough courses, harsh grading scales, and constant work. I want my students to understand the texts they're acting out. To know why they're important so they can bring that to the stage.

Anything less is irrelevant. Not enough.

Mother, of course, believes the rigidity of my teaching style means I'm especially talented. Or maybe she just wants to believe one of her kids is destined for greatness rather than the suffering everyone in Fury Hill seems to eventually succumb to.

"Gift." Beckett scoffs. "He teaches acting classes, Mother. A monkey could likely do it just as well as Sutton."

"Shall I put you in charge on the first day then?" I ask.

He makes a sound with his teeth, then scrambles up from the sofa, heading for the arched doorway that leads to the foyer and main staircase. "Whatever. I have shit to do."

"Beckett," Mother whispers fiercely as he stalks away. The embroidered poppy and theta design on his blazer—the Curators' emblem—is the last thing I see before he disappears around the corner. His footsteps echo through the house as he shuffles down the upstairs hall, and then a door slams shut, and silence befalls us once more.

I swallow over the lump in my throat. A decade ago, laughter and music disturbed the gold-framed art and photographs decorating the walls. Now, only the dust of sound remains.

"I'm concerned about him," Mother says. "I don't think Beckett's been right since the night in those caves."

"He took quite the beating, Mother. We should probably just be glad he's able to speak or see at all."

We should be grateful he's alive.

"Still." She casts a nervous glance past me, biting the inside of her cheek. "The reason I paid Dean Bauer to have him reenrolled was to get him out of this house. I don't think he should be around Jean-Louis."

"You bribed the dean?"

She scoffs. "Well, I'm hardly the first Dupont to do so, but that isn't the point." Something flickers in her gaze as she settles back on the sofa beside me. "Jean-Louis's mind isn't what it used to be. He's…very angry and confused these days. His illness is only exacerbating those qualities, I'm afraid."

Not that he was ever a pleasant man to begin with.

"He suffers these delusions of power imbalances and losing control over the city. Considering what that led to a few weeks ago, I just don't think it's wise to allow Beckett to live in such close quarters. Your brother is very impressionable, and while I've always admired that…"

"It also gets him into trouble," I finish, nodding. "I know."

"I swear, he reminds me so much of Bellamy. They both took Jean-Louis's word as gospel, even if she was a tad more rebellious in nature than Beckett is. Maybe I should've encouraged them to interact more—perhaps she could've rubbed off on him." She casts me a sideways look. "Though that didn't happen with you, and the two of you were practically joined at the hip."

"We were twins," I reply, voice tight. "It was only natural we be close."

She slides one hand over mine, hers warm against my chilled fingers. "Your sister would be so proud of you, Sutton."

"Can we not do this?" My heart twists, and I pull my hand away. Talking about Bellamy here feels wrong. Too soon somehow. "Staff apartments are cramped, you know. Beckett takes up a lot of room."

"These are extenuating circumstances," she says. "I'm sure you can make it work."

"And if I don't want to?"

She narrows her eyes.

Clenching my jaw, I exhale with a shake of my head. "I'll figure it out."

"That's all I ask."

I nod, because of course I do. Of course I'll take the responsibility of another's safety and well-being, even though I'm not actually *good* at it.

But this is my lot in life.

Caring even when I desperately wish to stop.

A pair of hazel eyes flash in my mind, temporarily pulling me from the moment. Like some parasite that infected me without my knowing.

Given that it's been years since anyone interested me at all, I'm beginning to think the woman really was some sort of viper sent to tempt and torture. Who knows what would have happened if I'd let her fuck me the way she was silently begging to?

But just because I didn't allow things to go further doesn't mean I didn't *ache* for it. That now, an hour or so later, I'm not still replaying the divine sensation of her cunt wrapped snug around my dick or the little noises she uttered when I was making her come.

Putting an end to things was the correct decision. I'm not used to desire. Normally, I don't want to be touched at all.

But stopping doesn't keep the soul from yearning. Not when someone leaves their fingerprints all over it.

I walk to the foyer, shrugging into my coat. Mother trails behind, babbling on about council meetings and concerns among the other founding matriarchs that I'm not attending enough in Jean-Louis's stead.

Pressure explodes in my temple, the feeling of being watched causing pain to ricochet up the side of my skull.

When I glance backward, I spot Jean-Louis leaning against the upstairs balcony that splits the level into several wings. The lit end of a cigar hanging from his mouth burns bright orange among the shadows.

Of course he's watching. I wonder if he was actually too sick to come down.

It's likely he orchestrated the entire thing to get Beckett back on campus, where he thinks he'll be able to play puppeteer once more. All my life, he's been the manipulator behind the family, pulling strings by planting ideas in our minds and letting us think we were the masters of our own fates.

But the truth is we're as bound to that damn Fury Hill curse as its supposed subjects. As linked to destruction as Cronus Anderson's descendants.

Just a different kind. One that destroys from within.

"Sutton?" Mother reaches up, pressing a palm to my face. "Are you all right? You're suddenly flushed and very warm. Should I call for a nurse?"

Tearing my gaze away from his, I give her a small smile and swat at her hands, needing the space. "I'm fine, Mother. You don't need to worry about me."

Chapter 7

Elle

I look at Quincy as I pull my knees to my chest to try and make the confines of her office seem larger. My stomach aches a bit, though it's hard to tell if those are my nerves or period cramps.

Asher's the one with claustrophobia, but the longer I sit within Quincy's small forest—potted ferns, flowering plants, and even a tiny tree line nearly every flat surface that isn't occupied by occult, botany, and classic leather-bound books—the more I begin to understand his fear.

"What do you need help with?" she asks from behind her desk without looking up.

"What do you mean?"

"I assume there's a reason you're hiding out here instead of prepping for classes tomorrow."

"Is there a lot I should be doing?" I frown, tapping a finger to my bottom lip. "It's been a while since I was in school, but I don't remember needing to do *that* much beforehand."

"College is a totally different playing field than high school," she says, sighing. "Tell me you've at least gotten your textbooks."

"Textbooks?" I parrot back, grinning when a muscle twitches in her jaw. "I'm *kidding*, Q, Jesus. Lighten up. I did get a list of materials I needed, you know. Like everyone else."

"You're not like everyone else here," she points out. "Our last name alone puts you at a disadvantage."

A disconcerting chill scrapes my bones at the reminder.

In truth, I'm hiding out because I didn't know where else to go. As people meet up with friends from previous semesters, it's hard to not feel like the odd one out since I'm joining midway through the year *and* as an older student.

Not that there's an expiration on the age at which someone can attend college, but still. Most of the students are fresh out of high school. There's no denying that or the fact that there's a difference between me and them in general.

Avernia's primary demographic is residents of Fury Hill and surrounding cities. I spent the last seven years in LA, and while breaking into a community there was tough, once you did it, you had friends for as long as you wanted them.

Here, I'm not sure trusting anyone outside my family is a good idea.

I've seen the sorts of trouble caused in the forest's shadows, and I know everyone thinks we're villains coming to ruin their school.

It's safer to stay here, where the only judgment that can be passed is Quincy's. I learned to tune hers out long ago anyway.

My sister exhales, closing the ledger in her lap and pushing a stack of spiral-bound notebooks to the corner of her desk along with a few hardback books. She arranges them neatly, setting the ledger on top—the plain black cover of which has *A Short History of Fury Hill, New Hampshire: Primary* written in bold text across it.

"Did setting fire to the dean's house lower our stock value?" I ask eventually, when she doesn't offer more commentary. It's scary how long she can go without speaking, just like our father.

She adjusts the rings on her fingers. The one on her thumb has a small obsidian bat in the middle, while the others are mostly solid gold bands or have abstract gemstone patterns.

"It's not about value, it's about paranoia. In general, people here will act like you're some kind of god to your face and plot your demise behind your back."

"So… How am I supposed to make friends if I don't know who believes in the curse and who wants me dead?"

"You're not."

"Oh, well, good. No regrets over enrolling then. So glad you convinced Mom and Dad this was a safe place to be."

"I'm not trying to scare you," she says, getting up and walking to the bookshelves framing the one window in the room, which overlooks the garden her student organization is working on. "I just want to make sure you're adequately prepared. Avernia isn't Hollywood. There are real, active threats to heed."

"Should I be wearing armor to class? You don't think anyone would try to Julius Caesar me, do you?"

She narrows her eyes. "Did you see Uncle Kieran before you came here? That's his humor to a T."

"He might have stopped by the Asphodel with Aunt Juliet and Eden a few times." I tilt my head, smirking. "Why, jealous I got to see her?"

"Hardly."

"It's okay to miss your first lo—"

"Noelle," she says between gritted teeth. "That's none of your business."

"Well, sure, but man is a curious species, right?"

"Curiosity kills. Something you'd do well to remember."

"You say that like you think I'm gonna do something stupid."

"I'm just saying. You're a student first and foremost, but you're also my sister. Your actions will directly impact me."

Glancing down at my chipped nail polish, I nod. "*Okay*. I get it. I promise not to tarnish your reputation more than it probably already is."

"Hilarious," she drolls. "Speaking of reputations… Are you ready to talk about why you left Hollywood yet?"

My stomach drops.

No. No, I'm not ready. I doubt I ever will be.

"I had my reasons." Lifting my chin, I shoot her an annoyed look. "What's with the third degree? You sound an awful lot like Mom right now."

Offense mars her features, and she points a fountain pen at me. "Take that back."

"There are *worse* comparisons, you know."

"Yes, but no one wants to be *just* like their mother." She frowns. "Although you look more and more like her every day."

My nerves twist into millions of little knots. Sure, I might look like her, but the difference between us is that Mom has talent—she writes bestsellers under a pseudonym—and Dad. Meanwhile, my accolades and love life are currently nonexistent.

Not for lack of trying. But not everything is meant to work out, I guess.

"So if the California dream is dead, what's your plan here?" Quincy asks.

"Don't know yet. Playing it by ear."

She grunts, unamused. "Asher's only attending because of Lucy, you know. He'll be gone in the spring when she graduates."

"I'm aware. I might not visit often, but I do keep tabs on our family. I even came up to help Lucy with an audition last year."

Quincy's eyebrows raise. "I didn't know about that."

"Well, you weren't around." I pause, refraining from adding *as usual*. No reason to let her know just how deeply her absence affects me.

Leaning forward, I peer at the spines of the other books on her desk. *The Mythos of Fury Hill, Hauntings and Ghost Sightings in the White Mountains,* and *The Rule of Three: What Hidden Catacombs Can Tell the Modern World.*

"Aren't you a classics professor?" I ask, reaching for the one on top.

"Does that mean I can only read the classics?" She snatches the book from my hand, glowering, as she sets a small journal on top of the stack. "You shouldn't touch things that don't belong to you."

"Maybe I want to read too."

My eyes fall to the journal. The cover is white and stained with what looks like smudged fingerprints, though the coloring is off. Dark brown or maybe red, and there are dozens of symbols—poppies, torches, and something else I can't make out—scrawled around a single word etched in permanent marker.

DĪRĒCTORIBUS.

It reminds me of the school's mantra, *mortui vivos docent*, which makes me think of the lake and the bodies that apparently go in but don't come out.

I think of the night eight years ago when everything changed here, then quickly shove the thoughts away.

After a moment, Quincy reaches into a drawer, producing a composition notebook with a series of dates scribbled on the front. Silent, she stares at it for several beats and then seems to decide against handing it over, placing it on the stack along with the Dīrēctoribus.

My interest piques, but I school my expression, unwilling to let her know I find her evasiveness intriguing.

"Look," she continues, removing her glasses to rub between her eyes, "just do me a favor and keep the trouble to a minimum, all right? That means don't go into the Primordial Forest for any reason. Missing persons reports are up by, like, a thousand percent this year, and we don't need another incident like the last time you were here."

Nausea pokes at the base of my throat. *I've never forgotten those eyes.* Instead of pointing that out, I straighten my spine and nod. "Okay, fine. I'll stay out."

"I mean it, Noelle." She looks at me. "Mom and Dad got a glimpse into how bad shit is here, but it's hard to really tell unless you're in it. Given what happened with Asher last semester, it's unlikely you'd be the target of such violence again so soon, but not an impossibility. Avernia sweeps *everything* under the rug. Don't expect any problems to get solved. They'll take your statement and then pretend you don't exist."

Unease filters through my veins. That seems like something we should be alerting our parents to, yet the rule here is that what's *really* happening doesn't get back to them.

"So then… Why do you stick around?" I ask. "If this place is so dangerous and awful, why come *back*? Why let Asher and me enroll and keep all the secrets from our parents?"

The floor lamp next to us flickers beneath its dark shade. Quincy's fingers curl inward. The temperature in the room seems to drop, a breeze bursting suddenly from the vent in the ceiling.

"Do you believe in ghosts, Noelle?"

My eyebrows arch. "Uh…I don't *not* believe in them, I guess."

"Scientifically speaking, there's no *real* evidence supporting their existence. But not everything can be explained by science. Some things transcend deduction. Phenomena that occur but can't be defined."

"That sounds confusing."

She shakes her head. "Sometimes I wonder if it's just easier not to believe. If it can't be explained, people just write it off entirely. Like maybe…they're not looking for the right stuff. Or in the right places."

"Are you trying to tell me Avernia is actually haunted?"

I've heard the rumors about supernatural sightings over the years, but I didn't think my sister would subscribe to them. She's always been so methodical and poised that it's hard to imagine her believing in things she can't see or explain.

"I'm saying it doesn't take belief to be true." She stares at the wood of the desk between us. "And what haunts doesn't go away just because you do."

Her phone buzzes, and she draws it from her bag, looking at the screen for a long moment. I wonder whose name flashes there.

When she lifts her gaze to mine as if expecting privacy, I push to my feet, then leave her alone in the office. The dimly lit halls in the admin building seem unnaturally narrow as I make my way to the stairs.

Pipes groan behind the alabaster walls, sending an eerie wave vibrating along the rafters. The steps feel endless beneath my descent, like they could go on forever just to keep me here.

I don't *think* I believe in ghosts, but if there was ever a home to them? This would be it.

A shiver ripples across my skin, and I grip my biceps, glancing over my shoulder as a door slams shut. The sound echoes through the stairwell, blanketing me in stillness.

Coming here was probably a mistake. Even if I didn't have the knowledge that we're being monitored, it's as if the walls themselves have eyes that follow me everywhere I go.

By the time I reach the exit, I feel like they're pressing in and strangling my lungs. Bracing my hands on the metal push bar, I shove out the front door, gasping for breath.

I double over, clutching my knees as something akin to panic pulses in my body, lighting me on fire. Hand to my chest, I struggle to regulate my breathing, and a shadow moves across the quad.

A tall figure makes its way out of the Lyceum, the massive castle-like building near the school's gated entrance. He walks with his shoulders squared and a briefcase held tight in one hand. His steps are purposeful, the courtyard statues bordering his path like a parade of marble.

Curiosity keeps me afloat; there's something *familiar* about the man, but I can't quite put my finger on what it is. His dark hair blows gently in the breeze, and his eyes are completely indiscernible from my vantage point.

Distantly, a clock chimes, reverberating off the trees and bushes flanking the stone paths. I swallow, standing still, waiting to see if the figure turns my way.

When I blink again, he vanishes.

Like he wasn't ever there in the first place.

Chapter 8

Sutton

"Salvete! Welcome to Acting for Beginners."

I walk onstage during my greeting as the auditorium murmurs its reply. Better than expected for an early-morning course on the first day back.

My fingers curl around the apricot I swiped from my apartment—a daily staple of mine for eight years now. Ever since the migraines first began.

The beginning of the semester is always my favorite, because everyone is still full of hope. No matter what's going on elsewhere, within these four acoustic-friendly walls, they have a clean slate.

Sometimes, that's all you need to really turn things around.

A student in the back of the large auditorium groans. "Professor Dupont, did we *really* have to learn all those Latin phrases you sent over winter break?"

"Vere. The title of the organization I run *is* technically Latin, you know, although a terribly imperfect translation. Does anyone know what the correct phrasing should be?"

"Visio Aeterna," my former TA, Sabrina Taylor, answers, swinging her blond ponytail from left to right. She sits dead center of the front row, leaning forward as if to physically capture my attention. "*Vision of the Eternal.* Because the students who join work at bettering the community for the future."

"Correct. And though our founders inaccurately named the organization, I think it's important we learn about the words that are etched into our school's existence. We want to respect the cultures that influence us, not exploit them, right?"

"But it's a dead language," someone else calls out.

"And this is an acting class," another adds. "What's the point?"

"I'm going to pretend you didn't just ask me that." I set the fruit on the portable desk onstage and point at a pasty, curly-haired student frantically scribbling something down in his notebook. "What's Avernia's motto?"

"Uh…" He panics, glancing at the girl with a dark brown complexion sitting next to him.

She makes a face, then lifts her chin. "Mortui vivos docent."

"Excellent. What does it mean?"

A few titters in the crowd, but no one comes forward with an actual answer. Not even Sabrina this time, though she at least has the decency to look ashamed.

Jesus. So much for a clean slate.

"The dead teach the living," I offer. "Avernia was founded on the idea of learning from the past and the dead. Everything we use to progress as a society comes from what we glean from our ancestors, their societies, and how we utilize that knowledge to evolve."

More silence.

I smirk to myself, clasping my hands together. "You all are in for a rough semester."

"Professor," the boy from before calls out. "Is it true that a bunch of students almost died in the caves this past winter?"

The question catches me off guard. I cock my head to the side, folding my arms over my chest. *Deny, deny, deny.* "Where on earth did you hear a rumor like that?"

He shrugs. "*The Delphic Pages* mentioned it a couple of times, although the posts keep getting removed."

"That's just urban legend," someone toward the back replies. "Same as all the bodies that supposedly go missing in Lake Lerna. When's the last time anyone was even close enough to that thing to fall in?"

"Yeah," a blond with three eyebrow piercings and a pinkish freckled face agrees. "You can't trust anything Pythia says. *The Delphic Pages* is just a site for gossip. Half the rumors end up not being true."

"Well, they were right about the program cuts last spring and reported that new Anderson kid before he even showed up for class in the fall."

My heartbeat grows louder, drowning out the noise as they descend into arguing among themselves.

Shit. This isn't good. Discord on the first day rarely produces favorable long-term results, and I don't need future castmates clashing already.

Nor do I need anyone poking around, looking for answers that will get them into trouble if found.

Holding a hand up, I wait for a hush to fall over the crowd. "Unless this discussion is directly related to Visio Aternae or has something to do with acting, I'm going to request you all put pins in the ideas and hold them until after my time with you is up."

"*If* it was true," the kid continues, ignoring my request, "I was just wondering… What would we learn from the dead students then?"

I stare at him for several beats, waiting for the erratic pace of my heart to relax. Gritting my teeth, I bend down, grabbing a stack of Visio Aternae pamphlets and philanthropic guides from my briefcase, even as memories flank my vision, threatening to drag me down into complete and utter desolation.

There's a reason the forest is supposed to be off-limits. What happened last semester is only part of why.

Hopping off the stage, I pass out the information to the class, ending with the inquisitor. As people chatter around us, he looks up and meets my gaze.

I don't like how easily he does so—like he's actually trying to figure something out.

Something he perhaps knows too much about.

"They'd probably learn not to believe everything they hear," I tell him in a low voice, turning away to speak to the class again before he can respond. "As you all are aware, Pythia is notorious for spouting mindless drivel on our school's online forum, and you should take what she says with a grain of salt. I would have petitioned to have her shut down years ago if she wasn't so damned entertaining."

They laugh, but it's true. My issues with *The Delphic Pages* date back to my undergrad years when it was still in its infancy.

In the wake of my sister's death, the forum allowed Pythia to publish heinous lies about Bellamy and her involvements at the school. Those were the only things written about her at all—that we could find anyway.

Pythia said nothing of me, which always made me question who runs the account.

Death's Teeth protects their own.

I hoist myself up onto the lip of the stage, reaching for the class roster and my apricot. "In the back of these pamphlets, you'll find an index card where you can request enrollment in Visio Aternae. Don't worry if you're not interested—I won't be offended—but *do* note we're the only philanthropic organization on campus, and we don't accept new members midsemester. This is your one shot to join until the fall."

Heads bow as they begin writing their answers, and I wait a few seconds, reveling in the sound of pencils scratching on paper.

"When I call your name, I want a quick 'present' and then for you to form a line in the center aisle right *here*"—I smack the space next to me with my free palm—"where you'll place your card and winter essays in a neat pile. Please use the name listed on your student IDs, as that will be your proof of attendance. Lexington Abbott."

Lexington is Angelica—the owner of Lethe's—and Zane's son, and he draws the attention of every student as he strides past: Tall, with light brown skin, loose curly hair, and a toned physique he often emphasizes in sleeveless shirts and athletic pants, he's easy on the eyes.

As far as I can tell, he's one of the few founding family members who cares very little about the school's curse or the rules of law revolving around Fury Hill. It's the first time I've seen him since he enrolled as a theater major, but as he drops his essay and blank note card on the stage, I wonder if he's planning on joining any organization at all.

It's not common in our circles for a founder to be totally

uninvolved, though if the higher-ups allow it, I can't deny the envy I feel over his freedom.

He looks me over with clear blue eyes. "Assigning essays over break was cruel and unusual punishment, by the way."

Straightening my spine, I nod. "That was the point."

He tsks, seeming to swallow a reply before spinning around and heading back to his friends—a girl with dark brown skin sitting in a wheelchair at the very back, furiously writing on her note card, and a ghostly pale blond guy who keeps stealing glances at Sabrina.

New faces. Acting for Beginners is a lower-level course, so I rarely expect to see many familiar students—although I'm not entirely sure why Sabrina's here, considering she's been in other classes with me before and was my TA.

But if I ask, she'll assume I care, and I don't need her getting the wrong idea.

Clearing my throat, I move to the next name on the list. "Noelle Anderson."

No one in the auditorium moves.

I take a bite of my fruit and scan the classroom, searching for a kid with headphones or one who's too busy talking to someone they're sitting by, but everyone's looking at me, dutifully waiting.

"Noelle Anderson?" I repeat after swallowing, a strange sensation slithering down my spine.

Asher Anderson was in my Staging the Greeks course last semester, and the new classics department head shares the last name. Both part of the disgraced founding bloodline, thus two-thirds of the prophesied curse.

Despite Dean Bauer's many shortcomings, I doubt he'd actually let all three enroll at once.

Chest tight, I call out the name one more time. When no one

comes forward again, I shake my head and cross it out. "There's always one who drops the first day—"

"Wait, no! I'm here!"

Exhaling, I lean back on my free hand as one of the doors at the top of the room flies open, the silhouette of a leggy woman appearing. She nearly stumbles over the first step but manages to catch herself at the last second.

"I'm so sorry. There was an issue with the showers in my dorm, and then I got stuck in the elevator," she rushes out, gripping the railing that separates the wheelchair accessible seats from the lower levels. "But I'm here now, so…"

That voice…

It's melodic and full, resonating throughout the auditorium like she's used to speaking for a crowd.

A voice I've replayed in my mind since I last heard it in the passenger seat of my car.

Suspicion claws at my bones, and I slowly get to my feet, rounding the front row. The apricot falls out of my hand, rolling as I walk past it. I stop at the bottom of the aisle, staring up at the newcomer as she white-knuckles the railing.

Soft, dark brown locks spill down her shoulders in gentle waves, framing a delicate face with pouty pink lips. Beneath a charcoal-colored overcoat, she's wearing a cream blouse tucked into a short, tight brown skirt, and I follow the length of her pale legs down to the block heels she wears, buckled over frilly white socks.

Somehow the combination works, and she almost manages to blend in a bit with the rest of the student body, most of whom prefer earth tones, solid colors, and blended fabrics.

It's a far cry from the siren I met at the gas station and again at Lethe's, though no less devastating.

Her eyes are obscured by shadows, making it difficult for me to confirm that this is in fact *her*.

The woman I've been dreaming about—and, if I'm honest, fucking my fist to the memory of—for the past week.

Here. In *my* classroom.

This must be some cruel joke. A prank put on by the other theater faculty or maybe even Death's Teeth. They've been known to fuck with someone's psyche to get them to do their bidding, so I can't put it past them.

Not that they'd know I had anything to do with her in the first place.

Perhaps the universe is merely out to get me.

Electricity buzzes in the lights hanging above us, drowning out my thoughts as I rejoin reality, noticing several beats of immobilizing silence have passed. I've just been staring at this woman while everyone watched.

Jesus *Christ*.

Clearing my throat, I lift the attendance sheet. "You're Noelle Anderson?"

Several lifetimes seem to pass before she answers. "I am."

My stomach lurches violently.

Did she give me a fake name? No, I suppose "Elle" is merely a lie of omission, but still.

Had she really been so concerned that her full name would elevate what we were doing, as if something serious with me would have ever been possible?

Being with her was the first time in eight years that I'd allowed anyone that close willingly. The first time that being touched didn't absolutely revolt me and even…felt *good*.

Too good. My dick had been *inside her*, which is why I didn't put up much of a fight when we were interrupted. Sex is a complication. A means to an end in a life where I'm bound to be a symbol—an example—and nothing more.

It wouldn't have been fair of me to drag her into that, even temporarily. Even if I wanted it more than I'd ever wanted anything in my life.

She'd been so soft, so pliant. Her breasts were heavy, her cunt so goddamn soaked, and the noises she made when I touched her threatened to incinerate me.

I'd been three seconds from coming in that shitty gas station condom, unaccustomed to such a visceral reaction to a woman. To *anyone*.

For a long time, I assumed Death's Teeth had broken me. She proved otherwise.

"You're Noelle," I repeat, as much for myself as for her.

"I go by Elle, but—"

"Which is on your student ID?"

She blinks. "Noelle, but—"

"In the event someone asked you to introduce yourself," I interrupt again, my mouth dry as if I packed it with cotton, "which name would you provide?"

I'm grasping at straws, and she knows it.

Slowly, she brings her hands together in front of her, interlocking her fingers tightly. "Elle," she replies, lifting her chin. "But as I'm sure you're aware, *Professor*, Avernia prints its student IDs according to the paperwork submitted by each applicant. I presume class rosters do the same, which is why you're seeing *Noelle* there."

"It's barely even that different of a name, sir," someone else calls from the front. "Is it really that big of a deal?"

"A fair point." Gritting my teeth, I take another calculated sweep of Elle before turning away and heading back to the stage, trashing the discarded apricot on my way. "'What's in a name? That which we call a rose by any other name would smell as sweet.'"

Sabrina bounces in her seat. "*Romeo and Juliet*!"

"Correct, but I wasn't asking. I merely hoped to convey the importance of names, especially in a class like this one, where so much of what we do will be taking on the roles of others. It's vital to know yourself and your peers past the surface level so you can perform well later on. *That* is why a name matters. It fosters intimacy and knowledge. Encourages relationships."

From the corner of my eye, I watch Elle take a quick seat somewhere in Lexington Abbott's vicinity and ignore the hyperawareness of my tongue as I scan the attendance sheet once more.

"Ms. Anderson, please bring your winter essay to the stage and pick up a Visio Aternae pamphlet so we can move on with the lesson."

Silence.

When I look up, I see her staring, frozen in place like a deer caught in headlights.

"Essay?" she calls out.

"The one on the differences between live and screen acting? I sent the prompt out weeks ago."

"Over break?"

Sighing, I scrub at the underside of my jaw. "Ms. Anderson, are you planning to question everything I say the entire semester?"

"Well, if it requires expansion, yes. Asking questions is important." She narrows her eyes at me. "Almost as important as a person's name."

For some reason, my blood feels like it's boiling. "After a certain point, questioning becomes disruptive. Insubordination won't be tolerated." A long pause, and I glance around the rest of the auditorium, looping them back in as if this is a public lecture and not a conversation I wish I was having in private. "Do you have the essay or not?"

"No. What kind of professor assigns homework to a class he hasn't met? How would a late addition even know what was going on?"

Someone snickers, and I know without looking that it's fucking Lexington. Maybe even the boy next to him.

"If you have a problem with the way I run my class, Ms. Anderson, I encourage you to take it up with the dean. Though I expect he'll give you the same answer as I'm about to."

"Which is?"

God, why does the way she talks back make me dizzy?

"This is a monarchy, not a democracy. I'm the king, and what I say goes."

A few students chuckle.

"Sounds more like a dictatorship," Elle spits back.

I shrug. "Call it whatever label you prefer. Either way, you're unprepared, and I'm done with this conversation."

She doesn't come to the front to get a pamphlet, so I quickly move on to the rest of the attendance sheet, noting that if I spend too much time going back and forth, it'll look suspicious. I can already feel Sabrina's eyes peering into my soul, trying to determine why I gave such an unflattering welcome to a new student when I'm typically more relaxed about interruptions.

There's no way I'd be able to explain it, so I just ignore her stare, slapping my hand on top of the stack of essays once I get to the end of the list.

"Beautiful. Now, take a good look at the person sitting directly to your left. They'll be your warm-up, improv, audition, and set design partner for the rest of the semester. Exchange names and emails on your own time, and take out your syllabus. We'll go over the bullet points and my expectations, and then we can talk about what I know we're all *dying* for: the final play of the semester, which is the only way you pass the course."

Lexington's friend raises her hand. Meg, I think her name was. "Will we get to vote on the play like previous classes did?"

I nod. "While this may not be a democracy, certain aspects are community efforts, and therefore I like to let the *community* determine them. But we'll talk more about that in a minute. Turn to page two in the syllabus—"

A hand shoots up, and I know whose without even looking.

"Ms. Anderson," I drone, clenching my jaw tight. "Do you have yet another question? This might be a school record you're breaking."

"I don't have a syllabus."

My fingers crinkle the corner of my packet. "So not only were you late, but you're lacking even the most basic materials? Is unpreparedness a common theme I should anticipate from you?"

If a pin dropped from anywhere in the room, I expect they'd be able to hear it in the hallway.

Elle tucks her hair behind her ears. "Well, my roommate's printer wasn't working."

"There are three libraries on campus. Not to mention an administration building and a plethora of student services. You could have asked anyone."

She drops her gaze like she's deeply embarrassed, despite having practically bared her entire soul to me the moment we met. Like she doesn't know what my fingers feel like curling inside her or my dick pushing in—

Tension threads through my neck, knotting in my shoulders, as I abruptly halt those memories. Fucking hell, this is a disaster.

Nobody in the class moves a muscle. I suspect many of them, likely freshmen, are afraid that my soured mood will spill onto them, and they'll become the objects of my irritation.

Returning my focus to the syllabus, I speak directly to Elle one final time. "You're dismissed, Ms. Anderson."

"*What*?"

"Three strikes. Please see yourself from my classroom."

She huffs, defiant to her very core. In my peripheral vision, I watch her gather her things but pretend I'm focused on the attendance policy in the syllabus, pointing at Sabrina to read it out loud.

While she talks, my skin feels like it's being stretched, goose bumps prickling every inch. My heart pulses hard in my throat, and I don't relax even a little until the sound of the door swinging shut behind Elle's exit echoes through the rafters.

Chapter 9

Elle

HUMILIATION BURNS MY SKIN, LIKE AN OPEN FLAME BEING held against me. I stand outside the auditorium while class continues, debating silently whether I should even stay enrolled in this fucking school at all.

I've never had anyone go so far out of their way to embarrass me—*three* times. Then again, nothing men do surprises me, so I'm not sure why I find it so bothersome now.

I certainly wasn't expecting *him*. He'd been leaning against the stage, his brown hair all slicked back and neat, making him look more boyish than the beige sweater vest and pleated trousers he wore.

But it was the severity on his face when he said my full name that caught me off guard. Like he was *angry* I hadn't shared the entire thing or pissed I was there at all.

Whatever. I'm a student, and regardless of some fleeting encounter, I have as much right to be in an elected course as anyone else. So when the class begins to file out, signaling its end, I slip inside and down the aisle, watching as the professor—*Sutton Dupont*, according to my course schedule—disappears behind the stage.

"If you're looking for Dupont," an attractive man with warm, light brown skin and bright blue eyes says, seeming to arrive out of thin air before me, "he hides in his office between classes. The whole theater department is in the annex of the Lyceum."

"Oh." I blink, nodding. "Um, thanks."

"He keeps syllabi in there too if you can convince him to give you one." The guy smirks, extending his hand. "I'm Lexington. The thorn in Professor Dupont's *other* side."

"Why's that?" I ask, taking his palm just barely, letting him shake once before his arm drops. *Has he hooked up with him too?*

Just how much do you really get around, Professor?

"Fury Hill founding family stuff. Feuds go back centuries. It'd take too much effort for me to really care though."

I make a noise of disbelief. "Yeah, I usually go out of my way to bring up things I don't care about too."

A big, goofy grin stretches across Lexington's face. "*Please* tell me you're staying in this class. I can already tell you're gonna be a lot of fun for Dupont."

"The only man I let tell me what to do is my father," I say, pushing past to move through the auditorium. "And he's not here right now."

There's just one door backstage, and when I shove it open, it leads to a narrow hall with the occasional dead cockroach and dozens of wooden doors that seem to go on forever.

Not much of an annex if you ask me.

I jump as the exit swings shut; the sound of the handle latching into place bounces off the corridor, and I follow it with short steps, reading the names mounted on the walls as I pass them.

An overhead light flickers as I walk under it. I grip my backpack tighter, reaching the last door on the left.

This one lacks a label, but I can see a faint glow beneath the frame. Swallowing, I reach for the knob and turn it quickly, inviting myself in.

Sutton stands just out of reach, the door missing him by a hair as it swings open. A bowl of apricots and overly ripe bananas sits on the corner of the large mahogany desk behind him, next to a small orange prescription bottle and a stack of *La Musica Deuxième* playbills.

His arms are crossed over his chest like he's been waiting for me, and he wears an unreadable expression. His wavy hair is now slightly mussed, like he's been dragging his hands through it out of frustration.

The image sends a shiver slinking down my spine, and I freeze in place.

Fuck me, I'd forgotten just how hot he was. Even standing at the top of his class earlier, I hadn't been entirely sure. My brain was still reaching for anything that could disprove this being the awkward man who made me come on his hand last week.

Standing here now, though, there's no denying it's him.

"What are you doing?" he asks, his voice carefully detached.

"I was told I could get a copy of the syllabus from you."

"Only students enrolled in my courses receive syllabi."

My head cocks. "I *am* enrolled."

"You were. I'm having that taken care of." He surges forward, reaching for the door and pulling it wider. "Now, if you'll excuse me, I've got—"

"You can't kick me out just because we hooked up."

"Jesus," he hisses, sliding a hand around my waist to pull me into the office as he slams the door shut. As soon as he touches me, though, he withdraws, curling those icy fingers into a fist and clenching his teeth. "Do you *want* me to get fired?"

"I have no particular feelings on the matter," I reply, lifting my chin in defiance. "All I wanted was a syllabus."

His eyes vibrate with his ire, but I lose myself in the mossy shade anyway. Soft yet firm, like a forest floor you could lie down on until it swallowed you whole.

Internally, I shake myself. I'm here for one thing and one thing only, and I can't let a cute guy distract me from that goal—not again.

After a long, heavy moment, he withdraws entirely, crossing his arms and walking to lean against the edge of his desk. "You could have just emailed."

"So you could ignore me? I don't think so, Boy Scout."

"I hardly find that an appropriate thing to call your professor."

"But you just said you were 'having that taken care of.' So… Are you my professor or not?"

He reaches up, closing his eyes and pinching the bridge of his nose with two fingers. I ignore how the tendons in his forearm, exposed by rolled-up sleeves, strain against his skin.

Somewhere in the perverted recesses of my brain, I wonder what he'd look like in glasses. A tie, maybe, or some suspenders. He could take the glasses off as he leaned in to kiss me and undo the suspenders to wrap them around my—

"What's your interest in my class?" he asks, interrupting my thoughts. The taut look on his face makes me think he can read minds. "Are you taking the course just to harass me?"

"Harass you? Like by, perhaps, making you repeat your name over and over in front of a class full of students as if you've committed some heinous crime?"

Pink crawls up his neck, flushing his cheeks. "I didn't intend for that to be so…" He exhales, shaking his head. "You have to understand my confusion. I mean, you said you were a tourist—"

"No, I said I wasn't from here, which I'm not."

He's quiet for a long time, seeming to mull something over. "Are you related to Quincy Anderson? And Asher?"

"They're my brother and sister," I finish, shrugging. "So?"

Exasperation colors his features. "If you're an Anderson, one of *those* Andersons, by default, we're supposed to have some sort of unspoken rivalry. At the very least, we shouldn't be speaking, much less interacting privately."

I frown, tilting my head. "Why is that?"

Sutton releases his nose, opens his eyes, and swallows. "Because of our familial history?"

I blink at him.

He braces his hands against his desk. "Ms. Anderson, how much exactly do you know about Fury Hill?"

"As little as possible."

"Because knowledge means responsibility?"

Blood rushes between my ears as I stare at him. The air expresses instantly from my lungs, and I clasp my hands together, squeezing tight. He watches the movement but says nothing.

It's unnerving how good he is at seeing right fucking through me. He probably doesn't even realize how transparent I really am, which would be comforting if *I* didn't know.

All my life, I've worn my heart on my sleeve. Once upon a time, I thought it was safe there so long as I played whatever role people wanted me to—any role I could get my hands on.

But sometimes you can do everything right, play every part, and still wind up used and discarded.

"If this is how you treat all your students, I'm surprised your class was so highly recommended."

"It's highly recommended because I'm a good teacher."

"Just a bad liar then?"

Pure, unadulterated fury burns in his gaze. His chest rises and falls rapidly, matching the urgency of my own breathing. "Are you implying I somehow tricked you?"

"I'm just saying. Why didn't you mention working here? You said you were a director, and you made it seem like the other night was…"

I trail off, heat bleeding into my pores. No way am I admitting that for a few moments, our little tryst in his car felt *special*.

A man has to earn that right.

"Had I known you were a student, I certainly would not have engaged. My behavior was incredibly inappropriate, and I apologize."

"What is that?" I ask. "A PR apology? I don't remember requesting your regret over kissing me."

"I didn't say I regretted it." His eyes flash, and a muscle in his jaw thumps. "I said I was sorry."

"How is that different?"

"Regret implies I wouldn't do it again."

Oh.

He sighs, letting his chin drop. I take a moment to look around, noting a few dying plants in the windowsill, a large bookcase next to it filled with various works of famous playwrights like Wilde, Aristophanes, and Euripides, and even some Behn and Kalidasa.

It's the collection of someone who not only enjoys acting but wants to fully understand the medium and its worldly history. Someone who takes theater *seriously*.

My heart thumps a little faster in my chest, but I ignore it.

A well-read man is attractive. Even more so when he's well-read on things that interest me. But that's not what I'm here for.

No matter how badly I might ache to learn more.

Beyond the books, a single filing cabinet sits beneath the window, holding a bust of Shakespeare and several cartridges of fountain pens. The cement walls are painted a forest green, a few shades darker than his eyes, and they remind me of the woods surrounding this school.

I shiver. All the more reason for me to leave without pursuing anything more.

"There was a fire at the dean's house," he says, glancing above my head. "Any chance you had something to do with it?"

"That's what you want to know?"

Slowly, he drags his gaze to mine. "I'm asking if it was you, Elle. Is that what you needed the lighter for?"

Crossing my arms, I look away. A coffee stain catches my attention, dried up on the dark green ombre rug under our feet. I trace the outline with my eyes until it starts to blend in with the fabric below, eventually turning into a memory.

One filled with the scent of sweat-soaked flesh. The sound of distant screams echoing through the forest. Eyes I can't unsee, ever, no matter how much time passes.

Fear scales higher along my body, sparks licking their way up my spine and limbs in a path toward destruction.

A different memory, this one tainted with sin, snowballing out of control. The need for attention—*distraction*—clawing at my brain, propelling me into strong arms, the scent of apricots and cologne invading my senses, making me dizzy.

And then…nothing.

Nothing at all.

He waits for an answer. A confession.

"I've never intentionally started a fire in my life," I tell him.

"I don't know about *that*," he mutters, and I have to wonder if he means a different kind of fire.

If he too feels this *heat* pulsing between us, beckoning and pleading.

Instead of elaborating, he redirects the conversation. "Are you aware that arson is a very serious crime?"

"I'm not an idiot." I slink forward a step. "But as I said—*I've* never started a fire. You don't have to worry about me."

"So far, you've instilled very little confidence in that being the case. Your preparedness skills leave much to be desired."

"A momentary lapse in judgment."

"That also seems like a pattern with you."

"It's cute that you're so concerned."

"I am. For both our sanities."

Fluttering my eyelashes, I edge even closer, clutching my hands behind my back and pushing my breasts forward. One of the buttons on my blouse came undone earlier while I was waiting, so my cleavage peeks through a slit in the top, tantalizing. "Do you worry about all your students like this?"

He swallows. "Yes."

"Really?" I slip into the gap between his thighs but don't actually make any contact. He smells just like he did in the car that night—some mix between crisp apricot and a touch of woodsy cologne—and I try not to inhale too deeply.

"A *good* professor shows compassion for those he's trying to teach."

"Compassion." I reach for his chest and start to drag my finger down the center. "Is that what you feel for me?"

His arm lashes out, and he catches my wrist, halting my movements. His fingers are as cold as I remember.

"I don't feel anything for you except contempt, Ms. Anderson. You're proving to be little more than a nuisance."

"That's no way to talk to a student."

"Nor should you be touching your professor." His green eyes blaze, rage bubbling in the irises. "I suppose we're both at fault here, *temptress.*"

The nickname he gave me the night we met. Heat sizzles against the surface of my skin. "Would you like to touch me?"

"No."

"Liar." I pout and try to pull away, but he holds me tight.

In place.

He doesn't say anything for a beat, but the way his gaze burns like liquid emerald sears me from the inside out.

The chill from his hands sends a spray of goose bumps scattering across my arms. "You're cold, *Sutton,*" I purr, shifting to wrap my fingers around his. "Let me warm you up."

Before I can, he releases me and stalks around to the other side of his desk. He snatches a stapled packet from the filing cabinet, tossing it onto the wood surface between us.

"There's your syllabus," he states, entirely devoid of emotion. That mask of his slides right back into place, shutting me out. "Now leave. I can't keep you from taking the course, but I can damn sure have you removed from my office if need be."

Chapter 10

Sutton

"HAVE YOU MADE A DECISION YET?"

Jean-Louis's voice is a constant fucking pain in the back of my skull, but especially so when he feels well enough to call me at school. Normally, I screen his attempts to reach me on my cell, but the office landline is a different story.

Only faculty have the number—or so I thought.

I would hang up, but I suspect he might make his way to campus, and I don't feel like dealing with him right now.

Anything a founding family member touches ends up stained with blood. There's no getting around that fact—it's as much a curse on this town as Cronus Anderson's descendants.

Something pinches in my chest, and I glance at the student files spread across my desk.

Quincy, Asher, and Noelle Anderson.

The three descendants are on campus together at the same time, just like the curse warns.

I wonder if Jean-Louis knows about that, but I don't ask.

Frankly, I'm trying to forget about it—and the hazel-eyed seductress—entirely.

She's a theater major, which is unsurprising, but her file is also stuffed full of glowing recommendations from her community troupe back in Los Angeles and several Grandeur Playhouse directors. Her roster of speaking parts is admirable enough, and she aced each of Avernia's entrance exams.

On paper, she's an exemplary student and actress, willing and eager to learn the craft, but at a certain point, her résumé just... *stops*.

About nine months ago, her work vanishes, and it appears she did nothing in the time since before coming here, which I find interesting.

It's not typical for an actor to just abandon their love for the stage out of nowhere, especially when it seems as though things are poised to take off.

I suppose she could've been preparing to enroll at our university, but the question of *why* still remains.

Even though I know I shouldn't, I find myself tucking her file in my desk drawer and stacking the others.

Bellamy's sits on the very top, though I'm not sure why I grabbed it from the archive building. Staring at it now with Jean-Louis droning on in my ear makes me tense, discomfort weaving through my muscles.

"*Sutton*." Jean-Louis's tone is weary, and he lets out a cough, his irritation evident. "Are you listening to me?"

"No."

I can practically hear his teeth grind. "Your insubordination is going to get you into some deep shit. Ask that twin of yours how it worked out for her."

Leaning back in my office chair, I prop my hands behind my head and stare at the ceiling. A part of me wants to snap at him for bringing her up at all, but I don't. In some ways, he's right—Bellamy's dissent from council and founder business made her a target, and I didn't realize it in time to save her.

If I push back too much now, it endangers Beckett. There's no telling what our father would do at this point.

A dying man has very little to lose.

"A decision about what?" I ask finally, even though I'm fully aware of what he's referencing.

It's the same fucking thing he's asked every year since Bellamy's death: a request to fully step into the role Death's Teeth forced me into.

"There's not much time now that classes have begun," Jean-Louis says. "You should have your affairs in order. Otherwise, who knows what you might become susceptible to. Or whom. The council won't wait around forever."

"That sounds like a threat."

He's quiet for a couple of beats. "The longer you refuse to fulfill your role as Incarnate, the more tainted your sister's soul grows. Death's Teeth cannot survive without a rightful leader and Maiden."

I roll my eyes, then dig my thumb and index finger into them, rubbing hard. "You and that goddamn organization. Do you realize how archaic and strange it is to have something that easily disman-tled, all because I don't want to be some slave to death?"

"You would not be a *slave*," he replies, pausing at the end to let out a string of thick coughs. When he returns, his voice is slightly weaker than before. "Incarnate is the embodiment of power. The harbinger of order and balance at Avernia—and by extension, Fury Hill. Death would bow to *you*."

"Strictly speaking, maybe. They'd have their prop, but it wouldn't bring Bellamy back."

"Death doesn't erase a person from this earth," he says. "Dying is an honor. It's the natural course of life. We are here right now because of those who passed before us."

I frown. "It almost sounds like you're trying to convince me what happened to Bellamy was a good thing."

"Maybe it was. Who gets to decide that?" He pauses. "Well, you would, I suppose, if you'd finish the Incarnate initiation. All you need is a warm body—"

"I'm not interested in binding myself to another person," I snap, my chest tightening. "In any way."

"Fucking Christ, it's just sex. It means nothing."

"It's not *just* sex, it's—" I cut off, choking on the broken shard of a memory as it lodges in my throat.

Commitment. A precedent of understanding and ruling.

Death's Teeth forces their chosen leader to join with their chosen Maiden and watches as they come together beneath a blood moon. It's a vow of faith and servitude to death and life, chaos and the eventual order. A lewd creed in the name of our ancestors and their gods.

Life, sex, and death: the three principles that the organization believes are necessary to maintain a balance.

The Incarnate ceremony had been interrupted when I was an undergrad, and instead of becoming their leader in totality, the higher-ranking members of Death's Teeth used my body for their own pleasure, inducting me as an Elder.

The thought of voluntarily participating now makes me fucking sick.

"Ignore it all you want, Sutton. If you choose not to pick a side, it will be picked for you."

"Don't you think it's time we put it all to rest? You almost got Beckett fucking killed with this shit."

"Beckett almost got himself killed," Jean-Louis replies, falling into another coughing fit. This one lasts longer than the previous and sounds like it brings phlegm up with it. "It is not my fault the boy has issues with follow-through."

"Well, you would know."

"If that's supposed to be some sort of slight against me as a parent, I won't hear it. I've done nothing but look out for your best interests your entire life. Death's Teeth is *your* destiny, Sutton. Whether you want it to be or not."

Glancing at my hand, I pull my sleeve up a bit. The scarring is faint these days, but I can see it as well as the day I got it.

I hang up, not interested in entertaining more of his delusions. A part of me wishes the illness he's suffering from would hurry up and take him out, because maybe then I'd be able to move on.

Maybe death would relinquish its claim if I wasn't Jean-Louis's son.

Later, I make my way through Avernia's campus as the clock tower in front of the Obeliskos chimes midnight. I cut to my right, heading toward the staff housing, which is an old conglomerate of apartments wedged past the dorms and the Lyceum.

An email comes through my phone as I let myself inside my unit on the second floor.

FROM: noelle.anderson@avernia.edu
TO: sutton.dupont@theater.avernia.edu

SUBJECT: Late assignment

To whom it may concern,

Attached you will find my essay on the differences between stage and screen acting. Unfortunately, the suggested printers were occupied, so I hope you'll accept this digital copy. I would not want my first impression to be that of someone who can't handle adult responsibility.

Thank you,
T

I squint at my phone, wondering why the hell she signed it that way, when it hits me.

T as in *Temptress*.

That cheeky little brat.

FROM: sutton.dupont@theater.avernia.edu
TO: noelle.anderson@avernia.edu
SUBJECT: RE: Late assignment

Noelle,

Apologies, but it seems I was not clear enough in class the other day. Late assignments will not be accepted.

This is a policy I apply to every student. Better luck next time.

Best,

Professor Dupont

I enter the apartment while I await a reply, opening up *The Delphic Pages* app.

Several posts from Pythia sit at the very top—mostly welcoming the new semester and recapping events from the fall, though leaving out all the violence and bloodshed despite leaking a lot of information about each incident in the first place.

But only one post catches my eye: a snapshot of a beautiful girl as she stalks across campus, headed for the observatory with a backpack slung over one shoulder. Her long hair whips behind her in waves, dozens of shadows watching in the background.

If you don't look closely, they resemble a plethora of trees, but the observatory doesn't border the forest. Squinting, the shadows begin to take on human forms: people passing along between classes, stopping to chat with friends, all existing in the orbit of Elle Anderson without paying her any mind.

Except *one* shadow.

It stands on the back steps of the Lyceum's annex, a briefcase in hand, staring directly at her. Stuck in place, watching, as if his feet are glued to the very spot.

Beneath the photo, just one single line of text: *Spotted—trouble on campus?*

Nausea churns in my stomach. Are they talking about her just being here, or—

"You're home late."

Beckett's voice slices through my thoughts and causes me to jump, dropping my phone. He scratches beneath his chin, looking up from where he's lounging on the sofa, reading *Persuasion* in black sweats.

I keep forgetting he's staying here.

Bending down, I scoop up my phone and slide it into my jacket pocket, setting my briefcase and keys on the small hutch in the foyer. "Any chance you actually managed to make it to a class today, or are you just reading *Persuasion* for leisure?"

"Jane Austen is a literary genius. Of course I'm reading her for leisure." Beckett glances at me from the corner of his eye. "Why, are you tracking me or something?"

"What?" I kick off my shoes, scrubbing a hand over my face. "No. I'm just wondering where you're at in the journey of recovery."

"You make me sound like an addict."

"Addiction isn't merely relegated to drugs, Beck. You can crave all sorts of things."

A pair of hazel eyes flash through my mind for the briefest moment, but I blink them away. I'm not addicted to her.

I *can't* be. I've only had one hit, and one hit does not a habit make.

Still, the buzzing sensation beneath my fingers hints at a different story.

Walking into the living room, I try not to cringe at how many of Beckett's things are strewn about; discarded clothes are tossed onto the brown leather furniture, empty glasses crowd the oval coffee table that used to be ring-free, and in the kitchen, I see his textbooks and pencils everywhere.

Despite the fact that he's missed most of his classes so far this week, and we're only a few days into the semester.

He watches me over his book. "So what, you think I'm addicted to Father's cruelty?"

I sit down in the armchair across from him. "Perhaps cruelty in general. What else could have possessed you to take part in that shit show last year?"

His face screws up, and he slams the book shut, tossing it onto the coffee table. "I don't need another lecture. I *know* I fucked up."

"'Fucked up' the gravity of—"

"I don't want to talk about this," he snaps, pushing into a sitting position. He throws his legs off the cushion, shoving his feet onto the floor.

"Well, neither do I, but Mother is worried about you."

A choked laugh sputters from his lips, and he stands up. "She should be more worried about her *golden boy*. You're the one in danger."

"What's that supposed to mean?"

"That you're not as discreet as you think you are."

I sit there for a while longer after he heads down the hall toward the guest bedroom, wondering if that's some sort of prediction.

Or if it's a warning.

FROM: noelle.anderson@avernia.edu
TO: sutton.dupont@theater.avernia.edu
SUBJECT: RE: RE: Late assignment

To whom it may concern,

No luck needed. I'll recover.

-T

PS: You shouldn't be up so late. Burning the midnight oil is bad for your skin.

In spite of everything, the email makes me smile. She shouldn't be flirting so openly, but I can't find it in me to care *that* much.

FROM: sutton.dupont@theater.avernia.edu
TO: noelle.anderson@avernia.edu
SUBJECT: RE: RE: RE: Late assignment

Your advice is duly noted, though a bit hypocritical. If you need anything else, please ask a classmate, as I will be turning in.

Best,
Professor Dupont

My thumb hovers over the Send button.

I shouldn't push it. Shouldn't indulge the woman more than I already have.

Noise from the other side of the apartment draws me away from the screen, and my thumb slips, hitting the sideways triangle just for Beckett to not even come back out of his room.

Well, that's that.

Groaning, I run a hand through my hair and remind myself that he suffered a traumatic event—orchestrated it but also suffered—and isn't handling the fallout well.

Bellamy was easier to deal with. She volunteered her feelings, and I didn't have to guess at things until she caved. Beckett's a different beast entirely. Like me, he bottles his problems and tosses them into the ocean, praying they don't return.

I have no idea how to tell him it doesn't work. The glass splinters and slices before it leaves your hands, and the scars are as unremovable as they are unremarkable.

No one else will notice, but you'll feel them forever.

Maybe I should start dragging him to Visio Aternae meetings. He wouldn't get school credit for them, but it might do him some good to give back to the community he was raised to only take from.

When the light beneath his door goes out, I make my way to the kitchen and grab a bite to eat. As I'm chewing a forkful of refectory lasagna, my vision starts to break, growing into sharp, jagged lines even when I try to blink them away.

I grit my teeth, recognizing my earlier nausea as a symptom of an oncoming migraine—something I'd probably have noticed more if I hadn't been absorbed in thoughts about Elle Anderson.

Christ, she's bad news.

After popping an anti-inflammatory and triptan pill, I brace my hands on the counter and close my eyes, counting the time it takes for my vision to return to normal.

The minutes tick by slowly. I drop to my elbows, waiting—it doesn't always work, especially if I've taken the pill too late.

Sometimes, the medication alleviates the tingling and numbness in my hands as well, though I never know if that's just a psychological effect or the actual drug itself.

When I can see straight again, I quietly make my way to the foyer, cracking open the hutch and sliding my shoes on. Glancing over my shoulder, I make sure Beckett isn't coming out of his room before slipping my cloak and mask from within and leaving.

Chapter 11

Elle

I'm twenty-five minutes early to Acting for Beginners.

Not because I'm eager to see Sutton—er, Professor Dupont—but because being late makes me nauseous. Even though I *do* love the spotlight, walking in when a class or meeting has already begun causes me to break out in hives.

I really hadn't meant to be late the first time around, but Aurora's snoring kept me up the night before, and then with one thing after another, the universe seemed to be trying to keep me from going.

Now I can't help wondering if it had its reasons.

When I notice I'm not the first person in the auditorium, I pause at the entrance, checking to make sure I have the right room in the Lyceum: 137-A at eight.

A girl with deep brown skin and neat black braids sits in a wheelchair in the back, doodling in the margins of a notebook. Quincy would hate that—she was always so weird about keeping her papers neat. Asher would love it, since he draws on anything he can get his hands on.

I plop down one seat away, eyeing the doodles. They're stick figures and warped flowers, almost like a nervous habit more than an actual hobby.

"This is Acting for Beginners, right?" I ask softly. Just to make sure I'm not fucking up again.

Her brown gaze swings to me. "It will be soon." A long, pregnant pause. Then, "You're the girl who was late on the first day."

"Oh good. I was hoping that would be my lasting impression."

Her thin brows arch. "You got chewed out by Professor Dupont and you're still coming to class? Do you enjoy being humiliated?"

"Depends on who's doling it out," I say, lifting a shoulder. She doesn't laugh or even smirk, so I move on. "I'm not scared of our teacher anyway."

"Well, it's not about being scared," she replies, folding the edge of a page in the notebook. "Professor Dupont is intense but not really mean…usually. I had him for another class in the fall, and when we did breathing exercises or vocal warm-ups, I felt like I was gonna pass out any time he focused on me."

"Yikes."

"Plus, if you look online, there's all kinds of stuff about him on *The Delphic Pages*. Gossipy drivel that's probably not true but still fun to read…if you like that sort of thing."

"*The Delphic Pages*?"

Her eyes widen, and she dives into her coat pocket, pulling out her phone. On the screen, she taps a maroon app with an A and C on the icon, bringing up an online forum. She scrolls with a manicured index finger, showing dozens of threads under an account with the name **Pythia** in bold.

Each post has hundreds of comments beneath, encouraging and begging for more.

"Pythia is Avernia's…*oracle*, in a way," she says. "For the most part, she posts rumors and relevant information, giving students insight and keeping us up to date on the weird stuff that happens around here. But she also posts a lot of outright lies, so it's hard to tell when she's being helpful or malicious."

"And the school just…allows it?"

"Sure. Dean Bauer will let anything slide if he thinks doing so will prevent an overall disruption. Sometimes I wonder if the dean himself isn't the one behind the account, just trying to constantly throw students off his trail."

"His trail?"

"Oh yeah. Everyone thinks he's in a murder-sex cult where the participants, like, worship the founders or something. I don't know, it's way too complicated for me to really care. I'm just trying to make it to graduation alive."

I take the phone and type my name into the search bar at the bottom. Only one post is about me, a picture taken sometime this week as I scrambled to the observatory.

My academic adviser suggested a few supplemental courses to all the theater I'm taking, so I'm dabbling in astronomy and philosophy as well. Ever since I was a little girl, I've admired the stars' guidance and their reminder of how vast the universe is.

In comparison, human tragedy doesn't matter. Or maybe it matters even more.

The website doesn't really say much else about me, which fills me with relief. Speculation is the *last* thing I need right now.

When I scroll back to last semester, I note that a lot of the posts have been archived, leaving only shells with timestamps in their places.

Meaning the school really did scrub all evidence of the deaths and kidnappings that happened. That makes Quincy's warnings from before blare even louder in my head, but at the same time raises my confusion as to why she and Asher came back.

The urge to call our parents and let them know things aren't actually that safe is strong, but I resist. If I do that, they'll start asking questions about my mental state again, and I don't have it in me to keep rehashing my screwups.

Avernia provides distance, if not clarity. I'm sure as long as I keep a low profile, things will be fine.

How dangerous can this place really be when there are new enrollees every semester?

I hand the girl her phone back, unease creeping slowly along my shoulders and digging into my skin.

"What's your name?" I ask.

"Meg," she replies, swiping out of the app quickly. Almost like she doesn't want to be seen using it. "You're Noelle, right?"

"Just Elle."

"Okay, Just Elle," she says with a nod. "Am I correct to assume you're related to Professor Anderson, the head of the classics department?"

"Wow, word really does travel fast."

The edges of her cheeks heat. "Oh no, I just happened to have her for a course last semester. You guys look a lot alike."

That almost makes me laugh. "Don't tell her that."

"She wouldn't think it's a compliment?"

"I think she just…finds comparison uncomfortable." I shrug,

like it doesn't matter knowing how offended she'd be if anyone linked us so easily.

A locked vault isn't supposed to resemble an open door.

"Well, you should try and join Visio Aternae if you're planning on sticking around this semester. It's Professor Dupont's baby, and he always favors students who enlist. Could help your current standing as his class punching bag."

"Visio Aternae?"

Meg gives me a slow once-over. "Man, it's a good thing you're pretty. Maybe that'll save you."

Embarrassment scalds my face.

Students have started filtering into the class, and as one drops into a seat in front of us, horror etches into his alabaster face. "Are you suggesting Professor Dupont can be bribed, Meghan?"

"Well, it never *hurts*. Pretty privilege is a real thing, you know."

Lexington slides in next to the other student, slinging his backpack onto the floor. "And I've got it in spades, let me tell you."

"Oh *brother*," Meg mutters.

"He's not wrong," the first guy agrees.

"I didn't say he was wrong," Meg says. "Just annoying."

"Technically, you didn't say that either." Lexington looks at me, his blue eyes sparkling. "Noelle, good to see you again. Glad Professor Prodigy hasn't run you off yet."

"It's Just Elle," Meg tells him, twisting her arm around to reach into the bag hanging on the back of her wheelchair. She digs out a purple pen with a fuzzy top, handing it over to the other guy. "This is Percy, by the way, since apparently these two have no manners and can't introduce themselves."

"I'm still trying to process your gross mischaracterization of our professor," Percy replies, shuddering. "Reducing a man's hard work down to the potential for scandalous behavior seems trite, don't you think?"

"Don't worry," someone else adds, a voice from a few rows up. "No one's accusing *you* of being able to sway the professor, Perciville."

"Nobody asked you to listen in, Sabrina," Percy says, blushing as he glares at the girl with dirty-blond hair seated in front of him.

Her suntanned skin is visible through the geometric cutouts of her white blouse, and her dark eyes are hard as they land on me. "As an important Visio Aternae member and Professor Dupont's former TA, it's my duty to ensure his name isn't being slandered by randos who've decided to plop down in one of his classes out of nowhere."

"Why is a former TA in an introductory acting class?" I ask, cocking my head to the side. "Shouldn't you have advanced?"

"It's a refresher course—not that I'd expect an old hag like you to understand."

I make a face. "I'm twenty-five."

"My points stands." Sabrina juts her chin into the air. "What's a supposed rising starlet doing in this class? Couldn't hack it in Hollywood, so you decided to actually learn how to act?"

Jeez. I may not have been on *The Delphic Pages*, but clearly someone's been talking.

Shaking my head, I let out a perplexed laugh and refocus on the nicer people sitting around me. "So does everyone know who I am then?"

"You made friends with the nosiest group in the country and fought with the professor on the first day," Sabrina replies even though it wasn't directed at her. "Doesn't seem like you were trying all that hard to keep a low profile."

"I resent that," Meg says. "Implying we're worse than Pythia is categorically untrue."

"You're gossipmongers, Meg. Let's be real here."

"We only gather pertinent information and discuss it among ourselves."

"Is that why you got caught searching through Professor Dupont's garbage in the fall?"

My eyebrows raise as I glance at Meg. "Stalker behavior. I like it."

"You would." Sabrina gives me a dirty look.

Meg presses her lips together as if to keep from smirking. "How do you even know about that?"

"When it comes to Sutton, I know everything."

"Oh, but *I'm* the stalker." Meg rubs her hands over her knees, rolling her eyes. "I'll have you know, the garbage incident was to look for a paper of mine he said he lost. He literally sanctioned my access."

"Whatever helps you and the new girl sleep at night." Sabrina gives me another once-over, disdain coloring her features. "How many homework assignments did you forget today?"

"I think we should give Elle a break, you guys," Percy interjects.

"Yeah," Lexington says. "It's hard enough being a founding family member without having to keep up with all the bullshit happening around us on top of it."

"Oh, please." Meg snorts. "The founding families are not an oppressed class."

"That's true, but there are very few of us at Avernia. I've been in Fury Hill my whole life, and I'm still trying to adjust to the expectations and scrutiny. And I don't have a curse attached to my last name, unless you count Lethe's." He looks at me thoughtfully. "Do you ever feel like you're being watched?"

"Not this again," Percy groans. "I've told you, dude, if ghosts are real, they're not interested in haunting humans. They have more important things in the afterlife to attend to. The only people terrorizing Fury Hill are the weirdo vigilantes who killed those girls last semester and left their sigil on every flat surface they could find."

"A sigil?" I probe.

Percy's face flushes, and he runs his fingers through his platinum-blond locks, his light brown eyes creasing at the corners. "Well, only first responders and the dean *actually* got to see the crime scenes, but a few fellow tech-theater majors were in the Curators last semester, and they swore on their lives that the group was being framed by Death's Teeth. Said they'd overheard stuff about three-headed beasts and names written in blood."

"Death's Teeth has a habit of leaving their calling card whenever they commit some kind of crime," Lexington adds, propping his legs up on the chair ahead of him and reclining slightly in his own. "I guess they want to make sure we don't forget they exist or something. Usually, the crimes are boring shit like vandalism or public indecency, but the names of the accused are never released, and no records are ever taken down."

"Pythia reports it though," Meg notes. "That's the only reason we know about Celeste and Frances from last semester. Others have gone missing before, and no one mentions them again."

"I bet Pythia's someone in the administration," Percy says. "Not Bauer, I don't think he's smart enough, but someone else. Someone with firsthand knowledge and protections."

Ahead, Sabrina cackles. "A faculty member? You think they have time to chase gossip and make a fuss online about it?"

"Sabrina's the Visio Aternae treasurer," Lexington says to me as if she's not even here. "She thinks she knows things because she's constantly up Professor Dupont's ass."

Her eyes narrow at him. "That's not the only reason, but I don't need to explain myself to you cretins."

"*Anyway*," Percy continues, tossing Sabrina a lingering glance when she turns to the front before he drapes himself over Lexington's lap, stretching his arms on the backs of their seats. Lexington threads his fingers through Percy's short hair, and I briefly wonder what the extent of their relationship is. "So the main ghosts on campus are the possibly at-large murderers and probably the students who killed themselves on the thirteenth floor of the Obeliskos centuries ago. We think there are some in the dorms too. Erebus and Rad Hall to be exact."

"Oh, and whatever's hidden beneath the Apollodorus," Meg adds. "Some people say you can get to the caves through the basement."

"Don't forget the forest," Lexington adds.

My palms grow sweaty.

"Too many people go missing or die on campus every year for there to be *no* ghosts," Lexington says. "Eventually, that sort of bloodshed becomes a part of the setting, right? Isn't that what the whole Anderson curse is about?"

The three of them fall silent, and when they look at me, there's an added weight of unease pressing down on the center of my chest, making it difficult to breathe.

It feels a lot like drowning, and that image brings with it the memories of my last time in the Primordial Forest and the eyes that have graced my nightmares ever since.

Still, I force a smile. "Look, I'm just here to get my degree. I'm not interested in ghosts or curses."

Several rows ahead, Sutton appears from behind the stage curtain, instructing the students to take their seats as more file in.

He doesn't glance in my direction at all. Not even a voyeuristic peep.

I don't know why that bums me out so much.

As the exit doors are pulled shut, Sutton pulls an apricot from his pants pocket and takes a bite. He focuses his attention on a rolling chalkboard, cleaning the debris from a previous physics class with a rag.

His shoulder blades are sharp as he scrubs the board, ruffling the material of his forest-green button-down. I shift in my seat and retrieve a pencil from my bag, nibbling on the eraser to stop myself from imagining what his bare muscles would look like, especially glistening with a sheen of sweat.

My eyes track the movement of his jaw when he rolls the orange fruit, the accompanying slurp as he devours it making my stomach twist.

After a moment, he finishes, tossing the pit into a nearby trash bin.

"Shakespeare's earliest published work," he calls out to the class, notating the playwright's name on the board. "Who knows it?"

A few students titter, and then a hand goes up near him. "'The Rape of Lucrece.'"

I roll my eyes, crossing my arms and slumping down in my seat.

Sutton scribbles the title beneath Shakespeare's name. "And his first printed play was—"

"Um." I shove my hand into the air, sitting straighter when he continues. He doesn't call on me, so I clear my throat and speak over him. "'Venus and Adonis' is technically even earlier than Lucrece, though admittedly not by much."

Sutton—*Professor Dupont*—eyes me, his face devoid of expression. "That was no longer the question, Miss…"

He waits for me to fill in the blank as if he doesn't know my name. Dozens of gazes turn toward me, their stares amplifying the spotlight my body so often craves.

Normally not in such a contentious way, but I'm flexible.

I will not be humiliated again.

Defiance sizzles against the surface of my skin. "That may not have been the question, but I think it's odd you'd allow an incorrect answer to embed in your students' minds, Professor."

"Perhaps letting misinformation marinate is a way to help them differentiate between fact and fiction later."

"Sure, but how many of us are going to be thinking about Shakespeare later?"

"Well, this is an acting class," he notes. "I'd hope you think about him a little. Especially since we'll likely do him at some point."

"Okay, but who's going to be thinking about you later?" I continue, unable to stop myself. Someone snickers, and I clear my throat, amending my statement. "Your class, I mean."

"I'd imagine the students who did their due diligence in order to earn a spot on my roster, versus the girl who apparently thinks her last name gives her a pass to do and say as she pleases."

Whispers erupt across the auditorium, and a furious blush fans my face. His remains expressionless, but I can tell by the vein pulsing in his forehead that I'm getting under his skin.

I smother a grin. He makes it too easy. "So you do remember my name then?"

Silence falls over us like a blanket of snow.

Sutton stares at me for a severe stretch of time, his intense perusal almost enough to make me squirm in my chair. But I keep my feet on the floor and my eyes on his, refusing to give in.

He can despise me all he wants. Controlling my emotions, though, is out of the question.

Never again.

"And *scene*," Sutton suddenly announces, pulling two fingers together in a downward motion before his face. The students blink, looking at one another, as he finally rips his gaze from mine. "Your first lesson on stage acting—the ability to switch in and out of character at the snap of the director's fingers will be paramount to your success as a live actor. Distractions abound, and as Ms. Anderson has demonstrated, sometimes nuisances can grow quite cumbersome. It's important you remain in character, no matter what, until cut is called."

Annoyance bubbles in my veins. I grip the armrests of my chair, grinding my teeth together while he uses the outburst as a segue into his lesson.

"Here I thought you weren't prepared," Meg whispers, turning to a fresh page in her notebook. "But you're literally part of his teaching plan."

My shoulders slump, but I give her a grin anyway.

At least he didn't kick me out this time.

Chapter 12

Elle

THE OBSERVATORY IS CLOSED WHEN I ARRIVE EARLY ONE MORN-
ing after the first week of classes.

I slump against its door with my philosophy book clutched
tight to my chest, huffing in defeat. Quincy *said* she'd ask a professor to let me in, but clearly she forgot. The astronomy program
is small and for some reason no one really uses the place except
for classes during the day, so I've taken to studying inside when
it's empty. It's much more peaceful than any of the libraries or my
own dorm.

Swiping my phone from my coat pocket, I send Lexington a
quick text. He gave me his number at the end of our last lecture for
potential group study dates, saying I could text or call if I needed
anything.

Since he's a founding family member, I figure maybe he'll be
able to help.

I could go someplace else, but studying under the stars has
always been a source of comfort for me. When I was little, I'd crawl

onto the roof outside Asher's bedroom window and sit for hours, telling him I was heading off on a date or something when the truth was I just wanted to be alone.

Spend as much time wearing a mask as I do, and you learn to seek out those rare moments where you can be yourself.

The stars don't judge. They'll shine no matter who sits beneath them.

As I turn away from the observatory's door, I run into a wall, pinching my eyes shut with a grunt. The book tumbles out of my grasp, falling to the ground with a thud, and the wall reaches out with both hands to steady me.

Wait. *The wall has hands?*

Rearing back, I open my eyes and meet mossy green ones, somehow harsh beneath the moonlight still illuminating campus.

Sutton's hair is messy, tousled as if he's been raking his hands through it for hours. My fingers twitch, quietly aching to do the same, but I simply pull out of his hold instead.

"Should you really be touching students like that in the dark?" I quip, more viciously than necessary. "What if I'd had a weapon and used it on you because I thought you were an assailant?"

"Then I suppose we'd be having this conversation in the school's infirmary." His face is impassive as he bends down, scooping up my textbook. "You're welcome, by the way."

Irritation spikes in my blood, but I accept the book when he hands it over. "Am I supposed to thank you for getting in my way?"

"As pleasant as ever, Ms. Anderson."

"Like you've earned the right to a friendlier attitude."

His eyebrows arch. "Have I done something to upset you?"

Asshole. "Besides going out of your way in class to embarrass me?"

He stares at me for a beat, then shuffles back a step. "You're imagining things."

"That's gaslight-y."

"I'm not sure that's a word."

"Well, I'm making it one." Crossing my arms over the book, I pin him with a look. "You can't seriously pretend like you're not trying to put up a wall between us as some defense mechanism. Relationships don't work that way, you know. You can pretend, but you can't unfuck—"

His eyes widen, and he snatches my wrist, dragging me into the alcove outside the observatory's entrance. I stay silent, watching as he slides a key card from his pants pocket into the lock and shoves the door open.

Seconds later, he's flipping on a switch inside and yanking me in behind him, his grip on my wrist punishing for a moment. As soon as the door shuts us in, he releases me, so quickly it almost feels like a burn is left behind.

I glance down at my skin, imagining what the icy print of him would look like spread out there. My sleeve falls back into place, interrupting the vision.

The inside of the observatory is clean and bright, with rows of theater seats situated behind the observation deck and a massive telescope at the center of the first level, disappearing through a slot in the glass-domed roof.

Sutton places his hands on his hips and glares at the sky. "You can't keep saying shit like that in public. If word got out about… I'd lose my job, Elle. It wouldn't look good to anyone."

"Why?"

"There are certain power dynamics in play, not to mention the school policy in general forbids intercollegiate relationships of any kind, except blood. I'd be fired, you'd likely be expelled... It would be a whole mess."

"Power dynamics?" I squint at him, inching closer with the textbook still clutched to my chest. "They'd automatically think you coerced me or something?"

"That's how it would look, yes."

"But the semester hadn't even started when we—"

"It wouldn't matter to the administration."

I'm not sure if it's the early hour or his presence alone, but my brain is struggling to wrap around the logic. "But... *I* propositioned you."

His throat bobs on a swallow.

"Didn't I?"

Sighing, Sutton leans against a metal table, extending his arms behind him. "Yes."

"Then what's the problem?"

He watches, silent, as I walk over and set Descartes onto the table next to his hand, stretched out on the cool surface. I slide back, stepping directly in front of him, and tuck my hair behind my ears.

"The problem," he answers softly, eyes straining as I slink even *closer*, until I'm between his legs and our clothes are almost touching, "is I'm your superior. I could have—should have—said no."

"You didn't know it at the time."

"That's not the point."

"So you do regret it then?"

"No," he replies, voice gruff. He meets my gaze, and his irises shimmer like raw jade under the stars. "It isn't...regret. I'm acknowledging what I should have done and explaining why I can't repeat my previous actions."

"Didn't you say you *would* do it again though? You're sending a lot of mixed signals here, Professor." As if it has a mind of its own, my arm lifts, and I brush some stray lint off his sleeve, intrigued by the way he tenses beneath even the slightest touch.

But he doesn't pull away.

"Elle…"

My head tilts. "Is distance *really* what you want?"

"I want you to behave."

"That's not true," I whisper. "Where's that honesty, Boy Scout? You were so *good* that night in your car, don't you remember?"

A few tendons in his neck bulge against his skin. "Mind and soul of the man is entirely different from the body."

Descartes.

I spread my fingers over Sutton's abdomen, feeling him flex as a familiar sensation pinches in my stomach.

That's the issue.

No matter how I explain the situation to myself, sense doesn't fully compute with carnality. Logically, I know I'm being an asshole here, pushing for something I don't deserve that would have shitty consequences for us both, not to mention the repercussions it would have for Quincy and Asher.

But the body remembers things the mind suppresses, and sometimes we seek assurance to cover the phantom memories. To create new ones.

Sometimes, we want just because we can.

"I can keep a secret," I tell him.

He gives me a small smile and shakes his head. "You shouldn't have to be one, temptress."

A knock echoes through the observatory, and Sutton springs away, diving into the shadows behind the telescope. I grab my book and whirl toward the entrance just as Lexington strides in, hands deep in his jacket pockets.

"Fuck, it's cold," he says, shivering visibly. He grins when he spots me, blue eyes brightening. "You rang, m'lady?"

I shift away from the telescope. "And you came."

"Of course. I told you I'd help you out with anything you needed." He walks over, slinging an arm around my shoulders. "Though it appears you didn't actually need my help getting in here."

"Ah, yeah." I let out a nervous laugh, trying to turn us away from the front of the deck. The toes of Sutton's loafers are visible beneath the giant machine, and though Lexington seems chill enough, I can't be sure he wouldn't report us for violating school policy. "I think I was turning the knob the wrong way."

"Not used to opening doors, I guess?" he jokes, giving me a shake before glancing around. I tense up as he slows on the telescope, but then he keeps going until he's looking at the sky. "How come you're here so early? Or, like, at all? The school's astronomy program is super small, and you're not in it, right?"

"Not in the program, but I am fulfilling a science credit with an introductory planetary exploration course."

"So you came to do homework for it?"

"No, just to study." I point at my book.

"Ah, philosophy. I dropped that course freshman year. Too much posturing for my liking."

"Not used to using your brain much, huh?"

Lexington snorts, poking my cheek.

My face heats as he stares down at me, and I quickly avert my gaze, checking to see if Sutton's moved at all.

His feet are no longer visible, but I can feel his eyes on me.

Lexington's hand falls away, and he blows out a breath. "Well, are you wanting to stay, or can we go get coffee? Gaea's Beans is open early."

"Gaea's Beans?"

"Vegan coffeehouse in town. My mom's friend is the owner, and he makes a *fantastic* cappuccino."

I hesitate, wondering what this sounds like to Sutton, and then immediately brush that off. It doesn't *matter*. He said nothing else can happen between us, so why should I care what he thinks?

"All right. But we can't be late for class."

"Leave your worries to me, m'lady. I have *impeccable* time management skills."

As we weave our way out of the room, I toss a quick look over my shoulder. Just to see.

Sutton stands behind the telescope, mostly bathed in shadows, but the displeasure etched into his face sends a shiver down my spine nonetheless.

By the time we get to Acting for Beginners a few hours later, the sun is peeking through gray clouds, and I've downed a large iced coffee, waking myself up. Hair sticks to my forehead, and everyone turns to gawk when Lexington and I slip in the back exit together.

My stomach churns as I drop into a seat next to Meg, who whistles under her breath. "You don't waste any time, do you?"

I frown, sliding a notebook from my backpack. "What's that supposed to mean?"

"Nothing *bad*, just an observation." She offers me a fuzzy purple pen to write with and reaches for a mint tin in the bag hanging off her wheelchair. "Lex is cute, but beware. There's a vicious streak hidden behind those blue eyes of his. I'm also pretty certain he and Percy are hooking up on the DL, but I have no proof to back up this claim."

My gaze flickers to Lexington as he leans in to whisper something in Percy's ear. "How well do you know him?"

She shrugs. "We went on a few dates in high school before I realized I was more into femmes. Nothing too intimate. He's a good dude but cagey and secretive. Founding family trait if you ask me."

"Huh." I smooth my fingers out on my desk. "Well, that's okay. I'm not interested in dating him anyway."

"Have your eyes set on someone else?"

"Ladies, do you have something to share with the class?" Sutton's voice booms from the bottom of the auditorium, echoing against the rafters.

He's staring straight at us, an apricot poised between two fingers. His hair is less messy than it was this morning, and he's changed out of the jacket and dark jeans he had on when I saw him at the observatory, having swapped for another earth-toned sweater and brown slacks instead.

My pulse thumps heavily in my throat. "Um, no."

"No, Professor," Meg agrees.

His jaw works from side to side until finally he walks to the edge of the stage, taking a seat on the lip. He swings his legs, studying us. "I suppose this is the usual time in the semester when I have to remind students that if you're going to be late, I'd rather you take a seat in the back and be as silent as possible. Tardiness doesn't look good, but it's especially egregious when it becomes a distraction for the entire class. I expect you'll be on time from now on."

The rest of the students murmur their agreement, and I sink lower in my seat as flames lick up and down my skin. God, how *embarrassing*—

"Ms. Anderson," he says, and when I lift my gaze, he's glaring at me. "Is that understood?"

No chance in pretending the message was for anyone else. "Yes."

"Yes, what?"

The fire burns even brighter, knotting together with this strange feeling in my stomach, like it's turning in on itself.

He's doing it again. Calling me out in front of everyone in a way that makes it feel like he's putting distance between us. Humiliating me so no one could possibly think there's something deeper going on, a desire he can't bring himself to indulge.

I grit my teeth, wishing I could smack the smug expression off his face, but instead I sit up a little straighter and let my knees fall open.

I'm wearing stockings, but they're only thigh-highs.

And because I was too busy to do laundry last night, nothing else above.

Shifting in my seat, I flip the hair off my shoulder and give him a salacious grin. "Yes, Professor, *sir*."

His eyes dip for the briefest second—almost too quickly to notice, really, except that I'm waiting for it. Dying for his reaction while hoping no one else is paying attention.

When his throat bobs, satisfaction weaves through my rib cage like moss on the forest floor.

He turns his head immediately, and I cross my legs as heat pumps between them.

"All right," he continues, the slightest notch of unease in his voice, "today, we'll be discussing the importance of making strong choices. Acting is more than the simple ability to memorize words. A script doesn't paint the entire picture, right? It's up to you to read between the lines and bring that character to life, which means what?"

He points at Percy, who scratches behind his ear with a broken pencil. "You're gonna make us write another essay?"

Sutton smirks. "Indeed, I am. But does anyone know why I have you write so many essays?"

"Because you don't have anything better to do on the weekends than grade papers?" Meg suggests.

"That sounded like you volunteering to assist on next week's assignment, Ms. Valdez," Sutton tells her. "And no, actually, my dance card is quite full. The essays are my attempts at understanding where you're at comprehensively and how to move forward in a way that you get the most out of any parts you're given this semester. Remember, it isn't all about acting here."

He meets my gaze for a moment before turning to drag himself onstage and head for the chalkboard. The rest of the class, I'm practically shunned, even when I raise my hand to participate.

Oh well. If he's making it his mission to embarrass me in front of my peers, the least I can do is have fun with it.

Chapter 13

Sutton

A Death's Teeth fledgling slides their hand up my calf as if inspecting me for injury. At least that's what it feels like tonight as debauchery descends on the party in Tartarus, one of the deeper caves within the mountains.

These are the easiest functions to dissociate from: It's neither a full moon festival nor the beginning of a new period, so death isn't lurking around the corner trying to decide which nonranking individual it should claim.

It's just dark, the vast cavern illuminated by lanterns and punctuated by whatever makeshift furniture the Director has managed to smuggle in over the years. Tonight will be filled with copious amounts of sex aimed at appeasing the god our organization bows to.

There isn't much other science to the group. They believe sex holds power because it can result in life, and when they don't have a vessel to manipulate or anyone to kill, carnal pleasure becomes the sacrifice.

Normally, I can distract myself while members explore my

body by retreating to the recesses of my brain where I feel and see nothing. I check out, as if watching myself be used from above, but tonight I'm having a hard time getting there. My skull pulses, the echoes of a migraine still wearing off even though I took medicine over an hour ago, and I wish I could peel the skin from my bones.

I tense beneath the fledgling's touch even as she takes my hand, shoving one of my fingers through the mouth hole in her white mask. White and gold are the colors of anonymity down here, usually depending on a member's rank. White is low, meaning this brunette with tan skin wouldn't normally even be granted access to me.

When I glance across the cavern, I see the Director standing with her hands on her hips, watching. It's clear she sent this patron my way and is waiting for some sort of reaction, though I'm not sure *what*.

I haven't rejected others in the past because they were too close in status to me. I simply have no interest in any of the people here.

Before the beginning of the semester, I didn't have interest in anyone at all.

The ache scratching my skull intensifies, and I grind my teeth, wondering if that's the test.

If they've been watching me.

It's not a secret Death's Teeth has eyes everywhere, and though I haven't *actually* done anything since Elle enrolled as a student, it's possible they've seen me somehow.

Seen her near me, which is bad. Pythia posting her picture likely didn't help, even if they didn't say who she was. I doubt it would take long to figure out.

The only thing Death's Teeth wants less than my refusal to cooperate as Incarnate is their Incarnate fraternizing with an Anderson.

Given our ancestors' pasts, the idea of a Dupont with an Anderson would be history repeating itself.

Considering the lengths they went to last semester to try and scare her brother and sister off, I don't want to know what they might do if they realize all three are at Avernia. Don't want to know think of how they'll try to keep the curse from manifesting.

The Director continues staring, arms folded over her chest. Always watching me through the holes in that snake-adorned mask.

Sometimes, I wonder if she was there the night Bellamy died. If she was one of the people who—

Throat burning, I yank my fingers from the fledgling's mouth and push to my feet, tucking my cold hands into my cloak sleeves.

"Is everything okay?" the Director asks in that strange, obscured voice of hers. Like she has some kind of modulator hidden inside the mask that distorts it.

Though there is anonymity outside and within the group, the Director is the only member whose identity is fully unknown. I'm not even sure how she came into her role or how they choose a replacement, nor do I particularly care.

Seeking information in this organization is dangerous. They want you stupid and complacent so they can engage in their lewd rituals and human sacrifices in peace.

And they want me to pick who fucks and dies.

"Everything is fine." I shuffle back a step, away from the chair and the fledgling. "I'm not feeling well is all."

"Ah." The Director reaches out, a pale palm pressing against the side of my face. "Indeed, you're quite warm. Perhaps you'd like to take a dip in the lake? That's been known to cool members down."

I swallow over the stickiness in my esophagus. "I'm afraid I'm not equipped for a swim."

"You know we don't taint Lerna's water with *equipment*. Only those who resemble the way they came to earth may enter her." She clicks her tongue, the exact shade of her eyes eclipsed by shadows.

"Swimming with a migraine is a bad idea," I note, even as the fledgling gets to her feet and slinks over, grabbing for my arm again. I pull out of reach, meeting the Director's gaze. "If you'll excuse me."

"Your father said you'd be squeamish this semester," she calls as I turn to the entrance. "I didn't think it'd mean you'd actually attempt to withdraw."

"That's not what I'm doing."

"You've not stayed through an entire ceremony in months. The organization sees you scaling back. They don't like it."

"Then tell them to release me."

"I'm afraid they won't allow that. You're in too deep, and they fear losing you. Perhaps if you did something to sweeten the deal…"

There's only one thing I can think of that would satisfy their curiosity instead of me. One person I imagine they're interested in enough to step off my neck.

"The new girl," I rush out. "Surely you've heard the rumors of a new enrollee."

"Indeed. She's caused a bit of unrest, and there have been whisperings of her identity, but nothing confirmed yet. It's made the council uneasy, and they're planning to look into it."

"Let me." I lift my chin, forcing authority into my voice.

"Let you investigate?"

"Officially, I'm demanding you allow me the space to do so. As your Incarnate, it's my job to regulate the order at Avernia, so it's my duty to see that any unrest is dealt with."

She stays quiet, and I curse myself internally for volunteering. That certainly isn't maintaining my distance from the group, but it buys me favor with them and keeps Elle out of harm's direct way.

For now at least.

"And if she's who we think she is?"

"I'll take care of it," I tell her.

"Fine," the Director says, nodding. "We won't actively seek the girl out on the grounds of you doing so yourself. Provided you continue attending these gatherings and we don't happen to accidentally run into her, that is. A curse can only be ignored for so long, you know."

Good enough. I don't reply, pushing past her to head for the cavern exit. The tunnels are damp and narrow, with pockets of water and cold air that feel like phantom fingers brushing against my skin, but I ignore them until I see a sliver of light and come out near the lake.

The sun will set soon. Since the Director called this evening's function a ceremony after all, I've no doubt in my mind they're planning some display, though it's hard to say what the severity will be: light vandalism or full-on sacrifice.

Either way, I don't want to be in the vicinity when it happens.

Once I'm back within Avernia's gates, I rub my temple with the heel of my hand, trying to massage away the ache. I pinch my eyes shut for a moment, collecting myself as disgust continues filtering through my nervous system, dredging up the memories I work so hard at keeping away.

Familiar laughter draws my attention, and my eyes snap open, instantly searching for the source. Elle stands at the doorstep of the Daughters of Persephone clubhouse, chatting with someone I can't see because they're tucked in the alcove.

Her sister, presumably, since she's the faculty sponsor and founder of the organization.

My chest pinches with an unidentifiable sensation when a smile lights Elle's face. A breeze rustles her hair, and I rake my gaze over the length of her: Under a long black coat, she wears a red blouse that ties at the center of her chest, accentuating what is already very ample cleavage. Her legs are on display in a tight black skirt with a small slit in the thigh, shown as she takes a step back, waving to whomever is on the receiving end of her attention right now.

Rules be damned, I hate that it isn't me.

She turns, tucking her hair behind her ears, then reaches up to toy with the snake charm necklace that constantly hangs at her throat. I catch her touching it in class and wonder if it's some sort of calming technique.

I could ask. There are no rules about that.

I'm certain the conversation will devolve, but that's just nature taking its course. My heart thuds against my ribs as I slide one foot in her direction, clouds of cold air appearing when my breathing grows ragged.

The reaction my body has to this woman should concern me, but right now, I find I just want to be near her.

Last time I went to a Death's Teeth meeting, she was the perfect distraction after. The *only* distraction that's ever worked in nearly ten years. I didn't vomit or recoil when she touched me, didn't want to slit my throat when she crawled on top of me.

In fact, all I did was burn for more, and I've been on fucking fire ever since.

She wasn't wrong when she accused me of making excuses. My position at Avernia be damned, I want this.

Want *her*.

Just as the sole of my shoe connects with its next step, a new figure rounds the corner of the building, immediately sliding an arm around Elle's shoulders. She giggles, turning toward the intruder, and I pull back.

Lexington. That son of a bitch.

He smiles down at her, grabbing her wrists, and an entirely different inferno blazes within me.

When he playfully pulls her hands beneath the flaps of his overcoat, my stomach drops like I've swallowed an anchor. Something visceral and white-hot scalds my chest, a heated brand searing straight through my heart.

They turn in my direction, their collective laughter sawing me in two.

I slip beneath the branches of a large pine tree, hiding from sight.

It shouldn't bother me when there's nothing I can *really* do about it. Even if I were to throw caution to the wind and recklessly indulge, where would it go? I can't do *just sex*, and she won't stay at Avernia forever.

I'm stuck here with my past while she has an entire future to consider.

Still, the pang that ripples through my abdomen as she and Lexington prance past makes me clench my teeth so tight, my migraine seeps in, triggered by the onslaught of stress and tension.

My fingers are uncomfortably numb as I drag them through my hair, staring while they disappear into her dorm.

So like many other nights after a Death's Teeth function, I make my way back to my apartment, turn off all the lights in my room, and wait for the pain to subside enough to fall asleep.

Chapter 14

Sutton

A KNOCK ON MY OFFICE DOOR SENDS A WAVE OF ANNOYANCE across my skin, and I quickly swipe out of *The Delphic Pages* on my phone, though the post I was staring at continues to flash in my mind.

WANNABE ACTRESS ON CAMPUS, KNOWN FOR SLEEPING WITH FILM EXECS FOR PARTS. IS THE NEW GIRL FUCKING THE DEAN?

They don't name her explicitly, which I imagine is simply to keep curse speculation at a minimum, but it's obvious to me who they're talking about.

The knock comes again, and I push thoughts of Elle from my mind. None of what she did before she came here matters really, even if any of it is true.

I glance down at the back of my hand as another knock comes, smoothing my fingers over the scar.

Everyone does what they need to in order to survive.

My chest burns until I clear my throat, shoving my hand beneath the desk and looking at the door.

"It's open," I call.

Quincy Anderson peeks through the crack she creates, her brown eyes darting around the room before she enters. "This a bad time?"

Shaking my head, I gesture toward the space in front of me. "Not at all. Come in."

She leaves the door open as she crosses the threshold, as if uncomfortable with the idea of being trapped in here with me alone.

Good sense, I suppose. We don't know each other really, aside from being here together during undergrad—she was a year or two ahead of me, but I was explicitly forbidden to speak to her.

Mother and Jean-Louise would keel over if they knew what I've done with her sister. What I'd like to *keep* doing but can't. Won't. Especially not now that I'm supposed to be investigating her to keep Death's Teeth off her scent.

Elle would've shut the door though. I know that much.

Quincy's gaze flickers to the stack of papers spread across my desk. "If I'm interrupting something, I can come back."

"Oh no, I was just needling at an old screenplay. I've been trying to complete one since freshman year of high school but keep rewriting the first act instead. It'll probably just be buried with me."

"I had no idea you wrote plays."

"Indeed. I, much like Walt Whitman, contain multitudes. But that's a story for another time. What can I do for you?" I fold my hands on the desk. "If you're here to ask me to sub for a class, I'm afraid I'm not terribly up to speed on my Roman mythology."

"Roman *and* Greek," she corrects, taking a seat in one of the two plastic chairs across from me. "And trust me, I don't need a theater kid philosophizing about the Byzantine Empire."

I smirk, leaning back in my chair. "Afraid I'd do a better job?"

"No." She doesn't elaborate, and I smother a laugh at her candor. That must be an Anderson trait. "How's my sister doing?"

"Ah…we're not terribly far into the semester," I say. "It's a bit difficult to talk about progress when there's little to have been made."

"But she's showing up? Doing her assignments? Participating?"

"Oh, she's showing up," I mutter. "Earlier than my other students most days. Though I do have to ask why that's your concern? Her application and references for enrollment were sparkling."

Quincy adjusts her glasses. "You looked at her file?"

The air in my lungs solidifies, panic pumping through my veins.

Fuck, did I just say that out loud?

No way can I admit to her sister that Elle's file is the only one I haven't returned to the student archives yet. It's currently tucked under the pillow in my bedroom, where I spend each night poring over the details, obsessively trying to commit them to memory.

Because despite my best efforts, I'm hanging by a thread here, trying to maintain distance.

She's the first thing I think about in the morning and the last before I go to bed. My soul feels like it's cracking in half every time I push her away, as if I'm splitting it down its seam and severing my own humanity.

It shouldn't be like this, the connection I feel to her, but it is. There's no escaping it. All I can do is pretend it doesn't exist at all. That's how I'll keep her safe.

So I hold on to the file in the hope that its contents will placate me. Thus far, I have not been successful.

"She applied to be in Visio Aternae, so I might have taken a quick glance," I answer, swallowing over the sudden dryness of my tongue. "Standard procedure for new initiates, as I'm sure you know."

"Wait, she applied to be in Visio Aternae?" Her brows furrow. "She didn't ask to be enrolled in Daughters of Persephone."

"Maybe campus beautification isn't her thing."

"That's not the only thing we—" She stops herself, snapping her mouth shut.

Her group is notoriously more secretive than Death's Teeth. The public at least knows the gist of what happens at our meetings—the sex stuff anyway. But nobody talks about Daughters of Persephone outside of their revitalization efforts.

If I believed in the curses and conspiracies, I'd be concerned. Around here, secrets are just a currency. Everyone's got them.

Shifting in her seat, Quincy toys with the rings adorning her fingers, seeming to work through something silently in her head. "I don't mean to make my sister sound like a troubled student. I just didn't think she'd want to get involved in anything here."

"Why wouldn't she?"

"Well, she never really cared much about school. She was good at it, don't get me wrong, but it wasn't a passion of hers. Learning by doing was her preference over sitting through lectures and doing classroom scut work."

"Seems like joining a campus-run organization would be right up her alley then."

"Sure, but then there was the whole…" Quincy trails off, glancing at me from the corner of her eye, as if refraining from revealing sensitive information. "Maybe you're right. I just…worry, you know? I mean, you get it, right? You're an older sibling."

There's a slight pause as we consider this truth. Neither of us mentions the connection between our younger siblings, which is good since I'm supposed to be pretending the cave incident never happened.

She continues. "My parents are amazing, but I've never been able to stop from feeling like I needed to watch over my brother and sister. Especially Noelle, who's always been sort of reckless and—"

"And what?"

The two of us startle at the addition of a third voice, and my gaze flickers in the direction it came from. Elle stands in the open doorway, a dripping umbrella tucked beneath one arm. Her hair is damp and a little frizzy, as if she'd been caught in the rain before she could shield herself from it.

She arches her brows, glancing between Quincy and me. Waiting for an answer.

"Ms. Anderson," I greet, keeping my words as even as possible. I'm not sure why, but as the two sisters stare at each other, I can't help feeling like I'm watching the moments before a predatorial attack. "What can I do for you?"

Elle's icy gaze slides toward me, and I ignore the ache in my chest. Even when I'm teasing her in class, there's never been a lack of warmth when she looked at me, yet it feels as if she could slice me to pieces with the daggers she shoots my way now.

"You can explain why you're talking about me behind my back," she says.

I guess I walked into that one.

Quincy turns around in her chair. "Noelle, it's not what it sounded like."

"Okay." Elle shifts her weight from side to side, shrugging.

"Then explain. Or continue. I'd love to hear what you think of me after eight *years* of us barely speaking. Reckless and what else, Q?"

This feels like something I shouldn't be witnessing. "Ladies, perhaps this discussion to be had in private—"

The chair legs scrape against the floor, letting out an uncomfortable squealing noise as Quincy pushes to her feet. "I've got a meeting I should be getting to. If you'll excuse me, Professor."

She doesn't even acknowledge her sister as she books it from my office, so quickly that the soft scent of her perfume still lingers after she's long gone. I sit forward, rubbing my eyes.

"Well? Are you fucking her?"

I pause, palms blocking my vision. "Excuse me?"

"My sister. Is that why you can barely look me in the eye during class, because you feel bad about it?" The door is open behind Elle still, yet she continues hurling these ridiculous accusations. "I get it, I guess. She's smart, calm, and convenient. Why go for the unstable mess when you can have the perfectly wrapped package?"

Slowly, I let my hands fall to the desk. I don't look right at her, not yet, because I'm afraid that if I do, only a string of swear words will come out.

There's not a world where I'd pick Quincy over her sister.

I can't even fully pick my career or sanity over her. Otherwise, I'd have escorted her from the room by now.

Instead, I'm stuck listening to her jealousy, letting it scald long-dormant pieces inside me that I never wanted anyone to see, much less touch.

"She's in love with someone else though," Elle continues, as if any of it even matters. "Not that she tells me directly. I have to hear about that stuff from our mother or one of our aunts, because when she came to Avernia, she stopped talking to me. Well, *really* talking.

We'd have a call once a week or so, but she never said anything of substance. Never asked me how things were. We talked about the weather, her classes, or our family. Anything to avoid the elephant in the room that destroyed our relationship, which was—"

"Elle."

"—when she told me that I wasn't good enough to make it out west. Said I was naive for moving there instead of going to school. Do you know how much it sucks to have the one person you look up to the most not believe in you? It's so—"

"*Elle*."

"—dehumanizing." She sniffles, and I glance over as she wipes her nose with the back of a hand, shaking her head. Her eyes are trained on the ground, and she looks more demure than I've seen her. This doesn't feel like the same girl I met at the gas station or the one who challenges me in class every day.

This Elle is different. Vulnerable in a way that makes me nauseous—because my fingers buzz with the need to console. To provide comfort.

I *ache* to reach out and pull her into my embrace. To keep her warm and safe.

But I *can't*.

She clears her throat. "Anyway, I'm just saying. If that's the kind of person you want to get in bed with, then you should at least know all the details."

I grit my teeth when she turns toward the door, balling my hands into fists. "Maybe she had a reason."

Elle pauses in the doorway, lifting one hand to the frame as if to balance herself. "What?"

"For saying those cruel things…for pushing you away." My heart thuds a slow, unsteady rhythm in my chest, my throat, my wrist. I feel it everywhere when I look at her. "Maybe she was trying to protect you in her own way."

"I'm not a child who needs to be constantly watched over," she snaps.

"No," I agree. "But sometimes it's not about what you need."

"Why are you defending her?"

"I don't know."

"Then *stop*." She whirls around, stomping over to my desk, fire blazing in those hazel irises. She slams a palm down on the wood surface, baring her teeth, and it takes every single ounce of strength I can muster not to draw her into my lap and plant a sloppy kiss to her mouth. "If you really care about your students and their well-being, you should stop talking about my sister."

"I'm not fucking her," I say softly.

"You don't have to speak to me like that." Her eyes shine, glassy with unshed emotion. "Like I'm some rabid animal you're afraid of."

"It's not a fear of being bitten," I tell her. My fear is that I'll ask her to do it again.

Her face grows bright red, as if she's just comprehending this entire situation. She drops the umbrella, crossing her arms over her chest, those perky tits hidden beneath an impossibly tight sweater. It's plastered to her skin like it was painted on, and I can see the faintest outline of her nipples, though I bite my tongue to keep from ogling.

Sitting up straight, I try to school my features. With decades of acting and directing experience, it should be a lot easier to do, but something about this woman just throws me off entirely.

"Was there...something you wished to see me about?"

She nods. "I'd like to join Visio Aternae."

I bark out a laugh. How long had she been listening to my conversation?

"No."

"No?"

"That's what I said. Conflict of interest."

"How so?" she demands. "It's been weeks since you were inside me."

My eyes swing to the doorway, my ears straining to hear footsteps or heavy breathing in the hall. "An anecdote I would like to keep *private*, by the way, and only after noting that I had no idea you were an Avernia student at the time."

"I bet it doesn't stop you from getting off to the memory," she says. When I don't immediately respond, she huffs a laugh, shaking her head and glancing around the room.

The smile falls from her face as she scans the bookshelves, pausing briefly on one area before slowly dragging her focus back to me. Whatever emotion burned there just seconds ago is gone, replaced by some sort of mask—slid into place as if she's done it a billion times before.

An actress playing a role.

I can't help wondering just how many different forms of this woman I'll get to see before the semester's end.

Without another word, she turns on her heels and stalks out of the room, so quickly that she forgets to grab her umbrella. I pick it up, balancing it on my knees, and spin toward the shelves, scanning the spines of my books to see what spooked her so badly.

My heart sinks to my stomach as I note the gold-embossed envelope I'd forgotten to file in the locked cabinet where I keep all Death's Teeth–related items.

Still, I'm not sure she'd necessarily know what it means just by looking at it. Though it's difficult to be at Avernia for longer than a few hours and not learn about the school's lore somehow. She didn't seem to be aware of much when we spoke on her first day.

Maybe she didn't see it anyway. Maybe she freaked out over how many volumes of completed Shakespeare works I own.

Regardless, I imagine I'll need to keep an eye on that, if only to make sure it doesn't progress.

Elle Anderson is a curious woman, and that's never been a good quality to have at this school.

Chapter 15

Elle

"You want my opinion?"

I give my cousin a long look as he stretches out on the couch in his apartment, his six-foot-six frame barely fitting in the scope of the camera. His brown hair is shaggier than I've ever seen it, and stubble lines his normally clean shaven jaw, but it's the brace on his arm that really throws me.

Foxe had been with Lucy and Asher in the Tenarus cave last semester. Apparently, it was a miracle he made it out—much less that he recovered from extensive injuries so well.

Minus the brace and a scar between his brows, you might not even know anything had happened at all.

"Would I have called if I didn't?" I reply, popping a french fry into my mouth. The campus refectory's food tastes like cardboard, so I dipped into the funds my parents send each week and had something delivered from town.

In LA, I waited tables and did stage work for Grandeur Playhouse, only using their money for emergencies. But they suggested I take time to focus on school and not work now, so unfortunately I'm twenty-five and living off their dime.

Not that I'm complaining, especially since there are people who'd kill for this life. It just sometimes feels like my independence is a sham, is all.

"That hurts, Noelle," Foxe whines. "You wouldn't call your own flesh and blood just to check in on him? Don't you love me?"

"Okay," I say slowly, chewing. "How *are* you doing? Written any new songs lately? I see the plants behind you are wilted, so your mom must not have visited recently. Does that mean you're well?"

Aunt Violet, a florist, believes heavily in the healing and therapeutic power of plants, so naturally she filled her son's apartment to the brim with every pot she could get her hands on.

Foxe faces the ceiling again, folding his hands over his tanned, tattooed chest. The ink is everywhere—it stretches up each arm and rains over his back in a plethora of patchwork designs, some fresh and some not.

Only one spot is blank, above his pectoral—lasered off at some point.

"My opinion is that you're too hard on your sister," he answers, ignoring my questions. Classic deflection. "She was probably just making sure your transition to a new school was going smoothly. This is how she's always been, so I don't really see why you're freaking out."

"Why would she need to ask my *teacher* about me? Why not go directly to the source?"

"Maybe she didn't want you to think she was overstepping. You tend to assume the worst, you know."

The fry drops from my mouth onto my bed, and I frown, scooping it onto the paper plate in my lap. "I do not."

"I'm not criticizing," he says. "Just observing."

"It sounds critical."

He waves a hand, dismissing the notion. "Some people hear whatever they want to hear."

"Ugh." I groan. "Why did I call you again?"

"Because I'm willing to pretend if you are." He grins, but it feels forced somehow, not quite reaching his hazel eyes. "Other than Q being her regular overbearing self, how're you liking it up there? I assume no one's tried to murder you yet."

"'Yet' being the operative word really bums me out."

"Hey, you chose to enroll."

"My parents thought it would help."

"Oh, I'm aware. Strength in numbers, or whatever. I heard them talking about it over the holidays. Kept waking me up arguing when I was in the midst of early recovery, the fuckers."

"Is that why you got your own place?"

Foxe shrugs, rolling his head to look at me. "Partly. And because my mom was suffocating me. Unintentionally, of course, but she was pretty inconsolable when I came back from Fury Hill." He pauses for a brief moment as if remembering something—replaying his return to Aplana Island in his mind. Then he chuckles to himself. "You'd think I almost died or something."

"Do you joke about what happened like this with your mom?" Aunt Violet is like sunshine in human form, so I can only imagine how hearing that stuff from her son would make her react.

The dead plants suddenly make sense.

"I am who I am, Noelle." He sighs, propping his hands behind his head. "Can't be changed."

"Remember when you used to think Asher and I were callous about death?"

"Callous about *others*' deaths. I think I've earned the right to feel however I want about my near one, don't you?"

I do, but I'm not sure Foxe understands the cost. He doesn't know what it took for us to get to this point. You practice ambivalence, growing those calluses, just so you can sleep at night.

So the memories of your past don't keep you awake.

"Anyway," Foxe goes on. "I'm on the mend, so I don't know why we're even talking about me. You're the one in danger. Everyone there thinks your family is cursed, and students go missing at Avernia like it's the trendy thing to do. The school acts like they're not even aware it's happening."

"How can that be possible if it's such a high number?" I ask. "People would notice if their roommates just stopped showing up."

"Good question. Chemical brainwashing? Maybe the tap water is laced with something."

I give him a look. "You're listening to too many true crime podcasts."

"Or maybe I'm listening to the correct amount and have been enlightened."

Someone snorts from the doorway, and I tense up, glancing over my laptop to see Aurora and Asher standing there. She's got one hand on the doorknob, the key still wedged in the lock, and Asher walks past her, making an immediate beeline for my food.

"What are you doing here?" I ask.

Asher bends down, stealing a fry and plopping it in his mouth. "Looking for my girlfriend. Thought maybe she'd come to see you, but now I have a bad feeling she's doing lake cleanup."

"It's, like, twelve degrees out," Aurora says, snatching the key from the door and coming inside.

"When has that ever stopped Lucy from trying to save the planet?" he replies around chewing.

My face scrunches up. "Don't talk with your mouth full, you troll."

Foxe grins, straightening. His entire demeanor changes with his best friend's presence, and I pretend it doesn't sting a little that I wasn't able to cheer him up.

"Ash-tree, my pride and joy! You haven't called me in…" Foxe sits forward, checking something off-screen, and returns with his phone in hand. "Exactly fourteen hours."

"Jesus Christ." Asher steals another fry, dragging it through my ketchup. "Do you just sit around counting the minutes?"

"I always miss your shining, sparkling personality when it's gone."

"God, you really are a fucking golden retriever."

"I'd prefer something a little more formidable. A husky, even, would work. At least they're musically inclined."

Aurora slams her wardrobe shut, keeping her back to us. I glance at Asher, feeling a small twinge of guilt knowing these two have a history and tend to avoid interacting in front of others.

Given Foxe's current predicament, I imagine things are even more strained than they used to be.

"Rory?" Foxe calls, pursing his lips as he pretends to search for her. "That you, cupcake? I'd recognize the way you slam a door anywhere."

She scoffs, dumping an armful of Japanese skincare products onto her desk. "Well, I've slammed enough in your face that I'd be surprised if that wasn't the case."

Foxe's grin widens, though I swear it still looks off. When we were growing up, nothing bothered him. He was like a punching bag that always snapped back into place no matter how many beatings it took, and he took many from my angry brother.

There's this sentiment that people don't change. Seconds ago, Foxe basically just said the same thing. Years back, I might have agreed, but looking at my cousin now, I'm just not so sure.

Maybe people don't change for no reason. But they definitely don't stay the same forever.

"What were you all talking about anyway?" Asher asks, perching on the edge of my mattress. "Foxe's supposed enlightenment?"

"Supposed," Foxe repeats, confirming. "We were just discussing the possibility that your school's student body has been brainwashed."

"So casual lunch conversation."

I shift, curling my arms around my middle. "Don't you think it's odd that people die or go missing so often, and the school's just operating like it's business as usual?"

Asher shrugs. "Odd? Maybe a little. But given how they believe in curses and other supernatural phenomena, it wouldn't surprise me if Avernia just thinks it's all part of the Fury Hill experience. A little death to round out their college careers. They do have an entire student organization named after the fucking thing." He pauses, considering, then points a finger at me. "Do *not* go poking your head around for answers."

"You're not the boss of me, *little bro*."

"Exactly. I'm not gonna take shit from Mom and Dad if you end up in trouble for being nosy either."

"Whatever." I shove him from the bed and then get up, walking over to Aurora. "You have studying to do?"

She snorts. "Does a bear shit in the woods?"

I reach for her hand, tugging her toward the door. "Great. Let's go."

We run into Lexington and Percy on our way into the Obeliskos. The former is wearing a thick black sweater while the latter's gray peacoat is buttoned all the way up, and I can't tell if they're coming or going.

"Neither," Lexington offers when I ask. "We were just arguing over where to get food before heading to the quarry for a Curator party."

"They're still throwing those?" Aurora asks, lifting her blond brows.

Percy shrugs. "School didn't tell them to stop, so why not?"

"It's the middle of the week though," I note.

Grinning, Lexington slings an arm around my shoulder, giving me a playful squeeze. "Which is exactly why faculty will be less likely to come and shut things down. They're usually at office hours or teaching night courses right now."

"That logic seems…flawed," I tell him.

"The professors and administrators don't want to step foot in the Primordial Forest any more than we do," Percy says.

Aurora frowns. "Then why are you going?"

"For the adventure." Lexington releases me, sliding his hands into his khaki pockets. "The start of the semester is usually pretty slow for theater majors, so I like to get as much fun in before we start play prep as I can. Professor Dupont monopolizes our time the minute auditions are over."

My stomach churns at the thought of him, and I scoff. "Dictators are like that."

Behind us, the revolving glass door swings open, and in walks Sutton at the head of a gaggle of students, as if summoned by the mere mention of his name.

He breezes past us, pointedly ignoring our group.

That Sabrina bitch from class is right on his heels, swinging her ponytail as they head for the study rooms blocked off by the main stairs beyond the circulation desk. She turns just before they're out of sight, giving me a sharp look of victory.

As if she's accomplished some great feat by getting to be Sutton's little ankle-biter.

Big fucking deal. I bet she hasn't ridden his hand to completion or had his cock inside her.

Nausea spins a web in my gut, something bitter boiling within. *Has she?*

No, no. That can't be right. He implied hookups were unusual and seemed to need to convince himself he wanted to be touched at all. That's not the kind of professor who makes a habit of fucking his students.

Aurora kicks my shin. "Dude, unclench."

I release the pressure on my teeth.

"Do you think she was looking at me?" Percy asks, a blush staining his cheeks as he stares after Sabrina.

"Definitely not," Lexington tells him, chuckling. He gives me a sidelong glance, one that makes me feel completely transparent. "You really get under Sabrina's skin, huh?"

"Bad habit of mine," I say. "Mean girls tend to clash like that."

"Are you a mean girl?"

"Depends on who's asking." Glancing at Aurora, I jut my chin toward the back.

She follows me into a closed stairwell, and I pretend I don't notice the sudden chill in the air as we head up a level. The higher we go, the cooler the temperature seems to get, and I can't help wondering about the validity of the ghost stories that swirl about here.

I'm not sure whether I believe in the supernatural or not, but certain physical anomalies make it difficult to rule the existence out entirely.

Below us, the stairwell door swings open and slams shut, and I pause, peering over the railing. Lexington and Percy stand at the bottom, heads tipped back as they look up.

Lexington shrugs. "Suddenly, going to the woods is less appealing."

Percy nudges him, then starts skipping the steps two at a time. "You just want to bug Elle about Los Angeles."

My face flushes as we reach the thirteenth floor, and I shove open the door, enshrouding us in darkness. Percy gropes at the wall, flipping a light that sends a row of bulbs sparking to life above an endless sea of books.

This level is sparsely populated, with us being the only visible souls around. Like the rest of the building, the floor is decorated with sporadic dark furniture that looks like it was crafted decades ago, and the faintest scent of vinegar and mothballs clings to the air along with the cool temperature.

The windows, likely arched and double-paned like many of the other buildings on campus, are boarded up. Nothing can get in or out.

My nerves tighten like drawstrings. Maybe coming here wasn't such a good idea, but all the curse and founding family talk has me curious, and the Obeliskos supposedly has the biggest catalog of Fury Hill's history.

"If we go any higher, I might get a nosebleed," Lexington says, panting by the time he gets to the top of the stairs. He bends over with his hands on his knees and glances at me, blushing. "I wasn't being nosy down there, I swear."

I lift an eyebrow.

"Well, okay, I was," he admits, straightening to his full height. "But not to be weird or anything. I just heard a rumor and wanted to know how much of it was true."

"A rumor." I pause, crossing my arms. "About?"

"You."

"Obviously. What *about* me?"

Aurora and Percy walk over to an area filled with study tables, the former dropping her bag on the top and flopping into one of the chairs. Percy makes his way to a glass display case against the far wall, studying the items inside.

"Why'd you come to Avernia?" Lexington asks, moving toward a solid wood bookcase. "Pythia says you got several highly competitive, merit-based scholarships before you graduated from high school, but you opted out of attending college to go to Hollywood."

I slide my fingers over the spines of a few books, noting the dated encyclopedias. Picking one up, I aimlessly thumb through the pages, scanning the entries about my ancestor Cronus Anderson, whose strange actions during a tuberculosis outbreak caused him to become a pariah.

Cursing his bloodline forever in the eyes of Fury Hill's residents.

Do the choices we make really have such extensive consequences?

"Higher education isn't for everyone," I tell Lexington. "And choosing to work instead isn't an unheard-of phenomenon. Lots of people go straight into the workforce or take gap years or live off their parents' dime."

"Not people who applied for college," he says. "Not those who *wanted* to go."

My pulse thickens in my throat. I don't want to talk about this.

Don't want to dive into how I spent *years* out west trying to make a name for myself, and even when I tried to do what others told me worked—so many swore up and down you could get a part if you made enough film executives *feel good*—I came up short.

Seven *years* and nothing except a little exploitation to show for it.

The embarrassing thing was that I *was* good. Acting is the only thing I've ever taken seriously, performance the one discipline I indulge. But out there, *everyone* was good.

So I started to feel like I wasn't. Not comparatively. Despite the logic of not wanting to base my talent on the success of others, I couldn't help it. Every time a friend of mine from the community acting company I'd joined got a part and I went jobless, something in me died a little.

Something vital that I'd been relying on my entire life to get me through the dark thoughts. The memories of my brief time here when I was seventeen and my understanding of the world changed forever.

That feeling propelled me to drastic measures. Favors, bribes, whatever else I needed to do to get work, because I was too afraid of failing. Too afraid of the memories swallowing me whole.

Acting was how I pretended to be someone who wasn't consumed by inaction, fear, and envy. I wasn't the girl who'd gotten lost in the woods or who witnessed something vile. Acting was my escape.

Until it wasn't.

When you sell out, your connection to the medium dies.

So does your spirit.

Lifting my chin, I glance at Lexington. No way am I telling him all that. "I applied to satisfy my family. My dad is obsessed with us having options."

"And why is that, I wonder? To make sure you'd never be stuck in one single place—similar to the way his mother was decades prior?" Lexington gravitates closer, looming behind me as I scan the paragraphs under Cronus Anderson's name. "The way your ancestor tried to trap the people of Fury Hill here?"

A chill skates across my skin, pulling goose bumps to the surface.

One of the six founding family members, Cronus is attributed with the conception of Avernia as a learning institution…

…survived the consumption crisis…

…no records of the death of Cronus Anderson…

…destroyed in a fire…or perhaps intentionally erased…

…often blamed by residents for having taken advantage of the situation to gain ownership of the school and town.

Frowning at the page, I wonder how someone manages to survive tuberculosis during a time when vaccines and antibiotics didn't really exist. Was my ancestor's immune system just stronger, or is it possible that the next paragraphs—ones that talk about blood drinking and night walking—hold some sort of truth?

Is *that* why Avernia is equally terrified and enthralled by our bloodline?

The curse says that having three descendants of Cronus Anderson on campus at once will bring instantaneous destruction, but it doesn't say how.

Do they think we're vampires?

I'd laugh if it wasn't so fucking ridiculous.

What kind of people would believe something like that?

Or do they just cling to their suspicion because inviting us in would be like forgiving Cronus's sins? Is it possible for people to be so afraid of change that they'd go to great lengths—threats, kidnappings, and even murder—to keep it from happening?

One entry under Cronus's name is marked out, and I squint through the pen lines, trying to decipher what it says.

The words *widow* and *Dupont* are legible, making me think back to what Sutton said about our families having history. But when I turn to the Duponts' pages and comb through dozens of entries about their economic and charitable contributions to the town, they don't mention the Andersons at all.

In fact, it becomes abundantly clear that the Duponts are Fury Hill's Kennedy family. The entries go on for pages, gushing over their accomplishments and implying they can do no wrong.

They're the chosen family, one entry says.

Chosen for what, though, isn't explained.

Two hands grab my waist, and I jolt forward, fear racing through my veins. The encyclopedia drops to the floor, its thud echoing through the quiet room. My head knocks into the bookshelf, and I wince, heart pounding as Lexington steps back, laughing too loud for a haunted library.

"Shit, sorry," he says, wiping a tear from his blue eye. "That was just way too easy."

I glare at him. "Asshole. Is that any way to treat the descendant of your town's Dracula?"

"Why?" He leans in, grinning wide, his handsome face ensconced in shadows from the overhead lights. "Gonna bite me? Teach me a lesson?"

Percy snorts from across the room. "Classy."

My hands shake as I bend, reaching for the book, which has fallen open to a random page toward the back. The encyclopedia runs from A through D, with a section highlighted by someone who checked it out previously.

It's a photograph of the caves carved into the White Mountains, deep within the Primordial Forest.

Beneath the photo is a caption colored in neon yellow: **Tenarus Cave, leading to the pits of Tartarus within. Death's Teeth sightings abound—photo taken by [redacted] just days after last known Ceremony of Life. Not pictured: missing student pulled from Lake Lerna, thought to be involved in secret.**

I blink down at the page. There's no date, so it could have been *any*time.

Crimson drips onto the page, blotting out the photo before I can get a closer look to confirm my suspicions.

I know that cave. That symbol, some sort of three-headed beast, painted above the entrance.

Those eyes—even if they're missing. I've been seeing them every night for the last eight years.

Dread settles deep in my gut; I barely notice when Lexington touches the top of my head, drawing my attention to him.

He stares down at me, pressing a finger to my hairline. "Fuck, you're bleeding, Elle."

Aurora comes over, shoving him out of the way as she hauls me to my feet. "This is why you shouldn't prank people."

He rubs the back of his neck, giving me a sheepish look. "My bad. I thought she realized what I was doing."

"Ew, she got blood on the encyclopedia!" Percy moans,

appearing in a crouching position beside me. "They're gonna have to burn this now."

I touch the cut on my head, instantly nauseous from the red staining my fingers. "S-sorry."

"Are you going to pass out?" Aurora asks, grabbing my hand so I can no longer see the blood.

My head swims, the image—now painted in crimson—making me dizzy. I don't answer.

"Is she okay?" Lexington leans in, tilting his head at me. "Should we have her lie down?"

"No, she just needs some air and to be cleaned up. I'll take care of it," Aurora says.

Percy frowns. "But the book—"

"Don't worry about it," Lexington cuts in. "I'll take the heat for destruction of campus property. You go get fixed up."

"They have handwritten accounts of this stuff anyway," Percy adds after a moment, though still a bit horrified. "If you ever want a primary source, just ask the librarians downstairs for a historical journal. There are a ton. Although I think they might have moved some of them to another library."

I nod, letting Aurora lead me to the stairwell. Once we're outside, she has me lean against the wall until I can see straight again.

But even then, my mind keeps spinning on an endless loop, stuck on the picture of that cave.

Quincy told me to stay out of the woods, but... It wouldn't hurt to go look during the day, right? Ghosts only come out at night or in creepy old buildings.

"We should go to health services," Aurora says, looping her arm through mine. "You're probably fine, but no way am I telling Uncle Kal if you have a concussion and don't get it checked out."

Silently, I roll my eyes. Everyone acts like my father—a former physician for the Mafia—is this big, terrifying man just because he has an undetermined body count. Most of the adults we were raised with have violent, bloody histories that no one talks about, though, so I've never understood why my dad was considered the scariest of them all.

Though given what lengths I've gone to to avoid disappointing him over the years, I can't really judge *that* much.

Either way, I'm barely listening as she drags me from the Obeliskos, too busy thinking about getting to that cave.

Chapter 16

Elle

Tightening the drawstrings on my hoodie, I close the fabric around my face as I slip through the broken gate of the wrought iron fence surrounding campus.

Mortui Vivos Docent is inscribed at the top, which makes my stomach drop. Maybe I shouldn't be doing this—or should have made Asher at least tag along.

But that thought doesn't stop my feet from moving.

According to the maps I've spent the last couple of days scouring, Avernia is bordered by the Primordial Forest on all but one side, where the entrance leads to town. The mountains stretch to the sky just beyond the trees, sealing the school off from civilization.

Even though it's a short drive to the city limits, it feels like we're all alone.

As I walk a worn dirt path through the tall trees, a gentle breeze grazes the leaves, making them rustle above my head. Despite the unease cramping my stomach, this stroll feels a lot different from the last time I was here.

I'm not sure what I'm hoping to find—maybe nothing. Maybe I'm trying to convince myself that this place is safe, and what happened eight years ago was just some fluke.

Until I get to the abandoned building and the half-burnt gazebo next to it. The structure is falling apart and should be condemned, but just beyond and visible through the rotted siding is the quarry. Walls and piles of rock stretch as far as I can see, eventually dropping into the ravine and landing at Lake Lerna below.

Legend says what goes into those black waters doesn't come back out.

I know better though.

Sometimes they crawl out to haunt whoever's near.

My feet move as if encouraged by invisible limbs propelling them forward, guiding me alongside the quarry to the base of the mountains. The lake is unsettled, its opaque waters rippling the closer I get.

The muscles in my stomach coil, and I reach up to smooth my fingers over my necklace, outlining the snake charm with my thumb.

Somewhere in the distance, a branch snaps, and I freeze. Fear roots me in place the same way it did eight years ago, and the urge to dive into the shadows pushes at my back.

It feels like a warning.

Energy lurks between the trees and bushes, slithering along the forest floor, waiting for an opportunity. I'm being watched. Preyed upon. I squint at the surrounding foliage, trying to tell myself no one else is out here at the moment.

The woods are silent beneath the sunset.

Somehow that's worse.

An owl's hoot echoes off the water, and I gulp audibly.

You're imagining things, Elle. The forest isn't going to hurt you.

As I come upon the embankment, my soles sink with each step I take, as if the lake has other ideas. When I glance down, I see hands reaching up, sliding over my boots and tugging—trying to consume me.

A pair of familiar eyes reflects on the water's surface, and my mouth parts as fear flashes through me.

My throat collapses in on itself. I scratch at it the way you'd try to relieve a rash, my fingernails scraping the column until it feels raw. The bite of pain is what clears my head, though, and I release a long, shuddery breath.

It's in the past, Elle. Everything is fine. This area is safe, and the fear is just in your head.

Manufactured by real events but made up nonetheless.

The mantra repeats as I scale the water's edge, droplets spraying my boots as wind pushes waves at the shore.

Goose bumps snake their way over my skin. I turn from the lake at the same time a horrid scream pierces the air, coming from the exact place it did eight years ago.

Nausea rolls through me violently.

No.

Not again.

I spin toward the sound, terror rendering me immobile. Another scream echoes through the trees, and my petrification mounts.

"Shit." I reach into my pocket with a shaky hand for my phone, checking the screen: 1 percent battery life and no service.

Weird, considering I charged it before I left.

Quickly, I type out a text and try to send my location to my brother before the juice runs out.

As soon as I hit the button, the screen goes black.

I stare at it silently, eyes wide, for several seconds. My heart thumps an erratic rhythm, the noise striking hard against my skull.

A bright light flashes through the trees in my direction, and I duck lower, glancing around frantically for cover. Laughter carries over to me, and when I scoot forward enough to peek through the trees, I see cloaked figures hovering close to another cave entrance.

Horror seizes my gut, solidifying it. How is this happening again?

Am I the problem? The magnet?

The catalyst?

I shouldn't be here—that's what the forest is whispering. Inaudible words, but I hear them nonetheless.

My lungs burn as fear skirts higher inside my chest, making my hands tremble.

Convincing my parents to let me stay after they took an injured Asher off-campus was hard enough, but there's no way they'll let me off the hook if they know I purposely ditched Quincy at the quarry party to go make out with some girl I just met.

But Quincy was busy, and I was bored.

Now I'm fucking lost.

Shadows flicker around me as I try to use the available glow from the party to climb through brush and bushes. I swear I hear footsteps every couple of seconds, but when I glance over my shoulder, there's never anyone there.

I'm not sure how much time passes before I make it to a clearing. It borders the lake, which the quarry above curves around, making just one shoreline accessible between it and the mountains. The moment my feet hit the softer earth and cool air cascades over my exposed arms, I'm shoved to the ground.

The buckle on one of my heels breaks, sending the shoe flying.

I don't see the attacker before I land on my hands and knees, but I can feel their palms digging into my shoulders as they push me. Terror pulses in my throat, making it impossible to emit any noise as I roll over, trying to get a glimpse of the person.

They're wearing an elongated gold mask and a dark cloak that covers their entire body. The mask looks as if it's been shaped from raw metal and has eye and nose holes but nothing else. Their eyes blend in with the surrounding trees—walnut or moss-colored, it's impossible to tell for sure in the dark.

For a moment, we simply stare at each other.

When they reach for me again, I scramble backward, my elbows scraping against the dirt, collecting evidence. Leaving it.

I can sense how close I am to the water, my plunge imminent.

Both their hands close around my esophagus, squeezing tight. My vision blurs a bit at the corners until all I can see is the moon above us, full and round as it watches me lose.

Desperately, I grope the ground, arms flailing as I search for something—anything. The attacker isn't using quite enough strength to incapacitate me, which either means they're dragging my death out…

Or they don't know what they're doing.

Still, they don't let up, and instinct kicks in.

My fingers brush against something smooth and skinny. I grab it, angling the object as stars dance in my eyes.

Theirs hover close, two frenzied, endless pools of darkness.

I don't think I'll forget them as long as I live.

A shiver skates down my sternum, terror embedding itself in my core. I look at the sky above, preferring that to the evil before me.

The stars are safe. Beautiful. Perhaps they'll protect me.

Swallowing hard, I lift my arm as their thumbs begin digging inward. Fire scalds my throat where they press, and I grit my teeth against the urge to surrender, instead rearing back and driving the pointed heel of my broken shoe forward.

Right into their left eye.

Anguish erupts from their being; they twist away, reaching for the shoe to yank it out. I retch as blood gushes from the wound, splashing against my face and chest. I can't afford to pass out right now.

The hooded figure falls forward, clutching at their mask as if trying to tear it off while their wailing shakes the treetops.

I push onto my knees, aware that I don't have much time before my attacker recovers. Struggling to my feet, I rub at my neck. It still feels like they have their fingers around it, and that coupled with the gore sends a surge of panic through my chest.

A shadow off to the side catches my immediate attention; a body lying on the ground seems to lift slightly. I inch a foot toward them, paralyzed by fear and confusion.

From the corner of my eye, I see the assailant stagger to a standing position, and then they start in my direction, letting out a scream that rattles against my skull.

Bracing, I wait for impact, ducking at the very last second. The masked figure, soaked in their own blood, loses their footing. They slip on the mud, and their limbs go slack, their body catapulting forward.

Plunging right into the lake.

Their body contorts, thrashing as they try to get their bearings. Their one good eye is frozen in horror as the water swallows them whole.

My heart pounds in my ears. I wait for them to come back up. For bubbles to appear on the surface, indicating their return.

But nothing else happens.

Silence blankets the forest. Even up above where the party is going on, all noise has ceased. For me at least. My chin quivers.

I open and close my hands over and over, trying to make sense of what just happened. Throat tight, I lean over the edge of the embankment to see if there's anything visible—running on the instinct to save instead of destroy.

The water's pitch-black. Opaque twilight looks back at me, each ripple a taunt.

Swallowing, I force myself to focus on the immobile figure a few yards away. They're lying on their back at the edge of the lake, one foot still submerged in the water. As I walk over, I can see their clothes—a thin sweater and slacks—are in tatters, having been shredded by who knows what. A beast or fellow man… There's no telling out here.

When I crouch down, pushing drenched hair from the man's forehead, I note the bruises and blood covering him and instantly withdraw. The entire underside of his jaw is blackened, his cheek swollen from some sort of abuse, while burn marks decorate him, visible through the torn clothing.

He's unidentifiable with the debris and abrasions.

The crimson on his skin is smeared, somewhat diluted, and I realize after a beat that he's soaked from head to toe. It's as if he somehow dragged himself out of the lake.

A lump forms in my throat at the thought of what put him there. How hard he'd have had to try to get out. I wonder if my attacker was his too.

With shaky hands, I clench my jaw and avoid looking at the blood, laying my palms on his chest to begin compressions. I'm not sure how much time has passed since he resurfaced, but action is always better than nothing.

The eyes of my assailant flash in my mind, sending a raw shiver across my skin.

I lower my mouth to the stranger's, desperate to get him breathing again.

I'm not sure why it matters, really. Death is as much a part of life as anything else in my family, so we were raised with a more calloused view of it. People die—or get killed—all the time.

But it's never been my fault before.

Perhaps that's what unsettles me. Or maybe it's the way the forest seems to stare, watching as I breathe between an unknown man's lips, judging silently as if the sole witness to the crimes committed here tonight.

As hushed voices carry through the forest now, I'm reminded of the immediate aftermath of that night—how I dove to the shadows the second the strange man began coughing up water, because I'd heard voices then too.

Crawling on my stomach as far from the site as I could get but not before glimpsing a crowd of cloaked figures swooping in and taking the man away. I'd stayed still, caught up in thorns and poison ivy, waiting for them to leave.

Hoping they didn't notice me while those eyes painted themselves into my memory.

Calling my father and Uncle Kieran, who lives just one state over and has his own bloody history, to come find me once I got far enough away and had service. I told them about the person falling into the lake, and they came back later to scour the water together, never finding anything.

After that, everyone seemed to move on, though Quincy never really forgave me for wandering off on my own.

Everyone except me, and seeing those figures plunges me directly into the past, only now I know slightly more than I did back then. I know there's a plot against my family and a host of death and violence lurking at this school.

I know the people who kidnapped Lucy and Foxe were wearing cloaks too.

Had that been their doing?

Did they know who I was back then, and that was their attempt at ridding Fury Hill of its curse?

Anxiety rushes through my veins, and I try to focus on the issue at hand.

They can't see me, I don't think. I can barely see them, although the sounds of their laughter grate against the hair on the back of my neck, making me tense. My fingertips grow numb the longer I stand there trying to get a glimpse at what they're doing—it doesn't *sound* like anything violent. In fact, I'm almost certain I see slivers of naked flesh and hear distinct moans of pleasure as they call out in Latin.

But still. I've seen this film before.

I've *been* here before.

And I need to get out.

Blood rushes between my ears as I spin on my heel and take off, huffing through the burn in my chest. The noise from the group starts to taper off, though I continually check over my shoulder, making sure I'm not being followed.

As I take a sharp turn, relying on muscle memory and ardent fear to get me back to campus, I trip. A strained grunt puffs past my lips as my foot gets caught on a lifted tree root, sending me sprawling onto the dirt. My face scuffs against the ground, a jolt of pain slicing against my flesh.

I touch my fingers to my mouth, feeling my teeth to make sure they didn't crack.

"You probably wouldn't trip if you wore more practical shoes."

The scream that erupts from my chest at the male voice is otherworldly, making my ears crackle. I slip the flashlight from my hoodie, holding it up in defense even as I pinch my eyes closed.

"Jesus," the voice continues, familiar irritation lacing his tone. "I didn't even fucking touch you. Get ahold of yourself."

Chest heaving, I peel open an eyelid. As I glance around, I notice I'm almost back to the abandoned building past the quarry.

I push onto my knees, brushing debris from my skirt. My hood falls back as I tilt my chin to face my inquisitor.

Sutton Dupont stands over me, his green eyes almost ablaze. As usual outside of class, his brown hair is a mess, like he's been dragging his hands through it for hours—or someone else has.

Swallowing, I scan the full length of him, ignoring how at ease his presence makes me. The green sweater vest he wears is familiar and comforting, but that warmth disappears when I let my focus fall to his long fingers—clasping a gold Bauta mask.

Chapter 17

Sutton

PURE, UNADULTERATED HORROR SLIDES INTO PLACE ON ELLE'S delicate face. My ears are still ringing from the scream she let out after tripping over my foot, since she was running without looking where she was going.

I'm beginning to wonder if that's just how she lives her life: diving in headfirst to whatever suits her fancy.

By definition, I should want to stay away from her. Especially right now—if she's running from something out here, there's no telling what she witnessed.

Heat scalds the edges of my esophagus as she shuffles away from me, like running would do her any good if I wanted to take her.

I extend my arm, offering her my hand.

She smacks me with her phone, causing a sharp sting to ripple across my knuckles.

"What the hell is your problem?" I snap, drawing back. "You ran into me."

"Who just pops up out of nowhere in the forest?" she counters, glaring, though there's an edge of something else glittering in her irises. It almost looks like fear. "What are you even doing out here?"

"What are *you* doing here? This area is off-limits to students."

"I know you're, like, probably a thousand years old on the inside, but there's this cool new exercise called walking. I sometimes participate."

"Well, you're terrible at it. Consider picking up a new hobby. And maybe do it someplace you're allowed to be."

Her eyes narrow, and she glances at my hands. For a moment, I wonder if she's remembering our night together, but then she leans in and grabs my index finger, holding it up as if inspecting it for something.

A small spark zaps me where she touches, but I don't try to withdraw. It's her warmth that keeps me in place.

That's all. She just feels good against my cold fingers. It doesn't *mean* anything.

"Why is a college professor traipsing through the woods by himself with a mask?"

Now I do pull away. "I'm not sure you're entitled to that answer, Ms. Anderson."

"Since you tripped me, I think I am."

"I *didn't* trip you—"

"Explain yourself, Boy Scout." She gets to her feet and aims the phone at me again. "Or else."

The irritation and determination on her face make my chest tighten. I inch forward a step, letting the toe of my shoe graze the heel of her boot. Walking, my ass.

Why she feels the need to lie when I can see right through her, I don't know.

My heart thumps heavily as I reach out, gripping her chin and tilting her face. Her skin is soft and warm against mine, and the gesture causes her mouth to snap shut.

I can hear my pulse raging like a river between my ears.

Fuck, I shouldn't be touching her, but…

It isn't like this with anyone else.

Initiating or receiving, it doesn't matter—my body normally rejects it all, my brain recoiling in disgust. The feel of someone against me dredges up nausea and migraines and nightmares.

But she's different. Has been from the moment we met.

My fingers ache to graze her. To caress her. To be inside her.

Is this heightened craving a result of the night we already shared? Or the realization that I can't actually have her—which in turn makes her safe.

"You really think you can fend off a guy who's got eight inches of height and at least fifty pounds on you?"

Her eyes widen slightly, confusion swirling in those hazel irises.

I lean down, moving her head back more, so she has to bend to keep from breaking in half.

"If I wanted to have my way with you out here, who's going to stop me?"

Defiance shines in her gaze. "Ah, so you're one of *those* guys."

"You wouldn't know, would you?" I ask. "You just keep manufacturing these moments alone with me without knowing what sort of man I am. I could be biding my time, waiting for the opportunity to pounce."

"That would be my luck."

Something in the way she says that—like she's resigned herself to an unfortunate fate—dispels the illusion. I drop my hand to my side, watching as she blinks slowly, trying to process the shift.

Dark red liquid drips from a cut on her forehead, likely from where she face-planted. It's next to an older scab, and I wonder how a woman who seems so graceful in class can also be so clumsy.

The urge to wrap her in Styrofoam and hide her from where she can get hurt surges in my chest, but I shove it away.

"You're bleeding," I mutter, withdrawing.

She pockets her phone and lifts her fingers, touching her hairline, and pulls them away to look. A pale green flush slowly transforms her skin, drawing beads of perspiration to the surface.

"Oh." She blinks at the crimson on her fingertips, her gaze growing glassy.

In seconds, her knees buckle. I drop the mask and rush forward, catching her around the waist before she can collapse. She clutches my forearm as if to steady herself, and I guide us backward into a clearing near the half-burnt gazebo.

After having her sit on a wobbly wooden bench, I reach into my coat, retrieving the pocket-size first aid kit inside.

Elle's eyebrows arch, though she still looks woozy. "God, you really are a Boy Scout."

"A simple thank-you would suffice."

Crouching so we're eye level, I brush some of the hair from her face. My stomach tightens, and a fierce blush climbs over her cheeks.

She hisses when my thumb grazes the cut, and I wince. "Sorry. Didn't mean to do that."

"It's fine," she says, swallowing. "I just always forget how cold your hands are."

"Raynaud's," I offer, tearing open an antiseptic wipe to clean the shallow cut. "Narrow blood vessels and limited blood flow. It's a whole thing, but I really hardly notice it anymore myself. Just when it hurts, I guess."

"How often does it?"

"Varies, really. Sometimes my fingers and toes are just cold. Sometimes they're numb. The tingling can get pretty irritating, but mostly it just is what it is."

"Yeah, I get that." She nods, averting her gaze as I drop one of the soiled wipes.

"Not a fan of blood, are we?"

"Not particularly, no." She exhales shakily. "Ironic given my family's history with it."

"Their history?"

"Well, you know. My dad's a doctor."

"Ah." I open a Band-Aid and cover the cut with it.

Her breath catches as I smooth my icy thumbs over the edges, but when our eyes lock, it doesn't feel like the cold matters much anymore.

She takes her bottom lip between her teeth. My nostrils flare as I move away, pocketing the trash.

"Do you always carry Band-Aids with you?"

"You'd be surprised how often students get injured around campus."

"Is that why you're out here then? Cruising for someone to rescue?"

"No. I was on my way to a Visio Aternae meeting. They sometimes ask to hold them in the quarry, even when it's blisteringly cold outside."

"So what's the mask for?"

"Best way to keep the ghosts from recognizing you," I tell her. It's a partial joke, but she doesn't seem amused. "The mask isn't mine. I saw it on the ground and can't stand litter, so I picked it up."

"A likely story."

"You're awfully accusatory for someone who said she was *just walking* through here. What exactly do you think I was doing?"

What did you see?

The real reason I'm out here at sunset is due to a rumor floating around about a possible Death's Teeth sighting, though there was nothing scheduled. I came out to see if there was any merit to the claim, hoping that my demands to investigate Avernia's new student hadn't caused them to grow suspicious of me.

The Director is supposed to be ornamental. She doesn't pick and choose when to host gatherings. Not without Incarnate's approval or attendance.

The fact that she might be going around me doesn't exactly bode well, especially for the woman in front of me. I haven't reported any real news to them about the new attendee, so it's possible they're growing restless. If that happens and they set out to find answers on their own, I won't be able to save her.

Elle shakes her head, her shoulder slumping. "I don't know. I just… The Primordial Forest freaks me out is all. Don't you think it's creepy?"

I shrug. "I was raised in it. Things are far less terrifying when you know them from the inside out."

Our gazes connect, something passing quietly between us. The tendons in my neck pull taut, my fingers itching to touch her again.

"Tell me more about this group," she says after a moment, breaking the spell. "Visio Aternae. Why are they so special?"

"They're the only ones at Avernia trying to do *actual* communal good. The other student organizations focus on their own goals and projects, but Visio Aternae expands past that. It's about looking at the future and building a community for everyone."

"Is that why I can't join? You don't think I can be a team player?"

My eyes find hers. "I'm not sure your presence would bring about the sort of attention those students are used to."

"Rude. Are you implying I bring negative press?"

"Not intentionally, perhaps. But given how the school feels about your family, it's sort of the natural expectation. Are you unaware of the stuff Pythia says about you online?"

A small smirk tugs at the corner of her mouth. "Reading up about me?"

"I make it a point to learn what I can about all my students. Helps me be a better teacher."

She laughs, tilting her head back.

My throat constricts as the sound caresses my ears.

"No wonder you're such an honest guy. You're a terrible liar."

Offense pulls at my features. "I am not. And I told you—I'm not that honest."

Her eyebrows arch, wrinkling the Band-Aid on her forehead as she gives me a look.

"Fuck," I breathe, chuckling as I push to my feet. "Guess I walked into that one."

"You're very easy," she agrees, hopping up from the bench.

"If that were true, our relationship would look a bit different right now."

Overhead, the clouds congregate directly above us, shrouding our clearing in shadows. Elle's gaze darts around the area, as if checking for potential beasts that might crawl from the foliage to attack.

Or something far worse.

"So what are you *really* doing out here?" I ask. "Don't say exercising. You're not dressed for it."

She hesitates. I swallow as her eyes trek over every inch of me, my soul torn between arousal and unease.

Fuck, it could be a crime how badly I want her. My entire body vibrates under the weight of her speculation as if my sole point of existence is to be seen by her. Like my reason for being alive is just for the *possibility* of more.

Finally, she shrugs. "I was trying to get to know the school a little. It'd be nice if I really understood the hatred for the Anderson bloodline, don't you think?"

"Ah, so you've brushed up since our chat on the first day," I say. "Not everything has concrete, rational reasoning though. And I'm not sure you'd find many answers out here. Have you checked the Obeliskos archives?"

"Yes. They're boring. I'm not surprised you recommended them."

"Perhaps if you spent less time hanging on the arm of Lexington Abbott, you'd be able to unlock the town secrets."

I regret the words as soon as they leave my mouth, hoping that maybe she'll ignore them and continue the conversation in the direction it was going. When she smirks, I know I've fucked up.

"You sound jealous, Boy Scout."

"Do I? How odd." I lift my shoulder, walking away to reenter the path from earlier. "I suppose some people will hear what they want to hear."

She trails after me. "Some people are determined to play pretend."

"Not everyone has such glamorous choices. For some, 'playing pretend' is the only way to survive."

"Aren't you, like, town royalty?" She appears at my side, keeping pace. "They wouldn't actually fire you for fraternizing with a student."

"Avernia's policies are very strict."

"But Dean Bauer's a gutless tool."

I cock an eyebrow, glancing at her. "How well do you know Justin?"

"Not well enough to know his name is Justin." She meets my eyes. "But I can tell he's the kind of dean who accepts bribes and back-alley deals. I find it very hard to believe you'd be in as much trouble as you say."

Something twists malevolently in my chest, making it difficult to breathe. I stop in my tracks, turning to face her. "How would you know *that*?"

Elle slows to a halt, confusion threading through her brows. "I just mean he's easily persuaded—"

"Is that how you managed to get into my class? By *persuading* him?"

She blinks, as if trying to process what I'm asking. I don't know why I'm asking it, why it matters, but the idea of anything transpiring between her and the dean sends white-hot vitriol spiraling through my veins.

It's one thing to subject myself to the sight of Lexington flirting with her every class for a few weeks now—and even outside it—but *Dean Bauer* putting his hands on her isn't something I can live with.

My sister's tear-stricken face flashes in my mind for the briefest moment, but it's immediately replaced by Elle's thoughtful one as she stares up at me, waiting for some explanation.

"You've heard the rumors then," she says softly, looking at the ground. "That I was sleeping with people for parts in LA?"

Blood rushes between my ears, making my temples ache. "Are you denying them?"

"I think… I'm not going to dignify that with an answer. Believe what you want, Professor Dupont. What's it matter when you say we can't do anything about *this* anyway?"

She starts off again, walking away from me, and I move without thinking. My arm lashes out, grabbing her wrist. She pauses, as if waiting to see what else I'm going to do, but nothing happens.

It's like I'm frozen in place, unable to do anything other than keep her here for a moment.

Of course I don't believe the rumors, I want to say to her. It wouldn't make a difference if they were true.

I just don't know if my disbelief is rooted in a genuine ambivalence toward all rumors curated by Pythia, belief in Elle's honesty, or because I don't want to believe them.

I can't very well admit all that. Revealing every card to the one woman who tempts me is a dangerous game.

"Let go," she demands, but I don't. Fury colors her face, and I find it so fascinating how easily she allows emotion to shine through, like a crystal ball warning. "What is your problem? You think if you hold me hostage here long enough, I'll, what? Offer you a ride for the lead in your next production?"

Horror etches on to my face. "Of course not—"

The sound of hushed whispers and crunching leaves spurs a wave of panic through my bones. I whip my head to the side, peering past endless trunks of trees to see who's coming.

They're close, whoever they are, and there isn't time to run. Not when I can't tell which direction they're coming from.

Elle's resistance falters a little as she perks up, apparently also hearing the noises. "Um, what—"

"Shh," I tell her, yanking on her arm. I pull us in the direction of the gazebo, scrambling to get behind it before someone pops out. She trips, stumbling over a rock, and goes down hard; I swing my body toward her, trying to soften the impact as we roll into the burnt structure.

She lands with her face in my lap, her cheeks pinkening as she attempts to pull away. An enraged expression colors her features, and I ignore the dual sensations erupting within while I maneuver us out of sight.

"Stop fucking touching me," she snaps.

"Would you shut up for a second?" I shoot back, clenching my teeth at the thought of us getting discovered out here.

There's no innocent scenario anyone would believe in which the two of us could have been alone together. It would create more questions than we have answers for, and frankly, if it *is* Death's Teeth—which is highly likely—I don't want her seeing them.

Or vice versa.

I scoot behind a solid piece of the structure, bracing my back against the bottom half of the wooden wall, and manage to drag her into my lap as the voices and footsteps grow closer. Alarm registers in her gaze, and she tenses, her knees digging into my hips.

"What—"

The look in my eyes must answer whatever was on the end of that sentence, because she cuts herself off, swallowing hard.

Her fingers cling to my sweater, and she ducks her head, pressing her nose to my neck.

Each breath she releases breaks on the surface of my skin, warming me against the cold air. I let my hands fall to the ground, trying to maintain a modicum of clarity with her straddling me.

My legs are stretched out but hidden enough.

Unless someone comes from the left, past the abandoned house. They'd see me for sure.

Bending, I draw both knees against Elle's backside. She moves, as if trying to keep me from blocking her in, and my dick takes notice of the squirming.

I grip her hips, stilling the motions. My bones suddenly feel too large for my body.

The footsteps enter the clearing. Elle trembles violently as they speak in quiet, almost inaudible voices—but voices I recognize regardless.

Fuck.

"See? I told you no one's out here." It's the Director, her obscured tone undeniable. "Your paranoia's getting the best of you lately."

An answering grunt, followed by words I can't make out.

Something slams against one of the gazebo columns, and Elle jolts in my lap, clawing closer to me. She makes a startled noise, and I close my eyes, hoping they didn't hear.

My hand comes up, cupping the back of her head. I press firmly, fitting her mouth flush with my neck even though the very action is distracting.

Better I be distracted than they learn she's here. It's improbable, but on the off chance Death's Teeth *doesn't* know of Elle Anderson's presence, I'd like it to remain that way.

"All I know is we can't afford a fuckup like last time," the other voice chimes, closer now, as if they're standing *inches* away.

Elle stops breathing altogether. I dig my fingers into her hip, pressing harder on the back of her head. It's as much to shield her as it is to maintain my sanity.

"Relax," the Director says. "It's all happening according to plan, all right? Everything will be fine. I'll make sure of it."

"Good. Because you know if we don't—"

"I am aware of the consequences. Do not mistake me for some

bright-eyed fledgling who thinks sacrificing herself for Incarnate's sake will have any bearing on my survival. I am not that naive."

My muscles clench. *What the hell are they talking about?*

There hasn't been an official sacrifice—the third piece of the Death's Teeth puzzle alongside Incarnate and the Maiden—in years. Since they have no acting Incarnate, just me standing in limbo, there's been no reason for one.

But the way they're talking now makes me think something's changed, and I don't like the sound of it. Is that what the rumored ceremony was supposed to be for? To force a choice from me?

Perhaps I should've looked deeper. Should've gone into Tenarus.

Eventually, their conversation grows quieter, and their footsteps fall faint before dying off. Elle moves, trying to twist out of my grip, but I hold her still—just in case.

It's hard to tell whether they'll come back or not. I don't want to chance it.

And if I'm honest with myself, I don't particularly want to move from this spot either. The scent of honey and vanilla envelops me, and Elle's hair is soft against the underside of my jaw, her breathing harsh against my skin, leaving damp patches where it brushes.

If we get up now, if we move before I'm ready, she'll see the evidence of my lies. That I want her—want to touch her—more than I've ever wanted anything in my entire life.

That I'd sacrifice just about anything—my career, reputation, you name it—for her to kiss me. Even if it was the last time.

"Who was that?" she whispers.

"No one you need to concern yourself with."

"You dove for cover, but you're telling me not to worry?"

"I dragged you in here because we were going to be caught."

"But we weren't even doing anything."

"It doesn't matter," I reply. "How do you think it would have looked for us to be out here together all alone? Avernia students and staff *talk*, Elle."

She shifts again, tilting her hips in a way that makes me bite my tongue accident.

A heartbeat passes, and she does it a third time, bearing down in a more concentrated effort. Like she knows what she's doing— like she can feel me beneath her.

Fuck. She can, can't she?

I shouldn't like it so much. In every other similar situation, only disgust filters through my veins when another person chases intimacy, yet I don't ever want her to stop.

Her lips curve against my neck as her hips continue their undulation, slowly working over me. "You're a liar, Boy Scout."

"Elle." I offer her name like a half-hearted prayer. "We shouldn't keep pressing our luck."

"Okay, but what if we just pressed right…" She slides back, then forward, practically riding me through my pants. "…*here*?"

My jaw unhinges, falling open as arousal spins through me. Her teeth nick my jugular, making me shudder, and I realize how close to coming I already am.

"Elle. This is a very bad idea."

"Bad ideas make the best stories."

I can't think, can barely breathe as she continues, dragging her cunt firmly along the rigid length of my dick. Deep down, I know I need to stop this, especially considering we could both be in danger or get caught, but I don't.

I'm not sure which would be worse right now, and I don't fucking care.

Instead, I scratch at the dirty gazebo floorboards and let her have her way with me. Desire spins a vast and colorful tapestry through my veins, and she pulls back to look in my eyes. Her fingers touch my chin, sweeping over my lips; I part them, allowing her to slip her index finger inside for a moment.

"I don't know what's going on at this school," she says softly, bearing down so hard a whimper escapes me. "But *this* is undeniable. You and me. Tell me you don't feel it."

"All I feel at the moment is your pussy soaking my pants."

"Don't say that like you don't wish it was wrapped around your cock right now."

Every muscle in my body strains. "You have a filthy mouth, temptress."

She grins, leaning in to suck at my bottom lip before flicking her tongue against it. "And you have *no* idea."

When she threads her fingers through my hair and switches angles, my restraint snaps. Like a frayed rope hanging by its last thread, I come, adding my climax to the mess on my clothes. Stars dance in my vision, swirling around my face like some sort of angelic aura, and it takes several erratic breaths for me to return from the high.

As I do, regret and fear wedge themselves between the euphoria.

Elle seems to register my feelings before I voice them. She frowns, climbing off my lap, and rolls her eyes. "Don't say it. Please. I don't…I don't want to hear about how this was a mistake."

A pang tears through my chest. "It wasn't a mistake. Just… something that could get us in a lot of trouble."

"Avernia can cover up literal murder when they put their minds to it, but you're trying to convince me they'd actually fire you over something so trivial?"

"It's the policy—"

"It's *bullshit*, Sutton. It's you trying to put up a wall between us, although I'm not sure why. Maybe the people we just hid from have something to do with it, but either way, you're a fucking liar. Maybe a coward too."

Raw emotion makes her voice crack, and I clench my jaw because I can't deny her accusation.

My fingers ache with the desire to grab her, feel her, make her cry out my name. But I don't, reminding myself of Bellamy. Beckett. The curse.

Things I can't really share but are thinly veiled excuses anyway. Ways for me to distract myself from the things this woman makes me feel and the things I've been avoiding for years.

I am a coward.

It's just that no one ever really calls me out on it.

When I don't reply, Elle glares at her hands, then brushes them off and pushes to her feet. "Okay. I'll leave you alone."

"Wait, I'll walk you—"

"No thanks. There are people on campus who aren't too chicken to be with me, so I won't force you to do it." She rips the Band-Aid from her forehead, letting it fall on top of me. Dried blood stains the interior, and I ball it into my fist.

"People like Lexington?" I mutter.

"Maybe." She shrugs. "But if you keep making excuses and refuse to admit you want me… I guess that isn't really your business, is it?"

As she starts to leave the clearing, I stagger into a standing position, willing my dick to soften the rest of the way and ignoring the cool sensation of dried cum in my pants. "You need to stay out of these woods, Elle. If nothing else I say resonates with you, at least promise me you won't come back."

Her spine straightens, tensing beneath her hoodie as she crosses her arms. She says nothing, no acknowledgment of my words whatsoever, before she takes off toward campus, leaving me there wondering how long my resolve will actually hold out.

And where the fuck my mask went.

Chapter 18

Elle

WHEN I FINALLY MAKE IT BACK TO CAMPUS, I'M GRUMBLING TO myself about how much I despise Sutton Dupont. I even make a mental note to consider withdrawing from his ridiculous class entirely, although that would throw a wrench in my academic plans.

It's not even him I'm really mad at but myself for being so needy. Of course he wouldn't want to get caught with a student. The consequences for him far outweigh anything that would happen to me if people saw us together, and I shouldn't be pushing the boundaries like I have been.

That doesn't make the rejection sting any less, but it does make me the clear asshole here.

Even if he *is* lying and making excuses. His half-hearted rejections when he leans in for more of me and his refusal to deny it make that much obvious.

I recognize the signs of distraction and self-denial. I'm guilty of them myself, even now as I consider Sutton's reasoning for hiding. He said he'd done it to keep us from being discovered, but I can't erase the memory of the cloaked figures or rid myself of the images they embedded in my skull eight years prior.

But if we'd been in danger, a founding family member like Sutton would know about it. He certainly wouldn't have kept me out there if that were the case.

Right?

As I pass beneath the broken gate, I nearly smack right into the dean and a tall, gangly man he's chatting with.

My heart feels like it stops beating inside my chest.

A tall, gangly man I've *definitely* met before.

More than that even.

At his side, a third guy—the spitting image of the ganglier fellow, with the same jet-black locks and glacial blue eyes—gives me a dirty look when I'm steadied by the dean.

"Ms. Anderson, how lovely it is to run into you. We've not had a chance to chat since you started classes," Dean Bauer says, his beady little rat eyes raking over me.

His smile is tight, and I wonder for a moment if he knows what we did to his house.

But he doesn't say anything—just like Asher and Quincy predicted. Nobody online mentioned it either, so I assume this is just another thing they'll pretend never happened.

"How are you finding Avernia?" he continues. "Excellent, I hope. We've really poured our hearts and souls into the quality of education at our institution."

"It's fine," I reply, twisting away from his grip. I avoid meeting the older man's gaze. "If you'll excuse me, I'd better get to my dorm before—"

"Anderson, hmm?" the older one drawls, and as he turns his

focus toward me more fully, I notice his cheeks are gaunt, adding to the sallow look of his facial muscles. Like the life's been slowly bled out of him for years. Decades even. He looks like a vampire, and though I don't necessarily believe in the paranormal, I *do* believe in scary white men who want to devour young girls.

And I know better than to get close to this one again.

"Ah, yes, this is Noelle." Dean Bauer claps his hand onto my shoulder, pulling me forward a little. "Our newest addition to the Avernia College roster."

The older man glances between us. "So the Anderson boy dropped out?"

"Oh, well…um. No." Dean Bauer's face falls. "Asher is still enrolled."

"I see." The older man sniffles, reaching into his pocket for a handkerchief, which he then proceeds to cough a lung into.

That cough echoes between my ears like an incessant drum. My fingers grow numb, my limbs taut as I wait to see if he mentions it.

Mentions *me*.

A sickly man sits behind a glass desk with a metal name plate that reads Jean-Louis. *The entire office is glass, revealing West Washington Boulevard and a smattering of other businesses up and down the street. If you look hard enough, you can see the domed roof of the Grandeur Playhouse, where my acting troupe has been putting on a highly anticipated production of* The Glass Menagerie.

I bombed my audition for Laura, but nobody knows except me and the director.

And now this stranger.

His eyes are like twin lakes frozen over, and as he slides a tablet across the desk, I see myself on the screen.

200 SAV R. MILLER

Naked. Vulnerable. Writhing beneath assistant director Aaron Buckley and his girlfriend, Thalia, who both promised secrecy if I could get them off at the same time.

They swore it was a stepping stone, and stupidly, I thought...

I believed them.

Fuck. I've been at this for so long with so little to show, and I just gave up.

Sold out. Wanted to prove to my family what I'm capable of and to myself that I'm not just a screwup of epic proportions.

I wanted to be more than the terrified girl who aided in the demise of some faceless stranger years ago, whose memory has been haunting me ever since.

Wanted too much.

"I'm sure you're aware this type of behavior raises questions about your ethics and talent, Elle."

I hate how he says my name. Like he's earned the right to.

Still, I bite my tongue, hoping for a warning. Or a second chance.

Instead, Jean-Louis—the owner of the Grandeur Playhouse, some hotshot from the East Coast with a long family history in the industry— sits back in his chair and waits for an apology.

If I was a man, he'd have congratulated me on working a loophole in the system. In doing whatever I needed to to make my dreams a reality.

But since I'm a woman, he undoes his belt buckle and cocks an eyebrow.

"This will ruin your career if it gets out," he says, scrubbing a bony hand over his chin. "You're a nobody, and I can make it stay that way. Or..."

He trails off, his jaw shifting as his impatience seems to mount.

I get up from my chair and walk out.

Less than twenty-four hours later, my spot in the production was given to the understudy and my face smeared on every third-rate gossip rag in the county. Nothing big enough really to leave LA since I *was* a nobody, but still.

The damage was done. I spent weeks talking to my agent—who wound up dropping me—and trying to get even basic stage work, but no one wanted me. Not even for *free*.

So I left.

And now it seems my past is catching up.

The man clears his throat, turning back to me, and extends his free hand. It's long and skeletal, and I blink at it without taking the offering.

"This is Jean-Louis *Dupont*," Bauer tells me in a low voice. "Chairman of the Avernia trustee board, founding family member, and esteemed town councilman. When he asks for a handshake, you do it, little girl."

The ice in my veins runs cold.

Dupont?

My gaze shifts to the younger man slightly behind him, who's been staring at me with a blank expression since I stumbled through the gate. They're almost clones, save for the shape of his nose, lips, and ears beneath the mop of black hair.

All features that resemble the handsome professor I've been lusting after for weeks.

No, no, no. This isn't possible.

The universe isn't this cruel, right?

Jean-Louis cannot be Sutton's *father*.

Exhaling a shaky breath, I lift my hands for them to see, forcing myself to remain calm on the outside even though my world feels like it's shattering. My palms are scraped from when I ran into

Sutton. "Sorry, but I had a nasty fall in the forest. I'd like to avoid making the cuts worse."

"That explains the dried blood," Jean-Louis states, leaning in as if to inspect my face. "Thought maybe you'd been attacked by some vigilante mob. They're rumored to hang out there, you know."

"Is that something you'd expect a little girl like me to walk away from?" I stare right back. "I hear those mobs can get violent pretty quickly."

His blue eyes narrow. Behind him, the younger guy slinks away a step, as if trying to disappear into the background.

What if Jean-Louis tells Sutton about me?

The only thing worse than those LA rumors being true is me lying about them, even if they're blown out of proportion. I didn't sleep with *everyone*: Aaron and his girlfriend were a one-time thing, and I paid the price for it.

But most people won't care about reality. They'll pick which part of the truth they want to be disgusted by and go from there.

A man wouldn't have to care. His value would increase to the general public, probably. God forbid a woman takes a page out of his playbook.

"Yes, well, it is true that a group of maybe-vigilantes have been causing issues for some time on campus," Dean Bauer chimes in. "That's why Jean-Louis likes to come check on things, make sure they haven't overrun us. He hasn't been able to get out here for a while, you see, due to illness and travel, but—"

"Justin," Jean-Louis says sharply. "We needn't fill the girl in on such trivial matters."

I shrug. "Maybe I like trivia."

"You seem like the type to be entertained by nonsense." He

pockets both hands, giving me a long look that makes me feel sticky all over. "How are you enjoying my campus, Ms. Noelle?"

"It's just Elle, actually."

"If you don't mind, I'd prefer to use your legal name. At least until we've established a relationship."

So this is the game we're playing. "I don't see that happening."

Jean-Louis's eyebrows hike up. "Pardon?"

Dean Bauer and the younger guy stare at me, and a beat of unease bears down on the four of us.

"What sort of relationship were you hoping for?" I ask, cocking my head to the side. "Most professional ones don't require the use of a first name at all."

Hatred bleeds through Jean-Louis's pores. "You're quite chatty. When I was a student, we didn't speak so freely with our elders."

"Well, I didn't grow up in Fury Hill," I reply. "Must be a difference in parentage."

"Must be." He sneers at me, then turns to the younger man, grabbing the guy's bony shoulder. "Not everyone can have such strong, important genes, I suppose. Right, son?"

"Beckett," the dean interrupts, running the backs of his fingers over his forehead, "maybe we should escort your father to the Apollodorus for his meeting?"

Beckett. Where have I heard that name before?

The younger guy nods, casting a sideways look at me, before turning elsewhere. "Sure. Father?"

Jean-Louis hesitates, clearly still interested in me as he glances at the forest before settling on me once more. "Were you traveling alone, Ms. Noelle?"

"Yes, I was."

He hums, nodding curtly, though I can't tell if he believes me.

"I'd advise against doing so in the future. You never know what sort of nefarious creatures are lying in wait near the lake. There've been instances where students came back mutilated…or not at all."

I slide my gaze to Beckett, who shifts on his feet. Guilt riddles his face, but I'm not exactly sure why.

"The Primordial Forest *is* off-limits," Dean Bauer interjects, pulling at his tie. "I can only hope Ms. Anderson takes heed of the numerous warnings before venturing back out."

"I'm sure you'll discipline her properly," Jean-Louis replies, turning away and pushing his son ahead of him.

Dean Bauer exhales loudly as they begin walking in the direction of the Lyceum. He looks at me like I'm a bug on the bottom of his shoe. "Antagonizing Jean-Louis is not a smart idea."

"Why, because I'm an Anderson? Doesn't seem like you cared too much about that curse when you let me enroll, now does it?"

"Perhaps a bit of an oversight on my part, but it isn't as if…" He trails off, glancing in the direction the other two disappeared in. "Doesn't matter. You're here, and I'm not in the business of expulsion except in extreme cases. And even then…well. You met Beckett."

"What does he have to do with anything?" I ask, voice tight.

The dean gives me a strange look. "Well, he nearly killed your brother on school property, but things happened and now he's back."

I blink, my throat closing in on itself as the realization of why his name sounded so familiar slams into me.

My parents hadn't told me who'd been in the cave last semester or who had abducted the students. Just that it'd been a group of Curators, and most of them hadn't left alive. One had been beaten so badly by Asher that they were surprised he made it at all.

That one—*Beckett Dupont*.

I must have been so distracted when I met Sutton that I never put their relation together, and I certainly didn't think he'd be allowed back on campus. Not so soon, at least.

Which just furthers my assertion of the Duponts being Fury Hill royalty. They really can get away with murder.

Chapter 19

Sutton

FROM: noelle.anderson@avernia.edu
TO: sutton.dupont@theater.avernia.edu
SUBJECT: Class location

To whom it may concern,

I've seen other professors take classes outside, to the Primordial Forest's edge or that decrepit-looking amphitheater past the Lyceum. Why don't we ever go anywhere except our stuffy auditorium?

A curious mind,
Elle Anderson

MY THUMB TWITCHES AS I SIT IN THE EMPTY AUDITORIUM she's referencing, most of the Visio Aternae students having filtered out already after our discussion of the semester's big fundraiser concluded.

I quickly swipe out of the email thread without replying, aware that she's only sending a message because I canceled our first class of the week, and she likely thinks it had something to do with her.

In truth, it was a migraine from hell, causing me to consider just bashing my own skull in to rid myself of the nauseating pain. But then I thought of Beckett finding my corpse and the trauma that would cause and decided to hole up in my darkened bedroom until the medicine kicked in.

Still, it's not like I owe my students an explanation. I rarely ask them to elaborate when they miss my classes, so long as they inform me as soon as possible.

I tap my index finger against my knee, wondering what Elle did instead. Did she sleep in or get breakfast with her roommate? Perhaps she met up with Lexington and the other friends she's made, going over the weekend's homework assignment or speculating about the upcoming auditions for the class's final play.

We're over a month into the semester now, which means we've fallen into the groove of things, and Death's Teeth has been eerily quiet, relegating themselves to their Apollodorus and cave parties only. The hyperfocus on sex is alarming, considering the volume of violence that occurred on campus last semester, and the increased number of gatherings sets me on edge as well.

It's as if they're growing desperate, trying to get my attention by acting out. Like they mean to force my hand, the way Jean-Louis said they would.

And no one's asked about the new student.

Exhaling, I work my jaw as thoughts of Elle creep back in,

pushing the potential danger aside. The idea of her hanging around Lexington fills me with an uncontainable malice, and I briefly wonder if there's a way I could permanently break them apart. Maybe I should tell his mother I'm concerned about his grades and have her set him straight.

But that would be interfering, and Elle would see right through it. Not to mention it would likely tip off Lexington, who's one of the top students in the theater program. It wouldn't be fair of me to take my frustrations out on him.

It's not exactly fair of me to take them out on Elle either, yet I can't seem to help it. Every time she comes on to me, I'm struck by a million different fears: of losing my job, of involving her in the dangerous underbelly of this school, and of the way her mere stare provokes something deep within me.

I don't know what it is, but my skin almost seems to buzz to life each time it grazes hers, and the desire is entirely unnerving.

I'm not used to wanting. Especially things I cannot have.

And even if what she said that day in the forest was true, even if I could have her, what in the world would I do with her?

A woman like that deserves more than the emotionally distant shell of a man. She deserves to be spoiled, loved, and taken care of.

Though the idea of someone else—

"Um, Professor Dupont?"

Shaking myself from the shameful thoughts, I glance up as Sabrina clears her throat in the row ahead of me. She clutches a clipboard to her chest, then tucks a strand of blond hair behind a pale-pink ear.

"Yes, Sabrina?" I answer, hurriedly locking my phone in case another email comes through. She's the kind of person to report that to the dean instantly, no matter how much she might wish for my approval.

"Were you waiting on someone? I can leave you alone if so."

Running my knuckles over my lips, I stare at the stage; a few students linger, mingling among themselves, one of them the ghostly looking kid from our class. Percy, I think.

He slides his gaze over to Sabrina periodically, glancing at her every couple of minutes, as if he thinks she might disappear should he look away.

I know the feeling.

Resting my hands in my lap, I shake my head. "I was just lost in thought."

"Oh. Well, I wanted to see if you had any idea what play we were putting on for 330's final yet? I know the auditions are our midterms, basically, so maybe you haven't really considered it, but…"

"Are you hoping I'll tell you so you can get a leg up on the competition?"

She purses her lips. "Is there anything wrong with wanting an advantage? The way your brother used to tell it, you had no problem fighting your way to the front for a lead when you were a student."

"I'm not sure you should be getting lore on me from Beckett," I tell her. "I may have been tenacious, but I wasn't unfair. I never cheated."

"Technically, this isn't cheating. You never *said* we couldn't ask about the play."

"Exigo a me non ut optimus par sim sed ut malis melior."

Sabrina frowns, blushing. "I'm afraid I haven't brushed up enough on my Latin to know what that means."

"We must not equate ourselves with the best but do better than the bad." I push to my feet, grabbing my briefcase. "Loosely translated, of course. It may be a foreign concept, Ms. Taylor, but I'm sure you can figure it out."

"Just be better than the bad? That's, like, the bare minimum expectation."

"Then it should be easy for you."

The sentiment is true, though certainly not one I live by as often as I'd like. In the classroom, I aim for whatever means necessary to help my students learn—which sometimes involves recognizing limitations and adapting accordingly.

Or pointing out when someone is trying to take advantage of a loophole.

One cannot make it in theater if they're incapable of change. The outside world even requires constant evolution to survive.

It's not always nice and pleasant, but neither of those descriptors is in my job position.

Flattery and cheating do us no favors.

A thought I remind myself of later that evening when I go to leave the apartment, strolling through campus as music from a quarry party drifts up over the forest, invading the quiet nighttime.

At the bottom of the stairs, Jean-Louis leans against one of the Roman columns holding up the balcony on the second floor, a long coat buttoned up all the way to his chin. Brown leather gloves cover skeletal hands, and the slight curve in his neck makes him appear inches shorter than his actual height.

He's the older, sicklier version of Beckett. I often wonder if the similarities are why my brother craves his approval so desperately.

My stomach twists, begging me not to approach. I know why he's here.

A Death's Teeth alumnus never misses the spring instauratio—a prestigious, highly secretive festival inspired by the Haloa of ancient Greece, where the start of a new semester brings rebirth and opportunities for depravity.

Basically, murder and sex. Their bread and butter. Sacrifices for death and the motions of life. Given the inactivity of the organization thus far, I'm not surprised Jean-Louis is making his attendance specifically known to me.

He probably believes he can sway me with his foul presence.

"Headed somewhere?" Jean-Louis asks as I turn, starting in the opposite direction, any hope of him not seeing me dashed.

"Anywhere away from you is a start."

"Still punishing me for things I had no control over, I see."

Pausing, I catalog the way his hollow cheeks practically hang off the bone, and the yellow glow of the streetlights makes his skin seem sallow and sunken.

That he finds himself innocent of Bellamy's death nauseates me. If I were a violent man, I'd take my guilt out on him. End my and Beckett's suffering once and for all.

You don't have to be the one holding the gun to pull its trigger.

"Mother says you're sick," I reply, slipping my free hand into my coat pocket. The other grips my briefcase tight. "How interesting you felt well enough to make an appearance tonight."

"Well, someone has to attend the meetings you and your mother refuse to. This place would fall apart without me." He brushes some lint off the collar of his coat. "I have good days and bad days. Today was the former."

"Very convenient of your illness to let up on the eve of an instauratio."

He lifts his head, running a hand over his thick black hair. The blues of his eyes are too dark to see from where I stand, but I feel his disdain regardless.

Always have. It wasn't something that needed to be spoken. When it came to Bellamy and I, he never shied away from the loathing.

When you're introduced to that young, you develop one of two ways: indifference or the need to prove the person wrong.

Bellamy's ambivalence was a shield. She only cared about what made her feel good. I thought I needed to make up for that.

"I suppose I am favored by my ancestors," he replies, his voice thin and devoid of emotion. "Am I wrong to assume you're headed for the celebration?"

Snorting, I glance at the forest. The glow of the Curator party reflects in the night sky, obscuring some of the stars. They have no idea what lurks out there this evening.

The darkness that will ripple through Avernia tonight and remain through the spring.

"If I don't attend, they'll assume I've forfeited my title," I say.

He nods. "They want you as Incarnate, but it's been *years*, Sutton. You've been in limbo this entire time. Your sister is probably rolling in her grave over how fickle you've grown."

My hands curl into fists as a sharp pain pierces my skull. He doesn't deserve to speak of her.

"How long do you think it will take them to shift to someone else? We need a leader. We need Incarnate to maintain the balance of power and order on campus and in Fury Hill. They *will* move on from you and find another. I've seen them do it before."

Beckett. Though they're leery of him because of his past unpredictability, they'd take him if only to keep leadership in the Dupont name.

Incarnate is their designated leader. The chosen one whom they believe is sent by Death itself to rule over their organization. Incarnate chooses the targets, the ceremonies, the messages scrawled on bathroom doors, and the narrative of the gossip whispered throughout campus.

I have no idea how they make that decision, but I know they've been waiting for me to officially accept so they could fill the Maiden position as well, since they don't want Incarnate to rule alone.

The Maiden is Incarnate's partner in darkness. It can technically be any gender but traditionally is a founding family daughter.

If they choose the sacrifice tonight, the three rings of their sacred cycle—Incarnate, Maiden, and Sacrifice, satisfying their rule of three—would be ready if they went with Beckett.

And I would have ruined my brother alongside my sister.

"Leave Beckett out of this," I snap. "They don't touch him."

Jean-Louis's mouth twitches. "I never suggested they should. But we both know it's a likely alternative."

My limbs grow heavy. Unmanageable.

I'm thrust back in time, bound and helpless while my body is used for the gratification of my captors. Nausea rolls through my stomach as the memories, mere flashes of that night between labored breathing and moans of pleasure, assault me from all angles.

But none worse than what came after. The way my vision blanked and my lungs felt like they were being incinerated from the inside out.

The feeling of drowning. Panic, fear, and desperation colluding in my chest and then utter silence. Waking in a clearing and realizing Bellamy was gone.

The immediate devastation that I hadn't protected her and would never get to apologize for it.

That guilt lingers to this day.

Jean-Louis juts his chin toward the moon, round and lumi-nescent as it hangs in the cloudy sky. "Better hurry now. This isn't a ceremony you want to miss."

Chapter 20

Elle

A WEEK AFTER MY ENCOUNTER WITH SUTTON IN THE FOREST, I drag Aurora, Lexington, and Lucy to the Apollodorus in the hopes of uncovering more about the Anderson curse and Fury Hill's lore.

"Ugh, I don't like this," Aurora mutters.

I shoot her a dirty look as Lexington shimmies open the door to the basement stairwell. We'd gone to the Obeliskos first, under the impression that all the archives and important town information were kept there. According to one of the student aides, though, an older part of the collection had been moved after some sort of vandalism incident. I'm not sure whose call it was, but when I asked Lexington if he could get us access, he'd been very excited about the prospect.

Comparatively, the libraries *look* similar with their dark wooden and carpeted floors that creak beneath every step, the ebony and oak furniture that looks as if it's been here since the school's founding, and high ceilings with various colorful murals painted on them.

Walls of bookcases, locked doors, and empty study rooms

decorate the main levels, and while the Apollodorus is smaller in size, it feels somehow even more haunted.

"No one is forcing you to be here," I tell Aurora as she grips Lucy's biceps, half hiding behind her smaller frame.

"You promised doughnuts," she whines. Her French manicure digs into the sleeves of Lucy's black long-sleeved shirt.

"Doughnuts? She told me there was a sign-up for a reproductive rights walkathon," Lucy says, narrowing her blue eyes.

"So I didn't want to go down here alone," I snap, crossing my arms. "Sue me."

"You guys are gonna scare the ghosts," Lexington says, holding the door open for us.

"Not funny," I mutter.

"Wasn't a joke." Though his smirk contradicts his words. He nudges me forward with an elbow, and I glare at him.

Swallowing over a knot in my throat, I lean past the doorway, peering down at the spiraling descent into the underground. The stairwell itself is dark, with seemingly only one dim wall sconce per level, and endless.

"Can we go already? I don't think we should prolong this." Aurora huddles close to me, breathing on my shoulder. Her hands find the back of my sweater, tugging, the thick scarf around her neck bumping against me.

"What are you looking for exactly?" Lexington asks as we head down, taking each step slowly as if they might give out at any moment. "Town lore? The archives are pretty boring, so you'll probably want to go for founders' journals or even the old *Delphic Pages* paper."

"Paper?" I ask. "That gossip site was a print tabloid first?"

"Oh yeah. It only went online maybe a decade or so ago? I have no idea who made the shift—some undergrad, most likely—but when my mom was a student here, Pythia's musings were printed and posted front and center in the dorms and on all the Lyceum's bulletin boards."

I hum, gripping the wobbly railing to steady myself. The picture I saw of the cave in one encyclopedia flashes through my memory, and I wonder if a Pythia of the past captured it.

Maybe that's why the photographer's name had been redacted.

We pass one floor, and I can practically hear Aurora's teeth chattering every time the plumbing in the walls lets out a groan. Goose bumps pepper my skin even though I'm no stranger to old buildings, since the Asphodel where I grew up was a remodeled hotel.

Not to mention my dad's shady past pretty much guarantees some level of bloodshed happened there, though neither of my parents talk about that part of their lives at all. Still, not talking about things doesn't mean they didn't happen, and the internet does have articles from early in their marriage.

Plus, what they won't say, sometimes my aunts and uncles will.

"Do all founding family members attend Avernia?" I probe.

"Historically? Yes." Lexington purses his lips. "Though I guess your dad would be the exception there. While not well received, your ancestors before him were still permitted to attend school—so long as it wasn't more than one at a time."

"Because of that stupid curse, right? What exactly do they think me and my siblings are going to do to them? Surely we know vampires aren't real."

"That's what they want you to think," Aurora mutters.

Lexington tosses her a smirk. "It's hard to say what people think the curse in manifest will look like. Cronus was rumored to have drained townspeople of their blood, so maybe they do think you're all vampires. He also married the Dupont widow after the other founding patriarchs died, so some believe there were extramarital activities happening there. Dude was knocking off the seven deadly sins like they were on his bucket list."

The Dupont widow? My heart thumps faster at that revelation, but I force myself to remain calm.

"Sounds a little satanic panic-y to me," I say.

"Also possible. The founders passed on their superstitions, and the belief in the curse predates a lot of the buildings within city limits. You can't really blame them for it."

"Well you can blame them a little," I note.

"That's fair, especially since these are beliefs held by the town alone. Outside Fury Hill, no one cares."

"Which is probably why no one in my family ever heard of a curse until Quincy enrolled."

He points at me, nodding. "Exactly."

Lucy scoffs. "Either way, Fury Hill groupthink almost got me killed."

"Yet here you remain," he says as we round the next floor, veering into a hall off the side that seems to get narrower the farther we go. "Honestly, you all lucked out somehow avoiding detection by Death's Teeth. They're the real threat to the Andersons."

That name sends a chill skittering down my neck. "How come?"

We walk to the end of the hall, passing multiple blank, inconsequential doors and one marked ARCHIVES. The last is a solid wooden barrier with slash marks slicing across the paint, making my chest tighten.

"Everyone thinks of Death's Teeth as this sexy vigilante group," Lexington says, slipping a lock-picking kit from the inside of his corduroy jacket. He bends slightly, fitting the tools into the door-knob. "But that would imply they're doing some sort of public service, avenging crimes or whatever."

"They're not?"

"No one's ever seen real evidence of it. That's kind of the point though—the obscurity. If you don't know enough to ask questions, they can get away with anything."

"Do you think what the Curators said about the murders last semester were true?" Lucy asks softly. "That Death's Teeth framed them?"

Lexington shrugs. "Maybe. I have heard they deal in orgies and human sacrifice among a host of other things Pythia likes to claim."

"Human *sacrifice*?" I stare at his fingers as they work. "Is there a religious component to this school that I'm unaware of?"

"I'm sure it's got its roots in something," he replies, finally pushing the door open to reveal a massive, unpainted room filled with dozens of bookcases, most of them only half-filled. "Growing up, my parents were always saying that death was the ultimate god to some people in this town, so maybe the sacrifices are their way of appeasing him."

"Or her," Lucy adds. "Death could easily be a woman. Or nongendered at all. I don't think we should confine its identity to Western gender norms."

"Fair enough," Lexington says, straightening to his full height once again. "Point is no one really knows anything about Death's Teeth, and they like it that way. But given all the weird shit that's been happening, and Avernia's long list of inexplicable student disappearances and deaths…" He looks at me, shrugging. "I'd say staying off their radar is your safest bet at survival."

"And I'd say yours would be not entering restricted areas on campus," a baritone voice asserts, shattering the air around us.

The four of us let out a noise of surprise, whirling around to face the intruder. Aurora clutches Lucy's bicep, and Lexington slides a little closer to me, hooking his foot around mine as if he plans on protecting me.

I glance at our shoes—mine a Mary Jane, his some kind of sneaker—and then at the voice's owner.

Sutton stands at the bottom step, arms crossed over his chest and a stern frown resting on his annoyingly handsome face. His jaw clenches as he looks at our group, slowing to a near stop when he notices how close Lexington is to me.

Good. Be jealous.

Especially since flanking his sides are Percy, Sabrina, and my sister.

The latter places her ringed fingers on her hips, narrowing her eyes slightly at me.

"Told you they were trying to break into locked archives," Sabrina says, twirling her blond ponytail with one hand.

Percy shifts the cardboard box he's carrying, averting his gaze.

"Jesus Christ, Sabrina, you're such a goddamn tattletale," Lexington mutters.

"Don't be mad at me because you broke the rules, Abbott," she says.

"Can I be mad that you're such a Goody Two-Shoes?" he quips back.

"We're not doing anything wrong," I say, meeting Sutton's eyes finally as I ball my hands into fists. "Research is a school-sanctioned activity."

"With proper permission," Sutton replies curtly. "Which you'd need from the library board and the dean. I'm going to assume by the lock-picking kit Mr. Abbott is holding that you obtained neither."

"You know what they say about assuming," I tell him.

Exhaling, Sutton reaches up and pinches the bridge of his nose. "Would you all just go back up to the main floor? You're not allowed to be down here without a faculty escort."

"And Asher's looking for you, Luce," Quincy adds.

I smirk. "How sweet. You have your own little lapdog."

She frowns, poking my side. "Hey, don't take your irritation out on my love life."

My shoulders slump. "Sorry, Lulu."

Lucy grins, wrapping her arms around my neck. "It's okay," she whispers in my ear. "I have a tendency to lash out when I'm around the man who pushes my buttons too."

Gripping her arms, I pull away, giving her an incredulous look. "That's not what's happening here."

Her eyebrows quirk, and she withdraws with a shrug. "If you say so."

"Ash-tree's always been like this anyway," Aurora notes, stepping toward my sister. "If Foxe is a golden retriever, Asher's a Doberman, and he's only gotten worse since everything last semester."

My stomach churns at the reminder.

Lucy grabs Aurora's wrist and pulls her toward the stairs. "Swing by the apartment this weekend. I'll tell you everything I know about…" She trails off, pausing as she glances between Sutton and Quincy. "The subject at hand."

Seconds later, the sound of their feet pounding against the steps as they head up echoes through the corridor.

I cross my arms, defiant.

Sabrina's eyes narrow into slits. "Hello? The exit order goes for the wannabe actress and her puppet too."

"Real nice, Sabrina," Lexington says under his breath.

"What? Is it untrue? Did she not come crawling back to the East Coast because she couldn't hack it—"

"*Hey*—" Quincy starts.

"Enough," Sutton says at the same time. My throat burns as they exchange a look, and he drags a hand through his hair, mussing it as he shakes his head. "Name-calling is unnecessary and more than a little childish, Ms. Taylor. I expect better from the Visio Aternae treasurer."

Heat blossoms on Sabrina's cheeks, but her face just grows angrier. She turns to Percy, pointing toward the stairs. "Whatever. Let's go set up for the philanthropy mixer."

He hesitates, tossing Lexington an apologetic look. As she stomps away, genuine pain colors his features, making his pale skin glow with a greenish sheen. Like he's powerless against denying her.

Lexington rolls his eyes. "Just go, man. I get it."

Percy blows him a dramatic, wet-sounding kiss, then takes off after Sabrina, tripping and nearly falling over a couple of steps before disappearing. A door slams shut, and the sound carries all the way down here, making everything feel emptier than before.

I pretend not to notice how dejected Lexington looks.

Sutton lets out a long breath as he turns toward my sister. "What do you think?"

She lifts a shoulder, adjusting her glasses. "Knowledge is power."

I clench my fists tighter, feeling the indentation of each individual nail as it cuts into my palm.

They look at us, and Quincy pushes past, flipping on another set of lights in the storage room. "You have ten minutes."

My face breaks out into a small smile, and I squeal, moving to sprint inside. Quincy grabs my arm, halting me.

"This counts as causing trouble, you know."

"But you're letting me in."

Her expression flattens. "Noelle, come on. Don't be obtuse. Breaking and entering into the school's archives is garnering unnecessary attention. Do you want more of a target painted on your back?"

"I'm still not entirely sure what the initial one entails," I admit.

Sighing, she slides her hand down, wrapping her fingers around mine as she drags me into the room. I grunt, disliking the force even if the physical contact makes my insides warm.

How long has it been since she led me around like this, inviting me into a world she knows better than I do? Decades, I'd bet. Certainly not since she left home for Avernia and all but stopped speaking to me.

And when she did speak, her comments were biting. As if she were hiding things behind ire.

When we were kids, I begged her to let me in. To take me where she went. Now I can't help wondering if that drove her away.

She deposits me in front of a long bookcase, its shelves filled with notebooks, some tattered and some newer. "This row starts with journals from last year and goes backward chronologically. The other side is past the 1900s. You want to learn more about your place at Avernia, take it from the primary sources."

I slip the last book from its slot, reading the cursive scribbled on the front. "This is last fall."

"The journals are a Fury Hill tradition aimed at preserving history in real time," she says.

"How do we know it's a primary source?"

Flipping to the inside front flap, she points at the name

inscribed there and the familiar handwriting. "You can trust me," she says, though it's hard to tell if it's only because that's her name written here or if she means in general.

A part of me wishes that were true—that I could confide in her the way I did when we were young, even if I was bad at keeping her secrets myself. She didn't hold it against me back then, preferring to maintain silence instead of retaliating, but Quincy's not the same girl she used to be.

And neither am I.

So instead I nod, pretending I don't hear a double meaning at all as I tuck the journal beneath my arm. I feel her stare at me for a few more beats, and then she lets out a sigh, turning on her heel and heading for the open door.

I watch as she pauses, just long enough to say something to Sutton, who stands guard at the exit as if someone could come down at any moment.

Though I haven't spent much time in the Apollodorus, I'd be willing to bet this area doesn't get much foot traffic.

My throat burns at their interaction, and I force my attention elsewhere. It doesn't matter who he talks to or is interested in, because he's made it clear *I* can't have him.

That doesn't mean I have to like it if it's my fucking sister.

Lexington appears at my side, the sleeves of his skintight athletic shirt pushed up, revealing thick muscles in his forearms. He reaches for the journal I'm holding, turning it in his hands.

"What exactly are you looking for?" he asks.

"I'm not sure."

And I'm not, really. If Death's Teeth is as elusive an organization as everyone says, I doubt even the most detailed journals will have much data on them.

Still, I'd like to try and understand why the school—and town—seems to hate us so much. What kind of brainwashing you need to convince an entire population that a singular bloodline is to blame for everything terrible that's ever happened and any terrible thing to come.

I suppose scapegoats are as much a part of the country's history as anything else though. Really, the practice is as old as the air itself: Where there is power to be kept, there are people to be exploited.

My question is how do the student organizations come into play here, and what is with the cloaked figures I keep stumbling upon in the forest? Are they conducting rituals like Lexington suggested that I simply happen upon, or are they orchestrated to make me feel like I'm losing my mind?

To keep me quiet.

And what was that about Cronus marrying the Dupont widow?

A woman's voice returns, softly vibrating through the room; Lexington and I glance at the door, spotting Sabrina with her hands on her hips as she leans in, her lips moving quickly with each word she utters to Sutton.

The tendons in my heart grow hot, and I snap the next journal shut, slotting it back into place with more force than necessary.

He doesn't even bother looking away from her.

"You think she'll get a big part in the class play?" Lexington asks. "For the final."

"What, like the female lead?" I scoff, snatching a different book and cracking it open to a random page. "Only if Sutton has no taste."

Lexington cocks a brow. "Didn't know we were on a first-name basis with the professor."

Sweat beads along my hairline, and I look up at him, attempting to school my features. "We're not, but you are, right? Isn't that a perk of being a respected founding family member?"

His expression flattens. "Not sure he'd be thrilled if I called him by his name on school grounds. Avernia's real weird about interpersonal relationships between staff and students. Even students like me."

"Why is that?" I focus my attention back on the shelves even as my gaze burns with the effort. "I mean, I know it's taboo in general for students and professors to have, like, sexual encounters and stuff, but Avernia seems particularly strict. The school handbook names every punishment short of a public execution should an unreported friendship or family tie be discovered."

"Dunno. I suspect they had problems with power dynamics and shit at some point. My mom went to school with the dean, and she said he was a repeat offender when it came to fucking students as a TA."

I shudder. "Of course he was."

"He does have that vibe, doesn't he?" Lexington stacks a second and third journal for me. "Only reason he never got into trouble was because he was so tight with the Duponts and Blackwaters."

"Blackwaters? As in the state prosecutor?"

"One and the same." He juts his chin at Sabrina and Sutton. "Word on the street is Sabrina has some sort of ties to him, but no one really knows what. The threat, though, is clear enough. Normally, Professor Dupont dismisses anyone who tries to get clingy, which happens probably more than you'd think. Yet he's with her *all* the time it seems."

Malevolence churns in my chest, setting the cavity ablaze.

"She'll probably make a good lead," he says thoughtfully.

I shoot him a glare. "I'm starting to not like you very much."

"What?" He grins, flashing his straight white teeth. "I've yet to see you *really* act outside of class exercises. If you're as talented as you say, then let's see it."

"You want me to break into a soliloquy in the middle of this basement?"

"Any actor worth their salt would be able to take on a role no matter the location." He waggles his eyebrows, and I realize how similar he and Percy actually are. That must be why they're so close.

Turning back to the shelves, I shake my head. "Quincy said I had ten minutes. I need to grab everything I can before she kicks me out."

"She's not here," he says, leaning against the bookcase. "Come *on*, Elle, I can tell you're good. Let me see those skills in action."

"Mr. Abbott." Sutton's voice is a quiet thunder as it strikes the air, rippling through the aisles. "Could you assist Ms. Taylor with something, please?"

Lexington frowns. "Right now? What happened to Percy?"

"Mr. Whitmore had an evening voice training class."

"Which he *could* have told me about when I recruited him." Sabrina groans. "Ugh, I didn't want Lexington helping. He'll get his slacker dust all over my project."

"You can't very well move three dozen metal chairs on your own before the mixer starts," Sutton says. "Besides, Mr. Abbott currently holds the highest grade in the class. I'm not sure 'slacker' is the appropriate term for him."

My eyebrows lift.

Lexington snorts, bending to place the journals on the floor next to me. "Don't look so shocked. You're not the only talent in the room, m'lady."

"Can't you just help, Professor? It's *your* meeting after all."

"Ms. Anderson's presence in the archives requires staff supervision. So no. I can't leave until she does."

"So *make* her leave."

My nose scrunches up. When I turn my head, I see her glaring at me through the shelves.

Sutton's expression matches hers, though I'm not sure why. He *could* make me leave if he really wanted to, but he was the one who agreed to let me in. Maybe he's trying to save face for it or hoping I'll forget our encounter in the forest.

Maybe my existence disturbs him, the way his has me since the day we met.

"Mr. Abbott," Sutton repeats, his tone firm, leaving no room for argument—and my knees wobbly.

Lexington grumbles something under his breath but heads for the door anyway.

"Are you serious?" Sabrina whines.

"Keep irritating me, and I'll revoke your status as treasurer," Sutton says.

She lets out a loud huff, turning as Lexington walks past her. Each stomp is audible as she ascends the stairs, rattling the lights dangling from the ceiling between exposed wooden rafters.

Leaving me alone with the man I'm supposed to be avoiding.

Chapter 21

Sutton

I'M NOT PLANNING ON SAYING A WORD TO THE TEMPTRESS across the room. I'm happy to just watch from afar where she's tucked between bookshelves in her little black dress with the bell sleeves and sheer tights clinging to her long legs, bending over to squint at the spines of journals like something straight out of a porno.

The snake charm she wears around her neck at all times feels appropriate.

She breaks the silence without facing me. "Did you have to send *everyone* away?"

I clear my throat, listening for sounds of someone else entering the stairwell. She has no idea just how close she is to the fucking carnage that would love to get its hooks in her. Down the hall and below us.

"Thought you could use a little distraction-free reading," I reply.

"Distraction-free, huh?" She snorts. "If you say so."

My chest tightens. I slide my hands into my pants pockets just for something to do while I wait.

Her shadow appears in my peripheral vision as she comes around one side of the bookcase. I resist the urge to look—or try to anyway. She bends again, dropping a new addition onto the pile of periodicals and journals she brought with her, and I get a flash of her ass in those tights as her dress rides up.

Fuck.

I swallow. Hard.

She spares me the slightest glance, smoothing her hands down over the fabric. Like she knows exactly what she just did.

I'm fucking starving.

Unable to sit still in the ensuing silence as she turns back to her task, I wander a bit closer, hands still in my pockets.

The pile of books grows at her feet, and I wonder if she even knows what she's looking for.

"Can I help you with something?"

"You can go away."

"What a different tune you're singing compared to last week when you were practically begging to ride my cock."

The words come out like vomit, triggered instantly for some reason by her disdain. Or maybe I'm still keyed up from having to watch her with Lexington. Or the fact that I can't have her despite settling between her thighs being the only thing I've been able to think about since the start of the semester.

It feels like I'm losing my mind, bit by bit, every time I'm forced to share the air with her but unable to do anything more.

She swivels those beautiful, glittering hazel eyes my way. "I begged, you chastised me, and I saw the error of my ways. Can we just forget about it?"

"So what? You're done coming on to me?"

Her jaw shifts. "Yep. I know better than to ask a man for something multiple times. My previous attempts probably set women back centuries."

"I wasn't aware you had that much influence on your gender."

"Sounds like something my sister would say."

Ah. There it is. I lean an elbow on one shelf, staring at her as she continues her task. "You think I came here with Quincy."

"You showed up at the same time she did."

"Coincidence."

"Whatever. It doesn't matter—I don't care. The only reason I'm down here right now is to try and piece together the puzzle that is Avernia and its many mysteries."

"Mysteries?"

"Yeah, like the students who go missing and are never investigated. The lack of charges in connection with the deaths from last semester. The strange network of student organizations and their ties to weird-ass cultlike practices. The curses." She shrugs, and I can't help wondering if she's seen things or if this really is just a basic curiosity. "Those people you hid from in the forest."

Most in Fury Hill are happy to believe whatever they're told if the truth is shiny enough. For centuries, Avernia's been a breeding ground for misinformation—a way for those running the town to test the waters and see just how much their people will overlook.

That Elle is trying to uncover things rather than go with the flow doesn't bode well for any of us. Especially should any higher-ups find out.

They'd see her as a threat. A manifestation of the curse.

The reason no one's done anything about the crimes perpetrated by her siblings so far is because they think they're under control so long as they can shape public narratives. Pythia does a great job keeping people *just* informed enough to think they know everything.

Elle looking deeper could unravel a thin thread tying the underbelly of this university together.

Something tells me that might be worse than losing my job or stepping in as Incarnate.

A book slips from her fingers, and she lets out a small breath as if exasperated. I crouch down, picking the journal up and putting it at the top of the pile.

"What would you like to find out?"

Her eyes find mine. "What do you mean?"

"I'm a founding family member from arguably the most prominent surname in town. Do you think there's information I can't get?"

"I didn't ask for your help."

"No," I agree. "I'm offering."

"Why?"

"Consider it a gesture of peace." I extend my hand.

She looks at it, makes a face, and pushes into a standing position. "No thanks. I'd rather just ask Meg or Lexington."

My body moves before I can command it to stop, following as she attempts to slip past me; suddenly I'm standing, guiding her back into the shelves behind us so we're mostly obscured from view at the entrance to the room.

Elle's eyes widen as her spine collides with solid wood, and I grip the edges of the shelf on either side of her head, irritation flooding my nervous system.

Goddamn. No one gets under my skin the way this woman does.

I drop my gaze to our shoes. She has those little block heels on again.

"Don't." It's the only word I can manage, and I'm not even sure what I'm saying. I shouldn't be this close at all. "Don't go to him."

"Why shouldn't I?"

"Because I'm asking you not to."

"You can't do this," she whispers, reaching up. Her palms flatten against my chest for a moment, as if she wants to push me away, but then they twist in the fabric of my sweater. "The hot-and-cold thing…telling me you can't act on what I know we're both feeling… If you can't be *in* this, I don't want any part of it."

"Since when?"

"Since I decided being an asshole wasn't very progressive of me."

I lift my chin. "After I sent you out of the forest."

She nods. "I'm sorry for how I've been behaving. I guess I didn't want to see your side of things, and it was selfish and rude of me. I don't want to be the source of your suffering. Pushing your buttons is one thing, but if you really think they'd take your job…"

Swallowing, I move my arms inward and step closer, trapping her. "Is there someone else you'd rather spend such valuable resources on?"

"Ugh. See? What am I supposed to think here, Sutton?" She ducks, trying to escape, but I just move with her. "I'm trying to do the nice thing, but then you… God, you're fucking exhausting."

"It's no picnic on my end, I assure you."

"Then let me leave."

"I *can't.*"

Her nostrils flare, and she lowers her eyes. "Someone will come back soon."

That's true, and I should release her based on that notion alone. Instead, I pinch her chin, tilting her head back until it hits the bookshelf and she's forced to meet my gaze. The longer I stare into those warm irises, the deeper I fall into a cycle of uncontainable desire.

My restraint, no matter what I claim verbally, is wearing thin.

"Fuck it," I mutter, shaking my head. If she wants to go back to Lexington, she can do so with my taste on her lips.

Inhaling that honey-vanilla scent of hers, I slink even closer until there's barely room for a breath between us. My hand slides back, cupping her jaw as raw need pulses through me, denial like a dam breaking and giving way to weeks of longing.

She lets out a tiny noise, something that sounds an awful lot like desperation, and moves toward me, angling her mouth in preparation for mine.

Footsteps thud in the stairwell. Our breaths mingle, and a momentary lapse in sanity glues me in place, mere centimeters from her lips.

I sway, temptation clouding my judgment, but she blinks, and within seconds, she's spinning out of my embrace and diving toward the journals on the floor.

I'm still standing where she left me, leaning against the bookshelf, when Quincy reappears in the doorway.

The older Anderson daughter glances between us but doesn't say a word.

For that, at least while I try to get the beat of my heart under control, I'm grateful.

Chapter 22

Sutton

"Do you think Mother or Father ever miss Bellamy?"

Beckett's question catches me off guard as he stares up at the sky. The sun's beginning to rise over Fury Hill, dewy oranges and pinks peeking through the trees, and even though it's winter, my brother insists on starting his mornings by meditating on the balcony outside my apartment.

In the nude.

My apartment is one of several dozen in the faculty dorm and any of the neighboring theater professors could waltz out and catch a glimpse of the once-great Curator president in his bare glory, but Beckett seems unfazed by the possibility.

Frankly, it's an improvement from him spending all his time in dirty, sweaty clothing on my couch, so I lezt him. As long as he doesn't attempt to leap from the iron railing barricading us in, that is.

Mother would never forgive me.

"Bellamy was their child, so yes, I imagine they miss her a good deal," I say, turning the page in the spiral-bound play I'm rereading for my course on writing and directing.

Throwing myself into class assignments is all I've been focusing on since I nearly gave in to my own depravity in the Apollodorus basement days ago. Elle likely has no idea just how much danger she would've been in had I kissed here there—I'm uncertain if I would've been able to stop.

It's ridiculous how easily she pulls me in. From the moment we met, it's like she's this flame and I'm a moth, powerless against her warm glow. Even denying her is a weak attempt at ignoring how my brain and heart feel, and the more I interact with her in class, the more I see she's not some pretty face who couldn't hack it in LA.

I want to learn everything about her. Listen to her talk for hours. Figure out what makes her tick, what lives beneath the mask she puts on for everyone except me, as if her true feelings—desperation and fear that manifest in snarky remarks and recklessness—are only safe with me.

But I can't, so I grade and study instead.

"They never talk about her," Beckett replies. "I mean, I wouldn't expect Father to, since he didn't give a shit about either of you growing up anyway, but… Mother acts as if Bell never even existed."

"Everyone has their own coping mechanisms."

He's quiet for a while, just staring up with his head resting on his bag. The balcony is barely large enough for him to stretch out on the floor, so his feet are pressed against the metal bars, and his arms are folded over his chest.

"How do you think she died?" he asks finally.

"Beckett."

He turns his head. "What?"

"I don't want to talk about this."

"No one ever does. Don't you find that odd? She'd be so pissed if she knew we were just forgetting about her."

"Just because she isn't discussed like gossip on *The Delphic Pages* doesn't mean she's not being remembered."

"Yeah, but... I'm forgetting her." He sighs. "The other day, I realized I couldn't even remember what color her eyes were, so I went to her old room at the manor to look for pictures, 'cause you know she loved snapping them any chance she got, but it'd been totally cleared out. Not even her bed is in there anymore. It's just... empty."

Something cold settles in my chest, a vicious pang spreading outward.

The situation surrounding our sister's death never did feel quite fleshed out, although I suppose that is the nature of a mystery. We never got to see a body, so there wasn't a chance for real closure. Instead, we were expected to accept things as they were and move on.

For a long time, Mother didn't come out of her bedroom. House staff filtered in and out, tending to the woman as if she were receiving palliative care, while Jean-Louis kept on with business as usual.

A year later, on the anniversary of Bellamy's death, we got the news that Jean-Louis was sick. Mother rejoined society, as if a fresh breath of life had entered her with the prospect of her husband's demise.

They've always had that sort of relationship, though—something toxic and vile, like two venomous serpents twisting around each other, trying to strangle the other and win the upper hand.

If they weren't Duponts, I suspect they'd have divorced a long time ago. The founding families frown upon that here, though, so Mother remains stuck in her loveless marriage.

But I didn't think she'd give in to his pleading to have Bellamy's old room cleaned out. For years, she kept it as a shrine, mummifying the whimsy that only my twin could create in a house built to entomb the people within it.

"Anyway, I just thought maybe it'd help jog my memory if we talked about her, since you were the closest to her. That's how you keep a person alive after they're gone, right? By telling everyone about them like they never left?"

My throat burns as I stare at him, wondering if getting beaten within an inch of his life actually knocked some sense into him. Or if this is some sort of warning sign I should be taking note of before he goes off the deep end and burns Avernia to the ground.

"She had Mother's eyes," I say, misery flooding the chambers of my heart when I pinch my own closed, thinking back to the last time I saw them.

That memory, so vivid even just weeks ago, feels like it's been replaced somehow.

"So your eyes?"

"I don't mean the color. Bellamy's were a warm brown mixed with green, but they were kind. Mischievous. You could always tell whatever she was thinking just by staring into them."

Slowly, my gaze travels over the treetops to the caves in the distance, not really visible from where we're located at the back of campus. But I know them well enough that I don't need to see them to remember the night my sister died.

The only reason I'd been at that party in the quarry was because Bellamy asked me to go. She could make me do anything, our connection forged in a distressed womb and fortified by a strict home life. I was guilty of constantly placating her.

Being around Bellamy felt like orbiting the sun though. It was a light source I sought when I was worn down from pleasing our parents and doing everything they said. I was a peacekeeper trying to get the four of us out from under our parents' influence and control, and it gave her the freedom to be chaotic and uncontainable.

I would have done anything she asked if it meant getting a taste of that freedom. Just for a moment even.

My desire for her to be that outlet is what got her killed. I shouldn't have gone to the party and shouldn't have let myself get taken advantage of, leaving her vulnerable for anyone who wanted to weaken the Dupont line.

I should have been stronger. That was my *duty* as her older brother—to protect her no matter what.

But when I came to, I was too weak to search. Too weak to do anything but wait for someone to rescue me, and even then, the flashes of people violating my body made me catatonic.

It was weeks before I returned to school. By that time, Avernia had fully moved on from Bellamy Dupont, and no one cared about the concerns raised by students. Not when the dean and higher-ups were saying our fears didn't matter.

Eventually, people started wondering if she'd ever existed at all. She became a ghost and has haunted me ever since.

Beckett glances at me, a thoughtful expression on his face. "Do you miss her?"

I'm not sure that's a strong enough word to describe it.

You don't *miss* a limb when it's forcibly removed from your body. You ache against the phantom sensations where it once was, your mind forever altered by the knowledge that there's nothing you can do to get it back.

"Every time I let myself," I answer, tilting my chin slightly toward the sky as a breeze coasts over the trees, whispering its secrets.

Except they're in a language I don't speak.

Having Elle in class is a lesson in fucking torture.

She answers as many questions as she possibly can, visibly irritating the other students, but it wouldn't be fair of me not to call on her. Reverse favoritism would be as much of a problem as anything else, and I don't want anyone questioning my authority as a teacher.

It's bad enough some people know about my relationship with Beckett. Too many connections, and people get suspicious.

I do my best to simply ignore Elle entirely, but her presence makes that impossible.

My fingertips yearn to smooth over her skin. My mouth quivers with the desire to have hers against it.

Any time I look away, placing the students into groups or allowing them time to start an assignment, it's her that my gaze seeks out. No matter what.

Our rendezvous in the forest and near-kiss in the basement did little to quell the mounting need inside my bones. I spend more of my time in class just trying to get through the lesson without recalling what her cunt feels like or thinking about how nice the imprint of her teeth would look on my skin. How nice she smells and the little gasp she inhales when my face gets close.

Now I sit on the stage, twiddling my thumbs, unsure of what to fucking do.

Acting on it would have catastrophic consequences for both of us, but ignoring the issue makes my migraines more frequent.

I've denied her multiple times at this point, but as my already-threadbare restraint thins, so does my bullshit reasoning.

I don't actually give a fuck about my job, but I *do* care about her. She knows that too, which makes this more complicated.

When I glance at her, she's just sitting in the front row, swinging her foot as she reads a passage in her textbook, biting down on the end of her pen.

Some sick part of me wishes I were that pen.

The more time I spend resisting her, the worse I feel, until my mind is spinning a tapestry of blistering longing with no end in sight.

As if she can sense my stare, she lifts her gaze, meeting my eyes. A smirk forms around the pen, and she sits up a little straighter in her chair.

Christ. It's pathetic the things I'd beg her to do to me if we were alone right now.

Breaking her stare, I lift my wrist and check the time on my watch.

"Thoughts on options for the final?" I ask, drawing the students from their studies. "From the list of choices, what are we thinking?"

"You gave us a list of Shakespeare plays to choose from," Lexington drawls from the second row. "Isn't that kind of limiting?"

"Anyone have an opinion on what play they'd like to do from the list and not an opinion on how I'm running my class?"

Meg adjusts a brake on her wheelchair, raising her free hand. "He has a point, Professor. Why vote when it's clear you just want us to do *Hamlet*?"

"Which is, like, the most clichéd of all plays," Lexington adds.

"Cliché has purpose," I remind them, glancing at the options written on the chalkboard. "It's not always a bad thing. And accessibility goes a long way with audiences. Need I remind you all that the theater department runs on donations and ticket sales, and our ability to continue next semester relies heavily on how well the play does? Your average Fury Hill citizen knows *Hamlet*. They enjoy the existentialism, the court drama, and yes—the familiarity."

"Doesn't make it any less mundane for us," someone grumbles.

I know that grumble though.

My eyes fall on Elle. She doesn't even flinch.

"All right." I fold my arms over my chest. "What production would you suggest then, Ms. Anderson? For a group of students who spend half their time onstage waffling in and out of character and seem mostly undriven by the prospect of the spotlight. I can't be sure these are the same students who auditioned for a spot in this class."

"Sartre's *No Exit*. Maybe *Vera; or, The Nihilists* by Wilde."

I try to stifle my surprise at how readily she had an answer. For some reason, I keep forgetting that she's not as much a novice as her peers. "Equally as existential as *Hamlet*, I'd argue. No less mundane in that regard."

"Sure, but it's fresh. By the time they get to college, every theater kid's done Shakespeare a dozen times. Nothing wrong with that, of course. He's popular for a reason. But since this course is mostly theater kids or a variant of them, why not mix it up, have us explore new themes and soliloquies? I bet the audience would love it too."

Pursing my lips, I nod, considering this. "You may have a point, but either of those would require permission from Avernia's board of trustees as well as procurements for scripts and extended costume budgets. I'm not sure we have the time to wait. The plays are already slotted in for performances at the old campus theater."

Elle rolls her eyes. "Then did you even need to ask?"

"If everything we did in life was relegated to necessity, the human experience would be boring." I clasp my hands together, clear my throat, and return my attention to the rest of the students. "Class dismissed."

They begin packing up, a hushed chatter falling among them. I catch snippets of their conversations—worries about midterms, ghost sightings in Erebus Hall—and even manage to absorb Elle's interactions with the group she's become quite friendly with.

"—the observatory is always closed by the evening," Percy tells her, leaning his elbows on the chair in front of him. "Which, yes, seems like a dumb rule considering you can't really see stars except at night."

"Most of Avernia's rules are dumb and arbitrary," Meg says. "That's, like, a thing with higher education. I think it's meant to distract from the actual discriminatory policies."

"Maybe they're trying to protect us from something shady," Elle jokes, smirking even as she says it—though I swear there's an edge to her tone, something sharp in the way she glances at the three of them, like she's waiting for some sort of confirmation.

"Nah," Lexington replies, shaking his head. "The only thing the school wants to protect us from is the Anderson curse, and I don't know if the observatory is a target."

"The Anderson curse?" Elle asks. "Is that what we're calling it now?"

"That's what we've *been* calling it, babe," he says, leaning forward to poke her cheek.

My nostrils flare as I watch the interaction happening in my peripheral vision. Swallowing, I dare to turn their way, feigning nonchalance.

Lexington's staring right at me.

A small grin pulls at his features, and he slowly drops his hand. *Fucker.*

But in truth, I'm the idiot. I wonder just how obvious my attraction is or if Lexington is just particularly good at deciphering my feelings because he's known me a long time. When you grow up around people, especially in towns as small as Fury Hill, their nuances are second nature to you.

He seemed to know about my attraction to people regardless of their gender before the rest of town did, sometime back when I was a teenager. It'd been a common question, as I devoted a lot of time to the Westwoods' only son, Zachary, and folks are naturally curious.

Giving Zachary my virginity had only solidified the fact that it wasn't just women I was interested in. I desired *people* and didn't spend much time taking gender into consideration past that.

I've never felt the need to formally address my pansexuality, as if it were some secret that changed who I was. Many of Fury Hill's residents are openly queer as it stands, so it isn't as if this made me different.

Wanting an Anderson, though, would cause them to stumble a bit. Especially one as formidable and disruptive as Elle.

I don't even notice she's standing before me until she's practically falling into my lap, leaning in with narrowed eyes. She rakes her gaze over me as though she's searching for flaws or evidence of some misdeed.

Instinctively, I jerk backward, my knees catching on the edge of the stage. She shouldn't be this close in general, but certainly not when there are other students still lingering in the auditorium.

"Someone's jumpy," she says.

"You shouldn't sneak up on people."

"I'd hardly call approaching you in class *sneaking up*. It's not my fault you weren't paying attention."

Sighing, I pinch the bridge of my nose. A migraine skirts around the outside of my skull, peeking in as Elle's presence taunts me. "What can I do for you, Ms. Anderson?"

"I've been thinking—"

"Dangerous."

She frowns, glaring at me. "I want to join Visio Aternae."

"Haven't we already discussed this?"

"No, *you* discussed it with yourself. You didn't even give me a chance to make a case for why I'd be a good addition."

"You wouldn't," I tell her, looking quickly around the room at her remaining peers. "They're a philanthropic student organization. Unlike the Curators, whose focus is networking, or even the Daughters of Persephone with their secretive enrollment efforts, Visio Aternae is entirely merit based, open to anyone who wants to join, and focused on bettering the community. But that opportunity cuts off at the start of the semester, and I'm afraid you wouldn't be a good fit."

Percy pushes Meg up the aisle, leaving Lexington behind as he speaks with a couple of Curators toward the middle of the room. Sabrina sits right up front, her eyes glued to us, and I wonder how much she can hear.

Elle crosses her arms. "Factually untrue, and I have a résumé to prove it. From ages nine to fourteen, I spent every summer at theater camps that 'benefited the community.' We put on plays to raise money for animal welfare, food pantries, and arts subsidies. From fifteen to eighteen, I volunteered as a counselor at these camps, so I know how to organize and delegate. I'm familiar with the acting world, and I'm *talented*."

"Yet you're the only student of mine who didn't audition for their place in my class. Something I require for all incoming enrollees."

"If you'd like, I can still do it."

For some reason, that idea makes my heart thump faster. I look at Sabrina from the corner of my eye, then focus back on Elle. "Perhaps this conversation would be better suited for a different time."

She blinks. "It sounds like you're trying to brush me off so you can pretend I agreed to drop it."

"I'm just suggesting that this may not be the best setting for a discussion that has nothing to do with our class. I like to compartmentalize so I don't lose sight of my goals."

She looks down and to the side for a moment, as if trying to understand where my attention drifted. Clearing her throat, she nods. "Fine. Tell me where you'd like to finish."

Warmth spreads its limbs down the sides of my neck. I wonder if she even realizes how often she engages in double speak.

"You may visit during office hours. They're posted on the schedule in the annex." I pause, groaning internally as Lexington turns, evidently waiting for her to join him. When I speak again, I lower my voice. "Though if you want to prove you're serious about the organization, you may want to reconsider the company you keep."

She glances over her shoulder, then back at me, her mouth twitching. "I wasn't asking for advice."

"As the faculty sponsor for Visio Aternae and the one who decides enrollment, I'm giving it free of charge. Lexington Abbott is trouble."

He isn't. Not any more than the other students, but I don't

like the way he's looking at her. I didn't like it in the Apollodorus basement, and that hasn't changed.

"Don't you think I'm trouble too?" she replies, lowering her voice as well.

I swallow, averting my gaze. "Different kinds."

"Interesting." She hums, leaning forward with her hands clasped behind her back.

My eyes snap to her, like she's some sort of inescapable beacon, and the blush that stains her cheeks makes my pulse quicken.

"Want to know what my advice would be?" she asks. "Generally speaking."

A knot lodges in my throat. I can't answer.

"If you're dead set on Shakespeare for the spring play, you should do *Othello*."

"Why's that?"

"I think existentialism already thrives in academia. Your students and audience don't need help reaffirming themes of mortality and revenge but the dangers of isolation and the importance of identity." Elle taps her fingers on the stage, right next to my hip. "And the risks associated with passion and jealousy."

With that, she grins, then spins and bounces back toward Lexington. He beams as she approaches, and a sharp pang slices across my chest, anchoring deep.

"Everything okay, Professor?" Sabrina asks, appearing before me in the seconds after Elle leaves. She swings her ponytail from side to side, blinking up at me. "You look a little shaken up."

Shit. I'm worse at masking than I realized. "I'm perfectly fine," I tell her. "You weren't at the last Visio Aternae meeting. Is everything all right with *you*?"

She nods, rocking on her feet. "Oh yes! I submitted an absentia request to your email a few days before, but I suppose maybe you didn't see it. I was helping the mayor with some spring equinox stuff and couldn't get out of it. I promise it won't happen again, and I especially promise not to miss any fundraising events or rehearsals once they've begun."

"That's good to hear. I appreciated your assistance with the mixer in the Apollodorus, either way."

That makes her smile. "You know, with how involved Visio Aternae ends up being in the productions each summer, I'm surprised more aren't in your classes."

"Well, acting isn't for everyone," I note, shrugging. "However, there are plenty of support roles that go into a play. Anyone who comes will find something to do."

My gaze wanders as I shift on the stage, bumping into something. I glance down at my hip, noting the little orange fruit sitting beside it that wasn't there a few minutes ago.

Beckett had eaten my last apricot, and I didn't have the chance to swing by the refectory for one on my way to class this morning.

I look up, meeting Elle's gaze as she stares back with an unreadable expression.

"That's because you're such a great professor and director," Sabrina gushes, a light blush staining her cheeks. "No one ever gets turned away from your shows because you recognize the importance of every last detail of a production."

Clearing my throat, I cover the apricot with my hand and refocus my attention on Sabrina. "It takes many cogs to run a well-oiled machine. Keep that in mind if you don't get a speaking role, Ms. Taylor."

"Oh, don't worry," she says, a sly grin tugging at the corner of her mouth as she tosses a look over her shoulder, then turns back to me. "I'm prepared for anything. That's the true mark of a talented actress: her adaptability."

It's clearly a jab, but I'm not sure I understand the intended mark. Though it hardly matters, since she skips away to join her friends anyway, and when I look back to the front row, Elle is already gone.

Chapter 23

Elle

Sutton's irritation is instantly palpable the moment he shoves open his apartment door to find me perched on the edge of his sofa, waiting patiently with my legs crossed, a short skirt high on my hips.

It's more thigh than I really need to show, but there aren't rules for this sort of thing. The way his piercing green eyes immediately fall to my legs makes me think I chose correctly though.

When he exhales, I wonder if maybe this was a bad idea after all. My nerves are shot, my confidence wavering, and this is the exact thing that got me into trouble with his dad, but… I also want this.

Spot or no spot. I want *him*.

I waited a few days before executing his request in case anyone had overheard, but for some reason, he looks surprised that I took him up on it.

"Perhaps this conversation would be better suited for a different time."

No subtext needed. I heard him loud and clear.

He sports a pair of dark brown slacks and a sage button-down, the sleeves rolled up to reveal corded forearms, and I wonder how long they've been like that.

If he taught his last class with them exposed so everyone could ogle him.

No, that would make him uncomfortable. He wants attention to be academic in nature—despite the glint in his gaze reflecting my own lewdness.

Just for a moment though. When he blinks, it's gone, and he closes the door behind him as he sets his briefcase on the cushioned green chair next to it.

"Just how long is your list of priors, Ms. Anderson?"

"Assuming I have a record is not very progressive of you, Boy Scout."

The apartment around him is dark, even with the lights he flips on as he comes into the living room. Every mirror within is covered with scrap fabric or some kind of furniture slip—even the standing one in his bathroom. The curtains contain about an inch's worth of dust, as if they're never drawn during the day.

It's unbelievably stuffy—everything inside barely touched, nothing ever disturbed, like a mausoleum of academia.

"Besides," I continue when he says nothing, "is it technically a crime if I have a key?"

"Where the hell would you have gotten—" He drags a palm down his face. "Never mind. I forgot who I was speaking to. Delinquency extends beyond restricted basements and prohibited forests, clearly."

I grin, leaning back. "You don't seem all that happy to see me."

Slowly, his eyes travel over my form, pausing for a single breath when he reaches the multiple undone buttons at the top of my blouse.

He clears his throat, pocketing his hands. Like he's physically restraining himself from reaching for me.

Our brief moments together outside class are mere memories. Ones I haven't been able to stop thinking about for a myriad of reasons—the main one being how badly my body craves him.

It's a disease, this want I have. Pathetic even. Normally, I wouldn't be so desperately trying to get him to admit there's *something* here, but my soul feels like it's being fed through a shredder each time he denies me.

I've never ached for anything like I do him. At first, it was just the physical attraction, a statuesque beauty that haunts my dreams. But beyond that, listening to him lecture each day only makes my admiration grow.

He's smart. Passionate. Endlessly unnerved by my existence.

Resistance is futile.

"You can't be here," he says, rubbing the back of his neck.

"Are we really still playing the *I could lose my job* game? I thought we agreed that was just an excuse."

"My brother is staying with me."

That makes my stomach drop. "I thought guests weren't allowed inside faculty housing."

"They're not, which doesn't help your case, by the way. But Beckett got a special exemption. He's sort of…in my custody for the time being."

"Custody? Is he a child?" Surely, not the Beckett I've met.

"No," he replies sharply. "It was just decided that given the circumstances of last semester, he should be kept under someone's watchful eye."

I purse my lips. "Because of the whole cave incident, right?"

He lets out a long breath. "You know about that?"

"Not all the details. My family works on a need-to-know basis, and apparently that didn't fully qualify." I slide my hands over my legs, considering. "My brother messed him up pretty bad, I heard. Though he seems to have recovered okay on the outside."

"Yes. Although I don't blame Asher so much as I do our father for influencing Beckett to act in the first place. And—wait." Sutton pauses, frowning. "You've seen him?"

"Well, I ran into him and your dad the day I saw you in the woods."

"What do you mean you ran into them?" he grinds out, jaw tense. "My father rarely leaves the family manor due to illness, and Beckett's been so despondent lately that he barely leaves this apartment. Frankly, the fact that you were able to sneak in the one time he was gone is a bit frightening, but I'm willing to overlook it for the moment. Stay away from my father, Elle."

Unease slinks down my spine. Now would be a good time to mention my history with the man, but I can't make myself do it. I don't *want* him to know—don't want him to think less of me. "It's not like I sought him out. I ran into him by pure chance. If you hadn't kicked me out of the forest, actually, I probably would've missed him altogether."

Sutton's laugh is humorless and made of glass. "You're blaming me for being put on his radar?"

"What is he, a UFO?"

"No, what he *is* is a major fucking influence in this town and a founding family member who believes your family is responsible for the downfall of ours. He believes in that ridiculous fucking curse, and he's the reason Beckett tried to kill your brother mere *months*

254 SAV R. MILLER

ago. Fuck. Do you take anything seriously, or is this all some big joke to you? Did you come to Avernia just to cause problems? Was LA not doing enough for you?"

I cross my arms, waiting while he seethes, ignoring the bite of his judgment. A part of me wants to walk over and offer him some sort of comfort since he's clearly spiraling, but I think that might make the final thread keeping him tenuously sewn together tear.

Finally, he sighs, dropping his head. "My father is not a good man, Elle. Stay away from him."

"Stay out of the forest, don't hang out with Lexington, stay away from your dad. Normally, I want a man to fuck me a *few* times before he starts trying to dictate my entire life."

"*Christ.*" Groaning, he scrubs his palms over his face. "Don't talk about fucking right now."

"Why not? You're the one who told me to come for office hours."

The air goes still. He spreads his fingers, peeking at me through them. "What sort of office hours did you think I meant?"

"Is that not..." I trail off, cocking my head to the side. Heat blooms in my cheeks, flushing warmth through my entire body.

Oh my God. That wasn't *a come-on in class.*

He wasn't offering sex in exchange for a spot in Visio Aternae. He really meant for me to come to his office *during* office hours.

Humiliation burns my retinas, blurring my vision.

I want to die.

"Forgive me for misunderstanding," I mutter.

Genuine horror registers on his face. "In what world would you believe I'd ask you to trade sex for group membership, Elle? Jesus Christ. You must think I'm a raging piece of shit if that was your first conclusion. Is that what Hollywood taught you?"

Tears sting my eyes as he scolds me, his words like a branding iron to the face. I feel utterly small. Infinitesimal.

My skin itches, and I scramble to fix the buttons on my shirt. Sniffling, I push to a standing position and grab my things, tugging my skirt down in the process.

"Like I said, it was a misunderstanding," I say, my voice robotic.

Stupid, Elle. You are so fucking stupid.

You fell for it again.

Sutton stares at me as I try to collect myself, an unreadable expression marring his features. "What aren't you telling me?"

I glare at my feet. "Nothing."

"Elle."

"What? We're just teacher and student, right? You don't need to know everything about me. An incomplete hookup doesn't make us friends, and you don't want us to be more so just drop it."

Keys jangle at the front door, and Sutton curses under his breath, springing into action. His arm collides with my stomach, shoving me backward as he practically drags me past the sofa and into a short hall with two side-by-side doors.

With a grunt, he dives into the one on the left, slamming it shut at the same time a voice calls into the apartment.

"Sutton! You home?"

His brother.

I let out a squeak when my back hits the mattress against the far wall, beneath a wooden headboard that's flush with a large window. Sutton falls on top of me, planting his knee between my thighs and slapping his palm over my mouth.

His fingers are freezing, and I suppress a full-body chill, though I can't be sure what exactly it's from—his touch or the fact that we might get caught.

"Hello?" A knock on the closed door makes my eyes bulge, and Sutton's jaw shifts. He glances over his shoulder, and we both see it at the same time: the unlocked knob, which twists before Sutton jolts back to reality.

"I'm naked," he shouts, louder than probably necessary.

The doorknob ceases moving. "Oh. Well, shit, you see me naked all the fucking time. Who cares?"

My eyebrows arch, and Sutton's grip on my mouth tightens.

Between my thighs, I'm throbbing, but I try not to focus too much on how good it feels to be pinned down like this by him.

"I—I'm not decent," he says weakly, meeting my gaze. There's something haunted living in his, and it feels a lot heavier than the reality of us being merely forbidden by school policy.

My heart aches to know what secrets he keeps hidden.

"What does 'not decent' mean?" his brother asks. "Are you, like…masturbating?"

Suddenly my mouth is dry, the image of him fisting himself too much for me to handle.

Sutton's lips part as he seems to settle atop me, his hips pressing into mine more firmly. I gasp through my nose, my pulse skyrocketing at the sensation, the hard planes of his body against the soft contours of mine.

I widen my legs a little more, allowing him better access. His nostrils flare, and he shakes his head.

Since he didn't pin my limbs down that well, I hook one of my calves around his waist, encouraging more. I don't force it, not wanting to make him do something he doesn't *actually* want to do, but I flutter my lashes as if to say *it's okay*.

Use me, I want to beg. The broken parts of me want the distraction, the urgency, the dependence. This at least I know I'm good at.

He drags his palm away from my mouth, sliding it down and turning his hand to pinch my chin between two fingers. A war rages in his irises, and I watch his throat bob, trying to keep myself from whimpering.

The way he looks at me feels like I'm being seared from the inside out. My body grows unbearably hot as he shifts, notching the pleat of his pants against my center.

Sutton leans in, his lips hovering so close to mine that I can taste the toothpaste he must have used recently. For some reason, that sends a spark of jealousy spiraling through my abdomen, wondering if he used it because it's a routine or if he was with someone.

I lift one hand, threading it through his hair. A muscle in his jaw twitches, and his eyes drop.

"Kiss me," I whisper, so softly that it barely even makes a sound. "We can worry about the consequences later."

His breathing deepens, and he floats an inch closer, mouth parting.

My tongue darts out, wetting my bottom lip.

He tracks the movement, and my stomach gets heavy. My breasts ache behind the confines of my shirt, hungry for his touch.

When he starts to move in again, his gaze hypnotic, I close my eyes and wait.

"Or… Oh shit, do you have someone in there?" Beckett asks next, chuckling. "I didn't really need anything, so don't bother coming out. I was just letting you know I'm heading to a Curator party in the quarry, so don't wait up tonight."

Within seconds, Sutton twists out of my embrace, launching off the bed and stalking over to the door. He positions himself so I'm shielded as he cracks it, peeking his head into the dim hall.

I glance around, trying to get my bearings. The shift happened so suddenly that it takes a second for my eyesight to adjust to the room, and as I do, I take in the covered mirrors on the bureau and hanging on what I assume is a closet door. There's a stack of papers on the nightstand beneath a ballpoint pen and a worn copy of some book.

Rolling to my side, I lean in to read the spine.

Othello.

I blink, sitting up. *Is he reading that because I suggested it?*

My eyes flicker to his back, rigid as he stands between his brother and me. His fingers grip the doorjamb in a way that makes my muscles feel weak, and I wish we hadn't been interrupted.

I wish he'd wanted more than *office hours.*

"What do you mean you're going to a Curator party?" Sutton probes. "You're not an active member anymore."

"Doesn't mean I can't attend. A couple of people from my Ancient Civ course last semester asked if I'd join. I didn't want to say no again."

"Again? They've invited you before?"

"A few times since the start of the year. But I've not really been up to attending, so…"

Sutton's shoulders slump. He doesn't immediately reply, and I see the shadow from the hall shift, and the top of Beckett's head appears. Cringing, I dive beneath the blankets, instantly regretting it when I'm enveloped in nothing but Sutton's scent.

"Who do you have in there anyway?" Beckett asks.

"No one."

They stay quiet for several beats. Someone clicks their tongue, and then Beckett speaks again. "Come on, just tell me. It's not like you to entertain guests. Honestly, I was starting to think you were just going to be celibate forever."

"My sex life is none of your business."

"But Death's—"

"Go to your party," Sutton cuts him off, his voice gruff.

My stomach twists into a dozen knots. *What was the end of that sentence?*

Is he seeing someone else? Someone in Death's Teeth?

I admit my understanding of that organization is still pretty fuzzy, but if there's some kind of requirement where sex remains between members only, I'm not sure I want to know more.

Surely not though. Sutton barely interacts with other people except when they're in an audience, a safe distance away. I've seen him go out of his way to avoid shoulder taps from colleagues and brushes against other students in the halls.

Still. Jealousy percolates in my gut regardless.

"Oh, is it a student? Someone Father would hate? Because—"

"Be home no later than midnight, or else I will drag you out in front of your friends."

Beckett's sigh is loud and obnoxious. "Whatever you say, Sutty," he grumbles, and then his footsteps carry off somewhere in the distance, making me think he's walked away.

After several minutes, the sound of the door clicking shut echoes through the room, followed by the turning of a lock. I peek out from the covers, watching Sutton as he walks back to the bed and flops face down onto the mattress.

Ask him. Ask him about what you saw in the forest, Elle. Ask what those people you hid from in the gazebo were talking about. Demand answers. Don't just wait around again until something happens.

"Hey, Sutton?"

He groans without moving. "Don't call me that."

Every other question I'd been about to verbalize vanishes on the tip of my tongue. "Your name?"

"I don't like how it sounds coming from you."

"Okay... Boy Scout it is then." I pause, waiting for something else, but he doesn't say more. The air shifts, and I don't really feel like now is the time to talk about curses or possible cults. "Should I go?"

"Yes."

My insides deflate. "All right. I'm sorry—"

"You *should* go," he continues, cutting me off. "Because the longer you sit here, the more I think about stripping you bare and taking what you've offered me multiple times now."

"Oh." I push the sheets off and toy with the snake dangling from my choker.

"Fuck. I shouldn't have even said that. Just... Give me a minute." He presses the heel of one hand to his temple.

"Are you okay?"

"Migraine. It'll pass eventually."

"Do you get them often?"

"A few times a week."

"Is that what the apricots are for?"

"Yes. They probably don't help all that much, but it's a bit of a ritual at this point." He pauses. "Thank you for the one you brought to class. That was very thoughtful of you."

"Well, I've used them myself, so I can attest to the anti-inflammatory properties. They don't work for everything or everyone, but I figured maybe you were eating them so often for a reason."

"You get migraines?"

"Endometriosis. Tissue grows outside the uterus and makes periods super painful. Among other menstrual and reproductive-related issues." I cringe as I speak, aware that I sound like a pamphlet you'd get at the gynecologist and that most guys probably don't want to talk about periods at all.

"Ah, yes, I remember you mentioning it before. That sounds... well, to be frank: shitty."

I laugh softly. "Yeah, it is."

"At least we can commiserate together. Perhaps next time, you can bring two apricots."

Flames lick at my cheeks. "The other one was just supposed to be a peace offering."

"Are we at war?"

"Well, no, but I've been coming on really strong, so I was just kind of hoping we could maybe...start over."

"Start over," he repeats. "And breaking into my apartment for sex was, what, a fallback plan?"

I don't reply, shame too heavy in my chest. The silence thickens around us, and I swallow, moving to dismount the bed in case he wants to be alone.

He lets out a small breath, like he's in pain, and I freeze.

"Is there anything I can do to help?"

"No," he replies. "Most of the time, I can sense them coming on and take the necessary precautions, but some things like stress can trigger them before I really notice. This one just happened to sneak up on me, but it will subside."

Guilt pecks at my bones. "Am I stressing you out?"

"Since the day we met."

Apparently my embarrassment knows no bounds.

"I'm sorry." And I am. I've clearly misread everything because I was too busy focusing on external, carnal sensations rather than putting any effort into caring about him.

He *should* reject me. I'd do the same if the roles were reversed.

"It's not just you," he adds, rolling onto his back, eyes closed. He folds his veiny hands over his chest with a long exhale. "My brother's been going through some shit, and I don't know how to help him. He doesn't talk, barely leaves the house…except for tonight, that is. And on top of that, I've got…things I can't really discuss."

"Forest-related things?"

One eyelid peels back, peering at me.

"Your dad told me not to go into the forest too," I tell him, pulling my knees to my chest. It's unnerving how comfortable and easy this entire situation feels, despite the fact that we were practically dry humping and arguing just moments ago. Like we've been doing this forever. "Does it have anything to do with Death's Teeth?"

He closes his eye again. "The less you know, the better. Trust me."

"Give me a reason to."

"I'm your professor. You should respect my authority."

Dropping my knees, I shift onto them and lean forward, letting my hair fall over my face as I hover above him, planting my palms on the mattress. Right next to him. His breath hitches when the ends of each strand brush over his chest and arm, but he doesn't look at me.

"Right now, you're not my professor," I say. "And I'm not your student. We're just two people in a bedroom. Talking. Resisting."

"Séductrice."

I smirk. "Is that seductress in French?"

"Oui. Very good."

My cheeks burn. "Are you just trying to distract me?"

"Is it working?"

"No."

He sighs. "Stay out of the woods, stay away from my father, and don't go poking around Death's Teeth. No good can come from any of that."

Chapter 24

Sutton

WHEN I ANNOUNCE *OTHELLO* AS THE SPRING PLAY, MOST OF THE students don't give a shit. Not that I was expecting them to, but the deafening silence that ensues after my big reveal is still staggering.

"What, no complaints? No comments or questions?" I hold out my arms, waiting. "This is your final, people. Speak now or forever hold your peace."

In the second row, Lexington shrugs. "Better than *Hamlet*."

"Definitely not obscure enough," Meg says. "Why not *Love's Labor's Lost* or *Titus Andronicus*?"

"No one wants to do *Titus Andronicus*, let's be real here. Plus, the way our semester is structured, we need something we can run through in a few short weeks, and that one requires a certain level of depth that might be too advanced for this course."

Soft laughter ripples through the seats.

"After everything that went down in the fall, wouldn't a comedy be sort of refreshing for the community?" Sabrina questions.

I point at her, nodding. "Indeed. This is why you're the Visio

Aternae treasurer—I appreciate your commitment to thinking of others."

She blushes, and someone mutters something incoherent under their breath.

"Does anyone want to hazard a guess as to why I didn't choose a comedy?"

"Because misery loves company?" Meg suggests.

"No, Meg, that was not my reasoning. *Love's Labor's Lost* would've been fun but…safe. Comedies are always safe—not *easy* and not even necessarily well-received at all times. There's a skill in translating words to actions that actually make people laugh. But so long as you're having a good time onstage, the odds of your audience enjoying the production are high."

"And tragedy is different?" Meg asks.

"By definition. We have to strike a balance—an understanding of your characters that reaches the audience beyond the surface. You want them sitting on the edge of their seat, wondering which heartstring you're going to sever next, even if they're intimately familiar with the source being pulled from. We want tears, passion, and people clutching their guts, wondering why we put them through such hell."

The class falls silent, staring back at me.

Fair. I feel a bit out of sorts. Since the night Elle broke into my apartment and we were almost found out, I haven't been myself. Beckett disappeared at that party for several hours and came back drunk after Elle left, bleeding from a scar he'd somehow torn open. He didn't tell me what happened.

Jean-Louis called the morning after to check in, and I still have this sneaking suspicion that he encouraged my brother to attend, but I didn't ask why.

266 SAV R. MILLER

No point when the fucker lies through his teeth 80 percent of the time.

"Ms. Anderson?" I quip after a moment, turning to where she sits next to Lexington, behind Meg and Percy. "You don't normally let me get through an entire sentence without interruption, much less multiple paragraphs. You have nothing to add?"

"Nope." She shakes her head. "You're the professor. The students are supposed to trust your judgment, right?"

My pulse thumps heavily in my throat, and I hold her gaze even though I can tell she's annoyed with me. "Glad we've finally come to that conclusion."

Elle scoffs, leaning forward to whisper something in Percy's ear.

I clear my throat, nostrils flaring as scalding hot pain lances my chest.

Sabrina raises her hand. "I'm curious—how many votes did *Othello* win by?"

"Enough."

She narrows her eyes but doesn't say anything more.

"All right, break into pairs. We're doing repetition exercises so you all can stop overthinking my decisions." A couple students glance at the front, but I actively avoid following their stares. "And remember—audaces fortuna juvat!"

They repeat the phrase, as has become custom anytime I introduce Latin to them at this point in the semester. I watch as they start grouping off, some hanging out in the aisle while others migrate toward the orchestra pit or take the stage behind me.

Elle grabs Lexington by the sleeve of his maroon knit swearer, dragging him toward the back, and the stabbing sensation from before reverberates in my chest.

Fuck me, she's beautiful. Her dark brown hair is tied back

today, giving me an unobstructed view of the slender curve of her cheeks and the plush heart shape of her lips as they curl for someone who isn't me.

I'm not used to envy stirring in my gut. I grew up with the ability to get whatever I wanted, though it was rare I sought much. Doing so made my parents fight, as if my desires reminded them I existed, and I didn't want to adversely affect my siblings. Peace of mind was more important than doing what I wished, and after Bellamy's death, it was tantamount to ensuring Beckett didn't get roped into the dark underbelly of the Duponts' legacy.

It happened anyway, despite my suffering. Now I'm not sure what the fucking point of denial is at all, especially with a woman who could be Aphrodite herself standing in the same room.

What I've told her is true—I don't want to lose this job. Sometimes, it's the only connection I have left to my sister, and it wouldn't get me out of the clutches of Death's Teeth. If anything, they'd take the sudden vacancy in my life as an invitation to force me into Incarnate's role, and I don't want that.

Elle's face lights up as she and Lexington begin their exercise, and it strikes me somewhere deep in the core of my being how animated she becomes. She's always fairly free with her expressions, but something truly sparks when she's acting, like she's this fire consuming the role completely. The mask of someone else slips into place effortlessly, making me wonder if we're more alike than I realized.

It happens like the flip of a switch, and I'd find it unsettling if it wasn't so goddamn hot.

I tear my gaze away, focusing on the other students.

But I feel Sabrina's stare no matter who I look at, and I tell myself that's how she's always been, not that she's actually suspicious. Even if I don't fully believe it.

Beckett hangs his head as he sits on the stoop outside my apartment, his hoodie pulled up and cinched tight around his face. He doesn't say anything as I approach, though I can smell the alcohol on his breath anyway.

I lean against the balcony railing and look out at the Elysian Dorms, wondering which one Elle's in as if I haven't memorized the exact floor and unit.

Not that I'm planning to do anything with that knowledge. It just happened to be in her file, which I've reviewed dozens of times since she showed up in my class the first day.

"You look like hell," I tell Beckett.

"Feel like it."

"Maybe you shouldn't be partying—"

"Did you know I got kicked out of my classes? I was only taking a couple this semester anyway, but the professors in my advanced history and drama courses dropped me within the first week."

Is that why he hasn't been leaving the apartment? "Were you absent at all?"

He shakes his head. "Nope. I guess they just didn't want this particular Dupont stain on their rosters."

"Well, we knew getting the rest of campus on board with your redemption was a long shot," I tell him, lifting a shoulder. "You did have a direct hand in several murders."

Exhaling, he kicks his foot, jamming his heel against the rail. "I didn't *actually* kill anyone though. I even saved one of the captives."

"You were the reason she was in the caves in the first place."

"Which no one *ever* lets me forget," he huffs. "Jesus. Haven't you ever done something stupid that you regret, Sutty? I know you're the golden child in the family, but I have to believe you've made mistakes at some point. Father even says so."

My jaw tightens. "You shouldn't be speaking to him at all, Beckett. The things he says…"

"Can we talk about my school situation?" he cuts in. "I'm having a crisis here."

"Have you thought about applying anywhere else? Mother and Father would—"

"Avernia credits are nontransferable, remember?" He flexes his hands, curling his fingers against his jeans. "What would the fucking point be?"

"Starting over might not be so bad." I scratch the back of my neck. "Getting out of Fury Hill could be good for you."

"It wouldn't matter, you know. The ghosts here… They haunt the people too. They go where we go."

Walking over, I take a seat next to him. Storm clouds are rolling in, casting a thicker gloom around campus than usual, filling the air with a film of anguish and resentment. The sky grows darker the longer we sit as nighttime settles in.

If I feel this shitty from the simple act of denying myself what I want most, I can't begin to imagine what's going on in Beckett's head.

Maybe I shouldn't have supported his return in the first place.

But a part of me had hoped it would do him some good, not make things worse. That being around his peers might make him feel normal again. Get Jean-Louis out of his head.

Clearly, I've not been paying enough attention, too occupied by a certain brunette to realize just how deeply brainwashed my brother is.

"The stuff that Father made you do…" I start, leaning my forearms on my knees. "That keep you up at night?"

He sends me a sideways glance. "I'm not actually a homicidal sociopath, so…"

"Why'd you do it?"

For several moments, he remains silent. Crickets sing their nightly tune, the sound carrying across the cobblestone and catching on the woods behind the apartment complex.

"I don't know," he admits finally. "Father made the Andersons sound so dangerous to Fury Hill as a whole and cited that stupid fucking curse over and over. Said it was my duty to the family to eradicate them. I guess I didn't ask enough questions. I just wanted what he said to be true."

A kid who trusts his father implicitly *wouldn't* ask any questions, and I'm certain that's what Jean-Louis was banking on when he roped Beckett in.

If you only see the world through one lens growing up, you might not know there are other ways to view it.

All the founding families raise their new generations to fear three things: outsiders, the Anderson bloodline, and change. They push the importance and superiority of Fury Hill lineage in order to keep people in line—an agenda supported and enforced by Death's Teeth in the background through whatever means necessary.

Without those power dynamics, the founding families would cease to matter. Avernia would be just like every other prestigious school in the country, and maybe fewer students would wind up dead each semester.

Maybe my sister would be alive.

"None of it means anything now anyway," he continues. "Mother thinks I should be institutionalized, you're livid with me, and Father is moving forward with things as if I did nothing last semester at all."

"I'm not livid with you," I say softly, though the last part of his confession sends an uncomfortable chill through me. "But what do you mean Father's going forward with things?"

"Didn't he come see you when he was on campus?"

"He didn't mention anything about plans." I release a long breath. "What was he doing here when you saw him?"

"Fuck if I know. He didn't tell me anything either, just made me help him walk around because he can barely do it himself. Dean Bauer was foaming at the mouth, though, so I'm sure that's not a good sign."

My stomach churns, nausea erupting in the cavity.

"He knows there are three Andersons here," he says, glancing at me. "We ran into that girl—the student, whatever her name is?"

"You had a thing for her brother but don't know her name?"

"I thought Asher was hot and wanted to fuck him. I didn't feel the need to learn his entire family history. The dean introduced her to Father, so I'm sure he's in deep shit for allowing them to enroll. Makes me wonder what the plan is." Sighing, he leans back. "Imagine how much simpler things would've been last semester if Asher and his girlfriend had just accepted my offer for a threesome."

"Christ." I shoot him a look, scrubbing a cold hand over my face. "I don't get you."

"Not sure you'd want to."

Agony pierces my chest. "Want me to talk to your professors? Get you reenrolled in classes?"

"Nah. You're right. I could use a break. Figure out what I want now that the stuff I *thought* I was planning for is basically unattainable."

"Opportunities do exist outside the Curators, you know. Outside Avernia and Fury Hill, even."

"For you, maybe. You've got acting and directing experience, philanthropic endeavors, and our name under your belt. If I'm excommunicated from the family line, where does that leave me? I can't network with my peers or otherwise, and my friends are…"

Dead.

He doesn't say it, but it's true. Of the three people who died in the caves last semester, two were his Curator underlings—one a Blackwater whom he'd known since they were born.

Founding family kids don't generally make many friends outside the inner circle. Bellamy was an exception—she collected friends like trading cards, soaking up attention and warmth wherever she went.

Like Beckett, I was mostly isolated, aside from Zachary Westwood and my twin. When the latter died, the former moved out west, and it was as if my world had crumbled too.

Here I thought getting involved with the underbelly of founder shit would be enough to protect my brother from a similar fate, but it's clear now that I've been neglecting him in the process.

No wonder Jean-Louis reached him so easily.

It's my fault. Again.

"Anyway. It's not a big deal," Beckett tells me. "I've got a couple of online classes that shifted because there weren't enough students enrolled, so I'll just focus on finishing the program so I can get my degree at the end of the year. Don't worry about me, Sutty. I'll be just fine."

"I have to worry," I reply, flicking the back of his head. "You're kind of a fucking mess."

He smirks, almost looking like the old Beckett for a split second. "Oh, you should be worried…just not about me."

Chapter 25

Elle

"SO SCHOOL IS GOING WELL? NOTHING ODD TO REPORT? NO kidnappings or violence?"

Mom's voice has its usual soft tone, though I can sense the worry even through the phone.

While she talks, I notice Quincy's brown cardigan is unraveling at the sleeve. As she leans forward, picking up the mug of steaming hot tea on the study table between us, the fraying fabric catches my attention and refuses to let go.

She could sew it or at least roll the sleeve up, but instead she pretends she doesn't notice. I try to look away, glaring at the astronomy textbook in my lap.

Apparently, dissatisfied with my weekly updates, Mom and Dad called Quincy and forced her to corner me in the Obeliskos for more. Luckily, we're in a corner far from listening ears, but I'm still trying to keep from talking too loud.

I don't need anyone knowing I still check in with my parents, or that they require it.

Mom rattles off more questions, and I imagine her standing in front of the kitchen sink at the Asphodel wringing her hands together. She's probably staring out the window at the beach behind the house and the endless rows of rosebushes and hydrangeas that Aunt Violet has helped her cultivate over the years, since Mom sorely lacks a green thumb and Violet owns a flower shop near the marina.

"Do you realize how weird that is to ask your child?" I ask when she finally pauses for a breath, forcing my gaze away from Quincy's cardigan. "No kidnappings or violence at *school*?"

"What's weird is that you didn't automatically answer."

"If you don't satisfy her curiosity, she's gonna crash your party," Violet says from somewhere in the background.

"Trust me, she's got a bag packed," Aunt Cora chimes in, sounding slightly farther away. "And if she goes, I have to go. Those are the rules now that Asher and Lucy are living together."

"Please. Those have always been the rules with you two. Then you drag me and Wolfe along." Dad's voice hovers close to the phone, and I imagine he's bending down to kiss Mom's forehead or smell her or whatever other weird gesture he has to do.

When I was growing up, they were always touching in some way, whether it was the brush of their pinkies or him slipping an arm around her waist or pulling her into an alcove for a kiss. And it wasn't just my parents. All the adult couples in our lives seemed so deeply, madly, incandescently in love that I spent half my life sick with envy and wondering when my time would come.

I wanted someone to look at me the way my dad looks at my mom—like she's hung the sun in the sky with her bare hands and is the sole reason he's alive.

"In almost three decades, I've never heard either of you complain," Cora says. "Vi, on the other hand…"

"Because you're always ditching me," Violet huffs. "My own brother, leaving me to fend for myself. Be glad he's your father and not a different relative, Noelle, because the dynamic matters."

I smile to myself. The main reason our family extends so far beyond blood relations is because of the connections my dad has and how secretly soft he is. Sure, Mom is the glue holding everyone together, but they were caught and adopted by him.

A former Mafia physician. I guess when you've seen the things he has, maybe you'd want to spend the rest of your life surrounded by goodness.

"Anyway," Mom says, and the background noise falls quiet. "So things are okay, my love? When you enrolled, you still seemed a little…off, so I'm just trying to make sure that school isn't making things worse. It's an odd place."

"Odd being the operative word," Dad adds, and I wonder if she has me on speaker. "You know the deal, Noelle. The slightest hint of a problem—"

"And I call you to come get the three of us," I finish, looking at Quincy again as she continues reading, pretending she isn't listening. And that I'm not lying. "I know. And if I do anything to jeopardize my safety or Asher's or Quincy's, you cut me out of the inheritance."

"Kallum," Mom chides. "We didn't discuss that as a punishment."

"There had to be something at stake, little one," he tells her. "But it won't be an issue either way. Right, Noelle?"

My heart thumps idly inside my chest, and I gnaw on the corner of my lip. I should tell him about the cloaked figures I saw in the Primordial Forest. I should warn him that this school is a lot stranger than he probably realizes, since Quincy's admitted to keeping the truth from them.

But if I do, he'll pull us out of Fury Hill faster than we can collectively blink, and I'm not ready to leave. Going back to my parents' house already proves what I fear most: that I'm not ready to be out on my own and not cut out for the real world.

Hollywood didn't want me. Fury Hill probably wants me dead. Sure, those are only two places in the entire world, but to me, it's starting to feel like I'm not destined to get anything I want.

"Right," I tell him, even as the dishonesty makes my throat constrict.

We hang up not long after that, exchanging a few more uncomfortable pleasantries, though it's hard to tell if that was my issue or if they could feel it too.

"You're being weird." Quincy interrupts my thoughts without glancing up from the *Botany of Empire* book balanced on her leg.

"Yeah, well, you're always weird."

"Good to see Avernia's done wonders for your rebuttal skills."

I make a face. "I'm not looking to become the next debate team captain."

"Right, that would be beneath you."

Something about her tone causes me to bristle. I sit up straight, my defensive walls rising. We've not spoken much since the day in the Apollodorus basement, and it's clear there's been tension from the moment I arrived in Fury Hill, but the blatant digs feel more serious than before.

"What's your problem, Q?"

"I don't have one. I'm just making conversation." A long pause ensues, and she sighs. "How're classes?"

"Fine."

"Good." She taps her fingers together. "Have you thought about joining any clubs or organizations? The Daughters of Persephone has an opening, if you're interested."

Disgust pulls my mouth taut. "I don't think campus beautification is something I'd be very passionate about as a long-term goal."

"Then what *is* your goal? I thought you wanted to come here to be closer to me, or Asher, or even Lucy, but now I'm not so sure." She purses her lips. "Why Avernia of all places?"

"Why does everyone keep asking me that?"

"Most people would see death and curses and run the other way. Yet you ran toward."

"I guess I'm not most people."

"No, you're not. I used to like that about you—how free and unrestrained you were, especially with your time and emotions. You loved acting, but it wasn't something that translated to real life. You used to be honest to a fault, yet I just watched you flat out lie to our parents."

"*You* admitted you've been lying to them about the degree of danger around here. Did you want me to tell them the truth?"

"There are responsibilities—" She blinks, cutting herself off and snapping her mouth shut. A few students near the desktop computers at the far end of the lobby glance over, disturbed by the raised volume of her voice. "Not everything is as cut-and-dried as you believe, Noelle. Some of us can't afford to be truthful."

Hurt clouds my chest. "What's going on with you? This place… You're different."

She scoffs. "You mean I've changed in the ten years since I left home? Shocking stuff, truly. And you're one to talk. After seven years of you hardly ever visiting and rarely speaking to us unless we called first, you just gave up on your dreams completely? I find it suspicious. What happened to you in California?"

"Nothing." Irritation flexes in my fingers, making them rigid. As if she didn't make me participate in the torching of the dean's house before the start of the semester, showing that I'm not the only one of us who's changed. "It's none of your business."

"Did nothing happen, or is it none of my business? Can't have it both ways."

No, and apparently I can't have it *my* way either when my big sister is a know-it-all who can't let shit go.

"There used to be this light in your eyes…" she says, cocking her head to one side as she studies me, like I'm some plant she's trying to determine the life cycle of. A specimen with quality issues she needs to inspect and fix. An ancient text she can't quite translate.

"Everything is fine, Q. Pinkie swear." I hold my hand up in offering.

She gives me a long look but eventually exhales and leans forward, hooking her finger around mine. For the briefest moment, we're little kids again, promising to keep each other's secrets.

As I discreetly unlink my middle and index fingers on my free hand, I note that I used to keep them crossed back then too.

"Hey, Elle!" Lexington shouts from the back of the Obeliskos. He waves, and out pop Percy and Meg from behind him. "Do you want to run lines for *Othello* auditions with us?"

Shoving my books into my backpack, I sling the strap over my shoulder and stand up. Quincy stares straight ahead as if I'm still sitting.

"What were you doing in Professor Dupont's office that one day?"

She glances up at me, narrowing her eyes. "Why do you care?"

"Do you like him?"

"Again—why do you care?" She stares for several beats, then clears her throat. "You know you can't sleep with him."

"Who said I wanted to?"

"Noelle."

"It's a fair question, I think. I'd hate for your relationship to interfere with my grades."

"I wouldn't let that happen."

Swallowing, I wait for her to elaborate. Quincy's always preferred girls to guys, but sexuality is fluid and personal. None of us kids are straight, mostly identifying somewhere between bisexuality and pansexuality with caveats in between, but I'm not exactly sure where she falls on the spectrum currently. She *has* dated men, so I can't put it past her to be involved with Sutton.

Maybe it's delusion talking, considering how strict he seems when it comes to school relations, or maybe I'm just a jealous bitch. I don't know.

I just don't want her to want him. Or vice versa.

My whole childhood was already spent in her shadow, where I so desperately craved to be like her or to be liked by her. I don't want that pattern following me eternally in adulthood too.

"Faculty can't have romantic or sexual connections," she says after a moment.

"Oh."

"And honestly, I barely know the guy. He was behind me in undergrad, and despite what you might believe, classics and theater majors don't really cross over much. Plus, there's the whole thing with that family curse, and his sister's death—"

Something cold fills my chest. "His what?"

"His twin sister died when he was a sophomore, I think? I can't remember the exact year anymore, but it really threw Avernia for a loop since it was the first on-campus death in decades. I didn't know who Sutton was until that point, and suddenly he was just *everywhere*, thrust into the spotlight." Quincy cocks her head, thinking. "Or maybe that's just when I started paying attention. I don't know."

Guilt pricks at the surface of my skin. Is *that* why he feels such a deep connection to this place?

If my ghosts are faceless, I can't imagine how difficult it must be to navigate life when you recognize the ones haunting you.

"Elle! Come on!" Lexington shouts again, earning dirty looks from a few people studying toward the front of the building.

Even though I want to probe Quincy about Sutton more, I leave her sitting there before Percy—whose face is a bright red, embarrassment clear on his cheeks—bursts a blood vessel.

I power walk across the floor, then follow the three of them to a glass room past the main staircase. They've pushed all the furniture back against the windows and have a circle of couch cushions set up in the center.

"Thank God," Meg says as I enter, tossing my bag to the floor. She fixes the brakes on her chair, shaking her head. "These two know *nothing* about auditions. I'm starting to fear for their grades in Dupont's class."

"You're just now worrying about that?" I snort, grateful for the distraction these three provide. "I could've told you ages ago that one's failing for *sure*." I point at Percy as he bends over, cuffing his loose-fitting jeans.

"Hey," he says, frowning at me from upside down. "I've aced all my essays so far, thank you."

"And the performance element?" Lexington questions.

"This is an elective *beginner* course, so I don't see why we have to get judged on that ability," Percy continues, unwrapping a green scarf from around his neck. "Shouldn't grades be based on our improvements over the semester?"

"Good luck convincing Professor Hard-Ass of that. You know he thinks everyone should be great right off the bat. That's why you have to audition for a seat anyway." Meg wiggles her eyebrows at them, then looks to me. "Though I guess Elle kind of bypassed that requirement."

Percy huffs, straightening. "Founders get all the favors."

"Do you want pointers or not?" I ask, wagging a finger at him.

He drops to his knees at my feet, clasping his hands together in a gesture of prayer. "Yes, please."

I giggle. "Men who beg rank high on my list, but I'm not sure how the professor will feel about it."

"Word on the street is he likes to do the begging," Meg notes. We all glance at her, and she pushes a braid off her shoulder, holding her phone up. "What? That's what *The Delphic Pages* says. Don't shoot the messenger."

I snatch the phone from her, peering at the screen. A picture of Sutton standing behind a partially drawn red curtain, mouth open as he says something to the people onstage, populates beneath Pythia's account.

My stomach grows heavy at the sight of him in directorial mode: Even from the still, it's clear that he's a firm, determined visionary. You can see it in his eyes and the hard set of his jaw—he *loves* what he does.

Beneath the photo in bold lettering, a caption states: SUTTON DUPONT PLEADS FOR MORE EMOTION FROM HIS ACTORS DURING THE FALL PRODUCTION OF MACBETH.

I make a face at Meg, passing her phone back. "That proves nothing."

She smirks. "Yet you practically broke your neck looking for the evidence. You so have the hots for our teacher."

"Are we going to start rehearsing soon or just spend our afternoon drooling over a robot?" Lexington quips, walking over with his hands on his hips.

"What, you don't see the appeal?" Percy asks, throwing an arm over his shoulder.

Lexington rolls his eyes. "Of course I do. I'm not dead—the man's gorgeous. But he also holds our fate in his hands, so I just think we should take that into consideration. We *barely* scraped by our auditions to get into the class, you know, P."

"Not me," Meg notes, lifting her chin with a grin. "My parents own a few community theaters from here to Concord, though, so I guess it's sort of baked in."

"Yeah, yeah, you're perfect," Lexington says, grinning. He slides out from Percy's grip, bending down to press a dramatic, sloppy kiss to her forehead. "But some of us aren't, so…"

He gestures toward the circle, and she laughs, nodding. "First point of order: loosening your lips and limbs."

"You should also be properly hydrated," I say, turning toward the door. "Anyone want something to drink?"

They decline, so I head down the hall by myself to the vending machines tucked next to an emergency exit. On my way back, plastic bottle in hand, I pause in the partially open doorway of a private study room, drawn to a stop at the sound of a familiar voice.

Sutton stands at the front of the room, surrounded by a wall of students. Most of them have jackets with a torch emblem printed on the back, and they all seem enraptured by the discussion he's leading.

"...once auditions have finished, we'll only have a few short weeks to prep for the production," he tells the students. "Volunteering is optional, but keep in mind I'm more likely to write recommendation letters for prospective internships and employment opportunities when you help out. We'll need set designers, costume coordinators, and the like."

There at the front, a familiar blond ponytail sways. "What about refreshments and lighting crews?"

"I'll let you handle refreshments this time, Sabrina," Sutton tells her. "The bloody-heart cookies you made for *Macbeth* were inspired and went over really well with the cast. I trust your baking ability."

Sabrina. Jesus, does she ever let the man breathe?

Though I guess I can't really talk.

Even that first night at Lethe's, there was this fine tether drawing me to him. As soon as I spotted him at the bar, I couldn't look away.

It was as though I unconsciously thought that doing so would cause him to vanish, like water vapor into the air.

The sensation was unlike anything I'd ever felt before. A temptation so strong that resistance was instantly pointless, even when he was rejecting me.

My mind flickers to Quincy's revelation about his sister, and I feel that familiar twinge in my chest.

Here I've been treating his employment as some throwaway thing, selfishly chasing my own gratification because he was lying about what he wanted. But what if the job is an excuse for him elsewhere?

Leaning on the doorframe, I lift my chin, scouring the heads of the students as they disperse, a few arguing about some canned-food drive. The room becomes obscured, and I search for the mess of dark brown hair or his sweater—

"Visio Aternae meetings are private."

Chapter 26

Elle

Sutton's voice is suddenly in my ear, nearly yanking a scream from my chest. I whirl around, my breath scattering in my throat as he moves in, planting his arm next to me.

He hovers close, our lips centimeters apart, and a flash from the day I begged him to kiss me in his apartment makes my stomach flutter.

With a quick tug, he pulls the door shut and backs up several steps.

I blink, glancing at his arm, which was just by my side and now rests at his. His face isn't flushed, and his eyes aren't that liquid green they only seem to become when we're doing things we shouldn't.

"You shouldn't sneak up on girls," I snap, pointing at him. "It's creepy."

"My apologies. I didn't mean to scare you."

The instant sincerity is disconcerting. My hand falls, and I clear my throat, trying to regain my bearings. "Well, announce yourself next time or something."

"It's not my fault you weren't paying attention."

"Most people don't think they're going to be accosted in the library."

He clicks his tongue. "Still haven't read up on your Avernia lore, I see. Am I to assume you don't have a warding amulet or salt packed in your pockets?"

"Uh…no."

"Pity. A sweet soul like yours would be candy to the spirits around here." He steps forward with one foot.

Pressing my back against the door, I try to shrink into myself, just so I can avoid that enticing scent of his. He normally isn't the one to initiate closeness, so his proximity is unnerving.

"Sweet?" I squeak. "That's a new one."

"You disagree with my assessment?"

"Normally you hit the mark pretty easily, but if you think sweet is a word to describe me, I'm afraid you must not be looking close enough," I reply, my gaze settling on the tendons in his throat, straining against his skin.

For some reason, the urge to bite them is strong.

I resist, even as he draws nearer.

"On the contrary," he says, dropping his voice. "All I do is look at you. For you. To you. It's become a real problem."

He leans in again, bracing his forehead against the door above me. Our bodies are inches apart, our clothes brushing, the heat from our skin mingling.

What is happening here?

My mind swims, the sting of his previous rejection still fresh enough for me not to trust whatever this is. Even if my body is on board with little protest.

"Well, I bet it's one you can easily take care of." I push up on my tiptoes, letting my lips graze his ear. "I hope you think of me later when you do."

His breathing hitches, but he seems to shake from the reverie, moving just out of my reach. It's almost a respectable distance, probably nothing that would alarm anyone *too* much if they wandered this way.

"Why are you here?" he asks.

"Uh, it's a campus library. I'm a student. Do the math, Professor."

"Right, right. Of course." He blows out a breath, and a part of me wonders if he isn't sure what to do or why he cornered me in the first place. "Well, what are you studying or reading? What, um, else interests you outside acting?"

My eyes narrow. "Are you trying to flirt again?"

"That you have to ask tells me I'm still not doing it right."

The glaring discomfort of his is satisfying. "Flirting requires levity. Humor. Shallow waters. Not minute detail."

"But I'm not interested in the surface when it comes to you."

Oh. My heart hammers faster in my chest. "Is that a casting tactic ahead of auditions or a personal agenda?"

"Personal." He presses his mouth into a thin line. "I'd like to figure you out."

"I thought you wanted nothing to do with me."

"Never said that."

"There's that honesty again, Boy Scout."

"It seems you bring it out in me."

"Can I ask what you're doing?" I jut my chin over my shoulder at the door. "Here, right now... Why are you talking to me? Aren't you afraid someone might see and get the wrong idea?"

"If I tell you, will you stop answering my questions with more questions?"

"I'll consider it."

The corner of his mouth tugs upward. His voice drops to a near-whisper when he speaks again. "I feel bad about the way we ended things in my apartment."

"When you turned down my offer for sex?"

He glances down the hall, then back at me. "Did that really need clarifying?"

As if we aren't standing too close for comfort as it is.

"Maybe not, but it was worth seeing you get all flustered."

His cheeks brighten with a blush. "That excites you?"

"I like that you sometimes don't seem to know what you want to do with me," I admit, even though I shouldn't. This is the opposite of how I wanted to approach things. "It's cute."

He huffs, as if that notion displeases him, then shakes his head. "You…challenge me," he says softly. "In a way no one has before, and I realized I may have been reacting poorly to this entire situation based on my own hang-ups."

My eyebrows arch. "So you thought you'd correct course in the middle of the Obeliskos?"

"Strike when the iron is hot, right?"

"You really do love clichés, don't you?" I grin, then chew on my bottom lip, the guilt from before pushing up into my esophagus. "Really, though, I should be the one apologizing—"

"Ah, ah." He shushes me, holding a finger close to my mouth without actually touching me. "You promised an answer to my question. What are you studying today?"

Again, I feel a strange tugging deep within my chest, but I ignore it. "Astronomy. Outside of the two acting electives I have this semester, it's probably my favorite. I was working on an assignment before with my sister. Well, she was here. Not helping me though."

Sutton laughs, which startles me. *Have I ever heard him do that before?* "Of course you're interested in the stars. Like calls to like, right?"

"Are you calling me a star?"

"I'm saying you want to be." He shrugs. "What better element to study than the ones so many look to for answers?"

This Sutton freaks me out. His unabashed interest feels like a major shift, even though I know he's far from done denying me. But as if he's also fighting an internal war against desire and logic, here he remains.

"Well, I spent a lot of my childhood camped out with my dad and uncles, trying to find and name different constellations. They'd tell me all the mythologies behind them and how so many people in history have used the stars to map out their explanations of the world or guide them through life. I like the idea of an ocean of knowledge just sort of existing up there for us to utilize."

"I see." He moves close again, making me dizzy. "That's why you were at the observatory that day. Have you been back?"

A custodian wheels a trash can past the hall toward a service elevator, their whistling causing both of us to freeze. My heart pounds in my throat, the threat of being caught—even though we're not actually doing anything—sending goose bumps along my arms.

The custodial worker doesn't stop or even look in our direction, though, so neither of us moves.

"A few times. I like going when it's closed. Makes it easier to study," I tell him. "But mostly I've been occupied with transitioning back into school. Turns out a lot changes in seven years."

"You didn't take any courses when you were out in LA at all?"

"Nope. I was really hoping I wouldn't need them. But you know, everyone out there is talented. It's a hard scene to break into." My face grows warm, shame coloring my cheeks.

Sutton purses his lips, then nods. "If not for my family connections, I doubt I'd have had much luck scoring professional gigs."

The mention of his family makes my skin crawl, but I don't say anything.

Instead, I scoff. "Please, you're insanely hot. At the very least, you could have modeled."

He makes a face, glancing at one end of the hall as if checking to make sure no one's coming. The blush returns to his cheeks, and I wish I could snap a photo of it for later.

"Not my thing," he replies. "If I'm going to be perceived, I'd like to be wearing someone else's skin for a bit."

"How very Ed Gein of you."

Another laugh, rich and throaty, erupts from him. "I knew as soon as I thought the words that you'd say something to that effect. I'd much rather not be associated with a real-life serial killer though. Can't we call me Titus Andronicus or something?"

"Are you eating your roles?"

"Hm. I suppose, in a way, there is a degree of consumption when you play someone else. Internalizing their struggles, finding what makes them human, and digesting their flaws so you can present them to the audience… One could argue that's a simulation of eating."

My face screws up. "That might be the grossest way anyone's ever described acting."

"Innovation, my dear séductrice, is half the battle." He grins, and it feels so out of place that I get a little dizzy staring at the curve of his mouth. After a moment, he clears his throat, rocking back on his heels. "So you've been studying with your sister?"

That familiar pang of jealousy pulses in my heart when he mentions her. "Well, no. I left her to prep for *Othello* auditions."

"With your classmates?"

Once more, the air around us changes, turning a bit darker. Headier. I shift in anticipation. "Maybe."

"Which ones?"

"Is this a conversation you really want to have here?"

"Just answer the question."

"Why does it matter?" I swallow, emotion clogging my throat. "Are you jealous?"

His jaw clenches. "Lexington and Perciville. Are they here with you today?"

"And what if I say yes? That we've skipped studying altogether, and I've just come from a superhot threesome to get a drink, but I'm heading right back in to start up again. Obviously, you know the rumors, and I've thrown myself at you multiple times, so clearly I can't keep my legs closed at all—"

He covers my mouth with his palm, cutting me off. The water bottle falls from my grasp, tumbling to the floor. "You are incredibly, *ridiculously* brazen, temptress, but that is not what I said, nor what I implied."

I roll my eyes, moving to escape, but he grabs my hip with his free hand, keeping me in place.

"It simply agitates me the way they're able to spend time with you. And yes, I know that is a line I've drawn, but it drives me *mad* to be relegated to stolen glances, pretending I don't care…fucking my fist at night, desperately wishing it was that insolent mouth of yours. All while they can interact freely."

Warmth spreads through my limbs. He slowly withdraws his other hand from my lips.

"After the incident in my apartment, I know I have no right to be standing here even saying any of this…"

"I don't mind."

A smarter, stronger girl wouldn't let him see her cards so readily, but I've never been very good at resistance anyway.

He tucks some hair behind my ear, his gaze softening a little. "What is this spell you've cast on me? Why can't I get you out of my head, no matter how many times I remind myself that you're poison to my life?"

"Some poison in moderation won't kill you," I whisper.

Shaking his head, he makes an irritated noise. "I don't want just a taste…or a bite…" His nose skims mine as he bends, and my stomach flips violently.

"Doesn't this go against everything you've been saying since I showed up on the first day of classes?" I ask softly.

"It does."

I squirm, glancing down the hall. *If somebody sees…* "Sutton, maybe we shouldn't—"

"Now you care?"

It's a similar question to what he asked me that evening in the basement of the Apollodorus, and I'm still not sure what exactly has changed. He was *just* rejecting me in his apartment, *wasn't he?*

"Are you finally admitting out loud that you don't?"

"Don't pretend you ever bought my excuses in the first place."

"Verbal confirmation is always a good thing."

"I can't stop thinking about you," he rushes out. "Right now, that's all I know."

My heart hammers in my throat, but I force my gaze away. "I don't want you to hate me."

"That's not possible."

The air around me dries up as he palms the back of my head with one hand. The other gently—*so gently*—brushes my chin.

He leans in, and I barely have time to process what's happening before his lips are on mine, damp and soft and lush as they mold against me. Like they were made to connect, to crush, to explore. My heart ricochets around in my chest, making me dizzy as heat races through my veins.

Every nerve ending in my body is on fire as he flicks his tongue against the seam of my mouth, seeking entry.

Even though I know I shouldn't, I let him in. I fold instantly, letting out a ragged breath when his tongue breaches the depths of my mouth, sweeping and tasting as if this could be his very last meal. Or maybe it's his first. A drop of water after an eternity of thirst.

His kiss obliterates all my concerns from before, shattering my attempts at resolve. This isn't the kiss of a man who's afraid someone might see or who's really afraid of losing his career. It's the kiss of a man who knows what he wants and goes after it. Who'll fight for his right to embrace passion.

It's the kiss of a man asking—no, *begging*—for more.

Distantly, the sound of a door clicking shut, followed by the clearing of a throat, yanks me from the moment. I jolt back to reality, disentangling myself with more effort than I've ever exerted in my entire life.

"Sutton…"

"Christ." Pulling away, he threads his fingers through his hair, tugging on the roots. "I know." Blowing out a breath, he spins around in a circle.

I don't move a muscle.

"I'd better get back," he mutters, his spine stiff, eyes on my lips.

He wipes his mouth but doesn't leave. There's a clear hunger in his gaze. A request for a repeat, damn the consequences.

Swallowing my feelings, I duck my head and go back to the study room where Lexington and Percy are now arm-wrestling on their stomachs on the floor. Still shaky from the entire thing, I walk over and take a seat next to Meg, who lets out an excited shout at my return.

"Thank *God*. These two have the attention span of hamsters." She frowns, glancing down. "Did you not have enough money for the vending machines?"

"Aw, poor Elle," Lexington calls, leaning up to try and leverage his weight against Percy. "We could've given you some cash."

Confusion knits my brows together, and I look at my hands—which are empty.

"Oh." I force a laugh and press my fingers to my tingling lips, shaking my head. "No, no, I just…wasn't thirsty anymore."

Chapter 27

Sutton

QUINCY ANDERSON TAPS HER FINGERS ON THE EDGE OF HER desk, as if uncomfortable with my very presence despite us having interacted several times previously this semester.

The look she gives makes me feel like a nuisance, and I wonder if this is standard. If she regards Elle like a bug on the bottom of her shoe and that's where the tension between them comes to a head.

It's one thing to tell your sibling you don't believe in them and a whole different one to look at them like you don't.

Still, I need her help, so I don't let her disdain intimidate me.

"I'm not sure I'm qualified to assist you with auditions for a play," Quincy notes after a long moment. "I'd suggest asking someone else."

"Aren't you the head of the classics department? Who could be more qualified?"

She pushes her glasses up the bridge of her nose, sitting back in her fluffy, rolling desk chair. Her entire office is covered in potted plants, some flowering and some just boring old leaves, which makes the floral aroma a bit overwhelming. I rub my nose with my knuckles, trying to dislodge the sudden itch to sneeze.

"Don't you think there's a huge difference between studying the classics and performing them?" she asks, her dark eyes searching mine. "Otherwise, why would we have separate departments at all?"

"Studying them should be the precursor to performance," I tell her, pointing at the copies of *The Iliad* and *The Aeneid* on the corner of her desk. "Acting is all about interpretation, and you can't really do that without understanding the texts you're trying to pull from. Thus, I think you'd be a great co-casting director."

"I don't know, Sutton. Shakespeare's a little different from Homer, and it feels like a conflict of interest." She shifts, glancing at the books. Quincy Anderson might be the only person on this campus more interested in the rules than I am.

"Given how highly Dean Bauer regards you, I find it difficult to believe you'd allow personal relationships to tie in whatsoever with your decision-making."

"The dean doesn't really like me," she says. "I know you're not dumb enough to believe his blustering, especially after what happened in the fall."

"How he really feels hardly matters if he's willing to pretend, right?"

"I suppose, but how long does that last?" She lifts a shoulder, shrugging. "Avernia's hanging by a very thin thread, if you ask me. Your sister's death was just the tip of the iceberg."

That stirs unease within my muscles, and they tense up. "Bellamy's death was an accident."

"Officially." She meets my gaze. "*Some* have suggested otherwise, and after what your brother pulled last semester, I'm inclined to believe it."

I say nothing.

"You don't have to agree out loud. I'm not usually wrong."

"It is what it is."

"Doesn't have to be," she says.

"What's that supposed to mean?"

"That not everyone is as comfortable letting a town curse and corruption from the founding families run rampant as you are. I know you were born into this world, so it's probably difficult to see a way out, but…I wasn't. I came here voluntarily."

"Do you stay voluntarily?" I ask, though I can already guess the answer.

No one around here talks about Avernia's underbelly unless they know too much.

Too much to be allowed to leave quietly.

I imagine it's why she's still here despite her brother's brush with death. Why she came back after graduating and, according to Pythia, swearing off this place entirely.

Death's Teeth or not, once Avernia sinks its claws into a person, it doesn't easily let go.

Quincy leans back in her chair, glancing at *The Iliad* and *The Aeneid*. "My sister gifted those books to me for my high school graduation. Mint condition, rare antiques she haggled with at least three collectors over because she knew I loved the stories."

Shit. I don't want to talk about Elle right now. She's the main reason I'm here, begging for a fucking buffer. After kissing her in the Obeliskos the other day, the feel of her lips on mine is the only thing I've been able to think about, and I know that if I'm left to my own devices with her, I'll start obliterating every line and boundary.

And though I want to, I also want to respect her wishes. I don't want her to feel like she's coerced me into something, especially when it's clear she's hiding things from her past that make her the way she is.

I don't care about the substance of the rumors, but I care if they've done irreparable harm to the woman I can't stop thinking about.

Which is why I'm hoping her sister's presence at auditions might cool her off a bit.

"That was kind of her," I offer.

"Noelle is kind," Quincy says. "Her temper sometimes obscures it, but she's kind, talented, and smart. Resilient to an absolute fault. I used to get so annoyed with her when we were younger because she told our parents *everything*, and I locked my secrets up in a vault like I was afraid they'd be used against me." She lets out a small laugh, shaking her head. "Which was ridiculous, because our parents aren't the type. They always trusted us, and Noelle trusted them."

I cross my arms over my chest, listening.

"When I came to Avernia... I was lacking something within, you know? It felt like something fundamental was missing, and I would look at Asher, who marched to the beat of his own drum with his drawings and obsession with his best friend, and I'd look at Noelle, who *loved* performing and being around people, and I'd feel defective somehow, because I preferred being alone. I didn't like to talk, didn't go out much... It felt like I didn't know who I was, so I thought maybe looking into my family history would fix that."

"It didn't?"

"No, it did. But I couldn't stop thinking about the look on Noelle's face when I left, like I was abandoning her. She'd been like a shadow to me, always wanting to go where I went with friends, borrowing my clothes even when they weren't her style, begging me to go to rehearsals or run lines with her. And when I left, she seemed so *horrified*, I almost didn't go at all. She had no filter, and I was witnessing my first best friend's heartbreak in real time. I didn't know what to do with it though. I'm not great at dealing with others' emotions."

I'm not sure why she's telling me this, but still, I don't try to stop her. Apparently, those Anderson girls have more in common when it comes to word vomit than they seem to realize.

"Anyway, my bright idea was to try and push her away, hoping it would hurt less when I didn't come back. I was pretty awful to her and said a bunch of things I didn't mean about her wanting a career in Hollywood." Quincy frowns, glaring at a worn spot in her desk. "I said I didn't think she could make it and that they'd chew her up and spit her out. It wasn't something I believed, I just… I don't know. It was a stupid attempt at keeping her at bay, because something in me said she'd follow me here if I didn't."

Pain seizes my chest, the conversation a near mirror to a similar one I had with Bellamy before we enrolled at Avernia.

I knew, even before we were students, that nothing good awaited us here. I tried so hard to keep her from doing it anyway, but she didn't listen.

She never listened.

Even now, I've been doing something similar with Elle.

"When I learned she'd moved out to LA anyway, I was so happy, but then she showed up here and she's just so different. Gone is the bright-eyed open book I grew up wanting to throttle, and in her place is a woman I barely recognize half the time. She won't tell any of us what happened to send her back to our parents last summer, but it's obvious *something* did. And I can't help feeling responsible for it."

"Okay…"

"My point is," she continues, pressing her index finger into the top of a book, "if you're trying to recruit me because you've crossed the line with her, you're going to have to find help elsewhere. I'm not going to help ruin something she loves. Not again."

A pit opens up in my stomach. "Why would you assume—"

"She might be different, but I *know* my sister. She's all those things I say, but her resilience often comes at the price of her own self-worth and others' sanity. Her being here is a step in the right direction, and I don't want her feelings or lust or whatever it is she might have going on get in the way of that. Not when there's enough moving in the shadows for her to deal with in the first place."

Swallowing, I force my head from side to side. "That's not it at all. My co-casting director went on sabbatical, and I just need someone to fill in. I can't handle auditions on my own, and I know you did some theater work as an undergrad, so this just made the most sense."

She stares at me for a long, tense moment. Nausea rolls through me, making my muscles tighten. *Can she see through me like her sister?*

"Well, if you want my assistance because you think I'd be a good addition, then I'll join you."

Chapter 28

Elle

"I KNOW IT'S WRONG AND WE COULD BOTH LOSE OUR SPOTS here," I say, pacing a dent in the carpet of the Obeliskos's thirteenth floor, "but it's like there's this insatiable need that just bleeds into my skin every time we're near. I can't stop it, and it doesn't help when he makes it so obvious he wants—"

"Jesus fucking Christ, Noelle," Asher groans into his hands, his head in Lucy's lap where they're sitting on a dark leather couch. Well, she's sitting; he's sprawled out lengthwise. "You have issues with impulse control, we get it. Can you please just let me nap in peace?"

Lucy tsks, pinching his nostrils shut. "You're supposed to be helping me study for this midterm, pretty boy."

"Did you take your ADHD meds this morning?"

"Yes." She releases his nose and pokes the silver hoop piercing one nostril. "Someone never lets me forget on days I have classes."

"Am I supposed to apologize for being helpful?"

She rolls her eyes. "You're not being helpful now."

302 SAV R. MILLER

"How can you even concentrate with my sister's villain monologue going at lightning speed over there?"

I frown, pausing midstep to glare at him. "I'm not a villain."

Asher snorts. "What do you think you are to him, Noelle? The heroine? Aren't they supposed to be selfless and considerate?"

Ugh. I knew I shouldn't have told them anything, but Lucy refused to relinquish me any of the Fury Hill lore or share the periodicals she found last fall unless I told her what was going on with Sutton, and it all just sort of tumbled out.

Asher's right about that much—my impulse control is severely lacking. I shouldn't have allowed him to kiss me at all, but I'm putty any time he looks my way. Even when he's awkward and stumbling over himself to get a point across, I can't help but be drawn to him.

"You're right," I admit, slumping into a chair against the wall. "Maybe I have been a bit of a villain. How do I make up for that?"

"Leave the man alone."

Lucy clicks her tongue. "Don't give advice you wouldn't follow yourself."

"Why not?" Asher grumbles, rolling so he's facing the back of the couch. He wraps his arms around her waist, crawling closer as he buries his face in her stomach. "Isn't that the point of advice? He's a professor, she's a student. End of story."

"I guess he's right. Wow, I don't like saying that twice."

"So don't let him be right." Lucy shrugs. "Asher doesn't know *everything*."

"Hey," he protests, though weakly.

"Plus, the whole professor-student thing doesn't make you incompatible. It just makes the situation forbidden, which makes things *hot*. Some of my favorite reality TV shows revolve around people who aren't supposed to be together but find a way to make it happen."

My stomach flips, a cramp making it seize up. I frown, pulling my legs into the chair, hoping the pressure might help alleviate the onslaught of discomfort.

"You said he likes you too, right? It's not like you're coming on to him out of nowhere."

"No," I agree. "Just after he explained how it'd affect him. God, I'm a bitch, aren't I?"

"Yeah." Lucy grins, lifting one shoulder. "But that's nothing new. You're also a great listener and strong. I didn't have a crush on you growing up for no reason."

Asher grunts, reaching up to slap his palm over her mouth. "Okay, time to go."

I smirk. "Do you feel threatened by me, Ash?"

"Well, apparently you don't always take no for an answer."

"That's not what…" I sigh, trailing off. I have no excuse for the way I've behaved. "I guess I just didn't understand the severity of it all. I thought the rules were more arbitrary suggestions, and he was hyperbolizing the consequences for effect."

I thought he was weaponizing reality to get more from me.

It hadn't occurred to me to care either, which isn't something I'm proud of. But if I didn't care about his job or his feelings, he wouldn't be able to use them against me.

The way his father had used mine over the summer.

"Maybe we should change the subject," Lucy suggests, tossing a leather-bound journal at my feet. "You said you were looking for more Fury Hill lore. That's an old ecosystem major's journal I found last semester while researching for one of my classes. Lots of stuff about the layout of the Primordial Forest, how Lake Lerna was made. They even detail some of the tunnels through the Tenarus cave, though a lot of those entries have water damage."

I flip through the pages, squinting at the chicken scratch writing. "And this helps me how?"

"There's stuff about the curse too," she says. "I don't know. Maybe it won't help at all."

"Do we believe in the curse or not?" I ask.

"Doesn't matter what you believe," Asher replies, sitting up. He drags a hand through his hair, exhaling slowly. "Avernia does, and that's all that matters. They'll do whatever they need to to keep that ridiculous prophecy from coming true. Last semester proved that much, so maybe you should focus more on studying and getting out of here than canoodling with that boring-ass professor."

"He's not boring."

"Half the school is in love with him, you know," Lucy says. "You've got a lot of competition."

Asher gives her a dirty look.

She grins, leaning her head on his shoulder. "Not me of course."

He grumbles something under his breath, but his face softens slightly anyway.

"I'm not trying to be with him," I tell her, my gaze falling to the journal again.

"Then what was the point of all that lamenting?" Asher asks.

"I don't know," I admit. I'm not sure *what* I want, and even if I did know, is it worth ruining our lives over?

Sutton seems to have had a change of heart, but that doesn't change *me*.

Doesn't he know I'm not worth the trouble?

Asher cocks his head to the side, then reaches into his pocket, pulling out a granola bar. He tosses it at my head, and I swing to the side, barely avoiding the hit. "Mom said to make sure you're eating, by the way. She said you looked like you'd lost weight in your last video call, and she was worried. Ballistic, actually, is the better word here. She's terrified of you wasting away at this school, and I don't know why, but for the love of fucking God, don't make me be on the receiving end of her hysteria again."

I smother a grin, leaning down to pick up the bar. She's right—I have lost a pound or two, but that's mostly been from the stress of adjusting to school, not anything to really worry over.

Mostly.

Still, I appreciate Asher for changing the subject.

Chapter 29

Sutton

"YOU WEREN'T KIDDING ABOUT THE SELECTION THIS SEMES-
ter," Quincy mutters, making a note in the journal she cradles
against her tan slacks. "Using auditions as midterms is brutal. I
don't envy you picking Desdemona or Iago."

"I'm thinking Schroeder for him," I tell her, pointing at the pale
kid down front chatting with a couple of Curators.

His brown eyes find mine for a moment, and he gives a slight
smile, clearly still riddled with nerves from his earlier audition.

"He wasn't bad," she agrees, taking a sip of her bottled green
tea. "Although not super villainous. Don't you think that requires
a certain aura?"

"A little coaching would push him over the edge, I bet."

We sit through half a dozen more auditions, each of them worse
than the last. I'm struggling to keep my eyes open when Elle finally
appears at the stage stairs, wearing a brown dress with a cream-
colored, long-sleeved shirt beneath.

Flanked by Meg and Lexington, she giggles at something the

pair says, and I suck in a silent breath against the sight of that smile on her face.

For him of all people.

Shifting in my seat, I watch as she leaves them and takes her spot in the center of the stage.

I don't know why it matters or why my eyes can't help but catalog everything about her—the exact way her hair falls over her shoulders, the neutral expression she maintains, how her chest puffs out proudly when she clasps her hands behind her back, waiting for her cue.

I'm in trouble here.

"Elle Anderson, reading for the part of Desdemona," she announces, the clarity in her voice and its projection more than a little startling. I'm so used to her low rasps and stolen words that this mask is a new one. "'O good Iago, What shall I do to win my lord again? Good friend, go to him; for, by this light of heaven, I know not how I lost him.'"

The blood ceases movement in my veins as her voice, strong and bold, erupts in the auditorium. My pen slips out of my hand as I take her in, admiring the way the stage lights illuminate her silhouette, basking her body in an ethereal glow that adds to the scene.

A hush falls over the audience. It grows so quiet I can hear a drop of water fall off a pipe backstage.

There's no pause needed for adjustment, no warm-up necessary. Elle slips directly into Desdemona's lines as if stepping into her skin. She flips the hair off her shoulder and cuts across the stage, commanding our attention as she continues.

"Here I kneel: If e'er my will did trespass 'gainst his love, either in discourse of thought or actual deed, or that mine eyes, mine ears, or any sense, delighted them in any other form—'"

"Next." I barely manage to squeak out the word, my mouth dry and chafed. She almost doesn't hear me, and I scrub my numb fingers over my pants, trying to regulate my breathing.

Her presence up there—I've never seen anything like it.

She's a breath of fresh air, and I can't keep watching from this distance.

The auditorium falls silent once more. Quincy glances at me.

"Um," Elle says, squinting out at the room. At us. Me. "Is there a problem?"

"I said next," I snap, my fingers trembling slightly. Discomfort burrows in my chest like a breeze caressing bare branches, and I swallow over the sensation, desperate to ignore it. "We've seen all we need to."

"But I didn't get to finish my mono—"

"Everyone got sixty seconds. Yours are up."

Her hands ball into fists at her sides, pink staining her flushed cheeks, and she stomps off the stage. Quincy looks at her watch but doesn't say a word.

Idly, I make notes in my folder about the auditions, scrubbing beneath my chin as Elle's voice travels up the rows of chairs, taunting me.

"—really unfair that you didn't get to finish," Lexington says, his poorly veiled attempt at comfort making my head throb. "You were the best of the class, Elle, honestly. I'd never leave you so... unsatisfied."

She laughs, and when I lift my chin, I curse myself for doing so. She's already staring right at me, awareness radiating from her body. As she smothers a knowing smirk, I break my pencil in half and avert my gaze.

Quincy's stare bores a hole in the side of my face, but I will myself not to take the bait. Fucking Andersons.

Did that kiss really mean so little to her?

My mouth is dry when I get up, dismissing the students for the day. I don't stay to chat with Quincy about the potentials or go over our expectations for set and costume design, instead taking the side door to the theater department and heading for my office.

I'm completely unsurprised when Elle's somehow already there, swinging her legs from my desk, leaning back on her palms. Her hair falls in waves, hovering above an open planner and a jar of highlighters she must have turned over when she hopped up there.

Exhaling, I toss my briefcase onto the green suede chair in the corner of the room and reach for my tie, loosening the knot. "Should you really be in here right now?"

"Well, given you cut my audition short, I thought maybe we could discuss why."

"I heard there was a student waiting for the opportunity to... What was it he said? Leave you satisfied?" Running a hand over my jaw, I round the desk, doing my best to ignore her presence.

"You know, I wouldn't have pinned you as the jealous type when we first met."

"It's not jealousy," I lie, though I'm not sure why. "I'm merely suggesting that perhaps your time would be better spent chasing after people your own age."

"You're two years older than me," she points out. When I cock an eyebrow at her, she shrugs. "Yeah, I was curious, so I looked you up. Physically twenty-seven. Spiritually, I know you're batting one billion. But back to my audition. Did Quincy put you up to this?

310 SAV R. MILLER

Don't think I didn't notice you using her as your co-casting director. She probably wants me to have a nonspeaking part."

I roll my eyes, slotting a folder into place on the wooden organizer sitting on my filing cabinet. "No, your sister didn't put me up to anything. She didn't even want to *be* here, but I managed to convince her to help out since my usual partner is on sabbatical."

"Why her?" Elle's voice grows small, and she toys with her choker, looking down. "Why are you always running to *her*?"

"Because, Elle!" I throw my hands into the air, exasperation coloring my tone and making me dizzy. *How does she not get this?* "I don't... Have you ever considered that maybe I gravitate toward her to get to know you better?"

She narrows her eyes. "Quincy doesn't know anything about me."

"That's not true, and you know it." I meet her gaze. "You think nobody notices you unless you're on a stage putting on a performance, but some of us are still watching even after the mask comes off and the curtain falls, Elle. Some of us like what's underneath *more*."

She purses her pretty pink lips, tilting her head. I bend down to the minifridge beneath the desk and take out a water bottle, unscrewing the cap and downing a drink. The bottle crinkles with the sudden loss of fluid, and I pull off with a gasp, unaware of how parched I was.

A metaphor if ever there was one.

Elle tracks the movement of my hand as I drag the back of it across my mouth. "How come you never drink?"

"What?"

"Well, the night I met you at Lethe's, you were just sitting there with your wine. You never tasted it," she says. "And in here, there's no hidden bottle of scotch, no decanter of whiskey like a lot of the other professors seem to keep. I was just wondering why. Is it the migraines?"

"Alcohol can exacerbate them, yes." My expression flattens. "Did you go through my things?"

Again, she shrugs. "I got bored waiting. Guess you took too long working through your frustration of seeing me with someone else…someone promising to make me happy for the first time in *years*."

"You came the night we met," I point out. "Seemed pretty fucking happy to me."

She grins. "That isn't what I meant. Lexington was going to let me finish my audition is all. Said I could go back to his dorm room in Cadmus if I wanted. So he could get the full effect."

Irritation spills into my blood. I set the bottle down, slowly edging my way back around the front of the desk.

"Is that so?" I ask, though it comes out much rougher than I intend. Almost a growl.

She nods, shaking out her hair and lifting her face toward the ceiling. "You know what they say. The early bird wins the leading actress."

"I don't think that's the phrase."

"Nobody asked for your opinion—"

Slamming my hands on either side of her hips, I grip the edge of my desk until it feels like my fingernails might splinter against the wood finish. She jolts, her hazel eyes widening as her face falls forward, level with mine when I lean in.

The scent of vanilla and honey is overwhelming, but I don't pull away yet.

"I believe you did ask my opinion," I tell her, moving so I can feel her breath skate across my lips when I speak. An indirect coupling of sorts that has to satiate this hunger I have for her, or else I might snap further. "You want to know why I cut off your audition. Right? That's why you've broken into my office again and are sitting on my desk in this short little dress, waiting for me like a decadent dessert desperate to be devoured."

"Your alliteration is impeccable—"

"You should know better than to assume I'd ever cut someone off because of petty feelings or to be mean," I continue. "I didn't end your audition early because I didn't want to hear the rest. In fact, I could have sat there through the night listening to only your recitation of Desdemona fantasizing about how to win her husband back, even after he's been cruel to her. If I never hear another rendition of a monologue again, I will be satisfied."

That goddamn word again. It causes heat to flicker in her gaze, making the nerves in my chest pull tight.

Her eyes widen, like two dark moons of iridescent awe. "You thought it was good?"

My brows pull together, confusion knitting between them. Has no one ever told her before that she's talented?

"So phenomenal that I wanted to keep it for myself," I whisper, suddenly acutely aware of just how close we are. How easy it would be to lean forward and seal our mouths together again. "I know it's selfish, and I know it goes against everything I've been saying this semester. You must be confused, and I regret…I regret that my own issues have caused this rift between us."

"I don't mind if you're selfish," she says softly. "I like knowing I'm not alone in this. But if anyone should feel bad, it's me. I've just been thinking of myself this entire time. I have this awful habit of overcorrecting and doing too much, and I'm sorry."

"Don't be." I don't touch her, though every muscle in my body aches to. "I'm not sure I would've had the courage to try had you not chased so thoroughly. I *was* using my position here to keep you away, and that wasn't fair either. Not with the extent of how terribly I long for you."

"Really?" Her voice is small, like she doesn't believe me.

"*Really.*"

"The rumors about me—"

"I don't care," I rush out.

"But I do," she says. "They're not…*totally* untrue, but they are greatly exaggerated. I wasn't sleeping with everyone for work. It was just once with this director, Aaron, and his girlfriend. They said they could get me a part, and I stupidly believed them. It was a big mistake. I'd take it back if I could."

"I'm sorry if I made you feel you needed to defend yourself," I say, my chest pinching. "Your past makes no difference to me. And there is *nothing* going on with me and your sister. She merely had the most open schedule, and I thought maybe a buffer would be a good idea after…well, you know."

"After you kissed me?"

"Yes, that incident. I wasn't sure how you'd feel going forward, all things considered. You were right to call me a coward."

She lets her eyes fall, and her tongue darts out, wetting her bottom lip. "Could I finish my audition? Just for you?"

My breathing hitches, oxygen scattering in my lungs. I nod, hypnotized by the way her eyes glisten with the praise. She gently pushes me back and hops off the desk, then turns and shoves me against it.

I catch myself with my palms on the edge, staring at her.

When she sinks to her knees, my heart skips a beat.

"Elle," I warn, my fingers curling.

"It's okay," she promises. "I want to. Please?"

Torn, my gaze flickers toward the door, then back. "This is a terrible idea."

"The best adventures usually start as one." She begins the short crawl forward, shouldering her way between my thighs. "'Here I kneel, if e'er my will did trespass 'gainst his love.'"

The recitation is soft, rasped low enough that passersby won't likely be able to hear, but I feel the vibrations in my veins anyway. I glance at the door, which is unlocked, as she sits up, reaching for the fly of my pants.

My hands cramp with the urge to turn her away.

They don't.

A heavy breath rattles from my chest when she pops the button open and slides the zipper down slowly, each tooth set free sending a spray of goose bumps over my skin.

There's a long, weighted pause. She looks up at me through hooded lashes. "Is this okay?"

I release a stuttered breath. Clear my throat. "Yes. Anything you do is, Elle."

Tucking pieces of hair behind her ears, she leans in. "'Either in discourse of thought or actual deed, or that mine eyes, mine ears, or any sense, delighted them in any other form,'" she continues, gripping my waistband and nodding for me to lift my hips.

When she slips my pants down to my knees, I feel like I might fucking die. I'm already hard as goddamn stone and can feel myself leaking, so unbelievably wanton and needy. She slides her fingers over my boxer briefs, then leans forward to run her tongue along the fabric, chasing the length of my cock.

Her gaze becomes ravenous as the contact makes me twitch.

"'Or that I do not yet, and ever did.'" Slowly, she pinches

the material and begins dragging it down my hips, revealing my erection.

I swallow.

She does too.

"'And ever will—though he do shake me off to beggarly divorcement—love him dearly.'" She drops her voice to a mere breath, as if mesmerized by the sight before her. When she takes it in her palm, giving me a firm pump at the base with fingers that barely touch around, I jerk into the movement, so unaccustomed to this kind of free exploration.

But gone are any of the thoughts of disgust or fear or memories that I usually dissociate with at times like this.

Right here, right now, it's just Elle.

Not a magical cure, but a soft balm against the tide of horror.

Her skin is so hot compared to the icy surface of my own as I lift my hand, cupping the underside of her jaw before sliding forward and rubbing her lips with my thumb.

A silent request. Something I've never thought to ask for in my life.

She parts her mouth, covering the tip of my digit. Sucking it in and laving her tongue over my fingerprint.

I grit my teeth, my cock throbbing painfully. My fingers are a little numb, but nothing that dulls the sensation of her. I'm not sure anything *could*.

"'Comfort forswear me! Unkindness may do much,'" she says around me, spreading the precum seeping from my slit around the crown. She teases the tip, and my eyes roll back into my head. "'And his unkindness may defeat my life, but never taint my love.'"

My breaths come in labored puffs. I remove my thumb, and

she pushes forward, nuzzling my dick with her cheeks—first one side, then switching to the other, all while maintaining eye contact.

"'I cannot say "whore,"'" she moans, though I'm just barely listening at this point. Barely hanging on to what little shreds of sanity I have left. Her tongue strikes me, swirling around my tip, before she dives down and drags it up the vein on the underside.

She spits on top of her fist, gripping my shaft tight, coating me in her saliva. Her lips part, and she pushes down, taking just a little while her hand continues working below.

"'It does abhor me now I speak the word…'" These lines are sloppy, slurred, spoken around a mouthful of cock as she moves deeper, pulling away to stretch her cheek with the length.

She repeats the action, working my cock toward her throat, whimpering a bit when she hits a spot that makes her gag.

"Fuck," she murmurs, though with her mouth occupied, it's garbled nonsense. Still, the vibrations are delightful, euphoria licking a path up my spine from my balls.

My toes curl inside my loafers. I steal a quick glance at the door, noting if I see any shadows pass underneath. When nothing changes, I thread my fingers through her hair and stand up, angling her head back a bit.

A beat passes. She pushes my hands away, pinning them back against the desk. As she does, she forces herself to take more, keeping me in her throat for a moment before pulling off.

"Finish it," she commands, her eyelids heavy as she swivels her head, capturing me and sucking me back in. Drool pools from the edges of her mouth when she gags again and again, the gurgling sound making my bones quiver.

My hands tremble beneath hers, going slightly numb. I wonder if she likes being restrained too or if the control is what excites her—if it could be both, the way it has always been for me.

In my fantasies at least. Before her, that was the only place I had any say.

I unstick my tongue from the roof of my mouth and close my eyes. "'To do the act that might the addition earn…'"

She pumps me hard, fast, in dizzying strokes and yanks her mouth off. "Open your eyes, baby. Don't you want to see the mess you make?"

Her lips return, her head moving faster as she bobs up and down, up and down. Stars explode behind my eyelids, and release barrels through my limbs, spreading like a goddamn fire—

Abruptly, she slows, and my entire world comes to a screeching halt. Adrenaline courses through me, my chest tight with impending climax that suddenly has nowhere to go.

My eyes pop open.

She moves in again, moaning louder than before, each forward thrust drawing an almost-pained, pouty noise from her throat.

My head lolls back, and I pant, struggling to keep my composure.

"That's it," she murmurs between ministrations, driving me to the brink and back. "This is what you've wanted since the first day of class, isn't it? Me on my knees, letting you use me however you want."

"Yes," I groan, my release shooting up and—

She yanks away once more, slowing to an almost halt, and my orgasm gets stuck on the precipice.

Chest heaving, head swimming, I snap my neck forward and glare at her. "Elle, for fuck's sake."

"What's the matter?" she asks, licking my tip like a lollipop, smacking it against her face. It twitches, and she gives me a devilish smile. "You don't like this?"

"I fucking love it," I admit, breathless. What's the point of lying?

Footsteps clamor down the hall outside, and I freeze, eyeing the door.

Elle has no such qualms, sucking me right back into her sweet goddamn mouth, increasing the pace of her previous efforts.

"Christ, temptress, maybe we should—"

Speaking becomes nearly impossible, though, when she fully seats me inside her throat, releasing my hand to reach up and rub against me from the outside. The tip of her tongue laps at my balls as she remains in place for several seconds.

I jam my knuckles between my teeth. Shit, shit, shit. Anyone could walk in right now and catch us.

I'm not even sure I'd mind.

My hands shake as climax scrapes its nails down my chest, begging to break free. But she holds me in the palm of her hand—literally—controlling my every whim. I want to shove my fingers into her hair and spill down her throat, but she doesn't let me, pausing anytime I go to touch her.

"Better come fast," she says, blowing across my slit before sucking me all the way down again.

Tears well up in my eyes, pleasure bordering on pain spinning through my stomach until it's taking up all the room. A pathetic whimper tears past my lips, like a siren erupting in the room.

"Elle, baby, I'm—can I—"

"Can you come in my mouth?"

"Fuck," I grind out, losing my mind. "That what you want?"

"Mm-hmm," she coos around my dick, nodding enthusiastically. Spit and precum cover her face, tears from all the gagging having smeared her makeup.

Her face brightens, sending me over the fucking edge.

My hands lock up, and I resist the urge to throw my head back as my balls seize, release shooting through me like a goddamn rocket. Electricity, white-hot and blinding, zips up my spine, and she lets out the sexiest sound when the first ropes of cum assault her tongue.

It's a greedy, almost anguished noise, almost placating as she coaxes more from me, squeezing tight and milking me dry.

I black out for a moment. She's still stroking me when I return to earth, keeping the crown just inside her lips, as if trying to catch any last drops.

Sweat slicks the sides of my face, over my neck, down my back. When she pops off me, she uses her middle and ring fingers to scoop what falls out of her mouth back inside, and then opens wide to show me the sticky white mess.

Goddamn, that's hot.

"Very good," I breathe, running my hand over her hair. "Think you can swallow all that for me?"

She rolls her eyes, like it's not even a challenge, but instead of doing so, she pushes quickly to her feet and shoves me onto the desk. My back slams against the wood surface, my body folding for hers as she climbs over me.

There's no time to consider what she's doing before she leans in. Her eyes meet mine, hesitating for a moment as she silently asks permission. I part my lips slightly, an equally silent agreement.

Salty, thick fluid drips into my mouth, and she presses her lips to mine in a wet kiss. On the one hand, most men probably aren't into their own spunk, but for some reason, I'm not even giving it a second thought.

It wouldn't be fair to ask her to swallow my load and not be willing to do the same. Plus, she gets really into the kiss, finally letting me put my hands in her hair and on her ass, and I realize I don't mind doing anything she wants.

She's owned me from the day we met anyway. I've just been unable to admit it until now.

The sound of knocking kicks us from the make-out session; she's sprawled atop me, her dress hiked up high on her hips, lips swollen. My hair is a tangled mess, my dick still hanging out and my pants around my ankles.

We don't move again until the footsteps walk away, and even then, we wait until there's no more audible movement outside at all.

Clearing her throat, she climbs off me, adjusting her outfit and fixing her hair. I stand, pulling my pants up and trying to collect my breathing.

"How'd that audition hold up?" she asks, tossing me a timid smile over one shoulder. "Better than with the audience?"

I'm not sure why, but the question makes me feel slimy. "Elle, I meant what I said about you out there. I wasn't trying to manipulate you."

"I know," she replies. "I'm the one who asked for the private audition, remember?"

"Sure, but I want to make sure you know I'm not…" Trailing off, I scratch my scalp, at a loss for words. "Well, I'm not the men you met in Hollywood. Roles aren't tied to sexual favors. Or any favors really. If you get one, you get it fair and square."

She snorts. "Relax, Boy Scout. I don't think you took advantage of me. This was inevitable, right?" Tossing her hair over her shoulder, she sends me one last grin as she heads for the door. "Next time, you can return the favor."

Chapter 30

Elle

BECKETT DUPONT IS WAITING OUTSIDE MY DORM ROOM WHEN I get out of astronomy, which instantly makes the hair on the back of my neck raise.

Does he know it was me in Sutton's apartment that day?

Or worse—did his dad tell him about me?

A shudder ripples through me at the thought.

When we were growing up, my dad was retired from his previous life, so we weren't necessarily privy to the bloodshed and violence that molded our parents and their friends. Still, Asher made up for what we weren't experiencing by getting into physical fights with practically everyone he ever met, his anger an unchecked flaw proving nature matters as much as nurture.

Even Quincy, who prefers quiet and peace, has been known to use her fists when she needs to. But for whatever reason, the urge seems to have skipped me—not just because I'm averse to blood in general, but because it just seems like so much effort to hurt someone.

Except in the quarry eight years ago, though that was self-defense.

Violence changes you. It's a callus that grows over time, and you're almost never better off for it.

Beckett's sorry state is proof of that. The cave incident seems to have taken its toll.

Lexington, Meg, and Percy trail close behind as I approach him, watching as he stretches out his legs.

"Can we help you?" I ask.

He glances up, the skin around his eye smooth, slightly raised, and shiny. Scarring from my brother's fists, I imagine. Exhaling, Beckett presses his palm against his forehead. "God, I can't escape you people, can I?"

I point at the little whiteboard hanging outside our door where Aurora's written our names in giant pink bubble letters. "Coming to my dorm will make that pretty difficult."

"Not here for you," he replies. "Should've known you'd be the one to greet me though. The universe has been quite cruel to me as of late."

"Karmic retribution got you down?"

Meg snorts.

Beckett's glare is icy. "Your brother almost killed me, you know. A little sympathy would be nice."

"Oh, well, that's where you've been misled. I'm not nice." Flipping my hair over my shoulder, I turn to the door and slide my key into the lock.

"She really isn't," Percy adds.

I shoot him a dirty look, which just makes his brows raise as if to say *See? Told you!*

"I'll never understand what he sees in you," Beckett mutters.

"Percy's not into Elle," Lexington says.

"And I wasn't talking about *Percy*," Beckett snaps. He pauses, frowning. "Who the hell is Percy?"

A pale arm extends straight into the air. "That'd be me. Perciville Whitmore. We had calculus together freshman year."

"Not sure that necessitated an introduction," Lexington interjects.

Meg leans forward in her chair, gripping her knee as it spasms slightly. An occasional extension of her spinal cord injury—surfer's myelopathy caused during a gymnastics stunt in high school, she told me a few weeks ago. "Could we take this conversation inside? The hallway is freezing."

"There's no way Beckett is coming into my room," I say.

"Okay, then you chat with him out here, and we'll wait for you in there." She rolls forward, pushing the door open.

Aurora, wrapped in a light pink bathrobe with matching slippers, is standing there with an unplugged curling wand. She leans out into the hall as the other three filter into the room, instantly spotting Beckett, and points the wand menacingly at him.

"I thought I told you to fucking leave," she growls.

My eyebrows arch, and I move to the side a little. I've never heard her raise her voice, let alone the animalistic sound that just came from her.

"And I said I would after you heard me out," he says, wiping his hands on his khakis.

"There's nothing you can say that I want to hear," she snaps. "You almost killed the two people I love most in the world. I want nothing to do with you."

"How many times do I have to say I didn't do anything? I was the one who got Lucy out of the caves, for fuck's sake."

"And where was Foxe?" Aurora's voice is pinched, slowly unraveling as it climbs in pitch. A door down the hall opens, the RA poking their head out to see what the commotion is. "After the grotesque things your friends, your club members, did to him? The only reason he's alive at all is because my uncles helped get him out of there. All you did was fuck up."

Beckett groans, leaning his head against the wall. "Don't you think I know that?"

Aurora's face is almost the same color as her robe. "If you know, then you shouldn't have even come here."

"I was just trying to apologize."

She clenches her jaw. "Yeah, well, I don't accept."

Turning around, she stomps back into the room, slamming the wand on the desk she's using as a vanity. The others have settled on and around my bed—Lexington sits on a pillow on the floor next to Meg, whose leg has stopped moving. Percy's sprawled out on my mattress but has at least managed to kick off his shoes and coat.

Exhaling, Beckett gets to his feet, brushing off his backside. He takes out a folded piece of paper from inside his blazer, holding it in my direction.

"If this is a written apology, I doubt she's going to want to—"

"It's for you," he says. "From Father."

Pressure closes in around my heart, squeezing the ventricles so tight that I think the organ might burst. Eyeing the note, I take a step back and shake my head.

"No, thanks."

He gives me a long, bored look. The detachment in his eyes sends a chill crawling up my spine. "How long do you think you have before he tells Sutton about you two?"

"I don't know what you mean."

"The rumors came from somewhere," he says. "Just 'cause the full extent of them hasn't made the rounds on *The Delphic Pages* yet doesn't mean it's not going to. There are people waiting in the shadows to expose you."

My mouth is suddenly arid. "Expose me for what exactly? I haven't done anything wrong."

"Not sure everyone else will see it like that. Plus, there's no telling what story Father will concoct. He loves hyperbole."

I ball my hands into fists. "What does he want with me?"

"Don't know, don't really care." He must not like the look in my eyes, since he straightens a bit and sighs, rubbing the back of his neck. "There's this prophecy he's spent his whole life trying to avoid, and your presence here threatens that. Threatens us."

"The curse, you mean. Is that why he tried to get you to kill my brother?"

Beckett winces slightly. "Yes. And I was stupid enough to listen to him. Trust me, I'm paying for it dearly, even if your roommate doesn't believe it."

"Yet you're still doing errands for him."

"I can't outrun everything." He lifts a shoulder, brushing off the sleeve of his black blazer. I notice the red symbol embroidered on the breast pocket—a theta at the center of a poppy—and wonder if he's still involved with his former student organization.

As he starts down the hall, suspicion claws at my sternum. One of my feet shifts of its own accord after him, but I call out and wait to see if he'll stop first.

He pauses at the door leading to the stairs.

"Do you think your dad knew who I was?" I ask, inching closer and lowering my voice so the group in my room won't overhear. "In LA. At the Grandeur Playhouse. Is that possible?"

"Anything is." Beckett meets my gaze, unflinching. "*Anything*, Elle."

He leaves me alone in the hall with that cryptic message, and I wander back to my room, closing the five of us inside as a million different thoughts swirl around my brain, trying to make sense of the clear warning.

The six of us, actually, because when I join my classmates on my bed, Aurora props her computer up on hers and turns the screen my way, revealing Foxe's beaming face.

It's a little surprising that she's interacting with him in front of us, but I don't question it.

"Well, well, if it isn't my favorite cousin." Foxe grins easily, seeming more like himself than the last time we talked, and I almost let that soothe the disrupted parts of my soul.

Almost.

"I'm telling Asher you said that." I settle against the headboard, tossing Meg a fruit snack pack from the stash I keep under my pillow.

Percy pouts as he settles next to me. I tear open another package and dump the gummies into his hand, then pluck out the orange and blue ones for myself, leaving the gross red ones behind.

"Dammit, you're still a bad secret keeper, huh?" Foxe says.

"I don't know, I think she's pretty good at it," Lexington replies, pulling a copy of *Othello* from his messenger bag. He cracks the spine and opens to a random page, fanning himself with it. "She's definitely hiding something."

"Lots of things, if I had to guess," Meg adds.

My eyes narrow. "Et tu, Brute?"

"If you're fucking the professor, I think we all deserve to know," Percy says.

I choke on a fruit snack. "*What?*"

Aurora's eyebrows shoot up. "The professor?"

"Dupont," Meg tells her. "Total babe if you're into the stuffy, awkward type. To be honest, I'm not entirely sure he'd know how to satisfy you, Elle."

Lexington grunts. "Is this where you offer your services instead?"

"Why, aren't you just waiting to offer yours?"

Percy sits up, his mouth full of red gummies. "Wait, you guys are trying to fuck Elle? I didn't know that. Give me a minute. I can probably switch my preferences from blonds to brunettes."

"There's a perfect solution to this, you know," Foxe offers, reclining on the sofa in his apartment. His foot kicks a plant on the coffee table, and I just know Aunt Violet put it there to discourage him from putting his legs up. "Orgies. Everyone fucks Elle."

"I'm going to pretend you're not selling out your own flesh and blood right now," I mutter, flipping him off.

"But it's a solution!" he cries.

Aurora cocks an eyebrow at me. "No wonder you didn't want to study in the library. You guys are *not* quiet."

"I'm also not trying to fuck Elle," Meg says, her cheeks darkening slightly. "I was just *saying* the professor might not be up to the task. I've never seen him date anyone." She looks at Lexington. "Have you? I mean, you've known him the longest, and your parents are friends."

"Our parents are associates," Lexington replies. "I wouldn't call any of them friends. Even among the married folks, I don't think there's much love between the founding bloodlines. It's mostly just a game of chess, each of them playing to keep as much power in Fury Hill as they can."

"Blah blah," Percy says. "Answer the important question: Does Dupont fuck or not?"

On the laptop, Foxe lets out a low laugh. One I haven't heard in ages. "Where the hell were you all last semester when I was drowning in boredom?"

"Attending classes, probably." Meg shrugs.

We all look expectantly at Lexington, who drapes his arms over his knees. He meets my gaze, hesitating, and I feel a familiar pinch of jealousy in my chest.

Do I want to know who Sutton has been with before me?

Not particularly. It doesn't matter, and it's not like I'm a virgin. But the masochist buried somewhere deep within me is a bit curious, so I just lean back, waiting for Lexington's response.

He rolls his eyes. "Again, I've never seen Sutton date anyone. Man, woman, nonbinary—doesn't matter. Does that mean he *doesn't* date? No. But you all know how Pythia and Avernia are. I wouldn't want to drag anyone into that scrutiny either."

"Not to mention that whole thing with his brother being linked to Death's Teeth," Percy notes.

I sit forward a little. "I thought he was a Curator."

"He was. Is? I don't know." Percy shakes his head. "But those deaths and vandalism sites last semester were riddled with Death's Teeth paraphernalia. Their insignia would be carved into the students or drawn on the walls in blood or—"

Meg clears her throat, glancing at Aurora and Foxe, the latter of whom is listening intently despite his face paling. "Maybe we should change the subject."

"But the Curators who kidnapped people are dead." Percy frowns.

"That doesn't mean everyone wants to relive the events," Lexington says, throwing his book at Percy's face. "Dumbass."

Percy grunts as the book connects with his nose, leaving a red mark on the bridge. "Sorry for trying to keep everyone informed. You guys are such haters."

"Because you're annoying," Meg says. "And we came here to run lines, not for a history lesson."

We don't have our parts yet, but we've been meeting up frequently outside class since auditions anyway, if only to strengthen our performances for the final itself.

Lexington and Meg break off into their own pair to go through a scene between Bianca and Cassio, leaving me with Percy.

"Go on," Foxe says from the laptop, waggling his eyebrows. "*Ask* him. You know you want to."

I toss Aurora a look. "Can you turn him off?"

"No," Foxe says, grinning wider.

Her cheeks blush the color of her robe, and she closes the computer before he can say anything else. She flops back on her bed, rolling over to continue reading some thick thriller book in silence.

A part of me wonders if she and Foxe are mending things between them more than either wants to let on, but I don't ask. It's none of my business.

"All right, Percy. Tell me what you know about Death's Teeth."

Chapter 31

Sutton

WHITE FLURRIES FALL AND MELT AGAINST THE COBBLESTONE as I stride across campus, weaving between the student service buildings and the libraries, and past the Lyceum toward the old movie theater that no one ever goes to. The film department still puts the classics on from time to time, but a couple other faculty members and I are the only ones who ever attend.

The crisp March air feels good against my skull, which has been pulsing since I left a faculty meeting that felt a bit pointed.

Dean Bauer spent fifty-four minutes talking about the importance of avoiding interpersonal relationships and not obscuring lines, and although he avoided eye contact the entire time, it still felt like he was speaking directly to me.

Maybe that's my own guilt seeping in. It's been weeks now since I had an official change of heart where Elle Anderson is concerned, though not getting involved with her never really felt like an actual option.

I've been feeding Death's Teeth bullshit about my investigation into the new student, but it doesn't feel like I've done enough, especially as her popularity on campus grows. At any moment, some part of me expects them to jump out of the shadows and snatch her from me the way they did my sister.

That guilt slots in place where the previous was housed, and I'm in a sort of limbo, torn between wanting to keep Elle out of harm's way—out of Death's reach—and *needing* to be near her.

Her chaos grounds me somehow. I find myself seeking it out involuntarily, like a tidal wave I can't escape.

A light in the observatory catches my eye. Even the night classes are done for the day, so the building should be empty and locked up. But there's one girl who seems incapable of playing by anyone's rules but her own.

My legs drag me in the direction of the entrance.

The door's unlocked; I enter quietly, flipping the lock behind me and pausing when a loud whirring noise echoes through the main area. Up a flight of stairs is the massive telescope that Dean Bauer was so proud of getting a few years back, sitting on a wide platform directly beneath the ceiling panels that are currently open, revealing the vast night sky.

At the far wall on the platform, a woman stands with her hand pressed against a red button, looking out.

She's in casual clothes I've never seen before—a pair of soft black pants that cling to her like a second skin, an oversize sweater, and a knit cap pulled down over her dark brown hair. That choker necklace never seems to leave her.

I watch from below as she walks to the telescope, letting out a big, contented sigh when she leans in. Again, as if they have a mind of their own, my legs take me up the stairs, ascending each step one by one until I'm on the platform with her.

People don't usually run into each other this many times outside their normal schedules. It's as if something is pushing, despite all the elements of our lives that should repel us, and I can't make myself stay away.

Fuck, I know I should. I know being alone with her right now is a mistake, considering the staff meeting I just left.

But I don't care anymore.

All I want is for her to touch me, and I want to fucking touch her.

After a near decade of shying away from the slightest caress or feeling disgust and shame whenever someone showed interest, this desire feels too significant to just ignore.

Even though I'm endangering her by getting this close, knowing Death's Teeth is watching and waiting for some fuckup. Knowing they'd love the excuse to drag her into our world and shatter hers.

Everything is so goddamn convoluted that the only piece I can focus on is the want.

The need. The absolute desperation.

"What's with you and sneaking up on unsuspecting women?" she asks, sensing me before I announce myself. She doesn't pull back from the telescope, just lifts her brows over the equipment and smirks.

"Boy Scouts are drawn to damsels in distress," I reply, shoving my cold hands into my pockets. "It's in our nature."

"Do I look like I'm in distress?"

"Well, you're breaking and entering again, so I can only assume something is wrong."

Elle turns, facing me. "Actually, my sister let me in, so no breaking required." She pauses, wincing. "But... Don't tell anyone please? I don't want to get her in trouble."

"Ah, so you do care when people's careers are in jeopardy."

"Didn't we already establish you were greatly exaggerating?"

"As if I needed to say it out loud. You saw through it instantly."

"Well, yeah, you came in your pants once when I dry humped you. I think that makes it pretty clear how you feel about me."

"Wait." I hold up a hand, frowning. "Who said anything about feelings?"

She makes a face, playfully pushing at my shoulder. "Anyway, that was one of the rules my parents had, actually."

"Rules?"

"For coming here. They encouraged me to enroll, but they said if I caused Q any problems, they'd pull all of us out."

"Would they see me as a problem?"

"Definitely. My dad has never liked any of the people I've brought home."

"Is that something you're considering doing?" I ask, moving behind her. My hands find her hips, and I revel in the soft gasp she elicits as I press into her. "Bringing me home to meet your parents?"

She laughs. "God, no."

"Rude."

"Trust me, I'm doing you a favor. My mom would eat you alive."

"I thought you said your father was the one to avoid."

"He is, but my mom would never let you leave. She'd want your entire life story, pictures of you as a kid, pictures of your parents, character references. Then she'd call her friends over to gossip right in front of you at supper and would probably try to get you to commit a crime just to see how you'd react under the pressure."

Jesus. "So how often do you bring people home then?"

"Never." She glances at me over her shoulder, and I reach up, tucking some hair behind her ear. "I've been out west since I grad-uated from high school, though, so it's not like there've been many opportunities."

"Anyone you've wanted to introduce them to?"

I'm being nosy, my curiosity about her past getting the best of me. I want to know everything about her though.

I want her to want to take *me*.

"Jury's still out," she says in a lilted voice, jutting her ass into my pelvis as she bends to look into the telescope again.

She slips away just as my grip on her tightens, walking to a table across the platform. I crouch lower, peering into the machine without moving it from the spot she had it in.

"Canis Major?"

"Yeah. I'm just, um, trying to go down this list I have and see what I can find." She holds up a sheet of paper where she's written down the names of multiple winter constellations. Orion and Canis Major are marked off.

"When you said you enjoyed astronomy, I have to admit I didn't think you meant it," I tell her.

She huffs. "Thanks a lot for the vote of confidence. Why wouldn't I have meant it? Acting isn't my *only* interest. Star power goes beyond the stage."

"Enlighten me."

"What do I look like, an encyclopedia? Do your own research." She bumps my hip, nudging me out of the way as she moves on to the next constellation on the list. "Besides, if you can't see the importance of being able to read the stars in the sky, then I guess you've never been at the whim of the cosmos. Getting lost is terrifying."

"I can imagine." I keep my gaze trained above us. "Imagine

only, of course, since a Boy Scout like myself would never get lost. Coordinates and compass reading are day-one survival stuff."

That makes her laugh a little. "So if you were plopped down in the middle of, say, some dusty desert, you'd be able to find your way out, no problem?"

"Sure. If I can't rely on myself to find my place in the world, then who the hell else am I going to ask?"

She eases back from the telescope, tilting her chin. "That sort of independence must be nice."

Unable to stop myself, I inch toward her, drawn by some invisible current. I don't touch her but lift my hand, pointing at Orion's belt with my index finger, then dragging it due west.

"See that bright point right there? That's Aldebaran. If you follow the distorted Y shape it creates above and below, you'll get the Taurus constellation."

"Oh." She leans into the telescope, sucking in an excited gasp. "Beautiful."

My nostrils flare as I resist the urge to look at her and agree.

But she is. God, she's fucking beautiful. Hollywood glam in a soft, delicate package that I want to tuck beneath my arm and never let go.

Up here, at least, it's nice to pretend none of the external stuff—her schooling, my job, Death's Teeth—matters. That I can just throw caution to the wind and take her anyway.

"Can you help me find Cetus?"

Nodding, I squint at the sky, searching for its tail. I point to the brightest star in a connected trapezoid. "Follow Menkar down, and you'll find the whale swimming in the celestial sea."

She turns the telescope to where I'm pointing. "I thought Cetus was a sea monster."

"Well, sure. Anything can be a monster if you don't under-stand it."

Humming, she moves back to her notebook, scribbling some-thing down on the page before returning to the scope. "You know, I got lost in the Primordial Forest when I was a teenager. It was stupid, really... We were here visiting Quincy, and I went off with this girl—"

"What do you mean, 'went off with'?"

"To hook up." She blinks, cocking her head at me. "Don't pre-tend you don't know what that means, Boy Scout. *We've* done it."

"No, no, I'm aware. Just clarifying terminology to ensure we're on the same page."

"So studious and precise," she teases. "Anyway, I remem-ber thinking it'd be really great if I could have used the stars to find my way back, but alas... All the experience did was give me nightmares."

I swallow. Those woods are as familiar to me as the back of my hand, and even then, they're vast and endless. Getting lost within must have been horrific.

"How'd you find your way out?" I ask.

Elle stands up straight. "I called my dad. My parents were still in town, waiting to come pick me up. He came instantly, no ques-tions asked. He's always saving us kids."

The last sentence comes out a little forlorn, scratching away at some hardened piece of my chest. As she clears her throat, she goes back to the telescope, plastering a big smile on her face.

I discard my coat and take a seat on the platform ground, drawing my knees up. I point to a cluster of stars between Taurus and Cancer. "My favorites: Castor and Pollux."

"Gemini?" she asks, walking over to where I'm sitting. She

stares up at the sky, her fingers instantly finding my hair and threading through.

Smothering a moan at how good it feels, I lean into her touch. "The twins. When I was young, my sister Bellamy and I would pretend to be them."

"Which one were you?" she asks, snapping her fingers. "Wait, no, let me guess. Pollux."

"Based on what?"

"Vibes mostly. I don't know much else about them."

"It breaks my heart how little you care about Greek mythology." Slowly, while she's still looking up, I slide my fingers around her wrist and draw her to the floor with me. Into my lap.

My heart races, my pulse thick and prominent in my throat, terrified that I'm making a mistake. That she'll pull away or resist or that the emotions I'm so used to when it comes to these interactions at large will resurface from where I've tried to drown them.

But she doesn't do anything except melt into my embrace.

Chest tight, I tentatively wrap my arms around her as she fits herself on top of me. The observatory is so still, so quiet, that I can hear every breath she takes and releases, and I allow the soft sound to steady me even as my mind swims.

She links her fingers through mine, warming my cold flesh.

I rest my chin on her shoulder. "Pollux was of divine birth, so I never would have ascribed him to myself. My twin... She was the magical one. Everyone loved her, and she could light up a room without even being in it. I was always sort of just there, watching over her, trying to keep her out of trouble."

Elle nuzzles against my neck. "You're a good brother."

I used to think that too, but a good brother wouldn't have let her die in the first place.

A good brother would've put an end to the organization that killed her instead of treading water within it for eight years.

"When I was an undergrad, she dragged me to this party," I say softly, admitting out loud things I've never told a soul. Not my parents, not the campus police, and not Beckett. "I didn't typically go to them, too busy with school or theater to waste my time drinking with peers I didn't much like. But she was convincing, you know? She had this way with words, and I wanted to be like her that evening. I wanted to be fun or have fun or whatever. So I went."

My throat constricts as the memories surge to the forefront of my mind. Bellamy's smile, her eyes glittering as she put a beer in my hand.

I only had one or two before things grew fuzzy, and even though I wasn't a big drinker back then, it still seemed odd for me to be so affected.

That was what I thought until I woke up drowning.

Submerged in water, bound and afraid. I'd struggled briefly before realizing it was useless and cursed myself for not being stronger. Fear bled into my body as my lungs filled, but then I was suddenly back on land, sputtering and coughing.

Hours seemed to pass at Lake Lerna's embankment. No one came forward to reveal they'd rescued me, and the darkness of the forest crept in.

A scream pierced the air, and I knew then—I knew it was hers. I wanted to move, wanted to find Bellamy, but couldn't. It was as if my body was sinking into the mossy earth, and I was too dazed to do anything about it.

"We'd been warned to steer clear of the woods," I tell Elle, staring at the back of her head. "From birth practically, everyone in Fury Hill is taught that the lake is haunted, and if things go in, they don't come out. We're told about danger lurking between the branches, catching in the trees, and that death waits for the founding family members. If we aren't careful, it'll snatch us up."

Elle tenses as I speak, and I press my nose into her hair, inhaling her soft scent.

"They assumed Bellamy fell into the lake, based on the drugs and alcohol they wound up finding in my system. I'd been... Well, someone had left their mark on me. Literally and figuratively. They'd slipped something in my drink, dragged me out to the woods, and..."

I trail off, gritting my teeth against the feeling of foreign hands violating my body. Forcing me to pleasure them while they crowned me with a role I didn't want.

Most of it is blurry or blocked out by my subconscious, but the *knowledge* that it happened remains.

"Who pulled you out?" Elle asks quietly, squeezing my hands. She pushes my sleeve back, smoothing her thumb over the faint scarring there, and I let my forehead drop to the back of hers.

That three-headed beast took years to fade. They'd burned it into my flesh, tying me to them permanently.

"I don't know, and it doesn't really matter. No one found her."

Elle releases me and twists, looping her arms around my neck. She looks at me for several long, tense moments before sliding her knees on either side of my hips, settling more firmly in my lap.

Swallowing hard, I let out a breath and flatten my palms against her ass.

"Is she the reason you're still here?"

"She's why I took the teaching job. It felt...wrong, leaving her behind. Then there was Beckett to consider. I..." I lick my lips, my mouth suddenly the desert. "I didn't want to fail two siblings."

When she leans in to kiss me, I can't tell if it's out of pity or comfort, but the air shifts anyway. I glide my hand around, cupping her breast, and let myself get lost in the moment.

Lost in her.

Chapter 32

Elle

THE WEEK AFTER MIDTERMS, A PARTY'S HELD IN THE BASEMENT of the Apollodorus, and even though I know I shouldn't, I agree to meet Lexington and company there. Aurora refuses to join, citing the fact that the basement is off-limits and in general creepy, though I hear the click of a phone call when I slip out of our dorm room anyway and the familiar rasp of a certain traumatized musician.

Neither of them are as slick as they think. Especially not when Foxe texts me constant strings about how in love with Aurora he is, though I don't need the news alert. It's been obvious since they were teenagers.

I used to be so envious that Asher had Lucy and Foxe had Aurora growing up. No matter how many friends I accumulated or how much attention I sought, it never felt like any of them were my person. Never felt like they understood me implicitly.

Maybe I'm still a little jealous, I don't know. Having someone look at me like I personally put all the stars in the sky wouldn't be terrible, I don't think.

Goose bumps line my skin as I enter the Apollodorus, and regret constricts my throat, but I push on. The upstairs is quiet, though there's an air about the lobby that feels tense and rife with anticipation.

Better than a quarry party at least. My history with those is what makes me slightly hesitant about attending tonight, but I push on anyway, needing to be among people. My siblings are drained by company, but I've always felt more alive in a crowd.

I spot Lexington and Percy arguing in line for the bathroom and head their way.

"Ah, a fellow founding family member finally makes her appearance!" Lexington cheers, instantly throwing an arm around my shoulders. "I was wondering how long it'd take for you to come to a Curator party."

"Wait, what? This is a Curator function?"

"Nobody *actually* knows who's throwing it," Percy answers. "Visio Aternae hosts *galas*, not parties. Daughters of Persephone soirees don't send out invites, though, and Death's Teeth usually puts theirs on in the forest." He pauses, squinting at me with his head tilted. "The Curators are just the most logical conclusion."

"So we're here, but we don't know why?"

"We know *why*," Lexington says, turning me toward the basement stairwell, where a girl in a Ghostface mask stands guard, stamping wrists as people pass through. "It's to have fun, m'lady."

I let the girl stamp my hand even as unease swashes in my stomach, and I don't protest when they lead me down the stairs. The levels twist as we navigate them in the near dark, and my anxiety ratchets higher and higher the lower we go.

"This place gives me the creeps," Percy whispers fiercely as we come to a stop three floors beneath the main lobby. "I feel like I'm going to puke."

"That's because you pregamed on an empty stomach, you dumb fuck," Lexington says, shoving his shoulder. "Which I *warned* you against."

"Blah, blah, blah," Percy replies, leaning against me. "You also made me pregame alone, so your point is moot. I bet Elle wouldn't let her friend drink by himself."

"I'm not much of a drinker," I admit. "One bad party in high school will ruin it for life."

Lexington grunts. "And one good party in college will make you think you're fucking Hemingway. Perce did *not* used to be like this."

"I'm not like anything!" he says, stomping his foot as we wait for the door to open.

It takes a moment, but then a masculine figure in a lacy maid costume appears, wearing a nondescript white mask that covers most of their face.

They glance at our wrists and then usher us inside, slamming the door behind us. The ballroom is packed, with vast crowds mingling throughout.

Soft piano music drifts from speakers mounted in ceiling corners, and as I look around at the vast ballroom-style floor, I note that all the attendees seem to be similarly dressed—some in masquerade garb and other scanty outfits as they mingle among themselves.

Well, some of them are just mingling. Others are engaging in varying degrees of lewd activities, and my throat grows tight as the sounds of slick flesh meeting and moans float around us.

"What the hell kind of party is this?" I mutter.

Lexington snorts, snatching several champagne flutes from a passing serving tray. "I don't know, but it looks like fun."

"Are you sure we should be here?"

"*The Delphic Pages* mentioned a rager open to the entire campus, so I don't see why not."

"Avernia's freaky as hell," Percy says, letting out a low whistle as he takes in a foursome, his eyes riveted to the languid motions as three men thrust in and out of a naked woman at the center of the room. "Remember what I told you, Elle? Some of the parties here get raunchy, especially ones thrown by Death's Teeth. Rumor has it that in order to be initiated, you have to fuck every member and even kill someone at the very end."

"Jesus Christ," Lexington mutters. "Now I'm not sure *whose* party this is."

I hesitate, discomfort crawling across my skin. "Do we have to participate?"

A short patron wearing a mask split in half vertically pauses as they walk by. "Nope, but feel free to watch. They love to put on a show."

Percy grins, handing me a glass while he drinks his. "See? It's like a secret sex club or something."

"Not much of a secret considering how many people are here." Lexington glances at the champagne warily but decides to swallow it anyway. "Fine, fine. We can stay, but only because I promised to help you forget about the woman who broke your heart earlier."

Grinning wide, Percy claps him on the shoulder, then moves away from us, drifting closer to the foursome.

I look over at Lexington. "Who broke his heart?"

"Sabrina."

"Really? I didn't know he was that into her. I kind of thought he was just teasing."

"Oh, he's been nipping at her heels since kindergarten."

Lexington smiles, watching his friend from afar. "It'd be cute if she wasn't such a dick to him all the time."

"Maybe he likes that she's mean."

Lexington shakes his head, something flashing in his gaze that almost feels like longing in its own right.

"Nah," he says. "Perce is a soft soul. He just doesn't know it could be any other way."

Something heavy settles between us, but before I have the chance to ask what he means, Percy wanders back over, throwing his hands in the air.

"'I don't want realism. I want magic!'" he squeals, and the piano music grows louder, as if to drown him out.

"Tennessee Williams," I say without thinking.

"I knew it!" he shouts, pointing at me. "I knew you'd know. Didn't I tell you, Lex? I said—I bet Elle can name any playwright with a random quote if they're popular enough." He beams at me, ruffling my hair. "You're so smart, Elle. How'd you get to be so smart?"

"Lack of things to do growing up," I say, flipping some hair over my shoulder. "Made me develop niche interests."

"You get it," he says, clutching his chest where his heart is.

"I do," I agree.

"Jesus, don't encourage him, Elle."

Laughing, I nudge Lexington with my shoulder. "You're gonna hate to learn that once I get a beer or two in me, I've been known to mouth off about the genius of *Machinal*. Real vibe ruiner, that one."

"God, you would be perfect for Professor Dupont," someone says from behind me. "It's too bad he seems to hate you."

I turn, coming face-to-face with Sabrina. Like us, she's not wearing a mask, and there are so few of us down here with bare faces that I can't shake the odd feeling gripping me.

Percy gives her a dirty look and then saunters off, presumably in search of more sex-capades to leer at.

I lift my chin, crossing my arms over my chest. "I've already told you I'm not interested in him, so what do I care if he hates me or not?"

Her mouth turns up at the corners. "You think I don't notice the way you look at him in class?"

"Sounds like you spend too much time paying attention to me." I slink closer to her, dropping my gaze over the tartan pants she has on and the oversize sweater that's falling off one shoulder. Reaching up, I tuck a strand of hair behind her ear, letting my fingers graze the outer shell. "Are you sure you're not trying to tell me something?"

She glares. "You *wish*, has-been. I'm merely pointing out that your crush on our professor is wasted."

"Because you want me instead." Sliding my hand from her ear to her neck, I lean in even more—enough to taste her bubblegum breath. Our lips are centimeters apart. "It's okay to admit it, you know. I don't bite *that* hard."

Her eyes drop to my mouth and then back up.

She doesn't immediately respond, which fills my insides with liquid heat. This close, I see the beauty mark beneath her left eye.

Impulsive, reckless behavior like this is what keeps getting me into trouble, but a point needs to be made here. I'm tired of doing this back-and-forth where we don't get along, and she needs to own up to her feelings if that's what they are.

I can tell when a person is attracted to me, and she's been giving that vibe since the first day of class. However badly she might want Sutton, when she doesn't pull out of my grip, it becomes clear she has other desires as well.

My gaze darts around the room to see if Percy's come back. I don't want to hurt his feelings, nor am I actually interested in pursuing Sabrina, but I *do* want to disarm her.

This is the quickest way I know how.

A tiny whimper comes from Sabrina's throat, and I smother a full-blown grin. Her eyes have grown pleading, desperate as I press closer, our chests rubbing together when my hand threads through her hair.

I grip her roots tight, angling her head where I want it.

"Apologize," I tell her softly. My head is swimming a bit, the general air of sex around us making me hot and dizzy.

Lexington is staring, and we've gained a bit of an audience, but it doesn't stop me.

Irritation boils in my chest, an accumulation of every emotion I've had since coming to this town maybe. Or maybe it's the heady rush of power as this girl bends to my will.

My lips are close. Her breath comes from her mouth in harsh, sporadic bursts.

She edges up, seeking more.

I smirk, tightening my hold on her hair.

"Say you're sorry, sweetheart," I whisper.

"I'm sorry," she replies instantly, eyes wide, like she wasn't actually planning to say anything at all.

Just before an actual kiss can happen, I withdraw with a satisfied grin.

"Now," I say, ignoring the stares we're getting as I cup her cheeks. "Friends?"

Sabrina lets out a little laugh. "You know, historically, the people vying for a lead in a play couldn't be friends. We'd be rivals."

Ugh, like I need the reminder about *Othello*. "But wouldn't it be so much more fun to not hate each other?"

To be good rivals, you have to be working toward the same goal. Sabrina wants to be the lead to impress Sutton, which tells me her heart isn't actually in it.

I want to be the lead to prove to myself I can do it, even after everything. That selling out didn't mean relinquishing my passion and talent.

We're not really the same.

Or maybe we are, and I'm oversimplifying things to make them easier to digest. I suppose that's possible too, given my own history.

"All right," she says finally. She extends a hand, cocking a thin brow. "Friends then."

When I take her fingers, she gives them a squeeze I feel in my stomach. Then we turn back to Lexington, who gives me a strange look.

"Do you almost kiss all your friends?" Lexington asks, handing me a beer.

"Just the ones I find attractive…sometimes." I glance at him and Percy as the latter returns with more drinks, then take a sip of my original champagne. "Don't worry. You two are safe."

Chapter 33

Elle

EVENTUALLY, THE SEXUAL ANTICS OF THE PARTY GROW REDUN-
dant, and the four of us look for something else to do. Sabrina gets a
mischievous glint in her eyes and leads us into the stairwell through
a different side exit.

"My dad used to tell stories about the tunnels beneath the
school," she tells us. "Said if you followed them long enough, you'd
reach one of the caverns where Death's Teeth holds its gatherings,
and I heard they might be having one to celebrate the arrival of
spring. Wanna see what they're all about?"

I hesitate. "That sounds like a terrible idea."

"You wanted lore, right? What better way to get it than to head
right into the belly of the beast?"

Even though my brain is saying not to listen, my curiosity wins
out. As long as we can peek in and not be noticed, it shouldn't be
a big deal.

Right?

The spiral stairs seem to go on forever; we wind around and

around until I start to feel dizzy, bracing myself against the wall when we've reached the bottom level.

It's even darker down here, and the walls are damp. Textured. They stretch into long earthen halls that my heartbeat echoes down.

We're no longer in the Apollodorus basement but *underneath* it.

Dread pricks at my skin. "I'm not sure about this."

Sabrina's mouth flattens. "What's with the weird expressions? You asked for something fun to do."

"We asked for *fun*," Percy says, scrubbing a hand over his blond hair. "Not to be led to our deaths."

She rolls her eyes. "Don't be such a baby. It's just a little tunnel."

"Spoken like someone without claustrophobia," Lexington mutters.

"God, you all are so annoying." She lifts her phone toward the tunnel, illuminating the immediate area. "Don't come then. Makes no difference to me."

"What happens if we get caught?" Percy asks. "This is a *Death's Teeth* meeting we're talking about."

Lexington nods, holding his phone up high. "Yeah, even if the rumors aren't true, we'll definitely get into trouble for trespassing."

"Oh my God, *shut up*." Sabrina reaches back, taking my hand. "You don't hear Elle whining, do you?"

"You guys just became friends, so don't start pulling the Elle card now," Lexington whisper-yells at her.

"Plus, she's an Anderson," Percy replies quietly as we delve deeper into the cave. "Whatever monsters live down here are probably her familiars."

I flip him off. "Stop believing everything your parents tell you."

"Well, you kind of terrify me, so I'm just assuming you might actually be cursed."

Lexington sighs, shoving him forward as Sabrina keeps dragging us along. The air in the tunnel is ice-cold and thick, the ground uneven and the walls narrow. Water drips distantly, and I wonder if that's from old piping or an extension of Lake Lerna.

Reaching into my coat pocket, I take out my phone, but the screen won't swipe because of how cold my fingers are. Sniffling, I let Sabrina guide me until we hear somber music filtering through the tunnels from somewhere.

The four of us freeze for a second.

Lexington's swallow is audible.

"You know the Apollodorus used to be a church?" Sabrina asks as we continue. "Early on, not long after the whole *plague* incident shook Fury Hill, some residents took over the building. Dedicated it to their god."

"Their god," I say, my shoulders tightening. "Not *God*?"

"Nope. Fury Hill's founders didn't subscribe to that monotheistic belief. They found god in their existences, the makeup of the world, and the cycles they observed within. Their god wasn't omnipotent or all-knowing but an inevitability. It was inescapable, and it was all around them."

"Death," I finish, my voice barely a whisper.

The music grows louder, rattling the cave walls.

"Exactly." Sabrina nods, squeezing my hand.

"So when you say church, you mean crypt. The Apollodorus was a crypt." I squint in the dark at the walls around us. It's hard to make out the shape of the texture, but something tells me they're not *just* rock and sediment.

"Avernia was a triage center when tuberculosis ravaged the townspeople. They couldn't keep up with the dead, so they dedicated buildings to their mass burials. Some of them never made it aboveground again though."

I pause, turning to face her. "Some of them. You mean the people who died in the Tenarus cave? The founding patriarchs, right?"

"All of them except Cronus Anderson. Legend has it that when he decided to make the Apollodorus into a library, he had the matriarchs bring the bodies of the townspeople through this very tunnel."

A chill slithers down my spine. "So these are the catacombs."

"Where some say…" Sabrina trails off, covers her flashlight, and dives into the shadows. I brace myself, and seconds later, she pops up behind Percy, grabbing his shoulders as she shouts "—*his ghost appears!*"

Percy's scream echoes down the tunnel, and Lexington barks out a laugh despite everything. Sabrina cackles, doubling over as her hyena noises assault my ears.

"I fucking hate you, and now I *really* don't want to be here," Percy says.

"Ugh, you're such a baby," Sabrina tells him, poking his stomach. I've never seen her act playful with anyone before, and I find it unnerving. The way he careens his body out of reach makes me think he feels the same.

Or maybe he just doesn't want to interact with her at the moment, considering Lexington said she broke his heart earlier.

"Look, Lex, I don't know about you, but I'm going back up." Percy holds a hand out, beckoning his best friend. "You coming?"

"We can't just leave them down here by themselves."

"I think Elle and I are more than capable of walking through some tunnels alone," Sabrina says.

"Yeah? Who's gonna keep you from getting bludgeoned if you run into a Death's Teeth member down here?" Percy snaps, grabbing her wrist.

He tries to drag her in the opposite direction, but she digs her heels into the ground, slowing him. "They don't bludgeon people," she insists, clawing at his fingers.

"Do you have firsthand knowledge of that?"

"Well, no, but—"

The music from before falls silent, and a harsh thudding noise takes its place. The ground vibrates beneath our feet, and we turn to look down the dark tunnel, peering into nothingness.

A rat scurries past, making me jump.

"Okay, maybe Percy has a point," Lexington says.

"Come on, Elle. You're not a chicken, right? I can see it in your eyes that you want to go to the meeting."

I glare at her. "Stop reading into my gaze so much."

"Why? Will you almost kiss me again?"

The music picks back up, caressing our ears and drowning out all reason.

Scoffing, I shoulder past her and turn, concentrating on the austere tune as it crescendos. "I only threatened to kiss you earlier to get you to shut up. Don't flatter yourself."

She makes an unintelligible sound behind me but then skips to catch up. "Just think about how cool it'd be to see Death's Teeth in their natural element. You'd basically be solving a campus-wide, centuries-old mystery. Maybe then you'd be able to clear your family name—"

"Well, well, well. What do we have here?"

An overly familiar voice materializes like a phantom before us, and I skid to a complete stop before I can run into the tall, gangly form of Jean-Louis Dupont. Two bigger, stockier masked figures flank his sides like bodyguards.

He's in a tailored suit, but his withered hand clutches a gold mask.

A mask like the ones I saw eight years ago. Like the one Sutton had in the forest weeks prior.

"You four know you shouldn't be here. This area is prohibited."

"O-oh, sorry, s-sir." Sabrina backs up a step, trying to pull me with her, but I don't move. "We must have taken a wrong turn, but we'll head back and get out of your hair."

He stares at her, his glacial gaze chilling.

My feet stay rooted in place.

"Lexington. Perciville." Jean-Louis looks at them over our heads, his expression unreadable. "Please see yourselves out of Tartarus."

Tartarus? I glance around, frowning at the fact that I can't see anything still.

If this is their underworld, we're in trouble.

"I don't think I can leave without my friends," Lexington says.

"You always did like playing the Good Samaritan role," Jean-Louis replies in a droll voice. "Don't worry, son. I'm just going to give them the tour they seek. If you want, you can stay here and wait for them."

"How did you know we were down here?" I ask.

Jean-Louis lifts a bony finger, pointing up. A tiny red dot blinks at us from the cave ceiling.

Cameras.

They were watching us from the moment we came down. Maybe even before.

He grabs my and Sabrina's shoulders, surprisingly strong for a man who looks so ill. Sharp fingernails dig through layers of fabric, and I glance behind me at Percy and Lexington, who stand in place, staring at us.

"Jean-Louis—"

"I'll bring them back," he calls out, his voice bouncing off the cave walls as he shoves us forward. The masked figures from before bar the boys from following, pinning them back against the wall with brute force. "Just testing out a theory." When I try to slide out from Jean-Louis's touch, he grips harder. "I wouldn't do that if I were you, Ms. Noelle. Play nice, and I'll bring you back to your friends soon enough."

Sabrina shoots me a look as if to ask how I know this man, but I don't say anything. Better we cooperate for the time being rather than cause problems.

He can't actually hurt us. Not with Lexington and Percy waiting, having seen him lead us out.

There's no conviction in that thought, though, because I already know better. He could kill us and have the crimes erased with the snap of his fingers.

I swallow over a lump in my throat as we're led deeper into the cave, the ground shifting downward. We pass beneath a narrow archway, and suddenly there are pockets of light illuminating the area.

Jean-Louis slips his mask into place, and fear coats my skin, making my teeth chatter.

We enter a massive cavern, larger than anything the town archives I've read mentioned. They scarcely talked about the caves at all, presumably out of respect for the dead.

Or because they weren't allowed.

From our vantage point at the top, the cavern snakes down

with different levels lining the walls in a spiral fashion, culminating at the ground. Hooded figures sit in seats carved from the stone itself, populating the layers like an arena. Standing water in some areas gives the air a musty quality, and I frown against the stench.

At the bottom of the cavern is a square stage with rope railings and crimson stains smeared across the rock.

In front of that, a table made of white, oblong objects, the joints fastened together with—

"Are those *skulls*?" Sabrina whispers.

Torches illuminate the area, with several propped against a far wall, where a three-headed beast is spray-painted in black.

"And other bones," Jean-Louis says matter-of-factly.

A moment later, two hooded, masked figures appear at the entrance we just came through.

"Mors vincit omnia, Elder," they greet in tandem, handing us our own disguises. "Are these your offerings?"

My stomach churns. *His what?*

Jean-Louis nods, silent, forcing the mask onto my face.

For a brief moment, I'm shrouded in total darkness as he situates the eyeholes correctly. One of the other figures does the same to Sabrina, then turns to me as if to assess my preparedness.

They meet my gaze, and I *swear* I've seen theirs somewhere before, but they turn away before I can get a good enough look.

A shiver coasts over my spine, notching in the vertebrae with its claws.

They gesture with their hands for us to follow them. Sabrina's breathing is heavy as we comply, because what the fuck other choice do we have?

We're led down a curved staircase carved into the side of

the cavern, Jean-Louis hot on our heels. Once we've reached the bottom, the sea of masks faces us, and Jean-Louis shoves us forward into a sudden bright spotlight coming from a level above us.

"Enjoy the Pit, ladies. Death welcomes you."

Chapter 34

Sutton

THE PIT MAKES MY MIGRAINES A THOUSAND TIMES WORSE, which is why, when the ranked Death's Teeth members drag two initiates down to the ground level, I'm too busy nursing a bottle of water to give a shit.

I'm only here for show anyway. To keep them from going after Beckett or Elle, since I haven't attended any actual gatherings in a while.

A few fledgling members flank my sides, kneeling on the ground. Their hands slide back and forth over my legs, my arms, down the center of my stomach. They stop just at the waistband of my pants, and I brush them away, not interested in even pretending to entertain them.

Not now that I know what pleasure's *supposed* to feel like.

As the two masked figures are led to a makeshift altar in front of the stage, I drop my head into my hands, willing the throbbing sensation behind my eye to go away. Any other group on campus would've respected how debilitating a goddamn migraine can be, but not Death's Teeth.

All they care about is satiating their debauched needs.

I lean back in my chair—one of the few not carved from the very rock we're sitting within and instead an ornate throne made of gorgeous mahogany and velvet cushioning.

"Death's Teeth presents a fine pair for our Incarnate-to-be's choosing, to whose lineage we owe our existence. Won't you take your pick and lead?"

One of my eyes pops open. "Quelle est la signification de ceci?"

My question is for the Director, who I know can translate it.

She says nothing.

Leaning forward, my other eye opens, and I fix my stare on the Director's back as it separates me from the newcomers. She stands between me and the offerings, as if purposely blocking my view.

"Deux? Comment deux d'entre eux ont-ils réussi le processus de vérification?"

"Silence, s'il vous plaît," the Director commands.

I clench my jaw tight. "Réponds-moi ou je marche pour toujours."

"Non." Clearing her throat, the Director turns slightly, still obscuring the pair from my sight. "If Incarnate will not choose, then the decision falls on the shoulders of the offerings themselves."

A few of the members at my feet caress harder, cooing under their breath as if I need soothing. Like I'm some wild beast about to break through invisible restraints and slaughter them all.

"Which of you then offers yourself?" the Director continues, adjusting her gold mask. The snakes slithering up the sides resemble devil horns tonight, which I find fitting. "To be Incarnate's closest companion, his trusted partner, the Maiden of Death through whom a new era can be ushered in, mos maiorum."

No one says a word. Even the members watching up on the stone balconies are silent.

Something feels off about this. Each semester and new season, they have these extravagant ceremonies that lead to a day of brutality, but nothing much ever comes of it because they don't have an actual Incarnate filling the position.

Normally they're satisfied with my presence alone, and the one offering goes ignored.

I've never seen two at once before.

Incarnate represents their god, the Maiden is his backbone, and the sacrifice is the connective tissue bridging the gap between this world and the next.

My stomach sinks as a realization hits me. That's why they're offering two candidates.

The discarded offering will become the sacrifice.

"If no one wants to pick, I shall do so for you." The Director's hand whips out, and a scream peals from one of the offering's throats, echoing through the cavern.

With my chest twisted in knots, I push to my feet and edge past the Director at the same moment as someone shouts, "Wait, wait! I'll do it! I'll go!"

I freeze, ice flooding my veins.

That voice…

The Director turns, glaring down at one of the masked figures kneeling on the stage. They're both in heavy, shapeless gold cloaks, their identities obscured, but a sliver of the speaker's neck is visible, and it's all I need to see for confirmation.

Black fabric.

Snake charm.

The Director appears unimpressed, her eyes narrowing slightly. "Speaking out of turn is a violation of our rules. My mind's been made up. Take these two to the—"

Without thinking, without considering the consequences of this action or the fact that it goes against everything I've spent the last eight years resisting, I step forward.

The offending masked figure's head turns in my direction, but we're too far apart for her to see my eyes. Still, a current of something unidentifiable ripples in the air between us, like a thread of fate raging against separation.

Fuck, what is she doing here?

Does she know what this is—what danger she's in?

Do they *know who she is? Would she still be alive if they did?*

Or maybe that's why they're letting her sit in. Maybe they think I'll choose the other offering, and they'll be able to remove her from the equation, saving Avernia from imaginary collapse, if she tries to violate the unwritten pact barring an Anderson and Incarnate from coupling.

The way our ancestors did—Cronus and Manon, the last two surviving members of the original founders.

Their union had caused destruction, shaking Fury Hill to its foundation. Even outside the belief in the curse, Duponts were expressly forbidden from interacting with Andersons, which is why I tried so hard to stay away.

Why I didn't want them to know about her.

But I can't just let them take her from me. I *won't* let them.

My options are limited. If I ignore her, they'll make her the sacrifice for sure. If I step in…

Clearing my throat, I walk toward them. The Director watches me like a hawk, unyielding in her perusal.

"Is there a problem?" she asks.

"Let them go," I say, approaching the infuriating, troublesome temptress hidden behind that costume. "Take them to the back rooms and I'll make my decision there."

The Director shakes her head. "It's not that simple. You have to—"

"I know what I have to do," I cut in sharply, bending so I'm eye level with Elle. From here, her hazel irises sparkle in the torch lighting, glistening with unshed tears as if she thinks I've somehow saved her.

When I reach out to take her chin, she relaxes slightly.

For some reason, it makes me feel a bit better too.

What happens next doesn't.

"I accept," I tell the Director over my shoulder, though I'm too nauseous to meet her gaze. "Sanguis meus tibi."

Surprise flickers in the Director's eyes. She lifts an arm, instructing the crowd to rise to their feet before sweeping it low. The crowd bends, bowing, each of them flipping over like dominos in favor of their new leader.

Their Incarnate.

"Welcome," the Director says, ducking her own head. "We've been waiting for—"

"I have a condition." Straightening to my full height, I turn to face her. "Since I've had this sprung on me, I'd like the opportunity to prepare more. Extend the deadline for my choice and allow me more time to decide which offering deserves to be at my side."

"That's highly unorthodox."

"I'm aware, but that is how I wish to do things. On my own time. This is an important decision, and it shouldn't be made in the heat of the moment. We haven't survived this long without proper vetting of our members, and we shouldn't cut corners for our leaders."

"I'm certain the recruiter did his due diligence—"

"You have my condition. In turn, should you grant this wish, I will take a more active role as Incarnate and…" I swallow, mouth dry, as I glance at the second masked figure. My chest aches. "I will personally deliver the sacrifice for the joining ceremony."

Chapter 35

Elle

THE REST OF THE NIGHT IS A BLUR.

I experience it in snapshots, like photographs being taken where the flash blinds my eyes. I'm not even sure this is a night I want to remember, but when I'm led to this small, secluded area off the larger cavern, leaving Sabrina somewhere behind, I realize there isn't much choice.

Keeping my gaze trained on my feet, I'm stripped of my cloak. Cold air scalds my body, licking the exposed skin.

Someone behind me reaches for the hem of my sweater.

I push my elbows down, trying to shove their hands off. "Don't fucking touch me!"

The masked person shows no emotion, continuing to try and remove my top. I ball my hands into fists, punching against them to no avail.

"Let go of me, asshole," I growl, rage boiling inside me—at their unwanted touch and at me thinking Jean-Louis wasn't pure evil.

I should've known better. Should've *told* Sutton about his father or at least told one of my siblings. Of course, his being on campus now isn't a coincidence.

None of this possibly can be. Fear is an orchestrated notion, an agent of chaos, and I've probably just played right into his deviant plans.

I'm not even sure what I volunteered for, but it's clear something sinister was going down. Since I imagine Jean-Louis would've let Sabrina go had I not been with her, I couldn't let her be punished.

Goose bumps crop up along my skin. *What have I done?*

"If you do not take your hands off her, I'll see to it you don't leave the caves with them intact."

The masked figure trying to undress me halts, glancing over their shoulder as a taller, broader, green-eyed masked man enters. I'm not sure what he's doing here exactly, but my fear lessens a little when I realize who he is.

I knew when he touched me out there, though it'd been a strange understanding to have while a crowd of masked strangers stared at me. It also confirmed my long-standing suspicion of him being involved with this organization, and given what I've seen happen in the forest, maybe I should be more concerned, but when he touched my chin out there, I didn't sense any hostility.

Surely, if he wanted to hurt me, I wouldn't still be here right now.

Nor would he be pursuing me during the day, telling me how much he wants me.

Maybe that's naive, but at the moment when the rug's just been torn out from beneath me, it's the only thread keeping me tied to sanity.

The masked figure attempting to assault me grunts, releasing me with a shove. I stumble, hitting the curved wall and catching myself with my hands. When the person leaves, I turn slowly, swallowing over the massive knot in my throat. He's close, directly behind me, and I feel slightly less panicked now that it's only us here.

"Are you all right?"

I nod. He slides my mask back, exhaling, as if relieved to actually find me underneath.

Warring emotions flicker through his green eyes, and I get a sense of déjà vu—not from any of the times we've been this close at our leisure, desperate to feel each other, but of something else. Something weighed down by all the secrets bubbling in the distance between us.

I open my mouth to speak, though I'm not exactly sure what I want to say. I have so many questions racing through my mind that it's impossible to pick just one.

A part of me wants to know why he's here, what his role is, although the display moments ago should be enough of an answer. The people out there listened to him like he was their god, and it was as terrifying as it was arousing.

Someone clears their throat behind us, and he turns his head slightly in their direction while keeping me shielded. A short, stocky masked person stands there, twirling their red hair around two fingers.

"Elder Dupont—er, *Incarnate*, sir," they say. "The Director would like to see you."

Sutton's jaw clenches. "I'll be there in a minute."

"She said to come immediately," they call out as they walk away.

When we're alone again, I let out a breath and meet his gaze. "So what exactly is Incarnate—"

"You need to leave," Sutton tells me in a low voice. "Now."

I blink. "Huh? I can just wait for you to—"

"Now, Elle. Do not test me on this. The longer you stay, the less likely it is you make it out of here alive. You had no fucking business entering these caves in the first place. I *told* you to stay away from this shit."

Being reprimanded like a child makes me see red. "Wait a fucking minute. I didn't *choose* to come here. Your—"

"We don't have time to argue semantics," he snaps, pure fury radiating off him in waves. He doesn't touch me, doesn't get any closer, but his heat seeps into me like a bloodstain, and I press myself to the wall, trying to make sense of its direction. "You're lucky I got to you before they could actually force you into one of their rituals."

"Rituals?"

"Yes. Death's Teeth is more than just some vigilante student organization. There are expectations. Roles to be played. I can't—I have to go figure out how to keep them off your back now that I've publicly offered to claim a Maiden."

"A Maiden?"

"Nobody saw your face, so that should be an advantage," he says, though as he pulls back a little, rubbing his chin, it seems more like he's talking to himself than me. "Do you know who the other offering was?"

"Sabrina."

His jaw clenches. The anger is so unlike what I've been getting from him lately that I'm not sure what to do with it. Not sure how to defuse it.

"All right. I will fix it. Somehow. Just promise me you'll leave here and go straight to your dorm."

"I'm not—"

"I will explain everything later," he says, urgency straining his features. "Please, Elle."

Even though I want to keep needling him for answers, I relent, acknowledging the desperation in his voice.

For a second, he looks me over, and something softens slightly in his gaze. But he doesn't give me any time to ask more questions before he slides my mask back into place and stalks out of the room.

The redhead from before comes back and grabs my wrist, leading me to the area we originally came through. A still-masked Sabrina throws her arms around me as we're joined by Jean-Louis, and she lets out a shaky sob.

She's unsteady, slurring her words, and I can't help wondering what the fuck they did while I was gone. There's a deep gash pouring blood on the back of her shoulder, and I pull away as my fingers slip through the liquid, glaring at Jean-Louis.

He shrugs, hands in the pockets of his suit. "I said I'd bring you back. I never said in what condition."

"And what exactly did you do?" I demand. "Does your son know you did this?"

"My son," he repeats, scoffing. "Does he know about *you*? Shall I be the one to enlighten him?" As we continue walking, he sighs, tearing the masks from our faces. "What a disappointing evening this turned out to be. I was hoping for more blood and sex."

I don't say anything, balling my hands into fists. I'm not sure what's going on or how important he is to this organization, so getting into an altercation likely wouldn't end well for me.

Jean-Louis grabs my shoulder, hauling me through the tunnel. I drag Sabrina along, tripping over her every other step, but heave a sigh of relief when Lexington and Percy come into view.

The men from earlier are still holding them at bay, but they step back once Jean-Louis gives them the all clear.

Percy runs over, taking a partially unconscious Sabrina from me. Lexington stays where he's at, eyeing Jean-Louis, whose hand remains on my shoulder.

"My offer from before remains," Jean-Louis says in a low, malicious voice. *His offer from last summer.* "You'd be better off fucking me than Incarnate."

"Still not interested," I reply.

"You've no idea what you're doing. What you're inviting. When they realize he potentially picked an Anderson to be the Maiden, you'll be torn to shreds. Literally."

I twist out of his hold, glaring. "Who's fault would that be? You dragged me in there."

His eyes crinkle under the mask. Like he's smiling. "I was hoping you'd be the sacrifice."

"What the hell are you talking about? What *sacrifice*?"

"I'm sure he'll fill you in soon."

With that, Jean-Louis spins and stalks off, the click of his heels against the ground loud in the tunnel as my heart races, confusion mounting.

Lexington comes over then, frowning. He grabs my jaw, inspecting my face. "What the fuck was *that*?" he whispers, checking me over and over.

I swat his hands away, irritation spiking as I continue staring at the space where Jean-Louis just disappeared. "Looks like I'm on Death's Teeth's radar after all."

Chapter 36

Elle

UNSURPRISINGLY, I DON'T SLEEP MUCH THAT NIGHT. WHEN I slog my way to class at eight the next morning, I feel hungover, even though I barely drank at the party itself and definitely didn't have anything in the caves.

Aurora spent the whole morning giving me major side-eye between the thirteen steps of her skincare routine, but she at least had the sense not to pry too much.

My stomach rolls as I take my usual spot in the front next to Meg, whose dark brows arch as she takes me in. "Jesus. How much did you guys drink last night?"

I lay my head on the small desk connected to the chair. "Let's not talk about it."

"Fine, fine." She sits back in her chair. "Prepare yourself though. Essays are being returned."

Groaning, I peek at mine as Sabrina sets it face down on my desk, expertly avoiding eye contact. I wonder how she's feeling and what she's thinking, but I don't ask. Not here, not yet.

"A C's not the end of the world," Percy says, leaning over to look at the big letter circled on the page.

"Hey, quit being nosy." I shove him back, flipping the paper over.

"That'd be like asking me to stop breathing," he says, shaking his head. "But you don't have anything to be ashamed of. Dupont's a tough grader, and it's not a failing grade. Ace the two big assignments we have left, and you'll be fine."

It's a little unnerving how easily Percy's managed to file last night away as if everything that happened was totally normal. I wonder how much he had to drink and if maybe the hangover is diluting the gravity of the situation.

Not that he really *saw* anything, but still.

"And one of those is the play," Meg adds, stuffing her A-plus into her bag. "Which you'll obviously nail."

If I'd thought my relationship with Sutton was going to have any bearing over my class performance, clearly I was wrong. Not that I'd want him to be unfair, *I guess*, but still.

Is he still angry about last night? Surely, this isn't a form of punishment.

"What'd you get, Lex?" I ask, leaning my head on the back of my seat.

"B-minus." He twirls a pencil between two fingers, not looking up. His attitude, dark and gloomy in contrast to Percy, feels more appropriate. "Seems like your boyfriend doesn't care for perfect prose or solid arguments that much."

Everyone looks at me, and I blanch.

"My…" I trail off, alarm swarming my insides. Sutton's all the way across the aisle, talking to a student who requested additional feedback on their essay, but his warmth is like a beacon to me—I can sense him wherever he's at in the room as if he's standing at my side.

I wonder if Lexington senses that too.

Or if he knows more about what happened last night than he's letting on. He *did* know that was Jean-Louis after all.

"Relax," he says, rolling his blue eyes so they're finally meeting mine. "It was a joke, Anderson. You've got to lighten up."

"Yeah," Percy chimes in, slinging his arm around Lexington's shoulders and giving him a shake. "You really do."

Tension threads through the air anyway, weaving between us as if we're back in those caves again.

"Come to think of it," Meg says, tapping her chin with a purple fingernail, "you're all acting kind of cagey. Did something happen you're not telling me about?"

The three of us exchange a look.

"No one's wound up dead this semester that we know of," Lexington answers. "So you can't accuse us of anything."

Meg's brows lift, and she glances between us slowly, narrowing her gaze. "I was thinking more along the lines of you three hooking up and then realizing it was a terrible decision. Or maybe that you and Percy were bad at it."

"Just us? You're not adding Elle to that possibility?"

"Uh, have you seen her? No way is she a bad fuck."

Heat crawls up my neck. "Well, sex with guys is pretty fool-proof. They'll come if you moan and squeeze enough—"

A throat clears, startling us. Sutton stands at the edge of our aisle, arms crossed over his chest. "Is this a conversation you four would like to share with the class?"

I lift my chin, catching his eyes with my own. His are hard as jade, unyielding and mesmerizing. "Only if the class is interested in learning how easy it is to make a man orgasm."

Percy coughs into his fist, his eyes bulging out of his head.

Sutton remains unamused. "Perhaps we should keep discussion confined to relevant talents, Ms. Anderson, and not hobbies we may engage in outside the classroom."

"Well, maybe you shouldn't eavesdrop."

A muscle in his jaw twitches, and my thighs clench. "Please see your assignments for *Othello* posted on the exit when you leave today. The short list is still being finalized, but you'll see which nonspeaking roles you've been given. Remember, we're putting this production on by ourselves. It's all hands on deck for the final." He starts to walk away, pausing briefly to look over his shoulder. "Ms. Anderson, I'd like a word after class."

Percy makes a *whomp whomp* noise with his mouth, sinking lower in his seat.

"Damn, he does not like you," Meg says, cringing.

Sutton's sudden claps fill the air as he stalks across the stage, instantly hushing the crowd to a silence. A bitter taste burns the back of my tongue when I look at his stupid dark hair and the stupid sweater vest he has on. Those stupid hands that ran over me last night to make sure I was okay.

The annoying mouth that hurt my feelings afterward.

He doesn't look at me at all as he begins the lecture, so I exhale and open my notebook, scribbling notes.

"…the importance of acting exercises cannot be overstated. If you want to continue to grow in your craft and preserve the talent you possess currently, it's imperative you make exercises like these a part of your warm-up routine," Sutton tells us.

My stomach twists into a million little knots. How easily he can compartmentalize is unsettling.

He points to the rolling chalkboard behind him. "Now, get into groups of…let's say four, and I want you to practice the first three of these in preparation for our impending rehearsals."

I join Lexington, Percy, and Meg and try my best to focus on the task, but my mind keeps drifting. A few times, I sneak glances at Sabrina as she works with her own group, but she never makes eye contact.

By the time class is over, I'm starting to wonder if I made up the events of last night altogether.

"Ms. Anderson," Sutton calls out from the stage as I sling my backpack over one shoulder. "Don't forget I requested a quick meeting in my office."

He disappears backstage, and I clench my teeth.

"Someone's in trouble…" Percy sings, grabbing the back of Meg's chair as he starts wheeling her up the aisle.

Lexington hesitates. "Need me to stay for moral support?"

I shake my head. His presence would likely make things worse.

Leaving Lexington there with a wave, I head to the annex, pausing outside Sutton's office door. I knock before entering, and he gestures for me to have a seat—but not in the plastic chairs right in front of his big desk. Instead, he points to the green suede armchair against the far wall, and I can't help feeling a little like I *am* in trouble, even though I don't know the full extent of what I did.

He folds his arms over his chest, leaning against his filing cabinet. "Do you know why I asked you to come here today?"

"Are you finally going to ask me to be your TA? I could really help whip your students into shape, you know. I have a lot of experience. With acting at least. Teaching, not so much."

Sutton exhales, pinching the bridge of his nose. "As if I could deal with that temptation."

That almost draws a grin out of me. "Well, we could test that theor—"

"You have no idea what you've done." He lifts his eyes, dropping his hand onto the desk with a loud smack. "What the hell were you thinking, going to a Death's Teeth gathering?"

Huffing, I drop my gaze to the floor, sinking lower into the armchair. "I didn't *choose* to go there, which you would know if you'd let me speak last night instead of berating me."

"Berating you?" He shifts on his feet, an incredulous expression etched into his face, but lets out a sigh. "Fine, all right. Tell me what happened."

So his dad didn't tell him anything?

I should feel a twinge of relief, but for some reason, that just makes me more anxious.

"We went to a party in the Apollodorus," I offer, though I can instantly tell that's the wrong thing to say. His face reddens, and he clenches his teeth, but I keep going. "No one knew who was throwing it, just that *The Delphic Pages* sent out an invite. As it started winding down, we wandered past the exit and kept going down, just to see what was there. If the rumors about a Death's Teeth meeting were true."

His nostrils flare. "So you *did* go on purpose."

"Yes, okay, fine. But not to participate. We just wanted to watch from a distance."

"Who's 'we'?"

"Me, Sabrina, Percy, and Lex."

"*Lex*," he spits, his anger mounting. "Is he the one that convinced you to go?"

"Not that it matters, but no. Sabrina was. Lexington was just along for the ride."

"I'll bet he was."

Squinting, I frown at him. "Are you seriously jealous right now?"

His jaw shifts. "Feelings aren't logical. And I may have heard a rumor about the party you were at. Someone said they'd seen you kissing another student, and I guess… Fuck, I don't know."

I swallow, guilt burning my insides. "I didn't kiss anyone."

"You didn't."

"It wasn't like that. I was just…proving a point to Sabrina. No lips touched. I wouldn't do that to you."

To us.

Sighing, he leans forward with his elbows on his desk, dropping his face into his large, veiny hands. "You make me regress into a person I don't recognize, Elle. It's daunting."

"So that's why you're mad?"

"No," he says quickly, letting his hands fall. "I'm mad because I tried to keep you from the scope of Death's Teeth, and not only have I failed to do that, but I've made you a target too. I'm mad at myself."

A lump forms in my throat, singeing the tendons inside. That word, "fail," again. He used it when he told me about his sister in the observatory, and it'd felt like he'd placed a cinder block on my chest without warning.

I know what it's like to crumble beneath the weight of your perceived failures. How easily everything can shatter if you don't succeed in your dreams.

"What exactly is Death's Teeth? Everyone keeps saying they're this secret organization, and I've read about their supposed vigilantism and sex parties in the school's periodicals, but there's not much written about them. Are they…actually dangerous?"

"Yes." He leans back, pressing his lips into a firm line, studying me with that gemstone gaze that makes my insides flutter, as if wondering how much he should tell me. "Death's Teeth was born out of fear. An initiative to restore faith and order in the town after Cronus Anderson debauched it with his greed and bloodlust. Some say they concocted the whole prophecy about your family, planting seeds in the minds of our people to make them hate the ancestral line, because they needed someone to blame for the death and sickness."

"And what do you say?"

"I wouldn't put it past them. These days, they front as a vigilante terror group, made untouchable by their blood oaths and anonymity. It's not a very large organization, you'll notice, as it would be very difficult to maintain their secrecy otherwise."

"If everyone knows about them, how are they a secret?"

"The secret's in the identities of the individuals. Even I don't know everyone. Only the Director does."

Tilting my head, I peer at him. "What's your role? Are you… Do you participate in the sex stuff?"

Something passes over his face, and he seems to shut down, withdrawing from the conversation. "Death Incarnate. Their leader, essentially. The one they want to maintain order and…pick who dies."

"Who *dies*?" My stomach flips, panic seizing my bones.

"They use sacrifice to appease the god they've erected. Incarnate and his Maiden act as a vessel connecting life and death, and the sacrifices keep the cycle going. Well, that and the sex."

"So it's all true then? All the rumors, all the stuff people whisper about?" I swallow, trying to make sense of the information and wondering just how Jean-Louis ties in. "That day in the forest..."

"I had nothing to do with whatever that was. Until last night, I was doing my best to keep my involvement at a minimum." he says, his jaw flexing. "Though this *is* why I advised you to stay out of the forest. I was trying to keep you away from them. Said I'd investigate the new girl myself just to keep them off your trail."

"But why exactly? What do they want with me specifically?"

"It's not that they want you. It's that they'd go out of their way to keep you from being my Maiden." He grabs an apricot from the fruit bowl on the corner of his desk, rolling it in his hands. "The very first Incarnate and Maiden are rumored to have been Cronus and Manon Dupont. That was why they wore masks: to obscure his involvement. The current members are fearful of what it'd mean to have history repeat itself in that way, especially since they believe your family wants to destroy Avernia as an institution anyway, which would cut off all their power in Fury Hill."

I sit forward, wrapping my arms around my stomach. I'd be lying if I said this wasn't dredging up all the terrible memories I've worked so hard at ignoring and that it didn't feel like I'm in way over my head here.

Maybe I should tuck tail and run. Rid myself of the problems once and for all. No way would any of this touch me under my parents' watch. Dad would never let it.

But that would mean abandoning Sutton and my siblings to fend for themselves, and I don't want to be the girl who only cares about herself anymore.

"You can't leave, can you?" I ask softly. "That's why you were there last night, why you participate. Why you said you'd be their leader officially."

"Yes. But something you should know, Elle, is that no one who joins gets to leave. You're in it for life, which is why I'm sorry for dragging you into this. Had I not intervened last night, they'd have…" He trails off, squeezing the fruit until it starts to smush, juices spilling over his fingers. "The harm they would have caused as some sort of message… I would not have been able to bear it. I am not a strong enough man to stand idly by while you suffer."

The cut on Sabrina's shoulder flashes in my mind. Would it have been worse for me, being an Anderson?

"It isn't your fault," I say, the urge to mention that it's his father's on the tip of my tongue, but he stalks around the desk, gripping my chin in one hand before I can.

He forces me to look up, meeting his eyes. "It *is* though. Do you understand exactly what I've forced you into?"

I swallow. "It's just role-play, right?"

"No." He plants his hands on the arms of my chair, leaning down until his green eyes look like flames, burning bright enough to see from outer space. "It isn't. The Maiden *belongs* to Incarnate. It's the equivalent of a marriage pact. An oath bound by consuming each other's blood, then marked by sex before the Director and her cronies."

My breath hitches when he toys with a piece of my hair. The way he reaches out tentatively, a hesitance lacing his actions, and gently takes a strand between his fingers.

"It isn't technically legal, but the city would uphold it regardless. Especially for a Dupont." He looks up, meeting my gaze once more. "There's a reason I've never wished to fulfill the Incarnate position, other than the fact that it requires sentencing innocent people to their demise."

But I just forced his hand.

His jaw clenches, a muscle thumping as he averts his eyes. I reach out, softly flattening my palm against his cheek and chin, and pull his face back toward me.

"This is not something I can ask you to take on," he says in a low voice, lacing his fingers through mine. "I didn't want you near any of this."

"I'm a lot more resilient than you think. Maybe it won't be so bad."

"The Maiden holds Incarnate's heart in her hands. She is required not to break it."

Why does it feel like we're not talking about Death's Teeth anymore?

"Because of the oath," I supply, breathless.

His gaze dips to my mouth. "Yes. The oath."

I lick my lips, my chest heating at the implication.

His movement is staggered as he leans in, swallowing thickly. I twist my fingers in my lap to keep from grabbing him, forcing myself to wait patiently for once. It's been so long since we last kissed that I'm starting to forget the slant of his lips on mine, the force of his breath against my chin, my nose—

A knock on the office door sends us springing apart; Sutton launches to the other side of the room, immediately snatching a stack of papers as a blond faculty member sticks her head in.

"Hey, Sutton, could I borrow you for a moment? We're having trouble getting one of the curtains down in the back auditorium."

Clearing his throat, he nods stiffly, shoving the papers into my lap. "Ms. Anderson, please see to it that your rewritten essay follows the format I laid out. I have rules in place for a reason."

Shame burns the edges of my face. "Yes, sir."

He doesn't linger, sliding past his desk toward the waiting woman. Leaving me totally alone.

Chapter 37

Sutton

Jean-Louis invites Beckett and I to brunch at the manor, but when I show up, only Mother is there to greet me. I'm not sure where Beckett is at all—haven't seen him since he left the apartment this morning, saying he was going to work out in the student gym.

I've been seeing a lot less of him lately, but I'm choosing to chalk it up to the fact that he's gotten some of his color back and seems to be going out more.

And the fact that there's a certain brunette student who's been occupying most of my free time as of late. Especially now that she's aware of Death's Teeth and practically a part of it.

Fuck, I still can't believe I did that, pulling her into this mess when all I wanted was to keep her out of it.

The only reassurance I have is that they don't know *exactly* who the offerings were that night. My goal is to convince them I've picked Sabrina as my Maiden and some poor unfortunate soul as the sacrifice, sating the members' desire for bloodshed and carnality at the hands of their Incarnate while keeping Elle from their actual reach.

Regardless, Elle is stuck with me now. Whether I can make her my Maiden officially or not, my mind's made up.

But she's not here at the moment, so I focus on this random encounter instead. I typically don't visit the manor much during the semester, but the invitation seemed important.

Color me surprised to see Jean-Louis couldn't be bothered to attend.

Mother had the chef make a spread of my favorites—pain au chocolat, Boursin omelets, asparagus-and-zucchini frittatas—and spends the afternoon trying to get me to eat everything on my own.

"Mother, honestly." I hold my napkin to my mouth, pushing away the tofu scramble she's sliding in my direction. "I'm quite full."

She pouts, taking a sip of her mimosa. "You look a bit thin, darling. I'm simply trying to make sure you get quality meals and don't rely solely on vending machine subs the way you did when you were an undergrad."

"Well, coming home back then felt a bit weird, so that certainly played a hand in my dietary habits."

Her green eyes find mine over her glass. "Yes, I suppose it did."

I wrap my fingers around my water. "Beckett told me you cleared out her room."

"Eight years is more than enough, Sutton. Are we supposed to remain stagnant forever? It never brings anyone back."

Sadness tinges her voice, and she downs the rest of her drink, signaling for a member of the kitchen staff to refill it. Chopin fills the courtyard, lilted notes filtering through an open window from an old record player in the main sitting room. I prop an elbow on the table and rest my chin on my fist, trying to identify the exact feeling within me.

Shame and misery, maybe, to an extent—those are nothing new when I think about my twin's death. But there's something else, a kernel of confusion surrounding all the mystery, that hovers close behind the rest of the emotions, preventing me from feeling the others fully.

I glance at Mother as she busies herself with the sourdough pancakes before her, spreading marmalade over top and cutting a bite off. She dips it in syrup but never quite manages to bring the piece to her mouth.

Perhaps she's as stuck as I am and clearing out Bellamy's old room was an attempt at pushing herself through the sludge. I'd venture a guess that moving on is much easier to do when you don't have constant reminders smacking you in the face every day.

"Her things are boxed up in the attic if you'd like to pick through them." Mother folds her napkin, placing it on her plate. "I'm not sure what you'll find there, but if the dismantling of her room bothers you the way it does Beckett, you're free to look for mementos."

"Beckett's upset about her room?"

She sighs. "Darling, it's very difficult to tell with that boy. Everything seems to upset him these days."

I pause, considering. "Well, he was almost beaten to death in the fall."

"Almost," she notes. "And as a consequence of his own actions. I hardly think he has the right to be upset about that."

"Whether he has a right to is beside the point. The brain and the heart don't always operate with logic at the forefront."

Sitting back in her chair, she presses the backs of her hands to her cheeks, as if trying to cool herself down, as the courtyard has two mirroring fireplaces providing warmth to the area. "Are you suggesting he see a therapist?"

"Maybe." I shrug. "If that's what he wants."

"You didn't need therapy after what happened to you," she says, waving one hand. "Besides, what would the Blackwaters and Westwoods think? The Abbotts and Julie Ouellette? Our social reputation around Fury Hill has taken enough of a beating recently without adding crazy people to the mix."

"Beckett isn't crazy," I say. "He said Father was the one who convinced him to lure those people into the caves. Speaking of, where *is* Father? I thought he was too sick to leave the house, yet he doesn't appear to be here."

"He has good and bad days," she says.

"Well, I'm just not sure any of them should be spent on campus. I have a hard enough time keeping Beckett from him as it is. I don't think—"

"On campus?" Her eyes widen, and she sits up straighter. "What do you mean?"

"I mean he's been there multiple times this semester."

She frowns, fear seeping into the lines on her face. "The rumors about the Anderson children… Are they true?"

"The curse? You know I don't—"

"No, that the three descendants are on Avernia soil this semester." She looks at me, her eyes pleading. "Tell me it's not. That you haven't been there this entire time while they run amok."

"Jesus, Mother, you act as if they're out to get me."

"It isn't you I'm worried about," she says, shaking her head. "It's *them*."

Chapter 38

Elle

With a little over a month until the end of the semester left, Sutton posts the casting list on a white sheet at the back door of the auditorium. Sabrina and I make a beeline for it after class, and I immediately wish I could combust at will.

I stare at the names, my face hot. "*Bianca*?"

Sabrina winces, and for some reason, that pisses me off more.

I shove my finger in her face, rage making me vibrate all over. "What, did you say something to make him not want to pick me?"

"Huh? Of course not! I wouldn't do something so low just for a part," she says. "Seriously, Elle, I've been trying to—"

Releasing a dissatisfied growl from between my teeth, I curl my finger back in and stomp down the stairs, ignoring her. The whole class watches, and I realize I'm acting like a petulant child again, but *Bianca*?

Is that really all he thinks of me?

My steps get softer as I push open the side door to the back halls, veering right for Sutton's office. He's leaning against the front of the desk when I stomp inside.

"Is there a problem, Ms. Anderson?"

"Your cast list. My audition was ten thousand times better than everyone else's in this class. You said so yourself."

"What's wrong with Bianca? She's a beautiful courtesan who enthralls everyone she meets."

My throat burns like he's poured acid down it without even knowing. "Is that how you see me? As a shiny toy that's fun to look at? You said the stuff with Aaron didn't matter, but—"

"I didn't say that's *all* Bianca is." His green eyes narrow slightly. "Though perhaps I took how well a person might get along with her castmates into consideration as well. Working in a production isn't all about raw talent. This isn't Hollywood. The play gets put on, and we have to come back to finish our class. Your castmates are your classmates."

My face flushes, and my hands drop to my sides.

"I'm teaching skills that go beyond the stage. Cooperation, determination, compassion—all of those are important tenets I'm trying to instill in my students. If I think an important role might impact that for someone, then I might not give it to them. Far be it from me to exacerbate an issue."

I scoff. "And here I thought we were making progress in our relationship. I guess you're still mad about the Maiden thing—"

"I had no malicious intent when I posted the cast list," he says in a dark voice that makes me cold all over. "But if you'd like me to punish you, I can think of more effective ways."

He walks around me, crowding me until I'm forced to shuffle forward against the desk. I'm staring at the wall and his chair and the plethora of papers and ink pens scattered across the surface.

My breathing hitches when his words graze the shell of my ear. "Is that what you want, temptress? For your professor to punish your bad behavior?"

I slide my fingernails against the wood. "Should we—"

"Answer the question."

My heart hammers inside my chest, tension threading through my muscles. "Yes," I whisper faintly. "Yes, please."

I hear him swallow. The change in our usual dynamic ramps up my pulse; I'm so used to being the one to initiate, in control, that I'm not totally sure what to do with myself. Breathing becomes a concentrated effort the longer we stand there, a hairbreadth away, before he presses a hand against my lower back.

Pushing forward.

"Bend over," he commands softly.

Resistance is a reflex. "But the class—"

"They won't come in."

"The door is open."

"Then you'd better be quick."

I'm breathing through my mouth when I obey.

"Stretch your arms out, and grab the edge of the desk."

Slowly, I do that too, gripping the wood so tight that my hands cramp. Excitement swims in my stomach, making me extra sensitive when he finally slides his fingers over my hips, down the sides of my thighs.

"You have no idea what you fucking do to me," he groans, moving all the way to my feet. He lifts them one at a time, dragging my boots off and letting them fall to the floor with a resounding thud I feel in my gut. "My productions are business only. I don't make personal decisions when it comes to casting, and I would never use your passion as some sort of correctional device—not your passion for the stage at least."

Both his hands glide up the outsides of my legs, shoving my skirt up over my hips. His palms are cold but warm the longer he caresses me.

"Not getting the lead isn't a reflection of *you*. It just means we had a lot of talented people, and I tried to be fair."

I raise up on tiptoe, blood pumping like lava through my extremities. He hooks his icy fingers in the waistband of my tights and drags them toward my feet with painstaking measures. Each new inch of exposed skin is caressed by his hot breath, making my pulse ratchet up between my thighs.

This is the most reckless he's ever been with me, and I can't deny that I like it. A lot. Or that I needed this.

"Doing okay?" he murmurs, right against the back of my thigh.

I swallow. Nod.

"Words, Elle."

"I'm fine," I breathe.

"If you want me to stop—"

"Didn't you say this was a punishment?" I ask, turning to look over my shoulder at him. "Quit fucking around and—"

The first blow comes out of nowhere, a stinging sensation that ripples the meat of my ass. I drop my head, my mouth falling open.

My toes curl against the floor.

"Good?"

Again, I nod and then remember his request. "Yes, that was—"

Another strike against my ass, slightly higher than the last but still in the perfect spot. A surge of annoyance pulses in my stomach at the thought of him doing this with someone before me, and I grit my teeth when he lands a third and fourth smack.

The hits are light, but their bite sends liquid heat through my limbs. Pressure builds in my pussy, catching me a little off guard with how quickly it shows up. Each subsequent slap makes my body quiver, and I'm practically trembling when he pauses next.

"In a small-scale production like *Othello*, I want a lead who can share the stage so everyone's part feels equal. You'd have eclipsed the entire cast if I made you Desdemona."

Sutton delves between my legs, rubbing my clit and then exploring me. I let out a strangled noise, barely able to concentrate on his words.

He tsks, wiping a drenched finger on my ass. "Such a temptress, getting wet so easily. Do you enjoy being punished that much, Ms. Anderson?"

When I don't answer, the spanking gets harder. He delivers another series of slaps, soothing my inflamed skin with his cool, soaked fingers.

His breathing is labored. It's all I can hear above my own as I grasp the desk so tight my knuckles are white and going numb.

My mind drifts to the hallway and auditorium. Will no one really come this way? He's stationed at the very end of the hall, but still. Worry and adrenaline pierce my mind, fighting with the bliss, until he inserts two fingers, drawing an orgasm out of me when he curls them.

I pant, breathless, as he eventually withdraws and barely notice him retrieving a bottle of lotion from his desk. I hiss when he slathers it over my inflamed skin, smoothing in slow circles.

"Feel better?" he murmurs, dragging his free hand over the back of my head like he's petting me.

For some reason, I find it incredibly comforting. I don't know that I agree with his assessment, but I suppose it's not my call either. A part is a part, and he's the director.

He smiles when I nod, then adjusts my clothing.

"Good. Now get back out there. We have a show to put on."

Chapter 39

Sutton

MY ARMS ARE BOUND TOGETHER BEHIND MY BACK, BUT THEY'VE purposely left my legs undone. If I could move them, even just a little bit, maybe I could maneuver myself off this platform, and—

A numbing sensation ripples through me when I try to lift a knee. Pressure is applied to my waist, bearing down as I struggle to open my eyes.

"Oops!" someone giggles, the distinct outline of a hand keeping me blind to the world around me. "Sorry, sweetie, but I'm not sure you want to see this."

Distantly, I hear someone else chanting about the power of three. Cheers erupt, filling the air, and a strange sensation works over me— something that's supposed to be pleasure but only feels hollow, as it's pulled from my body like a thread.

Hands claw at my chest, and I realize I'm beneath someone. I try to buck them off, but it doesn't work, and then I'm too dizzy, too over-whelmed by everything, to care anymore.

My body shuts down, searching inward for a kernel of peace. Sanity. Something to take me out of this nightmare.

I can't stop the biological reactions, but I can control where my mind goes.

Green eyes flash in my mind, striking a chord of panic in my chest.

Bellamy.

Where is she?

"She's not with us," the person above me whispers, licking my ear as they speak. "But don't worry. None of that will matter soon anyway. All you have to do is focus on me."

A scream echoes around us, filling me with more unease. I recognize that scream—I've been hearing it since we exited Mother's womb together.

It's the last thing I hear before darkness takes me again.

The last sound I hear of Bellamy's forever.

"—wondering if you think we should go with a modern twist on the costume design or keep it traditional?"

Blinking away the sickening memories that have just recently begun unraveling more fully in my mind, I focus on the two students standing at the front of the auditorium. They have a three-part poster board held between them with color swatches, style guides, and sample costume sets pasted on.

It's only the third rehearsal, but since we have mere weeks to put on the show, everything moves at lightning speed, including the questions.

"Well?" the redhead asks, pointing at the poster. "Which one?"

"Which will cost the least?"

They exchange a look. The brunette shrugs. "Letting students wear what they already own probably, but isn't that kind of tacky?"

"Our budget is small," I say, leaning back in my chair. Onstage, Cassio approaches Bianca, and a tinge of jealousy pricks at my fingertips when Atticus Lowell get a bit too close to Elle for my liking.

"So we have to make do with what we can. What's more important for this play specifically do you think—costume or set?"

The redhead hums, tapping her chin. "Costume," she says.

"Set," the brunette insists at the same time.

I laugh, scrubbing a hand over my jaw. "Wonderful. You ladies think it over and make your decision. We can lean more heavily on whatever we have left from the years prior, and maybe—"

As I speak, a quick snapping sound cuts through the air, and suddenly a light apparatus from above comes crashing onto the stage.

Fear leaps into my throat as the few students up there dive out of the way; Atticus snatches Elle, dragging her just out from the path of destruction as the lights explode on impact.

Everyone in the auditorium is silent, their attention on the malfunctioning equipment.

Mine is on Elle. Her eyes find mine above the wreckage, and something violent curdles in my gut—a cocktail of relief and utter terror.

My throat closes, barring access to oxygen. I reach up absently, trying to claw my way free, but my fingers don't seem to work. Horror keeps them at bay as it mounts within me.

That would have killed her.

It takes me a moment to collect myself and remember I'm the teacher and director. This is something I should be handling for them.

Getting to my feet, I hear the crunch of glass as I move onto the stage. "Is everyone okay? No injuries?"

There's only one voice I really give a shit about, but I manage to feign concern nonetheless. Hands on my hips, I tilt my head up to where the lighting rig was a few minutes ago; now the air is unbalanced, a hole sitting in the center.

"I'll call the custodial staff to do a thorough check on all the equipment," I say, scratching the back of my neck. "This has never happened, so I'm confident the issue will be easily resolved. Probably just a faulty wire or pipe."

"What about ghosts?" someone snickers.

"Or the Curators?" someone else chimes in. "Didn't they cause a bunch of problems last semester?"

"Don't let Fury Hill's propensity for paranoia poison your minds too." Clapping, I wave my hands toward the doors. "Go now so I can get this cleaned up. I'll see you next week."

Whispers abound as the students gather their things, the hush of their exit as unwelcome as the silence that comes after it.

I stare at the shattered glass and broken wires, my mind spinning like a rogue wheel, incapable of stopping. My hands tremble, unease spooling around them tight like thread, cinching until I can't focus on anything else—

"Professor?"

One student remains, hovering near the stage stairs.

Forcing a swallow, I turn my head slightly. Look into her hazel eyes. A strange wave of calmness settles over me, though the panic still exists right beneath the surface, like a fire temporarily extinguished.

"Yes?" I choke out.

"Are you okay?"

The calmness is like a beacon, bright and airy, drawing me to it. But I feel stuck in place—bound by the sensation of utter dread. One that's lived in me for much longer than I think I noticed.

"No," I tell her softly, shaking my head. "No, I'm not okay."

Chapter 40

Elle

"IT FEELS WEIRD BEING IN HERE WITH YOUR PERMISSION."

"Weird?" Sutton's mouth skims the underside of my jaw, one of his hands on my hip, the other flat against my back, keeping me as close to him as I can get with all my clothes still on.

"Well, it hasn't been all that long since you were telling me to leave," I breathe, my fingers tangling in his hair.

The leather couch in his living room is a lot comfier than it looks, which is good, because he hasn't let me off it since we arrived—separately, so as not to arouse suspicion, even though it was well after ten by the time we got the auditorium cleaned up and the faulty equipment reported.

He clearly wasn't okay after the incident, but I didn't want to pry, letting him deal with the shock or memories—whatever the incident triggered within—however he wanted.

This was his choice.

Since the whole Death's Teeth thing, it's like he can't keep himself from touching me when we're alone. Like he needs some reminder that I'm safe, which would be endearing if I didn't keep recalling the conversation we had in his office about the apparent danger I'm in.

They granted him an extension to make his decision, but I can't help feeling like a sitting duck still.

"In my defense," he murmurs, threading his fingers through the ends of my hair, "I was desperately trying to convince myself to stay away from you."

"You gave in surprisingly quickly."

"Well, you *are* my Maiden now, right? Between us at least. Why not enjoy the reprieve we have at the moment?"

It feels like an oversimplification, but I'm not sure how to tell him that. Sutton's the kind of person to shut down when threatened, and I don't want to ruin the progress we've made.

"Plus, that Lexington was always circling around you like a hawk, biding his time. I had to swoop in and stake my claim." He pulls back, looking into my eyes. His are a little unsteady, like he's got a lot going on in his head, and I wish I could reach in and stall the thoughts for a little.

"Your *claim*? What am I, a piece of property?" I say, leaning in and brushing my lips against his.

"I wouldn't mind conquering you." He grins, palming the back of my head and slanting his mouth onto mine.

Turning so I'm straddling him, I swallow every one of his breaths as if it were my own.

My palms flatten against his pecs, sliding up to cup both sides of his neck. His tongue slips inside my mouth, tasting and teasing mine; each flick sends arousal spinning webs through my limbs, making me clench my knees against him.

He lets out a little noise of desperation, his fingers inching beneath my sweater. The backs of his knuckles are cool on my heated flesh as he drags them from left to right, reveling in the way my stomach twitches, before slowly ascending to my breast.

Pushing my top up, he leans in and tugs the cup of my bra down. I exhale shakily as his breath skates across my nipple, hardening it to a fine peak.

"I love how responsive you are," he mutters, laving the flat of his tongue against me before closing his lips around it and sucking, hard. "Like I can give just the slightest touch and have you aching for more, my needy little temptress."

Crying out, I arch into him, clutching his head to keep him in place. A shiver races down my spine, pushing me into a brief flash of clarity as he swirls around my sensitive skin, sliding his other hand between my thighs.

"Wait," I say, grabbing his wrist before he can brush my pussy. My abdomen is tight, trepidation clawing at my muscles. Kissing him, being with him, doesn't usually feel like this.

The anticipation, the excitement, is off.

Something is wrong.

Sutton waits. I clear my throat, glancing over my shoulder. The thick brown curtains are pulled in his living room, along with the coverings in the kitchen and foyer. At the end of the hall, his bedroom door is shut, and no other sound is made while we sit there in silence.

Running his thumb over my nipple, he cocks his head. "Everything all right?"

No, but I'm not sure why I feel so uneasy. Maybe it's just paranoia seeping in from Fury Hill or the leftover adrenaline from the auditorium earlier.

"Is this what you asked me here to do?" I ask instead, avoiding eye contact.

He looks up from my chest. "Well, I'm not exactly opposed…"

"Maybe we shouldn't. I mean, don't you think the whole thing in the auditorium was a little oddly timed, especially considering the Death's Teeth stuff?"

"What's that got to do with what we're doing now?"

I shrug. "What if they know you're trying to push the Maiden duties off on Sabrina or that I'm the one you're really picking?"

"Doesn't matter," he says, shaking his head. "I'm Incarnate. They can't disobey a direct order to let me handle things. Sabotage would be insubordination. A punishable offense."

"Punishable how?"

"I'd…rather not say."

We spend several minutes sitting just like that, not speaking, not moving. I can hear the steady rhythm of his heart, but that's all. I let it ground me, shoving myself out of the narrative where something terrible is always about to happen.

It feels too easy that his dad let me walk away that night, especially if the organization hates Andersons as much as Sutton says. If my discovery could have resulted in my death without his interference, who's to say they won't try to off me outside the group functions and make it seem like an accident?

My eyes find Sutton's, and I grind my teeth together. He doesn't *want* me to be his Maiden, but he doesn't feel there's another choice.

And maybe there isn't.

Maybe I should just be content with what I've got and stop poking my head where it doesn't belong.

My mouth parts to tell Sutton about his dad, to clear that hurdle before it gets to him some other way, but then he's palming the back of my head. He pulls me into another kiss, this one startlingly sweeter than the last. When he withdraws, he strokes my cheek with his thumb, then places me on the other side of the couch.

I watch as he gets up and heads for the kitchen, tossing something into the microwave. A few seconds later, popping noises fill the air, and the scent of melted butter assaults my nostrils, making my stomach growl.

When he comes back, several thick throw blankets and a bag of popcorn in hand, I move to stand and give him that space.

He settles back onto his cushion, giving me a look as I start to leave. "Where do you think you're going?"

"Back to my dorm?"

"I don't think so. Come back here and watch *Casablanca* with me."

"*Casablanca?*"

"You know it?"

"It's one of my all-time favorites. I love all the classic movies, but that one in particular gets rewatched monthly."

He grins. "I knew you were perfect for me for a reason. Come on. We can have a movie marathon. I have *My Fair Lady* and *North by Northwest* in my collection too."

Licking my lips, I stare at him, then glance at the television when he switches it on. Within seconds, the black-and-white title screen comes on, though I still hesitate.

Is this a date? Can it really be considered one when we can't even do things publicly?

A part of me is terrified that I'm getting my hopes up. That going any further with this man will only end in heartbreak.

Maybe that's why I stopped things from progressing earlier. It's starting to feel a bit too real, and I'm much more comfortable in the land of make-believe.

Sutton leans forward, his eyes on the television, and grabs my wrist, yanking me down onto the couch. I fall into his side, and he immediately covers me with a blanket, holding me against him.

"This is now a hostage situation," he says, offering me a handful of popcorn.

I open my mouth, and he feeds me a few pieces. The earlier sensation is absent, so I write it off as nerves. "Fair warning, I'm a really bad crisis negotiator."

He laughs, his eyes softening. "Don't worry. I have no intention of letting you go."

Chapter 41

Sutton

"PROFESSOR DUPONT," IRIS CREIGHTON WHINES, HOLDING HER paintbrush between two fingers. "How come you didn't go to last night's meeting?"

It takes a moment for my brain to compute which meeting she's asking about—not the Death's Teeth gatherings I've been skipping but Visio Aternae, of which she's the secretary.

The former I'm avoiding under the guise of getting to know my Maiden, which they believe Sabrina to be. As long as I can keep them out of my business, I'm hoping I can protect Elle—at least through the end of the semester.

After that, once the Maiden ceremony has happened and a student has been sacrificed, there won't be an opportunity for them to protest when I announce my real pick.

Visio Aternae I'm not avoiding at all—they just tend to fall by the wayside as the end of the semester nears. They're pretty self-sufficient anyway, and most of them volunteer to help with the final play where they can check in with me as Iris is now.

"We picked a charity to sponsor this year," Iris continues, leaning in to add some fine, thin lines to the backdrop she's working on. "The Entertainment Community Fund. That's one you like a lot, right?"

I nod. "They do good work."

"See, I told Sabrina that when she suggested we do something with a wider appeal. Can you believe she thought a nonprofit focused on affordable housing would make a bigger impact?"

"Uh…" I cock an eyebrow. "What do you think the Entertainment Community Fund does?"

She blinks her big blue eyes at me. "Provides funding for theatrical productions, obviously."

At my side, Quincy lets out a low whistle. "Maybe you should think about vetting your organization's members next year."

I shift, scrubbing a hand over my face. "Can't. We're the sole non-invite-only group, and Avernia needs accessibility to decency now more than ever."

She says nothing, and I refocus on the task at hand—or try to at least.

Recruiting Visio Aternae members to repaint the sets from last semester's production was an easy enough task since they're so into reducing, reusing, and recycling.

But considering what happened last time we were here, I gave the cast the week off, with the explicit instructions to be off script at our next rehearsal.

"What?" I bark over my shoulder, glaring as Quincy crosses her arms.

"What do you think you're doing?" she asks.

Turning around, I frown. "Making sure these sets get painted correctly?"

Her eyes darken behind the lenses of her glasses. She takes a step toward me, bringing her nose toward my collarbone.

I shift back, holding my hands up as discomfort ripples through me. My fingers are numb today, the added stress of the play not good for the Raynaud's or my migraines. "Whoa, hey, I'm not into you like that."

"Oh, please." She scoffs, straightening back up. "You smell like Noelle."

"I'm afraid I don't know a Noelle..."

She clenches her jaw. "Don't play stupid, Dupont. You have a lot of nerve risking her reputation and status here."

"As an Anderson, wasn't that already a given?"

"So you think toying with her is okay because Fury Hill hates her? Jesus, I told you I wouldn't help here if you were messing with her, and you've gone and—"

Snatching Quincy's wrist, I drag her down the aisle, away from the turned heads and shushed students. "It's highly inappropriate to air your sister's business out in front of her classmates."

"You don't get to lecture me on what's inapprop—"

"I like her," I snap, giving her wrist a shake before dropping it.

"You like her." She narrows her eyes, scrutinizing me. "Or you like what she can do for you?"

"What the hell is that supposed to mean?"

"It means Elle is a person who loves being loved, and she's quick to do whatever it takes to feel a connection with someone. That resilience I talked about? It's a fucking shield. She wears it whenever she breaks her own heart, and I recognize the signs. She's smiling more, humming to herself in the mornings before class, even initiating calls and texts with our parents. It's the calm before the storm—the storm where she gets hurt and shuts everyone out, and then no one knows the truth about what's going on with her for eight fucking years."

"I'm not…" I swallow, shifting my gaze to the floor. "I don't want to hurt her."

"Then end whatever it is you've got going on. Before it's too late."

She shoves past me, shoulder checking me as she heads for the doors. I turn, watching her go, and just as her hands find the push bar, I speak.

"No."

Pausing, she shoots me a malicious glance. "No?"

"You heard me."

Several beats of my heart pass erratically before she straightens her spine, shoving open the door. "Then I guess I'll just have to report you both."

Chapter 42

Elle

WITH TREMBLING KNEES, I TAKE A SEAT BACKSTAGE, LISTENING to Sabrina deliver a flawless recitation of Desdemona taking credit for her own murder. My stomach is cramping *bad* today even though my period ended a week ago, so I asked if we could do my scenes last.

Through the curtains, Sutton yells cut, and the cast scatters to the back. I watch Sabrina in her beautiful gown as she sashays to the corner, gulping down some lemon water she keeps in a metal bottle.

She catches my eye in the floor-length mirror propped against the wall and turns toward me, an unreadable expression on her face. As she approaches, my entire body instinctively tenses up, and I scoot my legs in, as if touching her might drag me back down to those caves.

Sitting down on the closed clothing trunk beside me, Sabrina unfolds her hand, revealing an oblong, nearly translucent white rock.

"An apology," she says, offering me the object. "For getting you into that whole mess at the Apollodorus. I shouldn't have asked you guys to go down there. I wouldn't fault you if you blamed me for the emotional trauma."

It's the first either of us have brought up that night, seeming to choose to pretend it didn't happen. Out loud at least.

"Uh…what is it?"

"Moonstone. I found it at the quarry." She turns the object over in her palm, smoothing her fingers against the uneven ridges. "Fury Hill, decades ago, got into mining for raw minerals. A way to make a quick buck, I guess. The school actually shut it down due to environmental concerns, but the minerals are still there—including cool gemstones like this one."

Slowly, I take the rock from her and hold it up to the light; I can practically see right through it. "Thanks… But how is this an apology?"

"Lexington told me you like astrology and shit—"

"Astronomy."

"—so I thought maybe you'd find me more favorable if I found something cool that interests you." She shrugs, her blue eyes crinkling at the corners. "I realize now that it's completely cheesy, but you never know. Lots of people believe in celestial connections between the heavens and the earth."

"Life and death," I say.

She sucks in a low breath, nodding. "Yeah, that too." Bracing her hands on her knees, she looks at me through the curtain of her hair as it falls over her shoulders. "I'm really sorry about what happened at that party, you know. I swear, I had no idea what was down there."

My fingers close around the cool stone. "You seemed to know an awful lot about Death's Teeth though."

408 SAV R. MILLER

"Casualty of growing up in Fury Hill." She sighs, pushing her hair back. "You don't get through kindergarten without hearing tales of the masked shadows in the Primordial Forest. Then, with everything that happened last semester and the way it was swept under the rug… I guess I got curious. Started reading up about it."

I glance at the front of the stage, where Sutton is marking places for the cast to stand during different scenes.

"The man who dragged us to that cavern… Did you know him?"

"No."

"Really?" She glances at me, squinting. "He seemed to be familiar with you."

My gaze falls to my backpack again. I shake my head. "Probably just another curse nut. Who knows?"

"Stranger things have definitely happened. I'm just glad he let us go after. I've read some pretty fucked-up stuff that can go on at those ceremonies."

She doesn't mention that we were offerings or my own volunteer stunt, so I have to wonder how much she actually remembers. I'm about to ask for more information when Sutton cuts in from up front.

"Desdemona, we're ready for you again."

She exhales. "You should've been the leading lady."

"Nah." I give her a small smile. "Bianca suits me just fine. You deserve the spotlight—you've been practically begging the professor for it the whole semester."

Something flashes in her eyes, and she purses her lips, considering. "You know, I never really want—"

"*Desdemona*." Sutton's voice is louder, firmer, and I hate that the authority of it makes my thighs clench.

As she gets up and passes through the curtains again, I follow suit, hanging on to the fabric and watching the scene from behind. The auditorium is hushed and darkened, shrouded in an array of shadows as the spotlights focus on the cast members.

Sabrina crosses the stage, heading to the makeshift bed to simulate Desdemona's death. Everyone's enraptured by her elegance as she approaches, aware that she's about to be pretend-smothered by a classmate again.

She takes a detour as a couple of set designers work in the center to resituate the scene, all while our Othello continues his monologue, moving as if just entering Desdemona's bedroom to accuse her of infidelity.

"'Yet she must die, else she'll betray more men. Put out the light, and then put out the light.'"

Before he finishes the last line, the spotlights angled toward the stage go out, encasing us in total darkness. At the same time, a scream and subsequent crash echo through the auditorium, the fear reverberating off my skull.

"What the hell?" I hear Sutton say. He swears under his breath when the lights don't come back on, and panic murmurs through us as we listen to his footsteps rush toward the emergency switch on the wall.

Seconds later, the floodlights illuminate the room in a faint glow, and relief passes over us in a wave.

Until someone screams again. One of the set designers leans into the pit, a horrified look frozen on their face.

"Professor, come quick! Sabrina's hurt!"

Everyone rushes over to where they're at, looking into the secluded area. Sabrina's somehow flat on her back, staring up at the rafters with wide, unseeing eyes.

Blood pools beneath her head, soaking her hair.

Nausea rolls through me, a cyclone of terror.

"Oh my God!" someone cries, and the room begins to descend into madness.

Percy climbs into the pit, breathing hard, and reaches for her.

"No, wait!" I say, forcing myself to stop him. "You can't move a head injury. Someone needs to call the paramedics and campus police."

"Sabrina, can you speak? Or hear us at all?" Sutton asks.

She opens her mouth, but I jump down into the area and shove the others out of the way. My hands tremble, and I'm unable to look away from her eyes.

"I slipped," she manages, cringing as she tries to lift an arm. "Hurts."

Pointing at Percy, I still don't look away from her. Can't look away—fire scalds the inside of my chest when I try. "Call campus police. Get someone out here to treat her. Now."

Sutton stands above us and drags a hand through his hair. He hovers so close to me, like he's trying to silently offer support, but I wave him off too.

"Give her space," I bark, turning for a second just to shoot the hyenas watching a nasty look. "Stop staring at her like she's a zoo animal, and go figure out what the hell is wrong with your equipment."

"We did the full rundown on these lights at sound check, right?" Sutton asks someone, but I'm curled protectively over Sabrina's body and not willing to move to see who.

A tear slips over her cheek. "Am I gonna be okay?"

I nod, tapping her finger, even though I'm not totally sure. I'm only using the very basic knowledge Dad taught us about head injuries. I don't know what other signs to look for or what sort of response she should be having. But I feel the need to reassure her anyway, because as I'm maintaining eye contact to ensure she doesn't lose consciousness, I'm not in the auditorium anymore—I'm a helpless seventeen-year-old girl lost in the Primordial Forest.

I'm a girl who reacted without thinking and sent someone else into that lake. Someone who never came back up.

The body before me isn't Sabrina but the battered, limp form of a guy bound and soaked as if he somehow pulled himself out of the water.

Maybe that's why I sprang into action, the need to save Sabrina from a similar fate surging so thoroughly in my chest that I couldn't just stay still. A repeat of that night—of every time I've ever been fucking useless—couldn't happen. Not again.

Or maybe it's because when I look up into the darkened rows of the auditorium, I see the mangled silhouette of a man disfigured by brutal violence, and I know somehow that this is my fault.

Again.

Chapter 43

Sutton

"AND SHE'LL BE DISCHARGED IN THE MORNING?" I PAUSE, STAR-ing at my front door with the phone pressed to my ear as Dean Bauer relays Sabrina's condition. A concussion and some stitches from where she hit one of the music stands as she tumbled into the pit—frankly, much less severe than any of us expected.

"Yes, her mother's come to stay overnight. They're only keeping her for observation. Scans showed no signs of internal bleeding or swelling from the fall, but you know the board wants us to be certain."

"Anything to avoid a lawsuit," I mutter. It's why they're so eager to cover up anything that happens here—all the murders and disap-pearances, the claims of the supernatural, the unfairness across the campus organizations and their exclusionary practices.

Avernia is the greased wheel that keeps Fury Hill functioning, and it only manages that balance because of how hard people work behind the scenes.

Otherwise, I'm certain the school would no longer be in

operation. It likely wouldn't have seen much past its conception had the founders not been the heart of the corruption.

Hanging up, I let out a long sigh and exit my foyer, stuffing my hands into my pants pockets. Elle sits on my couch with her knees pulled up, arms wrapped tight around them, staring off into space.

There are no lights on, only candles lining the coffee and end tables, casting shadows across her pale skin. She's even more breathtaking surrounded by flames.

Quincy's warning blares in my mind, a bright red alarm telling me to make her leave. To stop engaging this way with this student before it ruins our lives, but I can't.

I don't fucking want to.

"The good news is the neurological staff at Fury Hill Medical anticipate Sabrina will be just fine," I say, moving toward the couch. "Bad news is she has to stay overnight, but all things considered…"

Flopping down next to Elle, I stretch my arm over the cushion back and reach for her chin, turning her face toward me.

"That's great," she says, moving away from my touch. She looks down at a loose thread in her skirt, wrapping it around one finger and tearing it from the fabric.

I hum in agreement, waiting for her to face me again. To melt into my embrace the way she normally does or at least let me get closer.

When I scoot forward an inch, she clears her throat and leans away. Rejection pulses in my forehead, and I narrow my eyes.

"What are you doing?"

She swallows, her gaze going to the coffee table now. "Nothing? I'm just sitting here."

"You're practically hanging off the couch trying to get away from me." I pause, smoothing my hands over my knees. "Did I do something?"

"No. I've just been…thinking."

My chest tightens. I rub at the sore spot in one of my pecs, a tendril of fear snaking around my spine. What if Quincy spoke to her already?

"All right. Thinking about what?" I force out, even though I don't really want to know.

She uncurls her fingers, staring at them as if they're not even attached to her own body. "What do you think this thing between us is?"

I scratch the back of my neck. "What do you mean?"

"You've said it before, right? That this… You don't normally do things like this. That from the moment we met, our connection felt *different* somehow. Like…fate, maybe, or I don't know." Her cheeks burn bright pink. "Maybe not *fate*, but something that keeps you from being able to stay away?"

"Yes."

"Do you…honestly believe that?" She glances at me for the first time since we came back to the apartment, her eyes distant. "You believe there could be greater forces at work and no matter how much we tried to resist, we'd still have crossed paths at some point?"

"I wouldn't agree if I didn't," I tell her, cupping her jaw before sliding my hands into her hair. "I believe it, yes. Destiny, fate, kismet—whatever you want to label it. I do not think for a second that we weren't inevitable."

"What if that isn't true though? What if you're just deluding yourself into feeling better about risking everything for me?"

She exhales, the sound a bit strained, and I realize a beat too late that she's panicking. Over what exactly, I'm not sure, but I find the fact that she's this unsettled completely unnerving.

"I wouldn't risk anything if I didn't think you were worth it."

She gnaws on her bottom lip, a blush staining her cheeks. "What if it's just this school making us think this way? Avernia clearly has influence over its students' thoughts and even their actions, so what—"

"Do you not think of me as a man capable of making conscious decisions? If I wanted sex, Elle—"

"You could get it, yeah, I know." She glares. "But what if—"

"We can hypothesize all day long, and the results would remain the same. I would still want you, and you would still want me."

She nods, leaning her forehead against mine.

I gently push her back until she's lying flat on the couch and climb over top of her, skimming my hand up her side. She shivers, accepting my touch as it slips beneath the hem of her sweater, over the flat of her stomach.

"Elle." I brush a strand of hair from her face.

She pinches her eyes shut, inhaling shakily. Two tears leak from the corners of her eyelids, and I bend down, kissing them away.

"What's the real issue here, temptress?" I whisper, pressing my forehead to hers. "Talk to me."

"I'm terrified."

My eyebrows hike into my hairline, and I pull back. "Of me?"

She shrugs. "Of everything. Weird stuff is suddenly happening at rehearsals. I'm supposedly in danger because of Death's Teeth. People hate me because of my last name. I don't know what I'm doing, I have no real plans for my future, and I'm…scared that something I did a long time ago is catching up with me."

"Something you did," I repeat, cocking my head to the side. "Like an ex? That idiot director you said—"

"No," she says. "That's definitely going to catch up with me. I accepted that a long time ago."

Tension threads through my muscles, drawing them so tight that it becomes hard to move. "If he were to ever come near you, I'd kill him."

That makes her laugh. "He's a pretty well-respected director, you know."

"He's nothing." Leaning down, I press a gentle kiss to her collarbone, aware that with every word, every kiss, every time I keep her in my presence, I'm just digging my grave deeper and deeper. But I can't seem to stop.

Finally, her fingers come to my head, twisting in the ends of my hair. I bite back a moan at how good her touch feels because it's more than a little pathetic how desperate I am.

"Don't worry about the play," I say into her skin, dragging my lips up the column of her throat. "The understudy will step in until Sabrina's well enough to return, and we'll move on as expected. It'll be great. As for Death's Teeth…"

I don't have anything good to say about them, but my earlier sentiment remains.

I'd kill them too.

Anyone who intends to hurt her at all.

"Everything will be fine," I say.

She doesn't answer, instead rising up to meet me as I dive down for another kiss, done with talking for the night.

Sweaty and shaking, I rip myself from a nightmare—from the fresh scent of burning flesh and blood and eyes that were carved out, begging me to consume them.

My throat is tight as I jerk awake, drenched and struggling to control my heart, which feels like it's going to beat straight from my chest.

The bedroom is dark, impossible to see even as I lift my hand in front of my face—just to make sure it's still there. Numbness tingles at the edges of my fingertips, and I rub a circle against my pec, trying to regain sensation.

Heat seeps into my side, short breaths puffing against my collarbone, and for a moment, I tense up. Reaching down, I smooth my palm over the soft head of hair, sliding over the side of her face, familiarizing myself with the contours I learned long ago.

Before I was allowed to really touch her.

Not that this is technically allowed, but here in the secrecy of my home, at least we can pretend.

She stirs, trying to get closer in her sleep; her calf hooks around my waist, bringing her hot little cunt flush with my hip. I'm suddenly very aware of the fact that she climbed in my bed with nothing but a thin T-shirt and cotton panties, and as I lie there trying to collect myself, I don't think I've ever craved something more.

Wanton desire is nothing new when it comes to Elle, but right now, my body hums at her proximity, still half-asleep and totally enraptured by her.

I run my hands over my face and exhale, settling back on the mattress. My heart thumps erratically behind my rib cage, and as I inhale slowly, I get a whiff of her—honey, vanilla, and a tiny hint of saline clinging to her skin.

When she shifts again, rubbing her crotch lewdly against me, I pinch her cheek to get her to wake up. It takes a moment; she pushes onto her elbow, one hand hovering just above the band of my briefs.

Too close for comfort.

"What is it?" she asks, her voice thick with sleep.

Fuck, she's sexy. Even the silhouette of her makes my cock throb, dying to be set free.

"Nothing, baby. Go back to bed. Sorry for waking you."

She nods and starts to lie back down, but her hand slips lower—too low, brushing over the raging erection waiting for her.

I grit my teeth as she pauses, keeping her fingers on me. "Elle…"

"Did you have a nightmare?"

An incredulous laugh tumbles out of me. "I'm not a child, temptress. You don't need to worry about my sleeping habits."

"Sex helps keep bad dreams away," she says softly.

"I'm fine, honestly—"

When she gives me a sharp squeeze over my briefs, I let out a noise of wicked contempt. The cheeky little brat knows what she's doing, and she seems intent on getting her way this time.

I've been denying her out of insecurity—the idea that once we take that step, the flames that burn so bright between us will extinguish. Or that any comparisons will hit too close to home and I won't be able to go through with it.

But that disgust, the feeling of absolute horror that persists when anyone else touches me or when I try touching someone else, is entirely absent when it's her. I don't even think twice about creating a physical connection, and I never have. Not since the first night we met.

That has to mean something. Even now, with the weight of my dreams and past sitting on my shoulders, tempting me into a spiral of total shame, the only thing I can really focus on is how badly I want this.

Want her.

So when she leans on her knee, sliding it onto the mattress to straddle me, I don't stop her.

She hums, content, as she settles on my lap, dragging her fingernails down my chest. Her cunt grinds into me as she moves, deftly unbuttoning my shirt. Each release of a button from its hole feels like she's plucking at the tendons beneath my skin, making them yield to her touch.

Once she's finished with all of them, she pushes the shirt aside, leaning in to lick my nipple. The sensitive peak hardens, and she nibbles around it, sending frissons of heat rolling through my abdomen.

Her hand crawls down the center of me, pausing right above the waistband of my pajama pants.

Without warning, she withdraws, climbing off me and then the bed to dart across the room.

My pulse grows uneven. "Elle?"

"Wait a second," she says, and a moment later, the sound of a match slashing against a striking strip fills the air, and a flame appears where she stands by my dresser.

She lights a few candles, coming around to place them on the nightstand next to the bed, and then waves the flame out.

I grunt as she scrambles back on top of me, pulling me up so she can push my shirt from my shoulders.

"Wanted to see you," she mutters into my skin, trailing her lips over my collarbone before shoving me back into the mattress.

"Good call." My hands find her hips, squeezing tight, and then move inward. I skim the tips of my thumbs under the elastic of her panties, just barely resisting the urge to tear them from her.

In the candlelight, she's exquisite. An ethereal goddess placed on the earth with the sole purpose of driving me mad.

When she shifts, angling her hips so her cunt glides more easily along my length, I suck in a sharp gasp. White-hot need pours into my chest, filling the cavity with its debauched fantasies.

Sitting up straight, she leans over to the nightstand and snatches one of the candles from its perch. As it burns, white wax drips down the stick, over her fingers—and onto my stomach.

I hiss as the initial scalding sensation ripples through me, instantly cooling as she inches up, tilting the candle to hit another spot. This time, it lands in the center of my chest, and she punctuates the connection with a slow thrust against my fabric-covered cock.

"That feels good, doesn't it?" she asks in a low, thick voice.

I nod, afraid my restraint might snap if I speak. The muscles in my limbs are taut, pulled to the edge and desperate to be set free.

She holds the candle up as she bends, sliding back toward my knees. With her mouth, she hooks her teeth into my waistband and uses her free hand to help shimmy them down.

That image alone is so erotic that I nearly come from watching.

It's embarrassing how gone I am for her.

Coming back up, Elle angles the candle above my hips, letting the wax drizzle onto my pelvis. My body arcs off the bed, the heat from the wax lighting my entire body on fire.

A dangerous glint appears in her eyes, nearly eclipsed by the shadows dancing around us. I move fast, snatching the candle from her hands and flipping so she's lying on her back with me over top of her.

With a sly grin, she wraps her legs around my waist, dragging me against her. Since my pants aren't pulled up, I can feel just how little material there is between us and how needy she is for me.

She wiggles out of her shirt, her breasts bouncing as she settles flat on her back again, tossing the clothing to the floor. Holding her arms together, she pushes her tits up and out in offering as she flutters her lashes.

Quickly, I shrug out of my clothes.

"Don't you wanna mark me?" she asks sweetly, softly, so deeply flushed that I feel like I might pass out.

"In so many fucking ways," I reply, switching the candle out for a new one—this one red. I tip the jar it's in gently, sucking in air through my teeth when the wax splashes against her smooth, pale skin and she lets out a low moan.

I follow the same pattern, drawing swirls and cross marks over her chest. When I'm finished, she's panting and covered in crimson. It's hardening quickly, but the picture of her drenched in blood, feral and waiting for more, is not one I can quickly erase from my mind.

Maybe ever.

"You…" I say, breathless, blowing out the candle and tossing it to the ground. I slide my hands over the wax, cupping her tits in my hands. "…are a vision, tentatrice. Je suis amoureux de ta perfection."

I cough a little at the end of my sentence, realizing a moment too late what I've inadvertently confessed to without even fully processing what I'm saying.

She gasps, threading her fingers through mine, making me squeeze her fully as she arches into the gesture.

The wax is hard on her skin, like it's trying to cast her body in a mold. She meets my eyes, hunger lighting hers. "More?"

"Wax or words?"

"Words. Please. I want to hear you."

Humming, I bend and drag my tongue up from the hollow of

her throat, all the way to her chin. "Tu as un goût incroyable. Je veux me régaler de toi pour le reste de nos vies."

Scoring my teeth over the underside of her jaw, I shift, rolling my cock against her cunt. She lets out a small whimper, tightening her legs around me in a silent plea.

My fingers trail up her thigh, coasting until I feel the fabric still covering her. With two digits, I find her soaked center, gliding slowly up her seam through those panties, reveling in how she writhes at the barest touch.

"Tu es belle."

It's intoxicating, how badly she wants this. How I ache to touch her, kiss her, be in her. How wet she is from a little foreplay, her body making it clear she belongs to me.

Fuck.

That's not right, but it's how I feel.

I want to claim Elle for myself—forever, all of eternity. Rules and pasts be fucking damned.

I want to bury myself so deeply inside her that it'd take multiple lifetimes for her to ever push me out. I want her under my skin, living in my blood, consuming me from the inside out.

"Dis s'il te plaît." I tug her panties to the side, delving between her sopping folds, skirting over her clit and hovering near her entrance. "Say please, baby."

"How do I say it in French?"

"How badly do you want it?"

"Really bad." She makes a strangled noise in her throat. "It's all I think about. You filling me, over and over, until I'm a sweet, sobbing mess."

My chest grows hot. "Je t'en supplie."

"Je t'en supplie," she repeats, licking her lips. She says it again, this time more desperate. "Je…t'en…supplie."

Leaning in, I slant my mouth across hers at the same time I plunge two fingers into her cunt, the immediate warmth and tightness as she spasms making me moan. She captures the sound, swallowing it as she slices her tongue against mine, her hands tangling in my hair.

Each time I kiss her, it feels like the world is stopping and starting all at once. Like time forcibly stands still, waiting for us to come up for air or die trying.

Our teeth gnash, scraping as the connection grows hungrier, needier, and suddenly what we're doing isn't enough. I tear my lips away with a low growl, shouldering my way between her thighs to add my tongue to the mix, lapping at her cunt like it's the only source of water in the desert.

Her hands pull at the roots of my hair as she drives her hips against my face, riding her way to pleasure. I pump my fingers in short, curled bursts, chasing the way her body moves and noting the exact things that make her clamp down around me like a fucking vise.

"Fuck," I groan into her slick, sensitive flesh. "Tu as un goût si doux."

"Oh, shit. Sutton—" Her hips arc up, seeking more, and I use my forearm to pin her back on the mattress.

"Look at me when my mouth is on you, or I'll stop," I tell her, sucking at her clit.

She cries out, eyes searching for mine as her grip on my hair becomes punishing. I add a third finger, curling and massaging, and spear my tongue into her alongside them. With my free arm, I push my elbow against her thigh to keep her spread wide and draw rough figure eights on that pulsating bundle of nerves, watching from her cunt as her entire body begins to tremble.

The moment she starts to come, though, I slow my movements, yanking her back from the edge. A frustrated grunt pushes from her chest, and I build back up again, stroking and sucking and rubbing until she's right there, over and over and over.

We're both drenched in sweat. My vision is blurring, desire swimming through my mind and blocking out all thought except how good I can make her feel. That's all my body wants to do right now.

"Sutton," Elle whines, tears pooling in those beautiful hazel eyes of hers.

"Goddamn, there she is," I coax, my stomach twisting violently as she tightens, cutting off my circulation. This time, I don't slow down, too desperate to feel her come around my fingers. "Let it out, baby. Take everything you need from me. You're so perfect and beautiful with my fingers inside you. Don't I deserve a reward for making you feel so good?"

Her mouth falls open on a soul-shattering moan, half prayer, half war cry. She goes rigid, shaking uncontrollably as her cunt clamps so tight that she almost pushes me out.

When her back arches, she breaks eye contact, but I don't make note of it out loud. Instead, I keep pumping, drawing every last spasm out of her until she reaches down and grabs my wrist, forcing me to stop.

I withdraw slowly, placing all three fingers on the back of my tongue and sucking them clean. The taste of her arousal mixed with the slight musk from her sweat makes me hard as a fucking rock, and I move up so I'm looming over her, wiping my mouth with the back of my hand before planting them both on either side of her head.

She's out of breath but manages a limp smile. "You're good at that. No one else ever—"

Wincing, I cover her mouth with my own, flicking my tongue against hers. She moans, tasting herself, and palms the back of my head, trying to bring me closer.

"Don't mention anyone else when you're in my fucking bed," I whisper against her lips. "You come on my hands, my face—that makes you mine. Got it?"

"You say that like I haven't been yours since the beginning of the semester," she says softly.

"Yeah?" Sliding my arm under her waist, I roll so she's back on top, my cock bobbing angrily between us. "Prove it then."

Humming, she guides me between her legs, slowly gliding back and forth along my length. Her underwear is still a barrier, but they're entirely soaked through, leaving so little to the imagination as the friction makes me harder than ever.

"There are condoms in the nightstand," I say, gripping the tops of her thighs. "Grab one and put it on me."

"You keep them on hand?"

"Well, normally, no." My face heats. "But I wanted to be prepared in case...you know. I got to do this with you."

She hesitates, sucking her bottom lip between her teeth.

I sit up on my elbows, tilting my head as a strange expression passes over her face. "Hey," I say, cupping her cheek. She turns, letting her hair fall, shielding herself from me. "What is it?"

Exhaling, she swallows. "I was hoping we wouldn't need one."

Silence, other than the slight crackling of a couple of the candle wicks, falls over us. My nostrils flare, my cock pulsing so thoroughly, I feel it in my throat.

Elle looks at me, her eyes cast downward. "It's just…well, I get tested every time I have a new partner, and I'm okay…if you wanted to."

"If I wanted to fuck you bare?" Sitting up more, I press my nose to her collarbone, inhaling deeply. "You'd let me in, just like that?"

"Well, if you're also—"

"I get a physical each semester. Avernia faculty policy. You'd have nothing to worry about."

She nods, grabbing my shoulders and pushing me back. "Then…yeah. I trust you. And as we know, I'm on the pill."

"Religiously since you were a teenager."

My recitation of her rambling the night we met makes her beam. "Exactly…and I really, *really* want to feel you with nothing between us. Please?"

"Christ, Elle. You're gonna be the death of me, you know that?" Her nod is my undoing; I hook my fingers in her underwear and pull, waiting for the tear of fabric. When nothing happens, I frown, glaring down at the material. "What the hell is this, some sort of chastity device?"

"It didn't do a good job of keeping your mouth from my—"

"Whatever. Get up and take them off so I can put this in you." I fist myself as she hurries to disrobe, settling back over my lap with her dripping cunt poised right at my tip.

"Go slow," she says, placing her hand over mine to help guide it in.

"You can handle it, baby."

She scoffs. "I know, Boy Scout. I just don't want you coming as soon as you're in me."

"The faster I come," I growl, raising up to suck at her collarbone, "the faster I can fill you up, then flip you over and do it again. And again. I haven't been with anyone in a very long time, temptress, so I've got stamina to spare."

"Oh." Pink crawls up her chest, ripening her nipples.

I move my hands and let her take over the direction—for a moment at least. She guides my tip in as I wrap my arms around her, and with one firm tug, I'm seated all the way, so deep and snug that I black out for a moment while she drones a low, hedonistic whimper.

"*Fuck*," she gasps, clawing at my skin, likely leaving marks. "That was not slow."

"You don't want slow," I mutter against her ear. "You want hard and fast. You want a harsh, brutal claiming and nothing less."

Her hips twitch, and she pushes me back, keeping her hands on my chest. "Claiming—like this?"

She lifts up, nearly removing me from her, and then slams all the way back down. Arousal surges into my throat, strangling me.

With a quiet huff, she leans forward, looming over me as she braces her hands on the headboard. I lift my chin, capturing one of her nipples in my mouth and sucking as she begins grinding and undulating on top of me. Her inner muscles are so tight, so warm, that I'm having trouble concentrating on not blowing, especially with her tits hanging in my face.

I take them both in my hands, kneading and nibbling the swollen, heavy flesh. She rocks up and down, back and forth, using the bed as leverage to really drive her movements.

My toes curl. I abandon her tits, my arms instinctively wrapping around her, pulling her so our chests are flush. She squeals as she loses her grip, tumbling into my embrace. My hips take over, my cock driving into her over and over and over from below.

Holding her waist, I anchor her in place as my thrusts grow punishing, the sound of our slick, heated flesh smacking together so loud that it'd be distracting if everything didn't feel so fucking good.

"Oh God," she moans into my shoulder, biting so hard I can feel my skin break. "Don't stop, please."

"Wasn't planning to," I grit out, using the momentum from her own grunts and groans to fuel my actions.

Her ass slams into the tops of my thighs, and her cunt feels so delightful—like it's getting more snug by the second. Each brutal stroke of my cock inside her brings her closer to the edge, and that knowledge has me spiraling quickly.

"That's it," she whimpers, sucking on the skin she just bit through. "That's so good, please keep going… I want to come on your cock. Mark you as mine… Oh, faster, *yes*…that's perfect… *fuck*, Sutton."

Sweat breaks out along my hairline, pouring into one of my eyes. "Shit, Elle, I'm—"

I'm running out of steam is the problem. Stamina is no match for the girl you've been dreaming about the last three months.

"Give it to me. I want it so bad." She makes a strained sound, breathless, and drags her lips down my neck, alternating between kissing and biting.

It sends release barreling up my spine, stretching out past my limbs like overgrown moss on the forest floor. It covers everything, blotting out the sun, until all I can see, think, and feel is her.

My head tips back as I pull her flush against me once, twice, and a third final time, my climax shooting through me so fast that there's hardly any time to process more than a blinding white light.

I groan, feeling myself spill and spill and spill, afraid I might never fucking stop.

She locks up, her cunt pulsing around me as her second orgasm seems to hit, milking me dry.

"Good boy," she says, collapsing on top of me, pressing a kiss to my forehead.

My hands fall to my sides, limp, as I return to earth. "Woof" is all I can manage.

Her laughter makes our bodies shake.

We lie like that for a while—so long that we start to drift off to sleep, with my arms wrapped tight around her waist and her face buried in my neck.

A strange heaviness takes root in the center of my chest. Something aches within, lessened only when she pulls away to look in my eyes.

She pushes hair off my forehead and smiles, and the ache intensifies. It turns into something bold and bright and completely alarming.

I swallow, clearing my throat in an attempt to shove it away. Now isn't the goddamn time.

"Do you feel it leaking out of me?" she asks, glancing at where we're still connected. My mostly soft cock stirs at the sensation, and she giggles.

"Want me to clean you up?"

Her eyes widen. "I don't think I can withstand another orgasm already."

I frown, confusion lacing my brow, and then realize what she thinks I mean. Snorting, I shake my head, scooping her into my arms and off the bed toward the bathroom. "No, silly, I meant with soap and water. You have class in the morning, so we should get you fixed up and back in the bed."

She's oddly quiet and compliant as I ensure we're squeaky clean before tucking her back under my covers. I get a glass of ice water and wait for her to drink, watching for any signs of her mind wandering while keeping an eye on my own mental well-being.

Not even my earlier nightmare feels like it's trying to make itself known anymore, as if displaced completely by her mere existence.

Sighing, Elle rolls onto her side, folding her hands beneath her head on the pillow. She watches me with soft eyes as I slip back in beside her, yanking her to me.

"So how many languages do you speak?"

"Fluently? Just English and French. Un pequeño español. Oh, and Latin, but that one's mostly just to impress my students."

"Does it work?"

"Not yet it hasn't." I arch an eyebrow at her. "Unless…"

She shakes her head.

Blowing out a breath, I shrug. "Ah, well, I suppose I'll have to find something else that gets you going. I can bake a little. Am pretty good at finding star patterns with my naked eye. An excellent director."

"You had me at baking."

We fall into silence again, this time slightly more tense than the last. I stroke my thumb over her shoulder absently, wondering what she's thinking about—if she has regrets or worries about how our relationship might affect her schooling.

For some reason, it's never really occurred to me to ask. I just assumed she didn't mind either way, since she was initially the aggressor anyway, but maybe—

"I've never done that with anyone else," she says after a while. "Not used a condom, I mean."

"I figured."

Indignant, she pokes at my chest, scoffing. "Hey, don't act like I'm so predictable."

Smirking, I shake my head. "It's not about predictability. I just feel like I see you." Lifting her chin with my thumb, I cock an eyebrow. "You know? Whatever this connection is—"

She nods, snuggling against me. "Yeah. I feel it too."

It doesn't take long for her to fall asleep, her breathing growing deep as it brushes across my abs. Leaning over, I blow out the few remaining candles, sliding lower in the bed and hooking my chin over the top of her head.

Quincy's words haunt me the longer I stare into the dark room. If this connection between Elle and I is what I think it is, maybe her sister is right.

Chapter 44

Elle

When my alarm goes off in the morning, I slap my hand onto the nightstand, pressing my fingers against my phone screen until the irritating beeping ceases. Rolling over, I stretch my arms and legs, expecting to feel Sutton still in the bed with me but instead finding only cool sheets.

This was the first full night we've spent together without me returning to my dorm, so I can't say I'm not a little disappointed to be waking up without him. Still, it's not like we set any expectations when we decided to cross boundaries, so I suppose the tiny pinprick of jealousy I feel over him not waiting for me is unwarranted.

Even if last night felt like a hell of a lot more than two people simply obliterating every line drawn between them. I won't get my hopes up for that either.

I lie in the bed for a few minutes, staring at the ceiling, taking stock of the state of my body. My muscles are a little sore, and there's a slight ache between my legs that I haven't felt in a long time.

Gently, I close my eyes and slide my hand lower, tracing along my seam as I try to re-create the delicious patterns Sutton drew and licked mere hours ago.

Arousal strangles my throat as the memories pulse against my brain; I push one finger inside, choking on a soft moan and tilting my head back.

A sudden gust of air pours over me like ice-cold water, and my eyes snap open to find Sutton standing over me, already dressed in a deep forest-green sweater and brown slacks. He perches on the edge of the mattress, fiddling with a sleeve, watching me with liquid heat in his green eyes.

"Don't stop on my account." The tendons in his neck strain against his skin. "Open wider and let me see what you're doing."

For some reason, I feel shy, and my legs go to close instead. "I don't—"

He palms both my knees, stopping me. "I didn't last long enough before to get to do everything I'd like to, but I'll watch one way or the other. Your choice, baby."

"And here you said you didn't know how to flirt when we first met."

"I didn't," he says, flashing me a goofy grin. "You just like me, so you respond to everything I say, whether it's corny or not."

"But I don't…" Swallowing, I force a shaky breath and pull my hand away. "I don't want this to be all we do."

His eyebrows arch. "Who says it would be? Can't a guy just want to appreciate his woman first thing in the morning?"

"I'm not really your woman, though, am I?" I chew on my lip, unsure of why I've chosen this exact moment but unable to stop the insecurities from tumbling out. When you leave a pot boiling for too long, it's bound to spill over. "I mean, we can fuck in private all we like, but what does that really mean if you can't even tell anyone about it?"

"I wasn't aware you needed to announce our status to the whole campus in order for it to count," he says, a tinge of hurt lacing his words.

Throat constricting, I sit up, pulling the covers over me. "It counts. I'm just wondering how much."

"Would it make you feel better if I offered you a role in exchange? Maybe we could explain to the class you should fill in for Sabrina because I like how you ride my—"

My eyes widen, and I blink as he abruptly stops speaking. There's a sharp sting against one of my cheeks, the sensation of being slapped reverberating off my skin even though he hasn't touched me.

I push the sheets off and throw my legs over the bed. "I should go."

He drops his face as I stand up, searching for my clothes. His hand lashes out, grabbing my wrist and trying to pull me back. "Elle, Christ, I didn't mean that."

"It's fine," I say, twisting out of his grip. "You can't be with me in public, I get it. It's not fair of me to ask for more anyway."

"Elle."

"Honestly, Sutton, it's *fine*." I give him a watery smile, leaning up on my toes to kiss him.

He looks as if he wants to beg me to stay, but I mention I have a test in astronomy that I can't miss, so he lets me leave.

There's a numbness in my chest as I go through the motions, attending the two classes I have scheduled for the day and finding myself in the refectory, wondering how Sabrina's doing. I spot Lexington and Percy arguing over the differences between beans and legumes and plop down at their table to see if they've heard anything.

"She's back in her dorm," Percy says, scooping some turkey chili onto a spoon and shoveling it into his mouth. "As of this morning, I think the dean said."

"Professor Dupont didn't tell you?" Lexington asks, cocking a brow.

I narrow my eyes at him. "Why would he have mentioned it?"

Lexington shrugs, leaning back in his chair. He smooths his fingers over the collar of his peacoat, giving me a lazy, taunting look. "You two were the last ones at rehearsal, I heard. Just thought maybe it would have come up."

Suspicion clouds my mind, but I force a neutral expression onto my face, plucking at the grapes on my plate. "I doubt it's within Avernia policy to discuss personal matters like that with students."

He snorts but says nothing else.

Percy glances between us and then shrugs. "You wanna go see her? I know where her dorm is."

"Why do you know that?"

"Oh, nothing weird. I dated her roommate last semester for a little bit. She's not as terrible as she seems in class, you know."

Lexington frowns. "No one said she was."

"I know," Percy agrees, nodding. "But you all always get this weird look on your face when she's around or when we mention her. Understandable, I guess, given how she's been and the whole Apollodorus thing, but…"

"That would sour a person's reputation a bit," I mutter.

"I'm just saying," Percy continues with a shrug. "I've known her since we were little. There's usually a method to her madness."

"You're just saying that because you love her," Lexington points out.

I get up from the table. "He has a point though. Plus, the *nice* thing to do is check on your castmate when they've been injured. Percy, lead the way."

He does, taking us from the refectory—only after stealing the rest of my grapes—and to Rad Hall. I can't help the wave of surprise that overtakes me as he swipes a key card, allowing us entry.

"She's in Rhadamanthus?" Lexington asks, whistling low as we're directed toward the elevators. "Unfortunate."

All the dorms are dark and dingy, but Rad Hall at least reflects its renovations a bit more, with sleeker hardwood floors and less of the overwhelming stench of fear, a combination of sweat and adrenaline.

Sabrina's room is on the second level, so I'm not sure why we take the elevator, but I figure Percy also has a method to his madness. He has yet to reveal it to any of us so far, but I'm holding out hope.

He knocks twice, and the door swings open, revealing a tall, broad brunette with dark eyes and a septum piercing. She's in plaid pajamas and glares down at Percy as she takes all of us in.

"Perciville," she greets in a monotone voice.

"Kelsey," he replies, nodding past her. "Sabrina has visitors."

She glares at him. "I thought I said not to bring anyone by. She's not—"

"It's fine, Kels, really," Sabrina says. "If we don't let them in now, Percy will just stick around until we do. The sooner you deal with him, the faster he leaves."

Percy lifts a shoulder. "An excellent point."

Sighing, Kelsey steps to the side, ushering the three of us in. Percy makes a beeline for Sabrina, shoving a chocolate chip cookie from the refectory into her hands.

She's sitting up, propped against the headboard, with her laptop balanced on her knees and a dark brown throw across her legs. A grateful smile lights up her face, which is unscathed, save for a small scrape beneath her left eye from the fall itself. White bandages are wrapped around her forehead, and she gives us a little wave, sheepishly inviting us closer as she pushes her computer to the side.

"The only good campus food," she announces, digging into the cookie.

Percy plops down on a wooden chair next to her bed, watching with soft eyes as she consumes the treat. "The lead in our class play should get only the finest Avernia cafeteria foods while she recovers from her injury."

Sabrina snorts. Behind us, Kelsey excuses herself, and I wonder if it's weird to watch her ex fawn over her roommate like this.

I imagine I'd have already thrown a chair through the window if I had to watch Sutton flirt so shamelessly with another.

"It's just a concussion," Sabrina says, licking chocolate off her thumb. "I'm supposed to be on total brain rest, but it's so boring that I've just been watching Professor Dupont's previous productions posted on *The Delphic Pages* all morning."

"I can't fathom how that wouldn't be more boring," Lexington jokes.

"Oh, no, our professor's a prolific director. Last semester, he had a super untalented batch of students, plus the whole thing with—" She cuts herself off, stealing a glance at me from the corner of her eye, and wiggles her fingers. "Well, you know. But somehow through all that, he managed to pull off a fantastic show and raised a bunch of money for the theater department through the tickets. Half the people come just for him."

My stomach churns, unsettled by the near-constant discussion of him. Even if I wanted to, I don't think I'd be able to escape Sutton Dupont.

There's still an ache between my legs from where he was last night; I wince against it as I sit on Sabrina's bed, pointedly ignoring the laptop screen.

I feel Sabrina's eyes on me and force a smile onto my face. "How long will you be out of commission?"

"About two weeks," she says, sighing loudly and falling back against the headboard. "Meg will have to take my place as Desdemona. At least temporarily."

Lexington snorts. "She'll be so thrilled."

Sabrina wrings her hands together in her lap. "Could I talk to just Elle for a second?"

"Sure," Percy says, leaning his head on the mattress. "We'll tune out."

Clicking his tongue in disapproval, Lexington reaches over and grabs Percy by the shirt collar, hauling him to his feet. "Elle, we'll be in the student gym if you need us."

"We will?" Percy asks, horrified by the prospect. "I don't like the way that place smells—"

His words are cut off as he's dragged from the room, and the door slams shut behind them.

I clear my throat, uncertainty swimming around my insides.

Sabrina cocks her head. "Are you okay?"

"Just swell."

"That bad, huh?"

Groaning, I slump forward, defeat lacing my shoulders. "Am I that transparent?"

"Probably only because I've spent the entire semester thus far watching your every move." She smirks, sheepish. "Not in a creepy way though—in an I-have-a-major-crush-on-you way."

"Like Percy does you?"

Her nose scrunches up. "Yeah, I guess that is what it's like, huh?" She looks up at the ceiling, exhaling. "He used to proclaim his love for me at every Fury Hill Fourth of July picnic. I'd sort of hoped college would open his world up to the other possibilities out there, but it doesn't seem like that helped."

I don't reply, wondering how she hasn't noticed the heat between him and Lexington.

"Actually, I encouraged him to date Kelsey, just trying to keep him away. People who get too close to me tend to wind up hurt." She runs two fingers over her bandages, pursing her lips.

"What do you mean?"

She gives me a knowing look. "Come on, Elle. You're not an idiot. Do you really think I didn't know who would likely be in the Apollodorus basement the night we went down to it?"

My stomach twists. "Considering you *told* me you didn't—"

"I didn't know for *sure*, but I had suspicions. The rumors suggested… Well. My curiosity about Death's Teeth didn't *just* crop up last semester. I've been studying them for years."

Silence descends on us, and my eyebrows knit together. "Why?"

"My brother—well, half brother on our biological father's side—was killed last semester in the caves. By your brother."

A hole opens up in my chest. I pull my hands into my lap, sure that my expression must betray the discomfort within.

"Look, don't worry about not knowing," she says, waving that thought off. "We didn't tell anyone about our relationship, and we didn't even really grow up together. Eli got to be a Blackwater.

I was raised by my mother and stepfather and apparently better off for it. But Eli was always sort of a loose cannon, so when we enrolled at Avernia, Henry—our father—had me tailing him constantly because he was afraid Eli'd do something to sabotage his own bloodline. He didn't want to fit into the Blackwater box, so he got involved with Death's Teeth pretty early on as a way to set himself apart."

"You can just join?"

"If you're a founding family member, yes. But that's why I've been watching them for so long. It was only a matter of time before Eli self-destructed, and Henry wanted to make sure he didn't drag down his other son. So I've been trying to keep an eye on that whole situation too."

"Who's his other son? How many siblings do you have?"

Sabrina pushes her laptop further away. "Do you remember what the Director said the night they brought us down there?"

"I don't speak French, so…"

"She told the group that there were two offerings, and that Incarnate needed to pick between us. If Professor Dupont hadn't been there, I'm not sure either of us would've made it out at all."

"You know about—"

"Sutton being Incarnate? Yes. I also know that had *you* not intervened, I would've eventually been sacrificed, because I couldn't have been his Maiden."

I blink, waiting for more. "Why not?"

She lifts an eyebrow. "You…don't know what I'm talking about?"

"Uh, no? You're speaking in fucking riddles."

"Oh, jeez." She sighs, wrapping her arms around her knees. "I don't want to be the one to keep dropping bombshells on you, but…it's Sutton. Sutton Dupont is Henry Blackwater's other son."

Chapter 45

Sutton

PYTHIA: What's this? The vapors speak of a certain hunky young professor getting down and dirty with one of his students—though nothing has been confirmed, of course. But who would blame the student for taking a Fury Hill darling for a quick ride? I know you all are daydreaming about it as I type this. Ooh la la!

WITH MY HANDS CLASPED TOGETHER, MY CHIN RESTING ON top of them, I glance up from the tablet screen at Dean Bauer.

He crosses his legs and leans back, waiting. Expecting something from me—a confession, presumably, but he won't be getting one.

"Why are you showing me posts from that god-awful website?" I ask, sitting up and letting my hands fall to my lap. "You know journalistic integrity is not *The Delphic Pages'* strong suit."

"That may be, but Pythia seems to have her finger on the pulse of this institution. Whether we like it or not."

"If you're going to accuse me of what she's claiming, then you'll need to draw up a formal complaint, launch an investigation, and bring me before the school's ethics committee. And, likely, find the student you think I'm philandering with."

Not that we've been going to that great of lengths to hide things, especially with Elle spending many evenings in my campus-funded housing.

But she wasn't there last night or any other night this week, which makes the sudden revelation from Pythia feel like adding salt to my wounds.

She hasn't even been in class or at rehearsal, citing illness. The pained, injured part of me wonders if telling Pythia about us is her way of exacting revenge.

No. She wouldn't have done that. If it were so simple a solution for her to just report our relationship, then she wouldn't have been so upset before.

She thinks I don't want to show her off to the entire world? That I don't wish to claim her as my own before the student body? To keep the wandering eyes and idle hands at bay by letting them know who she belongs to?

I'm not sure exactly how much more desperate I can become before she believes that I'd do anything if it were in my realm of possibility. Anything that didn't involve torching my career and ditching Bellamy's memory.

Even that… I'm not so sure work is worth the look she had in her eyes when she thought I wasn't giving her my all. That she'd turned herself over to me and wasn't receiving everything in return.

As if I wouldn't break open my own chest and tear out my heart to serve to her on a platter.

It belongs to her completely anyway.

Instead, I had to go and open my big fucking mouth and let my own insecurity spew vile words. The look on her face—dejected and distant, instantly withdrawing from me—could have sliced me in two.

Dean Bauer scrubs a hand over his face. "The administration is opening an investigation, pending the approval of one founding family member."

I work my jaw from side to side. "Jean-Louis."

He nods.

"You sure this is a road you want to go down?" I ask, raising my brows. "Avernia isn't the only one who can conduct ethics hearings."

Sweat beads along his receding hairline. "Nothing else has been brought to the attention of the school. That's the issue here, Sutton."

Pushing to my feet, I lean my palms on his desk, looming over him. He tilts his face up, a tremor working through him as if he thinks I'll turn a violent leaf and make him a victim.

It's not impossible, but at the moment, there are far more pressing matters to attend to.

"Just keep in mind that the rumors about what you did to those two girls when I was a student still run rampant among Avernia's back channels. Some even say there's video evidence." I rap my knuckles against his desk, winking. "In case you think I won't drag you down along with me."

I'd do it for the simple fact that he enabled Beckett and the Curators' bad behavior all last semester, but this would be the cherry on top.

In Acting for Beginners, I loiter around the auditorium, delaying the start of class, hoping that maybe Elle will show before the weekend. When she doesn't, I feel a flare of panic inside my chest, thinking I really fucked this up.

I don't even have her number to text and plead for her to come over or meet me in my office. She's ignored the multiple messages I've sent to her student email, and I'm afraid that if I don't scale back on those, the ethics investigation will be over before it's even begun.

Lexington sidles close to the stage after class, watching me silently as the students disperse.

"Mr. Abbott," I say in a deadpan voice, not in the mood. "Is there something I can assist you with?"

"You seem distracted today is all. Was just wondering if there was something going on?" He shrugs, slipping his hands into the pockets of his navy chinos. He really has an effortless charm, and the fact that he spends so much time with Elle just further irritates me.

"My personal issues are none of your concern," I tell him. "Your focus should be on the production and finals."

"Sure, sure, they are. Definitely." He glances at the floor, scuffing his shoe against it. "Class was pretty quiet this week, don't you think?"

My gaze cuts to his.

"Didn't realize how much effort Elle Anderson puts into participating, but you sure can tell when she's missing, can't you?"

The blood in my veins feels like it's boiling. "Rest is important when sick. As is not spreading germs. I appreciate her choosing not to come to class."

"Sick? Oh, then I guess when she said she'd be hanging out in the quarry this morning, she wasn't being serious."

My expression flattens. He's fully transparent, but now I have to wonder if he's the one feeding Pythia information or if he's just fishing for it now. I school my features, keeping them neutral, and close my briefcase, grabbing the handle tightly.

"Mr. Abbott," I say, heading to the back of the building so he doesn't assume I'm going to her. "I'll see you on Monday."

Lexington just hums, and though I've turned my back toward him, the smug look on his face burns into my retinas all the same.

Perhaps I'm not as discreet as I believed.

Certainly not when I drop my things off and head to the quarry, unable to spend even a second longer just thinking about Elle.

Having her in my thoughts isn't enough. It never will be.

I find her exactly where he said she'd be, alone with her legs dangling off the edge of the quarry. Her palms are flattened, arms outstretched behind her, as she soaks up bits and pieces of the sunshine peeking through the Fury Hill clouds.

It takes me a moment to gather the nerve to approach, sticking to the rock walls long enough to ensure she's out here by herself.

This is dangerous, considering the dean's questioning just hours ago, but resistance is fucking futile when it comes to this woman. My feet press harder into the rocky ground than necessary, but they carry me toward her anyway until I'm risking everything by being here like this.

She's wearing a red velvet skirt over tights and a thick black sweater beneath an overcoat. Her hair's pulled into a ponytail, a few stray pieces framing her delicate face; they rustle alongside the leaves with the wind, carrying the scent of honey and vanilla over to me.

"Stars aren't out yet," I say, pushing myself in her direction.

The slope of her shoulders straightens when she hears my voice, and she casts a pinched look over one of them, giving me a pointed once-over.

"Careful there, Professor," she replies, turning her nose up. "You being here during the day with a student might be *unseemly*."

God, that smart mouth. It strikes me standing here that I really fucking missed hearing it this week. Having it on my couch next to me. In my bed.

"I don't mind." Bending down, I take a seat next to her, hanging my own legs over the quarry's edge. The water below is as dark and still as ever, making me dizzy to think what it contains. "You haven't been in class this week."

"Sorry I couldn't be a nuisance, but I'm sure there was no shortage of students willing to take my place."

Venom drips from her words, striking me in the chest with its toxicity. "I was simply worried you'd fallen ill or maybe were having a bad endo flare-up."

That seems to make her hesitate in her fury. "If that's what you thought, why didn't you come check on me?"

Christ. This is not going well. "I was trying to give you space. You ignored my emails—"

"I didn't think it was an appropriate matter to discuss on Avernia servers. 'Hey, Dean Bauer, my boyfriend was an asshole. Do you mind if we talk through our issues here? I know we're not even supposed to be speaking much outside class, but actually we've been fucking, and I'd really like to continue. Thanks!'"

My eyes widen, my brain hitching on that one word. "Boyfriend?"

A furious fuchsia color crawls up her neck, making that choker seem even darker in contrast. "I misspoke."

"A Freudian slip?"

Her cheeks continue to burn pink, and she balls her hands into fists, saying nothing more.

We sit like that for a few minutes, silence bleeding into the air as if from an open wound. I suppose, in a way, that's true—it is I who wounded and left her untreated.

Boyfriend. It's not something I'd given much thought to as I rarely let anyone close enough to matter, but as the two syllables play on a loop in my mind, I enjoy the way it feels.

Reaching into my pocket, I pull out my small first aid kit, popping the top open. I fish out a pill packet and a folded stick-on heating pad and hold them out for her.

"I've been reading up on endometriosis," I say. "I'm not sure what your pain levels are at the height of a flare-up, but I've seen some people say it can sometimes be managed with heat and painkillers."

"Sometimes," she agrees. "But I'm fine right now. My period was short and light this week."

"From the sex, right?"

"I don't know, Sutton." She sighs. "It's possible, yes."

Glancing at the items in my hand, I set them on the ground. "Me paenitet," I tell her softly.

She turns her head slightly, frowning. "What?"

"Me paenitet—it causes me to regret."

"What does?"

"Well, when it comes to you, there is no shortage of things to choose from."

That makes her blink and shrink away. "Wow. Did you come here to make me feel worse?"

"No, that was not my intention. In fact, I don't really know why I came. I thought space was what you'd want after I made an ass of myself, and no, I didn't go to your dorm out of respect for your and your roommate's privacy. I could have stayed late outside your other classes and dragged you into the shadows, but I figured that would just be more of what you didn't want—more secrets, more sneaking around. But you know, you could have come to me."

"I didn't hurt your feelings!" she insists, pointing at me with her index finger, jabbing it into my chest. The pills and heating pad fall to the ground, and I catch her wrist in my hand. "I didn't imply you'd be satisfied with a sexual favor or make it seem like that's all you were capable of. Why would I need to seek you out?"

"You're right. But dammit, Elle, you can't just fucking run off and expect that to be the end of it. I don't mind chasing you, but I need you to *communicate*."

Her eyes are wide with the intensity of her rage. She lets out a strange noise, staring at me in horror as tears well up and begin sliding down her cheeks, like she isn't even sure why she's crying or how to stop it.

My heart cracks. God, what a fucking number Hollywood did on her.

Shame coats her features, and she yanks against my hold, trying to escape. "I'm sorry," she whispers brokenly, shaking her head. "I know that's what people think of me. It's what sent me away from LA, and I know I did that to myself, but I'd hoped you'd see me differently. I don't want to be some coed you can fuck and move on from. I—I want more. I want you to think I'm more, and I want to *be* more."

Wiping the tears away with my thumb, I press a harsh kiss to her mouth. "I was being an insecure ass when I said that shit. It has nothing to do with you and everything to do with me knowing I don't deserve even an ounce of your attention. And it wasn't right of me to use that against you, no matter what my own feelings were."

She sniffles, nodding. "I know. I think you just terrify me. I've never…"

I shake my head as she trails off, cupping her cheeks. "Me neither." Leaning in, I kiss the tip of her nose, slowly moving up to her eyelids. As they close, I press a kiss to each one, reveling in how she grows a little less stiff with each gesture. "Tell me what you want me to do if it'll help prove how sorry I am. I'll do it. Anything at all."

She remains quiet, allowing me to continue my trail of kisses on the underside of her jaw.

"You want me to announce myself as your boyfriend to the whole school? I'll do it. They're already investigating me anyway. Why not get ahead of the curve?"

Pulling back, her brows knit together. "They're investigating you?"

"Evidently, Pythia's been posting about some professor getting hot and heavy with one of his students."

"Pythia's a cunt," she breathes.

"That she is." My mouth descends on her neck, my fingers tugging at her sweater so I can kiss her collarbone, and then I keep sliding down her body. She catches herself on her hands as I drag my lips over the full swell of her tits, hidden beneath her clothing. Her nipples harden beneath a rush of cold air as I push the material up, exposing her lush tits to my hungry gaze.

"Sutton, we shouldn't be doing this here."

Ignoring the concern, I suck as much of her tit into my mouth as I can fit. My nostrils flare as her head falls back, the slender curve of her neck so enticing that I raise back up and sink my teeth into it.

Her hand comes to my hair, fisting at my nape, and I grunt into her skin.

"What do you need from me, baby?" I murmur, my cock throbbing. This was supposed to be a mere apology, but my body seems to have missed the memo.

Self-control goes out the window when she's concerned.

Overhead, the trees whisper with the weight of a cool breeze. Elle shivers, leaning back on her palms as she stares at me.

"I–I don't know," she says.

"You don't know? Need me to show you?"

She swallows, nodding, and I grin against her.

I'm not even thinking about the fact that we're in broad daylight and not particularly hidden depending on where you're at in the forest. I glance over my shoulder at the trees, aware that more activity happens during the evenings and we're probably not going to be alone long enough for it to matter.

But I also don't give a single fuck.

When she nods her approval, motioning toward her feet, I kneel on the rock and lift her left foot in one hand.

Slowly, I bring it up, watching as she leans back on her elbows more. I slip her Mary Janes off, peeling her tights off as well, and touch my lips to the top of her foot.

"Too cold?" I ask.

A single shake of her head is all I need.

Stomach tight with desire, I take my time, wetting my mouth before bringing it to her skin. As I withdraw, I let my tongue slip out, sliding up and over her ankle, keeping that leg in the air.

She jolts when my tongue caresses the inside of her calf. "Hey, wait, what are you—"

"I haven't gotten to taste you all damn week," I breathe, continuing my ascent, nibbling in different spots as I go. She bends her other knee, trying to bar me access, but I shove her skirt up and bat her hands away, planting a wet kiss to her lace-covered cunt, sucking the fabric in along with her clit.

Her sudden squeal of surprise fills the air, speaking to the trees. I hope they can keep a secret of passion as well as they do ones of violence.

Love is violence, though, in its own way. Love has the power to end everything, yet we chase it, expecting that it will fix and cure instead.

Shit. Why am I thinking about love?

My face heats, and I roughly tug her panties aside, sealing my mouth over her cunt to try and dispel the thought.

She cries out, and I moan into her, letting that sound cascade down my back in waves. Arousal spools tight, making me dizzy.

I'm fucking intoxicated by her—the scent of her skin, the softness of it beneath me, the noises she makes. All I can focus on is her.

Tearing myself from between her legs, I crawl up her body, panting heavily. She's flushed, glaring at me, and as I open my pants, fishing my cock out, I coax her thigh over my waist, unable to stop needing more.

I'm afraid nothing will ever be enough.

She bites down on her knuckles, sheepish. "This is a really bad idea. What if someone comes?"

"Let them," I say, fisting my length and nudging into her sopping entrance. That first inch sinks inside, and I grit my teeth, desperately clinging to whatever's left of my sanity. "I'm going to make sure you do either way."

Her inner muscles spasm around me as she chokes out a laugh. She captures her bottom lip in her teeth as I push deeper, sheathing myself fully with a languid moan of approval.

"God," I huff, squeezing my eyes shut for a moment. "You fit me so fucking perfectly, temptress. So fucking snug I should just stay here forever."

She forces herself to clamp down even more, and I see stars in my vision. With her bare foot, she prods at my ass, encouraging me silently. I slide my hands up the length of her arms, pinning them above her head and tangling our fingers together, and thrust slowly.

So slow and deep, ensuring she feels every single inch.

Her tits bounce with each shift of my hips. I realize a beat too late that the rocky ground probably isn't the most comfortable place for her, but when I go to move so she's on top, she just shakes her head, pulling me all the way back in and keeping me there.

"This is what I want to feel," she whispers, urging me to move, her mouth falling open when I obey. "You surrounding me, invading my senses, writhing on top of me—all of it. That way, if anyone is watching, they see it too. They'll know who you belong to. That *I'm* your Maiden."

"Fuck me," I say, scraping my teeth against her jaw, her cheek, her ear. Anything I can get access to as I piston harder, canting my hips until she's a trembling, soaked mess.

Releasing her hands, I grab both legs, cupping behind her knees and spreading them while I continue fucking her. I bite down on one calf, trying to stave off my arousal as it pumps through me, threatening detonation.

She swallows, toying with her choker necklace. "You're close?"

I nod, moving harder, faster, chasing that spot that makes her eyes roll back.

Grinning, Elle paws at her own breast, then reaches between us and starts rubbing her clit. She tightens around me, and I groan against her leg, my control unraveling.

"Do it," she commands, her own mouth slackening.

"Are you sure it's okay?"

"How bad do you want it?"

Something stutters in my chest. "*So* bad. Please, Elle, I need to come. I want to fill you up so much that it all just leaks out while I'm still plugged inside you."

"*Yes*," she hisses.

I feel her constrict, spasming around me, and am spilling before she's even finished cresting her own orgasm, like I can't deny even the simplest of requests.

My cum floods her cunt, and she greedily sucks it up, coaxing out as much as she possibly can with her own release. With her head tipped back, baring her neck to me again, I swoop in and bite down on the space above her necklace.

A red mark in the shape of my teeth forms, bright against her pale skin. I slide my tongue over it, soothing the sting, unsure why I need to mark her so damn bad. As if it's some primal instinct I can't resist.

Exhausted, I go to pull out and clean up, but her arms and legs lock around me. "Wait," she pleads. "Just…stay in me for a second."

"Even with my cum dripping down your ass?"

She nods, shutting her eyes. "I like the closeness."

Chuckling, I settle against her once more.

Whatever she needs.

Chapter 46

Elle

"So..."

I glance at Sutton as we weave through the Primordial Forest, feeling a strange sense of déjà vu even though it's still light enough out to see. Awareness pricks at my skin like the tiny bites of microscopic parasites waiting to devour us.

A shadow passes between the branches, sending me a little closer to Sutton. I'm trying to keep my distance because of suspicions that already exist, but this creepy fucking place makes it difficult.

"So?" I prompt, waiting for him to finish the question. I can still feel him between my legs, and I'd be embarrassed if the rest of my body wasn't so elated that he came after me.

That he wanted to talk and didn't let me off the hook with shutting down. That he still wanted *me*.

"So," he repeats, hiding a smirk. "*Boyfriend*, eh?"

My eyes widen, warmth drizzling across my face like honey. "I swear, I didn't mean anything by that. It just slipped out."

"Would it be so terrible?"

Pausing midstep, I stop completely, my feet crunching on dry, dead leaves in the dirt pathway. "You want to be my boyfriend?"

He lifts a shoulder. "If that's what you want."

My pulse grows erratic. I start walking again, falling into step with him. "I've never had a boyfriend before."

"Never?"

"Not a real one." I shake my head. "Back home, everyone was too scared of my dad to ask me out. Not too scared to slip backstage between rehearsals for a quickie but too afraid to risk being seen with me publicly. Then when I moved to LA, well…acting and moonlighting at whatever gig I could grab for extra cash took up most of my time."

He doesn't say anything, processing quietly.

The silence makes my skin itch. "You got to explain why you are the way you are, kind of, so I just also wanted to make a case for myself. You know, in the event I say something mean and hurt your feelings. I'm new to this."

"I like when you're mean," he says matter-of-factly.

"You know you're, like, severely repressed, right?"

He tosses me a grin that makes my chest flutter like a swarm of butterflies, and I spend the rest of our walk studying him from the side, trying to commit his entire profile to memory.

I consider asking about the Blackwater family. From what I can tell, there's not much interaction between the Duponts and them, especially given the death of their only son last semester.

Or only *known* son.

Instead, I keep the questions to myself and meet up with Lexington in the Obeliskos later that evening—except he's not alone. Asher and Lucy are lounging about on the thirteenth floor

456 SAV R. MILLER

with him, while Aurora and Meg sit in the corner charting mushrooms for some fungi class they share.

I take the empty seat next to Lexington, lifting my brows in surprise when no one else pops out of the shadows. "No ball and chain tonight?"

He grins, flexing his biceps in the thin T-shirt he has on, leaning against the table. "Don't ask what he's up to. All I heard was fireworks and Sabrina and figured it was best if he stayed away."

"Is he…setting off fireworks or making his own with her?"

He levels me with a look. "I didn't ask. Don't need to know."

"Okay, here's all the shit you asked for." Asher slams down a stack of thick, cloth-bound books in front of me, blowing some hair out of his eyes. "Can I take my girlfriend and go now?"

"You don't want to stay and help me sort through these? It's your heritage too, you know."

"Unlike you and Q, I don't really give a shit where we came from. All the past seems to do is get people into trouble." He shoves his hands inside his jacket pockets, shaking his head. "I'd much rather focus on the future."

"Aw, my baby brother: ever the optimist."

"It's not optimism. I'm just being practical."

"Doesn't learning from the past help keep you from creating future mistakes?" Lexington asks.

Asher slides his dark gaze to him, unimpressed. "Who even are you?"

"I'm a friend of Elle's."

"Okay, well, next time I want your opinion, I'll make sure to ask for it."

Sighing, I take the book off the top of the stack and crack it open to the first page. "Jeez, just go, Ash. I'm not going to force you to stay here."

"Lucy," he barks over his shoulder at where she's skimming through an encyclopedia at another table. "Are you ready to go?"

"I think I'll stay here for a bit," she says, not looking up.

Asher's hands ball into fists. I'll bet he wishes Foxe were here to use as a punching bag.

"Fine," he snaps, stomping back over to where Lucy's seated. He slams his ass into a chair, muttering something under his breath. She reaches up, threading her fingers through his hair, and he instantly softens at her touch, toying with his nose ring as he rests his head on the table.

A pang of envy splits my chest in two, so I glance away, refocusing on the book in front of me.

The first few I flip through aren't of much use—they're overall Fury Hill history, detailing things like how the infrastructure was initially intended to be built higher to deter lower-class citizens from venturing into the mountains. Avernia began as the center of town, but when deadly illness rolled through, eliminating a major portion of the population, the limits moved, and older plans were slashed and burned.

Like Sabrina said, Avernia College *was* used as a triage center during those founding years, lending to the rumors about ghosts and hauntings that exist even to this day. A few entries talk about the student organizations—although only the Curators and Visio Aternae.

"Seems a bit odd there's nothing in here about Death's Teeth," I mutter.

"Well, even the stuff about the founding families feels a little… contrived," Lucy says, clearing her throat. "They practically write about the Duponts and Blackwaters like they're the sole driving forces of the town while everyone else is background noise. And the Andersons…"

"Are cursed," Aurora finishes from her corner.

Asher snorts, glaring at me. "What an exciting history we have here, Noelle."

I roll my eyes, going back to the books. There has to be something that gives more information about how and why things turned out like this.

Mentions of Cronus Anderson and his strange healing remedies during the mass disease spread seem to be likely culprits; people often fear whatever they can't make sense of. But to be honest, it's not really *my* family I'm trying to find out about.

I scour the archives for anything on the other founding families: almost an entire line wiped out by paranoia, death worship, betrayals, and sin. That's what it all seems to come back down to—the people of Fury Hill may believe they honor their gods, but really, everything they do is tainted by their vices.

Eventually, Asher and the others get up to leave, citing weekend plans that they want to get a good night's sleep for, and then it's just Lexington and me.

He's playing some game on his laptop, not paying any mind to the copious amounts of research I'm trying to catalog.

A librarian makes his way up to the floor, carrying a leather-bound notebook under one arm. He pauses, glancing around, adjusts the round glasses sitting on the bridge of his nose, then scratches at his pale skin. "Did Ms. Wolfe leave?"

"Lucy went home, yes," I answer.

"Ah. She asked if I had anything on the history of Fury Hill locked away in the back rooms up here. I found this, but maybe—"

"I'll take it!" I say, scrambling to receive the journal he offers.

"Please remember to return that to the circulation desk in the lobby," he instructs, turning on his heels to head back downstairs. "Or else you'll be suspended from school until it's been retrieved."

Giddy, I skip back to the table and flop down, placing the book gently on the wooden surface. It's old and stiff, covered in a thin layer of dust that indicates it hasn't been checked out much before. Lucy had said she'd try to find something rare, and it looks like she delivered.

Leaning back in my chair, I crack open the spine, startling when a small rectangular packet slips out, falling to the table. They're stapled together, and the packet is pressed so thin I'm afraid to touch it at first.

Lexington glances over as I stare. "Wait. That's a *Pythia* journal."

"A what?"

"Pythia's journals. She used to write on this really fine carbon copy paper, staple it together, and leave them like little pamphlets all around campus."

I trace over the bold signature carved into the front and glance at the dates below it.

My heart stops dead in my chest.

Eight years ago.

Autumn.

The same year I came to visit Quincy.

It could be a coincidence, I suppose. Stranger things have happened.

I turn the page, intrigued anyway.

And immediately wish I hadn't read any of it at all.

Looking up at Lexington, I swallow hard, pushing down the

bile rising swiftly in my throat. His gaze meets mine, concern lining his eyes.

"Are you okay?" he asks, leaning close. "It looks like you're about to pass out."

Shaking my head, I press my fingers to the page, nausea pumping through my bloodstream. The scratch of pencil marks on the paper almost transports me in time, and I'm back in the forest as I read the entries, desperate to find my way out.

> — The rule of three applies tonight: it's the first time any sophomore class has had three founding family members enrolled at once. Prophecy coming to fruition.

> — Targets drugged, moved to Tartarus. Continuing death's rite ceremony.

> — The group has pivoted. Incarnate now the center of their attention. Their pick for Incarnate—S will be claimed physically as theirs while they wait for a Maiden and sacrifice.

From there, the entries begin to feel a little more personal, less clinical, like whoever was watching the events unfold had suddenly gotten much closer.

My stomach lurches as I read through, reliving each entry not as something I've concocted from my imagination but from my own memory.

> — His screams of agony are unbearable. Even more so than the wailing from the sacrifice. They've claimed him and now take

turns brutalizing the rest of his body, purifying it to appease their god. He's unconscious. Bound. Incarnate without his Maiden.

— They've moved him outside the cave, close to the lake. They toss him in—a test. Lake Lerna never releases its offerings.

— Shadows dance across the waters, and somehow, his body is returned to the embankment. He is violated further, a testament to their pick. They think they've made Death proud.

I press my hand to my mouth, bile teasing the back of my throat.

— A figure moves in the distance, obscured. Is this who fished him out?

— Intruder approached by sacrifice, who has somehow escaped the Elders' restraint. Sacrifice attacks, trips—or is pushed? Hard to tell.

— Sacrifice tumbles into Lake Lerna and does not resurface.

Does not resurface.

A pair of wide, terrified eyes flashes across my vision like a lightning strike. Eyes that kept me up for weeks after they sank into Lake Lerna.

Eyes that, upon reflection…

Look a lot like Sutton's.

I'd begun to suspect after he relayed his experience in the observatory, but I didn't want to pry. Didn't want to confirm the terrible, *horrible* truth.

That was why he'd seemed so familiar that day in the gas station. I'd already met him before—sort of.

And I'd caused the death of his sister.

"I need to go," I announce, my lips barely forming the words while my brain struggles to process this information.

His sister.

My fault.

"All right," Lexington says, closing his computer. "I'll walk you out if—"

As soon as he moves to get up, the lights on this floor go out. My heart hammers inside my chest, panic seizing my throat, making me feel like my organs are suddenly too heavy and large to exist within my skin. I grip the edge of the table, trying to steady myself when no emergency floodlights come on either.

"Shit," Lexington grunts, turning the flashlight on his phone toward me.

Jeez, why didn't I think of that?

With trembling fingers, I fish my phone from my pocket, fear coating every nerve ending in my body. I send Quincy a text, asking if there's a power outage we should be aware of, but she doesn't reply.

"Come on," Lexington says, grabbing my hand. He drags me to the stairwell, shoving open the heavy metal door and pushing me inside. "The automatic locks time out a few minutes after an outage. If we aren't careful, we'll get stuck in here."

Swallowing, I grip the journal tight to my chest and follow him down the thirteen flights. Our phones at least provide enough light for it to not feel quite as suffocating.

Sacrifice tumbles into Lake Lerna and does not resurface.

I can't get that line out of my head, even with the darkness pressing in around me.

"Elle."

Lexington's voice pulls me out of the spiraling thoughts, and I realize we're standing at the front entrance. He grabs my shoulders, shaking me.

"The doors are already locked."

I blink at him, the words not fully registering in my Jell-O brain. "Locked?"

"We're trapped in here."

Shaking my head, I glance around the lobby quickly. Where is everyone? The Obeliskos hadn't closed for the night yet, but I don't see anyone hanging around or panicking to find an available exit.

Did they leave as soon as the lights went out?

Or before that?

Anxiety swells in my chest, like a cloud of air pressing on my lungs and closing off my esophagus. I unlock my phone to call one of my siblings and see my service is nonexistent.

Clutching the journal, I grit my teeth, spinning around in a circle and taking in the various tall, pointed windows.

"We can't be trapped," I tell him, even though my tongue is so dry it feels like it's cracking when I speak. "Building fire codes require manual exit doors. We just have to find one."

Lexington points to the faint red sign above the rotating doors. "This is the fire exit. Normally, the push bar works, but…" He reaches forward, trying to shove the glass barrier with no luck. "It's jammed or something."

Heavy footsteps thud on the floor above us.

We glance at each other. Are we alone or not?

"Something feels off about this," he whispers.

I nod. No shit.

At that moment, a text comes through my phone, and a little spark of hope flares in my stomach. Except it's not Quincy.

Unknown: Stop snooping.
Unknown: Whatever you're doing at Avernia ends now.

I reach for Lexington's forearm, dragging him toward a flashing light at the back of the building. We weave through rows of bookshelves and oversize leather couches, passing the glass study rooms and club meeting areas until we get to an alcove around the corner from the elevators.

"I'm not rotting in here, waiting for someone to notice we're missing," I say, handing him the journal. I search the staircase, looking for something large enough to bust us out, finally finding a hammer in a custodial cart tucked in the corner.

With both arms, I pull the hammer above my head.

"Are you sure you want to destroy Avernia property?" Lexington asks.

"Would you rather wait for someone to come rescue us? Or for whoever's upstairs to find us?"

"What if the people upstairs are harmless?"

"And what if they aren't?"

Waiting around for people to save me is what got me into this whole mess in the first place. The more I do it, the more my life just wastes away, and I spend it living in fear that I'm not actually capable of anything.

I don't want to be a slave to the terror in my bones. I want to conquer it.

Lexington sighs.

Swinging my arms forward, I drive the hammer into the surface of the glass. It cracks a little but does not break.

Sweat slicks down my neck. The footsteps upstairs sound like they're getting louder, a stampede threatening us from above.

I swing again, causing more of the glass to shatter. Fractured spiderwebs obscure the tempered, frosted material.

"Do you want me—"

Ignoring him, I study the cracks, trying to make sense of how best to get it to break completely. The quicker, the better.

Distantly, the sound of a fire alarm begins blaring, but when I shake myself a little, it becomes nearly inaudible. My thoughts are loud, white noise humming between my ears and drowning everything else out.

I turn the hammer in my hands, staring at the claw on the back. Squinting at the door, I raise my arms again and aim for the center fracture. The moment the edge of the claw connects with the stressed glass, the entire door shatters, revealing the outdoors and freeing us from inside.

Several people mill about on the Obeliskos lawn, staring up at the building. Lexington and I file out quickly, breathing like we just ran a marathon unprepared.

Otherwise, everything outside seems normal. The air is cool beneath the night sky, but I still feel flushed from the trepidation of getting stuck inside.

"What the hell was that?" Lexington pants, turning back to look at the library. The lights flicker and then come back on completely, illuminating all the windows. "Are we being pranked or something?"

The fire alarm inside still blares, and glass still covers the ground where I busted the door open, so I know we didn't imagine what just happened. Somehow, that makes everything feel worse.

"Elle?"

A sigh of relief tumbles past my lips at the sound of Sutton's voice. My body hitches toward him the moment I turn and see him approaching, but I catch myself at the last second, remembering we're not supposed to be seen together.

Hugging him is definitely out of the question.

"I heard the fire alarm was going off at the Obeliskos, so I came to check it out…" He trails off, glancing at Lexington beside me. His jaw clenches, and he swallows, swinging his jade gaze back to mine. "Is everything okay?"

"We just got locked in the library," I say, breathless still, the aftershocks of fear coursing through me. "The power went out, and then the automatic locks latched, and we had to break out."

Sutton looks past us at the broken door, sliding his hands into the pockets of his long overcoat. "I see. And did you pull the fire alarm?"

"I did," Lexington answers. "I figured it might draw attention were we unable to escape."

Frowning, I shoot him a confused look. When did he do that?

"So it was just the two of you…stuck in the dark." Sutton sucks on the hollow of his cheek, suspicion lining his eyes. "Together."

"Well, there wasn't time to have my way with her if that's what you're getting at," Lexington snaps. Clearing his throat, he shoves the journal into my chest; I slap my hand against it to keep it from falling.

"What a strange thing to suggest," Sutton says. "Your mind certainly has no qualms going there."

"At least I'm allowed to go there if I want," Lexington replies coolly. "Wouldn't have to hide the fact that I'm in love with Elle if I wanted to pursue her or make things really fucking weird when she's trying to tell me she was endangered because I'm an insecure piece of trash who lets his job dictate what he does."

Sutton's expression darkens.

Cursing under his breath, Lexington scuffs his shoe on the ground and turns to me. "I'm gonna get back to my dorm before more weird shit happens. Try not to get picked up by Death's Teeth again, all right?"

I nod, a strange pit opening up inside me as he walks away. Guilt? Shame? I can't ascertain what it is exactly—just that his leaving unsettles me.

Chapter 47

Sutton

I'M POUTING.

It's probably incredibly unattractive, but I can't seem to help it. Once we've snuck away from the Obeliskos to my office, where at least we'll be able to explain away our sudden meeting late at night, I can't stop thinking about Lexington Abbott and the fact that he's always around my girlfriend.

Who looks angelic with some of her hair tied back loosely with a green satin ribbon, matching the tight little sweater she has on. Her thigh-high boots land a couple of inches beneath her pleated, black skirt, and as she leans over my desk to flip through some old notebook for me, I can't erase the image from Lexington's point of view.

There's this effortless charm that Elle possesses, where she captivates people without even speaking. It's what makes her such a powerhouse performer; the audience feels her presence long before she even steps out onstage.

She's intoxicating to watch do the most mundane things.

I can't blame Lexington for being enthralled.

I'm not sure when I became such a jealous fucking caveman, but it's as if Elle's very existence has wiped me clean of everything. I know she wouldn't cheat after we established boundaries—I know that.

Yet the fact that he might have entertained such a notion, even for a moment, is what pisses me off—more so the fact that I can't do anything about it by claiming her publicly.

Elle glares at me over her shoulder. "Are you listening?"

"Yes."

"What was the last thing I just said?"

I stare into her eyes, scraping the recesses of my subconscious for something. Nothing comes up.

"Fuck," I breathe, reaching and pulling her into my lap, rolling us closer to the desk. "Okay, I'm sorry. I just can't stop thinking about your prick of a friend."

"Pretty sure you were the prick out there tonight," she mutters into my hair. "He helped me escape the library I was trapped in, you know."

"Yeah." I open my mouth on the side of her neck, tasting her with the tip of my tongue. "He just seems so perceptive. It makes me worry he's paying too much attention to you."

"So what if he is?" she asks, her fingers sliding beneath my jaw, pushing my face up. "The only man I'm paying attention to is you."

Smothering a smirk, I give her ass a squeeze and nod at the journal on the desk. "Okay, tell me what this is."

She hesitates, then flips it shut, moving to show me the cover.

I squint, the air in my lungs evaporating as I read the dates scribbled there.

My sophomore year at Avernia.

"How much do you remember from the night Death's Teeth... marked you as Incarnate?" she asks softly.

"Nothing, really," I say, although that's not entirely true. The bits and pieces I do recall are scattered though. Just dangerous enough to keep me uncomfortable and haunted without showing me any full pictures. "It's fuzzy, and I've purposely blocked a lot of it out, I think. Or at least... I haven't tried to remember."

She remains quiet as I pull the journal forward, turning to the first page and skimming the neat, half-cursive writing. It's mostly the ramblings of a past Pythia, nothing I haven't seen or heard before.

Life and death are the ruling principles of Death's Teeth, so it makes sense they'd have an obsession with cause and effect, karma, and symbiosis. Even their selection process is bound by that school of thought—which leads into the first real journal entry.

The day of that party.

The last time I ever saw Bellamy alive.

I speed-read through the next entries, horror mounting in my stomach like an abyss of darkness as I relive the events through someone else's eyes.

Someone was watching the entire time and did nothing to stop it?

My fingers tremble as I get to the final page of that night's entry—when one of the figures falls into the lake while someone else stands there, watching.

Doing *nothing*.

The words start to blur as tension threads through my forehead, a sudden agonizing sensation splitting my face in half. Nausea pulses at the base of my throat, and I lean over my chair, dragging the wastebasket close as bile rises, spewing from my lips before I have a chance to stop it.

There's no doubt in my mind that this is detailing what occurred with me and Bellamy that night. Down to the description of how the other members shifted their attention to me, using my body—

More vomit pours out of me. Elle slides from my lap, retrieving a cold water bottle from the minifridge. When she presses it against the back of my neck, I suck in a sharp breath, something unsettling swimming through my veins.

I close my eyes, placing the wastebasket in its spot, and reach into my desk for a stick of spearmint gum. Without me asking, she walks to the door and uses the dimmer switch on the wall to lower the overhead lights.

Dropping my head into my hands, I take a sip of the water she offers, shaking my head. "Where did you find this journal?"

"A librarian brought it to me at my cousin's request."

"Your cousin specifically asked for this book? How did they even know it existed? This is the first I've seen or heard of anything like it, and it's…" I trail off, at a loss for words.

What in the hell is this book, and why is it only just coming to light?

"It's about you, right?" Elle asks, folding her arms over her chest. "The stuff they did to you…"

I don't answer, staring at my hands. They tremble beneath the weight of the memories, disgust twining tight around them until it feels like I can't move.

"The person who showed up. Do you remember anything about them?"

"No." It's barely a word, whispered through disbelief.

She pauses for a long time. "You opened your eyes at one point. You don't remember what you saw?"

"It's all so hazy that I—" Abruptly, I cut myself off, swinging my gaze to hers. She's pressed against the bookcase across from me, wearing a hole in the corner of my desk with her laser focus. "That isn't mentioned in the book."

Confusion makes a volatile cocktail in my throat, choking off my air supply.

"Elle?"

Tears pool beneath her hazel irises. One spills down her cheek. She won't look at me.

The Andersons are cursed.

All they bring is bloodshed and violence in their wake.

They must not be allowed to thrive at Avernia, lest we lose the rest of our founding families at their expense.

Warnings I grew up hearing but paid no heed to, considering the Andersons weren't even a part of Fury Hill.

Until Quincy enrolled at Avernia.

Changing the course of history again, the same way her ancestor did.

"How?" I ask. It's all I can manage. "How were you there that night?"

"We came to visit Q for family weekend," she says, the tears pouring now.

My forehead pulses, stirring the nausea again.

"Something happened with Asher, so my parents ended up leaving early with him. I convinced them to let me stay behind because I knew Q was going to some party, but that was the night I got lost in the forest."

"And you just…happened upon me?"

"I made it to the lake before anyone else was there," she replies. "It was dark, I was scared, and I saw you… I'd heard rumors from our tour guide about the caves being off-limits because of nefarious gang activities or something, but I figured it was mostly bullshit. I didn't think I'd actually stumble upon any of it."

Running my hands over my face, I try to place a teenage Elle there in my mind. She says I opened my eyes, indicating I was conscious at some point outside, but the memory of it past what they did to me inside is fuzzy at best, pitch-black at worst.

"You were tied up," she continues, her voice growing softer. "Soaked to the bone. I didn't know if you were even alive. You stirred, I think, and I hid, terrified that you'd be angry or draw attention, and I'd be next. A half hour passed, so when I finally got phone signal, I called my dad, since he was coming to pick me up anyway, and he's…familiar with that sort of thing."

"The messes left by cults?"

"Cleaning up unsavory acts," she says, shaking her head. When she meets my gaze, hers is glassy. "My dad never talked much about his past—well, neither of my parents did—because they wanted to focus on the future instead, but everyone growing up knew what he'd made his money doing in his early adulthood. Everyone was scared of him, and I knew that if I asked, he'd help me."

"So you were just going to have him clean me up and be done?"

She nods. "I didn't know what else to do. I couldn't move you myself, so I resigned to wait while we were rescued. That's all I've ever done really: let my parents step in and fix my messes. It's why when I left Hollywood—"

"You kept the whole scandal a secret," I finish, closing my eyes. "Yeah, I get it. Constantly needing help feels infantile after a certain point."

"I just got tired of being a disappointment," she adds. "Everyone else in my family holds their own no problem, but it's like there's something missing in me. Like whatever desperation I have for attention and the spotlight pushed out my independence. So when I made some mistakes in LA, I thought, okay, now's my time to fix them. To get my shit together. But the thing about mistakes is that if you're navigating them without any sense of direction, they'll just snowball out of control."

My mind is still looping on that night eight years ago and the fact that she was there all along.

She maybe even saved me. Or tried to at least.

But…

"Bellamy," I say, lifting my chin. "Did you see what happened to her? The journal said she fell into the lake."

"No." Her voice hardens. "She was pushed."

I pull my hands into my lap, digesting that. And the implication.

"Elle." Emotion burns in my chest, a thousand different revelations vying for prominence, but the only thing I can really focus on right now is her. She's still crying silently, as if afraid of what the noise might do to the stagnant air around us.

With her in the room, I can't fucking breathe. Can't think about anything except comforting her, making the tears stop, kissing her happy again.

The truth about my sister's death is staring me in the fucking face, and it's not even her eyes I'm thinking about.

Christ. I'm pathetic.

Standing on wobbly legs, I clear my throat and round my desk, grabbing Elle's face in my hands. I brush the tears away, unable to just let them stain her skin.

"I'm so sorry," she whispers, leaning into my touch. "It was an accident, I *swear*. A knee-jerk reaction that—"

"It's okay," I mutter, pressing my thumb to her lips. It's not okay, not even a little, but God, I can't stand her crying. My heart feels like it's being shredded into a million little pieces, and I can't tell which woman I'm dying inside for.

"No, it isn't," she insists, her voice catching on a sob. "You can't just say that and ignore this. You have to feel, Sutton. Or else it's going to eat you alive even more, and then what happens five, ten, fifteen years from now, when your heart is just dust because you refused to ever nurture it?"

Despair enlarges her pupils, and she begins shaking her head, losing focus. I squeeze her face and press my lips to her forehead.

"Lecturing me when you've just changed my entire life feels a little hypocritical, don't you think?"

A wheeze escapes her. "But you—"

"Need time to process." Lifting her face, I force her to meet my eyes, swallowing over the hard knot in my throat. The pulsing behind my brow intensifies, making me lightheaded, but I ignore it.

"Time?"

"Yes." A long, painful pause. "And some space."

She lets out a watery exhale, removing my hands from her cheeks. "You're breaking up with me."

"That isn't what I said."

When she closes her eyes, it takes every ounce of willpower I have not to wrap her in my arms again. I resist, stuffing my hands into my pants pockets.

My soul aches with the distance already.

Finally, she nods, sniffling into her sleeve, and opens her eyes once more. Turning on her heels, she heads for the door, shoulders slumped and head down. With her hand on the doorknob, she pauses, looking to the side.

Waiting for me to come after her.

My feet twitch. I almost do.

Almost.

"Should I not have told you?"

I shake my head. "I think it's important you did."

"Time and space, huh?" She scoffs, wiping two fingertips across her cheekbones. They come away wet, and I feel like I'm being swallowed by the earth.

She opens the door and takes a step out, slicing my heart into a thousand little bite-size pieces.

"Did she say anything?" I ask quickly, before she's over the threshold. "Before…"

Elle pauses again. Shakes her head sadly.

The bite-size pieces are diced even smaller. There're millions of them now, and I'm bleeding out on the floor, staining the rug.

"No. She didn't get the chance."

Chapter 48

Elle

"TIME AND SPACE. WHAT NOVEL CONCEPTS. DO YOU THINK boys are aware that both of those things can exist without shutting other people from your life?"

Aurora paces back and forth in our room as she breaks in a new pair of designer heels. I shouldn't have confided in her about the whole Sutton situation, but it'd been going on three days of no contact, and I was starting to lose my mind.

I even went back to class this morning just for an excuse to see him—only to find out he'd canceled for the week.

They said it was his first time ever canceling a class so close to opening night. Some of the students whispered about the ethics investigation, saying that was keeping him holed up in his campus housing, but of course they don't know better.

The people here will just believe whatever they're told if it comes from an authority figure. So much for Avernia being so different from every other college in the fucking country.

"Besides," Aurora continues, pausing in the mirror to adjust the

478 SAV R. MILLER

outfit she'd been working on for some fashion class. "Who hasn't accidentally killed their lover's sibling before?"

Groaning, I shove my head under my pillow. "Aurora, please shut the fuck up."

She makes an offended noise. "I'm on your side here."

"There is no side. We're all standing in the same confusion."

"Well, what're you gonna do?" she asks. "Sit around and sulk all week over a man?"

"Remember when you ate so many saltwater taffies in high school that you puked all over your mom's superexpensive art collection because you thought Foxe was seeing another girl?"

"Being mean to me won't solve your problems."

A few seconds later, I hear the door to our room open and close, her footsteps falling faint as she leaves.

Sighing, I roll over and fold my hands on my stomach, staring up at the ceiling.

Time and space.

Logically, I can accept that he needed both of those things to process the information I provided. It makes perfect sense and is maybe a healthy way of dealing with things.

But my feelings aren't ruled by sense, and I can't escape the ceaseless pressure gnawing at my chest that this actually was a breakup.

What if he can't stand the sight of me anymore? Or decides whatever use he was getting out of me doesn't matter now that he knows what I did?

My breathing hitches, my pulse ratcheting in speed. I lift my fingers, watching them tremble against the backdrop of the white popcorn ceiling.

How many times can you break your own heart just by ruminating? Is there a limit to the number of stress fractures the organ can take before it shatters?

Mine seems so goddamn fragile compared to everyone else. Like it's been waiting for the final blow to end its cycle of misery. Quincy, failure, and Jean-Louis weren't enough, but this doesn't feel like something I'll survive.

Sucking in a deep, cleansing breath, I roll onto my side and pull out my phone, opening a star-map app. No matter the time of day, pointing the camera at the sky will reveal the constellations above. I close one eye and aim over my head, watching little dots appear and connect in the blue background.

Oddly, the act is calming—the fact that no matter what's happening here on the ground, those stars remain.

Some die, some transform, but they're still there. Offering guidance. Comfort. Something to look at when it feels like everything else is lost.

Closing my eyes, I take one more deep breath before getting out of the bed and shrugging into some clothes. If Sutton wants space and time, fine. He can have it.

I'm not going to wallow while he makes up his mind. It's not like that changes the outcome.

Tying my hair back and applying some makeup, I shoot Lexington and Meg a text saying that I'll be at the early rehearsal since I skipped last week. But when I go to open the door, a little scrap of paper is taped to the front with my name scribbled on it.

In Sutton's handwriting.

My heart leaps inside my chest, excitement pumping through my limbs as I take it down, unfolding it quickly.

the course of true love never did run smooth.
meet me at Lethe's in one hour. I want to see
you.

I blink at the words. The first line is a quote from *A Midsummer's Night Dream* and so unbelievably Sutton, but does he realize what he's implying by using it?

That specific line out of dozens of others that would have worked for a tryst?

My stomach twists in on itself, knots forming within.

Well, whatever. He wrote it.

No takebacks.

Chapter 49

Sutton

No part of me wants to be here right now, but I need answers.

There's a statute of limitations on how long someone can go without understanding their past before it starts to eat away at their soul. My limit is three days, apparently. Three days of awareness at least, since the repressive instincts kept everything locked pretty tight up to that point.

My hands ache around nothing, desperate to fill their emptiness. In spite of everything, not a moment has passed in which Elle's soft skin and smug smirk haven't provided me a sense of comfort. Normalcy. Purpose.

Love.

That's why I'm here.

Because I'm weak.

Irritated, I toss my phone onto the floor of my car and scrub my hands over my face. Shit. I shouldn't have sent her away in the first place.

What was there to think about, really? To process?

I've been dealing with my sister's death for eight years. I'm not sure who played a hand in it really even matters anymore.

God. What am I even saying?

Of course it fucking matters. My girlfriend murdering my twin matters.

But it's clear I don't have the full picture, and there's only one person I can think of who might be able to fill in the gaps. Perhaps if I'd asked earlier, all this could've been avoided.

Or maybe what I'm really destined for is heartbreak.

My phone buzzes to life as I climb out of the car. The parking lot is practically empty, the cloudy gray sky casting a film of unease in the air around me.

Beckett's name lights up the screen as I take a look, but I ignore it for the time being. All he'll do is put me further on edge, and I want to focus right now.

Stuffing the phone into one pocket, I take a deep breath and walk to the entrance, pulling the door open slowly before slipping inside.

Chapter 50

Elle

At Lethe's, I get out of the cab I took and make my way inside. The neon sign out front is turned off, presumably since it's still the middle of the day, and the parking lot is only sparsely populated, so I can see why Sutton chose this place to meet.

Fewer prying eyes here, which is more important now, since he's being investigated by the school.

Inside, the lights are dim, and I don't see anyone behind the bar, but I take a seat at it anyway. I feel like a fucking teenager getting to see her celebrity crush for the first time at some meet and greet, which is ridiculous, but apparently I'm quite enamored with the stuffy professor.

Three days is a long time when you aren't sure where you stand with someone.

No one comes out to take my order, but I hear them in the kitchen messing around, so I don't mind. I didn't come here for a drink anyway. Alcohol in the middle of the day feels a little too much like a crisis, so I'd rather just sit and wait.

Ten minutes pass. I glance at my phone, frowning. Did I miss him already? I assumed that the note had been taped only briefly before I discovered it, but what if he wanted to see me this morning? Or last night even?

An hour isn't a very good distinguisher, which I plan to make known whenever he finally shows up.

Thirty more minutes tick by. Still nothing.

Forlorn, I stare at the front door, silently willing him to enter. When he doesn't, I slide off the stool and go to the bathroom, just for something to do.

Coming out of the stall, I wash my hands, noticing a beat late that there's something scribbled on the mirror. I look up, stepping back to get the full picture, and my heart plummets to my stomach.

Et tu, Brute?

The words drip down the glass in thick crimson liquid. Like they were just written.

Another Shakespeare reference, but I can't imagine Sutton trying to freak me out like this, no matter how mad he is.

Grabbing my things, I power walk back to the door, my fingers closing around the knob at the same time something shoves against me from behind. My forehead connects with the wall, blurring my vision as I'm accosted and wrestled to the ground. I flail, trying to find a weak spot in my attacker, but they're stronger and have the element of surprise on their side.

My head swims, unfocused. Something pricks the side of my neck, and the unfocused bits become darker and darker until I can't see anything at all.

Chapter 51

Sutton

JEAN-LOUIS ISN'T AT THE MANOR WHEN I SHOW UP.

No one is in fact, which irritates the fuck out of me. Our family seems to only want to appear at the most inopportune times and not when I might actually need something.

I came to ask if he'd known—if he'd known Bellamy had been *pushed*, and if he knew she'd been the sacrifice.

If that was why he always suggested her death had merit. That she had honored it in that way by becoming just another facet of the organization.

He had to know. There's no other explanation as to why he pushed so hard for me to become Incarnate. With a sacrifice already having happened, there was a gap in the control, and he couldn't stand the disarray.

A gap meant vulnerability in the Dupont line. No wonder he was so eager for Beckett to fill my shoes should I fall short.

I'm not surprised to find Beckett sitting on the balcony when I return to my apartment.

He won't stop bouncing his knee as I approach or twisting the baseball cap he's wearing. I walk past him, putting my key in the knob, and head in.

Beckett scrambles after me, nearly tripping over the threshold as he sprints to get inside.

"Father's not home," I say as I make my way to the kitchen, pouring some diet soda from a can into a glass of ice. "In case you were curious."

He scoffs. "Like I give a shit."

"Oh? That's a new development." Settling on my sofa, I take a drink and place the glass on a coaster.

Beckett hovers in the archway between the foyer and living areas. He tugs on the drawstrings of his hoodie, shifting from one foot to the other.

"Quit being annoying and come sit. Distract me with the musings of your day," I order.

Swallowing, he walks over and sits on the arm of the recliner next to the couch. As he does so, he pulls the cuffs of his sleeves down over his knuckles—but not before I notice the broken, dark red skin.

I sigh, leaning my head on the back of the couch. "What the hell, Becks? Have you been fucking fighting? How are you planning on applying for a Curator appeal in the fall if you're getting into trouble like that still?"

He clears his throat. "What if I don't apply?"

"Why wouldn't you?"

"Maybe I want to take your advice and get out of Fury Hill. Get out from Father's shadow."

"Just because you're here doesn't mean you have to live by his rules, you know. He would get over it."

His shoulders slump as he falls into the chair, reclining it. I watch him curl into a ball, shaking his head. "No, I don't think so. I've done too much for him at this point. Even if, by some strange miracle, he took his last breath tonight and I didn't have to worry about him anymore… I'd still remember, right? The shame and guilt don't go away if he does. I'm still here. Still me."

Something about the way he says that makes me uneasy. I reach down, grabbing a stack of paper-clipped essays, and drop them at his feet, tossing a pen on top. "Well, while you're here, why don't you do something useful and grade some of those?"

He lifts an eyebrow. "You trust me to do that?"

"Hey, you've got the same theater background as me. Either one of us could act circles around even the upper-level students."

After a long moment, he shrugs, bending to scoop the papers up. Better he do something productive with his mind than keep letting those parasitic thoughts fester.

That way only lies disaster.

I watch him for a long time, trying to place exactly what it is about his movements, his avoiding eye contact, that bothers me, but I keep coming short.

My gaze falls to his broken knuckles again, and I pause, folding my hands in my lap.

He refuses to look up at me.

Tension threads through my stomach, knotting the organ. I swallow, my mouth arid, and force a deep breath. "Becks. What did you do?"

Chapter 52

Elle

I WAKE WITH A START ON A HARD SURFACE, MY EYES COVERED, and drenched from head to toe in sweat and urine.

A part of me wants to believe it's water, but the acrid scent assaulting my nose leaves no room for interpretation.

The second thing I smell is smoke with a hint of burnt flesh— that isn't an aroma you can forget, no matter how hard you might try. Chatter echoes around me, quiet but present enough that I can use it to determine where I'm at exactly.

My heart plummets as I concentrate, noting the way the noise seems to carry down narrow passages and bounce off solid overhead structures.

I'm in the caves.

I can feel it in the cool air that lashes against my skin when I'm hauled to my knees by my armpit. The ground is harsh on my joints when I land, but I swallow my wince, unwilling to reveal anything to people I can't even see.

Only a coward strikes someone when they're not expecting it—because they can't risk their victim fighting back.

When I get my hands on the person who attacked me, I'll gouge their fucking eyes out.

A solitary thought crosses my mind, temporary reprieve from the nightmare: Did Sutton show up for me? Is he waiting, hoping I come?

What will he think if I don't show?

And then, a more horrible thought than that: He didn't write the note.

He wasn't trying to meet up with me at all.

Agony strikes my heart, and I hang my head a little.

Idiot. And now look what fucking trouble you're in.

Why is this stuff always happening to you, Elle?

Footsteps approach me, soft and short, stopping a foot or so away. I peer through my blindfold, trying to get even just a hint of a silhouette past the fabric, but it's too thick to see anything at all.

"Noelle Rose Anderson. Granddaughter of Deidre Anderson. Descendant of Cronus Anderson. Anathema. Have you come to stake your claim in our organization?"

Fear grips my muscles. "I'm not sure who you are exactly, so…"

The blindfold is ripped away, and I'm met with thick, putrid darkness—so dark, the only thing I can see is the iridescent, oblong gold mask three inches from my face. A serpent winds around the outer edge, curling up so its mouth extends into the air just above the wearer's head.

"Avernia's long awaited a proper Death's Maiden. You volunteered your service and, as such, are expected to carry out the responsibilities of loyalty and honor. Do you accept this role?"

It's a woman's voice, distorted by some sort of technology.

Who brought me here?

How do they know it was me who volunteered?

Though I want to believe it was a random member, someone simply coming to collect a debt they were owed, the fact that the whole note from Sutton was likely fabricated makes me highly suspicious. That person would've had to know we're an item and would also have to know we're having issues.

They'd be close.

My veins seem to constrict as the possibilities race through my mind in an endless parade of anxiety.

Also, the person before me used my full name, even though the whole point of Death's Teeth is anonymity.

They know me. Intimately.

They know I'm an Anderson.

Unease sparks on my shoulders. On either side of the serpent-masked figure, lanterns flicker to life, illuminating just enough so that I can see we're situated in one corner of the square stage built into Tartarus.

I can feel a crowd below, watching the action up here. Anticipating their show.

Nausea rolls through me, sudden and alarming. I don't want to be here.

Leather cracks against itself, the sound reverberating in my ear. A beat later, I feel a tingling on my lobe, and when I reach up, I feel a drop of blood beading on my skin. The serpent-masked figure leans in, and I notice the whip they clutch in one hand.

She just whipped me.

If I previously had any belief that Death's Teeth was a farcical organization, even after what I've seen with my own eyes, that idea is fading rapidly.

"What happens if I don't accept the responsibility?" I ask in a low, quiet voice.

The figure chuckles softly. Their voice is somewhat familiar, but I can't be sure of their identity because the cloak hides everything. And I can't imagine anyone I've met being this willing to pull me into deep shit.

Not even Sabrina, who dragged me into it in the first place. She wouldn't do this.

Right?

There it is, still hacking away at my resolve: the kernel of hope I've carried that whispers maybe everyone isn't out to get me. Maybe I can get ahead by merit alone, and maybe people don't give in to their selfish urges when left to their own devices.

But I'm living proof of the exact opposite. When given the choice between fighting and taking the easy way out, I opt for the latter with hardly any questions asked. It's why I wound up lost that night eight years ago, why I ran off to LA and fucked up majorly there, and why I'm sitting here even now.

The path of least resistance is paved with insecurity.

"If you refuse," the masked figure says, reaching to grab my chin with their bony fingers, "you die. And so does he."

Brow furrowing, I try to jerk away from her grip, but she squeezes my jaw and motions with her hand to someone behind her. Two more anonymous members enter the stage area, rolling some sort of apparatus between them. It takes me a second to adjust as they emerge from the shadows.

A large wooden pole supports a man's weight. He's bound to

it, his legs encased in a rectangular barrier. The scent of kerosene or gasoline becomes pungent, invading my senses as I stare at the new additions.

Based on the lighter color of his skin, it's not Lexington. And I know it's not Sutton—these people may be chaotic, but killing their esteemed member seems a little unruly, even for them.

Which means it's either Asher or—

Percy's face is a mix of horror and confusion when the hood is ripped off him. A cloth is tied around his face, shoved between his lips, keeping him gagged even as the situation registers.

His body trembles when we make eye contact, and he screams, the noises tearing from deep within his chest.

Tension knots through me, making breathing difficult. He didn't even come with us that night, so he has no clue what's happening.

Pure panic laces his eyes, and tears begin streaming down his cheeks as a piece of cardboard is lit and brought close to the pyre he's bound to.

"You can't burn a person in here," I say, forcing the words past my own fear. "Having any fire in a cave is reckless and stupid, but one that big would kill us all."

"Death's Teeth may be guided on this plane by the rules its humans have constructed to maintain a semblance of order and power," the original masked figure says. "But our ultimate ruler is Death. Delaying the inevitable is all we were created for in the first place."

"It makes no sense to torch something just because you didn't get what you wanted."

"Strong opinions from a woman known for doing whatever she pleases, damn the consequences." The figure releases my face, reaching around to grab a fistful of my hair and yank my head back. They lean above me, our faces dangerously close. "Tell me, dear. When you volunteered yourself, did you have no intention of following through? Did you think Incarnate wouldn't care if you were unfaithful? Did you think this was a joke, or that we wouldn't find out who you were?"

"No," I whisper. "I didn't, and I haven't been unfaithful."

"A pity then that your friend will die for nothing."

They bring the burning cardboard closer to Percy's face, and he begins thrashing against his bindings, dislodging the gag long enough to shout my name. It echoes around the cavern, making my eardrums bleed.

"Elle, please!"

His sobs rattle my bones, and when the masked figure lets go of my hair, I kneel, pressing my face to the ground. "*Please!*" I cry at their feet, clad in nylon stockings and nothing else. Slender, feminine feet with a silver toe ring peeking through the material. "Please don't hurt him. He has nothing to do with any of this. Let him go."

The figure stares at me for several long minutes, as if contemplating my plea. "Centuries ago, we had another Maiden beg for the life of someone she loved. It did not end well for her, but you already know that, don't you?"

I lift my head but not my face, focusing on their ankles. "I don't. I have no idea what you're talking about."

There's only one campus entity who claims that sort of omnipotence. I curl my hands into fists, my breaths growing ragged as the cogs continue churning, my mind tentatively putting pieces together.

"What a shame you didn't bother to read any more of my journals," the figure says, stroking my hair.

My stomach drops.

Pythia.

This is Pythia standing before me.

Her identity remains a mystery, but still she reveals a piece of it.

"I'll ask again," Pythia says, digging her nails into the back of my neck. "Do you accept the responsibility you volunteered for, or are you relinquishing your claim to the your title and thus Death's Teeth as a whole?"

"I don't understand," I say, trying to buy time. Her words are barely audible over the blood rushing between my ears, but I still want to try.

"You don't need to," she replies. "The machinations are of no consequence. You just do what you're told, or you forfeit your right to be here. Choose wisely."

"But I..." Glancing at Percy, who's been gagged again by the masked figures next to him, a pit opens up inside my chest. My emotions fall inside, lost to the ether of terror reigning within.

The figure turns abruptly, nodding toward the members flanking Percy. His screams start up again through the fabric in his mouth as the fire comes closer to his face.

Tauntingly close, without touching.

They're toying with him. A cat playing with its meal before devouring it whole.

And it's my fault he's here in the first place.

My fault we're all about to die.

I glance around, wondering how many other innocent students are among the masked crowd. How many students were tricked or forced into pledging their allegiance to a group that promised to do one thing and refused to release them from its clutches when it became clear their promises were nothing but lies?

Anxiety slices my stomach, but I sit up anyway, gritting my teeth. Sitting idly by isn't an option.

Sutton doesn't want me to participate, but the alternative is unacceptable.

Inhaling, I look up at the masked figure. Swallow over the acid burning my throat. Lift my chin.

"I don't reject the Maiden. I'm going to do it. *Let* me do it."

The figure's smile is palpable as she speaks. "Fledglings, please assist the Maiden-hopeful in her preparations."

Two or three masks appear around me, instantly grabbing at my clothes and tearing them from my body.

"Hey, wait!" I grunt, trying to keep them off as they scrape and burn, their touch leaving an inextinguishable fire in their wake.

They don't listen, and within seconds, I'm stripped bare. My underwear is torn off, leaving me totally exposed. A tremor racks my body as I place my hands over myself, discomfort lining every nerve ending, making it hard for me to move.

Being naked in front of dozens of strangers—strangers you can't even see—is more horrifying than I'd have expected.

It's different when you're in control. When you're the one shedding the clothes, deciding on how much others get to see. Having that choice torn away is dehumanizing.

They leave only my choker, and I push my finger into the snake charm, trying to soak up some sort of motivation from it.

Serpents are resilient, sneaky, and misunderstood.

I shiver as I stand there, wondering if this is what they did to Sutton. To Bellamy. How long did they suffer knowingly? How long before the drugs or whatever they fed the pair took over and blocked out most of the actions?

A fresh wave of nausea ripples through my stomach. I try to

focus on my breathing, doing my best not to hyperventilate despite the panic swelling in my chest like a tsunami wave.

"Bring in the beasts," Pythia orders, and for a second, I'm terrified they're going to make me fight some sort of wild animal.

Instead, two large, equally naked men are brought out, chained together at the ankles. They're wearing full-face golden masks, structured differently from the others I've seen so far—theirs have no holes anywhere. The masks are solid, constructed with the likeness of a human face but otherwise unaltered.

Funerary masks. I've seen them in the anthologies about ancient Greece and Egypt in my parents' home library, though never in person. They're not meant to be worn but to memorialize the faces of the deceased.

Unease trickles down my spine, like tiny spiders crawling over each vertebra.

Maybe that's exactly what they're doing.

I shuffle back, bumping into the rope barrier surrounding the stage. They can't make me fight men that large—especially at the same time.

Right?

"Cold feet?" Pythia asks, though she's no longer visible. She hides within the shadows, watching me with a note of amusement lacing her words. "Don't worry. It will be over before you know it."

"*What* will?"

"Since you're of cursed birth, we cannot trust that you'll be faithful to Incarnate, so it's only fair the rest of our members are allowed to taste you before you're bound to him forever."

The crowd gets a little louder, chattering excitedly. Hungry for blood.

Sweat pours down my face. I look over the two men: They're at least half a foot taller than me and probably over a hundred pounds heavier. Scars and cuts mar their naked forms, indicating a history of these situations.

They want to force me to have sex with them in some display of loyalty?

I vaguely recall Sutton's comment about there being some sex-related things involved in the Maiden induction, but I hadn't expected something so violent.

My gaze flickers to Percy, who's watching me with wide, glassy eyes. He gives a small shake of his head, as if trying to discourage me, even as he remains bound and gagged.

I nod slightly at him, hoping it feels reassuring.

The first blow comes out of nowhere—a fist against the side of my skull, knocking me onto my knees. In the seconds spent looking at Percy, the chained pair approached from behind and caught me off guard.

My vision blurs as my hands slap against the ground. I blink, not fully comprehending the sheer magnitude of fuckery that just happened, but when I manage to lift my face enough, I find Percy's once more anyway.

At the same time Pythia drives a small knife into his chest.

Chapter 53

Elle

PERCY'S AGONIZING SCREAM SHREDS MY EARDRUMS.

Or maybe that's mine. It's hard to tell because of how numb my entire body is.

Shock registers on his face in the seconds between our eyes meeting and when the knife slicks through him.

My sight swims, but I reach for him, attempting to crawl in his direction like the snake around my neck. My limbs are numb, but I try slithering toward him anyway, hissing when I make contact with the ground.

The beastly men grab me from behind, edging dangerously close to the space between my thighs. I feel sick, but if this is what I have to do to get Percy out of here, then I'll have to endure.

It will probably be over quickly…I hope.

Blood gushes from the wound as Pythia retracts the knife. She dips her fingers into it, drawing a three-headed beast on Percy's chest.

He blinks rapidly, still somehow conscious.

"What the hell?" I shout, my heart heavy on my tongue. "I'm doing what you fucking asked!"

Pythia looks at me for a moment, then turns back to Percy, pulling her elbow back before driving the knife into his stomach—over and over and over.

The repetitive motion makes me dizzy, and I let my head fall to the ground as a pitiful noise escapes Percy's gag. Tears slip down my cheeks, burning as they drip onto the ground below.

"I'm afraid Perciville has seen far too much," Pythia says, tossing the knife to the side with a shrug. "I'll take your cooperation into consideration henceforth."

A foot comes down on my back, flattening me onto the ground and violently stealing the breath from my lungs. The pair of masked beasts flanks me, one twisting my arm around while the other applies his weight to my spine.

My mouth falls open on a silent wheeze as I struggle for air. Just when I feel myself fading, they release me, chanting something in Latin to the crowd around us.

Rage boils up inside me, making my limbs tremble with its ferocity. I glare at Pythia, imagining how good it would feel to wrap my hands around her neck and squeeze.

I've never fully felt that urge until now. My fingers itch, quivering with the desire to end her life as cavalierly as she has my friend's.

That was his only crime—being my friend.

I am the common denominator.

But I'm certain if I did attack Pythia, the rest of the Death's Teeth members would put an end to me immediately. She clearly has their loyalty in a way I can't comprehend.

Instead, I turn and stagger to my feet. My face smarts, and there's blood in my mouth, but I don't pay much attention to that.

Bracing myself, I launch at one of the beasts' back, hooking my arms around his neck and holding tight. He stumbles, gripping the rope barrier, clawing at my forearms.

I grit my teeth and use every ounce of strength I can muster, imagining his head popping off like a bobblehead toy.

The other man stumbles as the one below me continues to struggle, trying to punch at my sides. He lands a couple of blows, but the mask must be more restricting than I thought, because he's turning to panic quickly, as if losing consciousness already.

His arm slips from the rope, and the three of us go tumbling off the stage; the breath instantly expels from my lungs as the other beast lands on top of me, smacking my head into the ground.

A grunt is audible as I lose my hold on the man, and I lie there trying to squirm out from beneath him. Then I feel something warm seep in around me.

Turning my head, I meet the dead eyes of the beast whose mask dislodged in the fall. His stare is cold, vacant, as blood pours from an apparent wound in the back of his head—if the sharp rock next to it is any indication.

Adrenaline courses through my veins, but there's no time to dwell on the moment because in the next, a strong, masculine voice cuts through the air, silencing everyone.

"Enough."

My eyes pop open wide. The beast scrambles off me, and I push up on weak arms, instantly meeting the green eyes I've been in love with for weeks now.

Shit. Love. That's what this is, isn't it?

I wouldn't have accepted this for anything less.

He's wearing a gold skull mask that looks like it was forged from the actual metal and a thick crimson cloak. His gaze burns as he takes me in, and I imagine his nostrils flaring, anger heating his skin.

"Incarnate. Anathema," Pythia says, appearing at his side. "You're just in time. We were ensuring your pick was worthy of—"

She cuts off as his arm lashes out, his hand grabbing her throat. The mask lifts a little, revealing pale skin, and my nerves vibrate with anticipation, waiting to see if it falls all the way off.

"If she's *worthy*?" Sutton spits, and she clutches at his fingers, trying to pry them off. "You kidnap her, threaten her with violence and death, and have the audacity to say you're doing this for my benefit?"

"Since she's an Anderson, we just had to be—"

The woman's words get choked off, and she wheezes. No one rushes to her aid.

"*I* chose to spare her. Didn't I?"

She nods.

"So what gives you the right to *test* her in any way? She's *mine*, not yours. *My* partner, the life to my death. My Maiden. You do not touch her. You do not so much as look at her, or I swear on these cursed school grounds I'll burn all the skin from your body and use your bones in *my* next sacrifice. Under my authority as Incarnate, is that understood?"

"E-elder—"

He shoves her to the ground, a noise of disgust puffing past his lips.

I glance around the room, noting how every masked figure seems stricken in place, like they physically can't move.

Like whatever beliefs they hold actually keep them from retaliating against their chosen leader.

Sutton exits the stage, pulling a spare mask and cloak out from a pocket inside his. He shuffles closer to me, holding the mask out—it's a pretty white one decorated in dozens of different flowers, the embodiment of springtime.

The Maiden's mask.

"How did you know I was—"

He shakes his head, offering the mask. "Do you accept your role as Incarnate's Maiden? His ultimate partner? His other half—in this life and the next?"

My heart skips a beat. This sounds an awful lot like a wedding proposal, but I'm not really lucid enough at the moment to decline. I know he'd mentioned something of the sort, but in truth, I hadn't thought it was real.

It's only now settling in that he meant it.

I nod, just barely, my vision swimming as his arms come around me. He fits the mask onto my face and lifts me while a small round of cheers erupts around us.

Sutton drapes the spare cloak over my shoulders and sets me on the stage edge. I avoid looking at Percy, pressing my palms into the ground to keep from falling over.

Behind his back, Sutton brandishes a shiny dagger, and the breath stalls in my throat. He crouches before Pythia, tilting her chin up with the dagger's tip.

"Since you've injured my Maiden, I won't be participating in the usual ceremonial practices. But she dons the mask, so she *is* the Maiden. Which means only one person can decide if she's worthy—and if she gets to live." He taps her skin, his voice dark and low, unlike anything I've ever heard before. "I decide it *all.*"

With that, he angles his arm, driving the dagger through her stomach, and I lose consciousness.

Chapter 54

Sutton

I'M FALLING.

Tumbling straight toward an abyss, unable to stop as my body picks up speed, hurtling into an endless sea of nothingness.

That's what it feels like when I extract Elle from Tartarus, instructing a few fledgling members to get the injured members whatever medical assistance is necessary based on their condition.

Beckett had the decency to offer to stay somewhere else tonight—just as well, considering I have half a mind still to kill him. He'd been withholding the fact that he'd seen Elle heading for those fucking caves again with one of her friends, and I could've throttled him then and there for not telling me immediately.

Then again, I suppose he couldn't have known I'd be interested in her whereabouts—not for *certain*, at least. I'd told him everything, begging him to reveal whatever he knew, and that's why I wound up walking in when I did.

Any later, and who fucking knows what the Director would've done.

If I would've had a body to extract at all.

Now, as I get her settled on my couch to assess her injuries, I ignore the erratic pulse in my throat. Reaching out, I push some of the hair from her face and instantly recoil. The entire right side is swollen and quickly turning purple.

Crimson stains mark a huge portion of her body, soaking the fabric of the cloak I wrapped her in. Cuts and bruises decorate the skin I've spent so much of my time cherishing.

Heart in my throat, I force my hand out again, this time just gently palming the back of her head.

She sucks in a strained gasp, shoving me and twisting out of the way. When she bursts into tears, curling against the railing, I just blink, my hand suspended in midair.

"Elle?" My voice is soft, barely above a whisper. My fingers tremble; I let my hand fall to my lap, not wanting to make things worse. "Elle, baby, it's okay. It's just me now. You're safe."

It takes a second for those beautiful hazel eyes to focus. She vigorously wipes her tears, staring at me as if she's looking at a ghost, and then launches herself into my arms.

I catch her easily, wrapping myself around her. She clings to my neck, stiff and unyielding.

"Elle, baby. Let me clean you up."

She doesn't respond. I gently pry her arms from around me and go to the kitchen to prep a warm rag.

When I return, she's just blankly staring at the coffee table in front of her. I crouch between her legs, dabbing lightly at the corner of her mouth where her bottom lip is split in two.

She doesn't react at all, though I'm certain it can't feel good having me poke at her wounds.

She pinches her eyes shut, leaning away as I begin dabbing

at the stains on her skin. Patches of dirt, streaks of blood, crusted saliva—I wipe it all away until only the cuts and bruises are left to mar such a beautiful picture.

"Elle," I say softly, pushing her hair off her shoulders. "Tell me what happened."

A tiny sob escapes her, and she shakes her head. "It was so stupid. I found a note asking to meet at Lethe's, and I thought it was you. Since we haven't exchanged numbers or anything, I just assumed…"

Agony pierces my chest. Why didn't I text or call or bother giving her my number?

To keep up the farce that there was nothing going on with us, just in case our phones were compromised.

"So I went, because I was really happy that you wanted to see me. And I sat at the bar, the same seat I sat in the night we met, and waited. Then waited some more." She pauses, wiping the corner of her mouth with her knuckles. "I had to pee, so I went to the bathroom when you still didn't show, and someone—they grabbed me from behind, put some bag over my head, and drugged me."

I freeze, my hand on her arm, mid-swipe over a cut there.

"So fucking stupid." Her laugh is hollow. Devoid of humor entirely. "If you'd wanted to see me, you would've just come to my dorm. Right? But I wasn't thinking, and then…"

When she trails off, I pull away, dropping the rag onto the floor and folding my hands in my lap.

"I don't know how long I was out for, but when I came to, I was in Tartarus. On that stage, surrounded by a sea of cloaked, masked figures."

Her voice cracks a little, and she lifts her chin, though she still won't meet my eyes.

"I know you didn't want me to do it. To be the Maiden. But that snake mask lady? She said if I didn't accept the role I'd volunteered for, she'd…"

My heart pounds like thunder in my chest. "She'd what?"

"Kill me and my friend." She inhales a stuttered breath, her voice trembling with the memories. "Percy… They dragged him out on this pyre, and I said…I said I would do it. I'd participate. I tried to save him."

Settling back on my heels, I scrub a hand down my face. *Tried.*

Despair storms across her features, anguish twisting them into tight spirals. She looks down at her hands, opening them slowly, her eyes so wide I think they could fall from the sockets.

"I didn't…I didn't want to do it, but I thought they'd let him go if I did. Then she stabbed him anyway."

"Christ."

She looks up, and I press my fingers gently to her mouth, swallowing hard when she flinches. "All I could think about was how it was my fault Percy was there in the first place. They knew my name. They threatened my friends. He tried to leave the basement the night we… He wasn't supposed to get caught up in any of this."

None of them were.

"But…I d-didn't want to d-die," she utters, so broken that listening feels like being stabbed with shards of glass. "I didn't want to die, so I…I did it."

My chin lifts. Discomfort wedges between my ribs. "Did what, baby?"

Tears fall freely, splattering across her stained fingers, sluicing through the cuts on her palms. She stares in horror, like she can't recognize them, and a wet noise of absolute misery rips from her throat.

"I killed that man," she sobs, trembling now. "I killed him." There's a long, pregnant pause. "I *killed* them. I killed them. I killed them. I killed them."

At no point do I think to ask her to clarify who exactly she means—her assailant, Percy, Bellamy. It's likely she means all of them.

The sentence repeats on a loop, a record skipping on the one spot you hate most. I close my eyes, opening them at the exact second she crumples, falling to the floor with the weight of shock and exhaustion, still repeating those words over and over like a compulsion.

"*I killed them. I killed them,*" she cries, even as I wrap my body around hers, tucking her head into my chest to let my shirt soak up her tears.

We sit there for so long that I convince myself the words are coming directly from me. So long that she tires herself out, eventually falling asleep within the cocoon of my embrace.

Picking her up as gently as possible, I move us to the bedroom. As soon as I set her down on the mattress, her eyes spring open, panic striking those beautiful hazel irises. Her hands whip out, clutching my shirt and dragging me close.

"I'm here, Elle," I say, pressing my lips to her forehead.

It takes a few more minutes for her to fall back asleep, and when she does, a part of me wishes Death's Teeth would just end my goddamn life.

Agony colludes with anxiety in my chest, bearing down like a thousand-ton weight, threatening to crush all the organs inside.

This is my fault. I was so dumbfounded by that fucking journal that I didn't think about how vulnerable I was leaving her by asking for space.

And what the hell kind of space did I need anyway? This girl could shoot me in the chest, and I'd forgive her over and over.

I look down at the bruises scattered across her face and chest, the cuts and abrasions on her knuckles, her cheeks, her jaw. Taking one fist in my hand, I bring it to my mouth, kissing each finger softly.

"I'm sorry." Closing my eyes, I let the misery mix with pure rage, unable to keep either of them at bay. "I fucked up big-time."

She stirs, her eyelids peeling open. "I fought back," she whispers, a glassy look carrying her far away from me. "I won, right? It's over… I'm… I did it. I'm yours forever now…"

My heart pinches.

"Yeah. You did so good, baby."

The words taste like acid, even if there is a modicum of truth within them. I didn't want her to get involved, but if she was going to, I can't deny the sliver of satisfaction I feel knowing she held her own.

That maybe she's not as helpless as some believe.

No, she's not helpless at all. She's kind, funny, talented, and honest when she trusts someone. I can't shake the feeling that I've ruined the last bit for us—that the ease with which I've touched her previously is gone, replaced by the skittishness caused by ghosts you can barely remember.

A feeling I know all too fucking well.

I remain in the bed with her for another hour, focusing on the soft, regulated sound of her breathing deeply. As if just to reassure myself that she is in fact alive.

Something about her recounting of the evening niggles in the back of my mind, though, and I can't let it go.

Beckett said he'd seen her go to the caves voluntarily, but she said she was attacked and dragged there against her will.

Eventually, once I'm certain she's in a deep enough sleep, I leave the room, closing the door behind me, and make a few calls.

Chapter 55

Elle

SUTTON STAYS WRAPPED AROUND ME THE ENTIRE NIGHT.

I know because I wake every half hour to check.

Each time I shoot up, panic shredding my chest wide open, he presses the weight of his arm against my head and curls into me. It's a little overwhelming how close he tries to get with each surge of fear, but even though my body is sore all over, I find his suffocation comforting.

I don't realize I'm crying until Sutton stirs, making my cheek shift against the wetness on his bare chest. He cups my jaw, so softly as to not cause further harm, and I can feel his inspection.

"Are you in pain?" he asks. He's already given me the allotted dose of medicine for the next couple of hours, but the pills haven't done all that much.

I'm numb mostly. His cool hands are a relief, and I lean into his touch, aching to put the memories from tonight behind me.

"How did you make yourself forget?" I reply quietly, staring at the base of his throat. "What they did to you… You really don't remember any of it?"

"Well, I was drugged, so I have the advantage of unconsciousness. If you want to call it an advantage. But to be honest, Elle, I don't know if it really mattered. Not addressing the things that haunt you is no way to live. The memories were sporadic, fractured, but they affected me nonetheless. Especially when it comes to intimacy. I forced myself to sit through their ceremonies, trying to feel something other than disgust even though I couldn't fucking place why exactly I felt that way. I knew, deep down, but I never let myself think about it too much."

I exhale, closing my eyes. Every time I do, I see it all—Percy. Bellamy. Pythia. Her laughter reaches deep, gripping my heart in its claws and puncturing slowly.

Not thinking about it doesn't feel like an option.

"Until you, that is," Sutton continues, his voice barely above a whisper. "You weren't some magical cure, but suddenly when I was around you, I…wanted to be better."

Opening my eyes, I blink at him as he moves, tracing back and forth across my forehead with his lips.

"But your sister—"

"Doesn't matter. Well, that's an oversimplification, but right now you're the only thing I want to think about."

"How can you stand to look at me?"

"That night at the Stop N Go and then Lethe's… I remember being so confused about why I was instantly enamored with you. I hadn't let anyone approach me in nearly a decade, and even then, touching outside the organization was out of the question. But I never hesitated when it came to you. All the resistance was merely a front. I wanted to touch and be touched by you more than I'd ever wanted anything. I've been looking at you ever since."

That, despite everything, makes my chest feel warm. "Maybe you recognized me, subconsciously, from our first meeting."

He pulls back, considering. "The body does remember what the mind won't. Perhaps I knew all along you were destined to save me."

The despair in my soul grows like a black mold, but I let him surround me again anyway, burying my face in his neck. It's easier than admitting that the only person I've ever actually saved is myself.

When I wake in the morning, Sutton's gone. I grope along the cold sheets, terror claiming my esophagus. Blood coats the cotton fabric, and a blush crawls up my face as I realize it's mine.

Maybe I should've taken him up on the offer to get checked out at the hospital last night, but all I'd wanted at that moment was to sleep and try to forget. Exhaustion and misery blotted out everything else, making me think somehow I'd come out of those caves unscathed.

Now my entire body hurts, but I ignore the agony slicing through me as I climb out of bed and pad into the hall in search of him.

I feel like a lost puppy seeking her owner, which would be totally embarrassing if the pain wasn't so severe. Bracing against the doorframe, I cast a nervous glance around the living room and kitchen, noting Sutton's absence. Fear twists in my gut, immobilizing me. My feet feel rooted to the spot, even as a breeze from the foyer carries over, like the front door is open.

That thought does little to comfort me.

But I force myself to keep going, peeking around the dividing wall, and stop dead in my tracks.

Sutton stands in front of the open door, unmoving, hands stuffed deep inside the pockets of his sleep pants. I frown, stepping forward, confused as to why he's letting the cold air in.

My foot lands on a creaky floorboard, and I swallow when his green eyes cut to mine. They're angry, and it only takes a second to learn why.

The mouth of a pistol presses flush against his forehead, gripped by a large hand. I can't see who from this vantage point, but the hint of a familiar red tattoo peeking out from beneath the assailant's jacket lures me in.

"Elle," Sutton warns, his voice laced with an edge I've never heard before. Not even when he found me in the caves last night. "Go back to the bedroom. Now."

Despite the pain I'm in and the panic freezing my limbs, I find his authoritarian persona appealing in a way that's probably inappropriate for the moment, but oh well.

"Noelle," the assailant chimes in, his cold tone indicating his displeasure with the entire situation. "Care to explain why a stranger is answering the door and ordering you around?" He leans in to glance at me, his brown eyes darkening immensely. "And why you look like that?"

I cringe, glancing down at Sutton's T-shirt, its hem hitting me mid-thigh. Most of the bruising is hidden beneath, but there's a decent amount still on my arms, plus all the cuts and dried blood.

My fingers hastily tug at the material as I make my way to the door, slipping between them.

"Noelle Rose," Dad spits through clenched teeth, unmoving.

"What the hell is going on here? You have thirty seconds to explain before I put a bullet between this man's teeth."

Sutton tenses. I feel him reach for me, even in the midst of danger. "Elle, you can't—"

"He has nothing to do with why I'm in this shape, Daddy."

A long, uncomfortable silence settles in the air.

"*Daddy*?" Sutton curses behind me. "This is your *father*?"

Dad's finger twitches on the trigger. The gray hair around his ears has spread more along his hairline, threading intricately through the inky-black locks Quincy and Asher got from him. "Is there a problem with that?"

"Well, it's not every day a student's parent holds me at gunpoint," Sutton replies glibly.

"Do you often find these students parading around you in nothing but a T-shirt? If that's the case, I'm more than happy to take action on the other parents' behalf."

Groaning, I shove Sutton backward and motion for Dad to step inside. "Can we please not make a scene in front of the entire campus?"

Dad glances over his shoulder at the empty, early-morning landscape, but he comes in anyway. He doesn't lower the gun, though, even as he puts a finger under my chin and turns my face, inspecting the damage.

"Fucking hell, sweetheart. What happened to you?"

I pull away, tucking my hair behind my ear. "Nothing Sutton had anything to do with, so can you please stop pointing the gun at him?"

His jaw shifts. "Sutton. What kind of name is that?"

"Okay, *Kallum*, maybe relax a little."

Growling under his breath, Dad lets his arm fall, tucking the gun inside his black trench coat. He gives me a long look, his expression unreadable, and pushes past me to the living room.

"Come. Sit. Explain."

Tension threads through my stomach, drawing awareness to the amount of pain I'm in. I pause, swallowing hard, and watch as he settles on the couch, waiting for us to join.

Sutton sighs, shaking his head. I grab on to his shirtsleeve as he heads toward Dad, stopping him.

"Did you call my parents?" I ask softly, unable to look at him.

He doesn't respond for several rash beats of my heart. "I called your sister."

"They don't know," I say, squeezing my eyes shut. "About anything, not really. Not LA, not Death's Teeth. I've been lying about how things were since I left home."

His brows arch. "Well… Maybe it's time to let them in on your secrets?"

Glaring at him sends a sharp pang across my face. I wince, grunting against it, and shake my head. "You don't know what he's capable of."

"Pretty sure I just got a glimpse."

"No, that was only the tip of the iceberg. If I tell him I've been lying this whole time…" Tears well up in my eyes as I imagine the concern that will etch into my father's gaze—and the disappointment.

It's the fear of that which haunts me most.

The acknowledgment of failure.

Dad's foot taps against the floor. His impatience grows the longer I make him wait, and the less patient he is, the more he'll press for information. I'm not sure what all Quincy's told him so far, but the fact that he showed up without Mom doesn't exactly bode well for me.

Or this town.

Sighing, I try to roll my shoulders, but the movement causes me to double over in agony. My ribs are sore, my chest tight and inflamed.

"Elle," Sutton says, brushing his fingertips across my cheek. They come away wet with my tears. "If you're in trouble—"

"He's not going to hurt *me*," I say, the thought almost enough to pull out a laugh.

"I might hurt him though," Dad says from the living room. "Depending on how long it takes you to get in here."

Shoulders slumped, I withdraw from Sutton's touch and cross the room, perching on the edge of the coffee table. Dad doesn't say a word, his six-foot-five frame too large for the leather couch, even as he tries to make himself smaller for me.

My fingers tremble violently as I twist my thumbs together, staring at them between my knees. I wait for some kind of lecture or words of wisdom but then remember that's Mom's MO. Dad waits in silence for a confession, content to sit as long as necessary—especially when it's something he already knows.

And Kallum Anderson knows everything.

A part of me wonders if that's how I've gotten away with the lies for so long. Has he been waiting all this time for me to come clean?

When I look up, heart in my throat, he's staring back. His eyes aren't harsh or soft but a neutral emotion that feels somehow worse.

I fucked up.

Percy's gaze flickers in my mind, and an ache spreads from my rib cage upward. Painful reminders of what I've done—what I didn't do.

Choking on a sob, I lean forward and rest my forehead on my father's knee. Every emotion I've been covering up over the last decade resurfaces like an activated geyser, blurring my vision.

His hand comes to the back of my head, large and sturdy. My sob escapes, puffing past my lips, unable to be contained. Relief I haven't let myself feel in ages floods my system, and I buckle.

I cave.

For the first time since I was a little girl, I cry in my father's lap and spill every single secret I've been keeping.

Chapter 56

Sutton

IT FEELS LIKE ENCROACHMENT TO BE IN THE APARTMENT WHILE Elle breaks down in front of her father. I want to stay and provide some comfort or soak up my own from her, but there are other matters I need to tend to first.

She's safe with him, that much is obvious.

I most definitely am not.

Grabbing a change of clothes from my laundry, I pull on a coat and quickly exit. Campus is still quiet this early, an eerie haze coating the cloudy air. A text comes through my phone, requesting my presence in the Primordial Forest, and I take a deep breath, wondering what the hell my brother can possibly be up to at this fucking hour.

On my way, Quincy practically runs me over, spilling the latte she's clutching on my shoe.

She opens her mouth as if to apologize but seems to think better of it when she notices who I am. "Oh," she says, pushing her glasses up. "I didn't see you there."

I resist the urge to roll my eyes. "Good call asking your father to fly in by the way. I came to you for advice, not intervention."

"Do you even understand what being the oldest sibling means?" she snaps. "You told me my sister was injured after I told you to stay away from her. Of course I called my dad."

"Were you aware she's been keeping things from him?"

Quincy's face falls, and she shifts, working her jaw from side to side. "Well, everything comes to light eventually. I'm just helping her along. The sooner she owns up to her lies, the sooner she can move on with her life."

Cocking my head, I study Quincy's face, her ringed fingers brushing the bangs out of her lenses. She shifts, in constant motion, as if she doesn't enjoy the speculation.

Everything comes to light eventually.

"You told the dean about us," I say finally, slowly, processing each word as it leaves my mouth.

She doesn't reply at first, her eyes narrowing further until they're nothing but angry little slits. Her grip makes the cup in her hand buckle, more latte spilling out.

"I mentioned there was a professor who should be looked into," she answers matter-of-factly. "I didn't give specifics."

"You sold your sister out. She was happy, and you tried to ruin it."

The way she flinches when I say "tried" isn't lost on me. An irritated, dangerous expression crosses her face, and she steps toward me, jabbing a finger into my chest.

"Look. I spent years keeping my mouth shut because I didn't want to scare her away, and I didn't want to keep watching people drain the life out of her. I wanted her to get everything she dreamed of in Hollywood, and I…" Quincy blows out a breath, shaking her head. "Doesn't matter. The past is moot at this point. But I will be damned if I sit back and watch someone else take advantage of her, especially when I have the power to put a stop to it."

"I'm not trying to take advantage of her," I say, shoving her finger away. "Why the hell can't you understand that? Your sister is not the weak little girl you're painting her out to be."

"You barely know her."

"No, *you* barely know her," I shoot back, my own ire growing into a ball of fiery rage, incinerating the inside of my chest. "She got abducted and brutally beaten by one of our campus organizations last night, and she walked out of those caves. She stayed with me and never asked for you. I wonder why that is."

Quincy's eyes harden. She clenches her jaw tight.

"Maybe you've spent the last eight years thinking she was lost and afraid, and now you're trying to distance yourself from the fact that you didn't believe in her. Or perhaps you think you're the reason she stayed away for so long."

Her throat bobs as she swallows, looking at her feet.

Ah.

That's it then.

Still, she says nothing.

"Getting her into trouble won't repair whatever is broken between you," I mutter, scrubbing a hand over my jaw. "Don't use me as some scapegoat for your issues."

"At least I tried to help my sister." Her voice is low as I start to walk away, pausing as it reaches me.

"Did you?" I quip, cocking an eyebrow. Reaching into my coat, I pull out the journal from the other night, the one that revealed everything, and toss it at her feet. "Let me know if you recognize that handwriting. If you need a refresher, might I suggest the sign-in logs of Erebus Hall during your time as an undergrad?"

She bends to pick up the journal, murder in her eyes.

"Maybe you'll remember more than you think."

Beckett's standing at the edge of the quarry when I finally make it to him, and unease slithers into my stomach. He's staring down at the lake, swinging a set of keys around his index finger, whistling jovially.

He looks more like the kid I recall—even from just a year ago, before our father sank his claws into his heart and tried to ruin everything. It's the first time since his own cave incident that I can remember him smiling when he notices me approach.

"Oh good, I was worried you wouldn't come." The smile is lopsided, marred by scars, but I count it anyway.

"Why wouldn't I?"

"Well, I heard your girlfriend was in pretty rough shape," he says. "She should really be careful about the caves she wanders into. Or the high-rise offices out west."

I give him a look. "You're being awfully cryptic."

"Maybe you're just an idiot."

Clearing my throat, I glance around the wooded area, kicking at some loose dirt on the ground. "I'm getting bored. If you're trying to play mind games, you'll need a different partner. I wanted nothing to do with Father's, I certainly don't want anything to do with yours."

Is he going to admit what he did?

"I'm not doing anything," Beckett insists, grabbing my shoulder. "Just making idle conversation with my big bro."

I shake off his hold. "You seem different from last night. Did something happen?"

He drops his head back, groaning. "Did you badger Bellamy this much before you snuck out to go to that party with her, or did you just fucking go because she was your sister?"

"I went because she asked, yes." A pause, regret solidifying in my chest, my heart. "But I wish I'd asked more. I wish I'd not taken the drink I was offered and stayed closer to her side. I wish for a lot of things, Beckett."

"Hindsight is twenty-twenty."

"Yeah, and Bellamy is dead. I can't rectify any of that." Bending down, I look him in the eyes, though his dart around me to avoid direct contact. "After you came close to a similar fate, I don't want unspoken regrets hanging between us. I'm your older brother. If something is wrong, tell me. If you've done something bad, *lean on me*. Let me help fix it."

I'm tearing a page from Quincy's book, but whatever. She was right anyway. As the oldest sibling, my job is supposed to be making sure my brother and sisters are safe and taken care of.

Our parents certainly weren't doing it.

I failed Bellamy, but I'll be fucking damned if I lose Beckett to anything the same way.

Beckett runs his hands over his face, scratching at his skin as if frustrated. I take a step back as he lets out a series of disgruntled noises, rattling the trees with his ire.

"Why do you have to be such a Goody Two-Shoes?" He walks in a circle, his face still covered. "Most people would hate me after I nearly got their students killed and definitely after what I did to their girlfriend."

He comes to an abrupt stop behind me at the same time the air grows thick around us. Slowly, I turn my head to meet his gaze.

"So you're admitting it." Each word is gritted through clenched teeth, dripping with malice.

"You knew?"

"Elle said she was attacked and brought to the caves. I had my suspicions."

"And you're still standing here, begging to help me?" He scoffs, incredulous. "You're something else, Sutty. Truly the golden child. It's a shame Father didn't appreciate you more."

"Tell me why you did it."

"Father… I was just trying to make my father happy. I didn't want him to die without satisfying his wishes, and I thought…I thought going along with it would make him proud of me." His blue eyes grow heavy with tears, making him look so fucking young that it's almost painful to see.

My father. For some reason, the distinction there feels odd, and I take a step back, trying to make sense of the sudden breakdown. Beckett's spiraling out of control, and maybe it was only a matter of time, but I'm also not sure what to do about it.

We're in the middle of the forest, where no one else will likely traverse for hours. If he hurts me—or worse, himself—I'm not sure how I'll subdue him and protect myself at the same time.

Christ, I shouldn't have come out. Should've had him meet me somewhere more populated, although then his meltdown would be witnessed by others. They'd judge him more than they already have, and that would just make everything worse.

I reach into my jacket for my phone, pausing as leaves rustle behind us, and the sound of them crunching suddenly grows closer.

"You've done a great job here, Beckett. Anyone would be proud of your loyalty to the Fury Hill founders."

My blood runs cold at the addition of another voice. A familiar voice.

As Jean-Louis steps out from between the trees, my disgust with his existence resurfaces. He strolls forward casually, hands in the pockets of his suit pants, as sickly looking as ever.

"I should've known you'd be here. You never did like to manipulate from afar." I glance at my brother, who's no longer looking at me but at the ground, and force a laugh. "What'd he promise you this time, Becks? A spot in the Curators again? His love? Council favor?"

"Oh, please. Like it'd take that much convincing. He was already on board the moment I mentioned another Anderson would be joining our campus this semester."

My blood runs cold. "What?"

"Dear, dear, did the slut not bother mentioning me? How we met when I had her kicked out of the Grandeur Playhouse production she was starring in because she'd slept with the director for that part?"

"What the hell are you talking about?" I snap, shaking my head. "She didn't—she would've told me if you'd been the one—"

I cut myself off, closing my mouth.

Maybe she wouldn't have told me. Not those details at least, especially after I made it clear how I felt about them interacting. What if I scared her into silence, and *that's* why she wound up getting hurt?

"Suppose she didn't tell you I was the one who brought her and the Blackwater girl as offerings to you that night," Jean-Louis continues, disgust lining his features. He pauses, coughing harshly into his fist, and his skin comes away covered in blood. "A shame you had to go and fall for her. I really had hoped she'd be rejected and our plight with the Anderson curse would be over."

"The curse isn't real," I say.

"It's real. You can try to convince yourself otherwise, but misfortune doesn't favor fools for no reason. Just ask Beckett over there. You think your soul is stained, son? Surely, multiple attempted homicides is the sort of thing that alters a man's character."

Ice solidifies in my veins, sending a wave of nausea through me. My heart hammers erratically against my ribs, and I look at my brother—my baby brother, who used to smile more. He used to be happy, and now, with tears pouring down his face, he looks like he's being eaten alive by the weight of his poor decisions.

The desire to be loved is dangerous when the people around you use that emotion as a weapon.

"Think you can forgive him still?" Jean-Louis asks, walking closer. He slings an arm around my shoulders and slips something out from the inside of his jacket, wedging it into my ribs.

A gun.

My eyes find Beckett's, whose own are wide and horrified. Which means Jean-Louis didn't let him in on the entire plan, pushing a tiny sprout of hope inside my chest.

I can't forgive him for what he did to Elle. I haven't even had time to process the fact that he attacked her and forced her into that ceremony before she was ready. But the fear etching his face right now is something.

Maybe he's not completely lost.

"See, I got Ms. Noelle blacklisted from Hollywood in the hope of sending her right into our waiting arms. My intent was for her to be here when Beckett killed the Anderson boy last semester, and we could just take the three of them out and be done with the bullshit line forever. But neither of those things happened, so when I learned she was here *this* semester, I started hanging around more.

Attending meetings. I figured she'd be drawn in by Death's allure eventually. It's like catnip to an Anderson."

Nostrils flaring, I jerk my head to the side, trying to dislodge his hold.

He jostles me, gripping my chin. Rage boils in my blood, but I don't react. Don't give him what he wants.

"I watched you two together. Noticed how you couldn't seem to keep your eyes off her, so when she practically dropped in my lap in Tartarus, I decided to try and kill two birds with one stone: I offered her as a Maiden. If you rejected her or the Director learned her last name, she'd be sacrificed just like your sister."

My stomach lurches. *So he did know.*

"And if you still somehow managed to claim her, the Director would reject *that* and kill you both. Which would free up Incarnate's space for Beckett, giving *me* power by proxy. I knew you'd never do what I asked as their leader. Didn't want to risk losing more control."

Mustering as much strength as I can, I drive my elbow into his side, hitting the tender area beneath his ribs. He grunts, losing his hold on me, and I hurl myself away from his immediate reach. The gun falls to the ground, and he dives for it at the same time as Beckett, who seems to have pulled himself together enough to join the scuffle.

Despite being so sickly, Jean-Louis lands a punch to Beckett's jaw, but my brother manages to headbutt him in the mouth, momentarily stunning him.

I freeze when Beckett grabs the pistol, clutching it between trembling hands. He's on top of Jean-Louis near the quarry's edge, his eyes wild and manic, like he isn't fully aware of what he's doing.

Face caked with dirt and bruising fast, Jean-Louis lets out a crazed chuckle. "Who are you working for now, kid? Me? Sutton? Do you have any independent thoughts inside your brain, or do you just do whatever anyone says? What's it like to be so spineless?"

Beckett's gaze hardens. "Shut *up*."

Lifting his arms, Beckett presses the mouth of the gun beneath Jean-Louis's chin.

I edge closer, not sure this is something I feel like cleaning up if Beckett goes too far.

Not sure I'll be able to pull Beckett back if he does.

"Pathetic, both of you." Jean-Louis hacks up more blood, glancing at me. "You're lucky I never got my hands on that slut of yours. I'd have ruined her pus—"

The heel of my shoe connects with his cheek, making his head snap to the side. Grunting, he vomits pure crimson and spits out a tooth before smiling up at me, one canine missing.

"One day, that jealousy's gonna get you into trouble."

"Why did you come here?" I ask. "Just to taunt us?"

"I wanted to see if Becks here had fulfilled his end of the task, since he fucked up so royally last semester with the other Anderson kid. Unfortunately, Pythia seems to have failed me this time as well."

"Pythia?"

He gives me a strange look. "You didn't recognize her last night?"

Familiar eyes flash in my mind, though they don't match the owner of the journal. The one I gave to Quincy.

How many Pythias are there then?

Beckett brings his wrists back, abruptly slapping Jean-Louis across the face with the side of the gun. "You talk too goddamn much. Apologize to my brother or else."

"Your brother. That's still the official party line, huh? No one's ever going to ask why Sutton and Bellamy didn't resemble me at all?"

Staggering back a half step, I frown. What the hell is he even talking about?

His laugh is tinged with wetness, and he spits more blood, letting it run down his chin. "Guess not. You two keep paddling along in your deluded little worlds, oblivious to everything around you." He shifts, trying to buck Beckett off, but my brother maintains his position. "When Avernia and Fury Hill burn to the ground, you'll only have yourselves to blame."

Beckett smacks Jean-Louis again, earning a growl from his throat as his head is whipped to the side once more.

Before he can recover, Beckett's hands come down a third time. Then a fourth. A fifth, until Jean-Louis's entire face is marred by crimson liquid, making him less recognizable.

"This is all your fault," Beckett cries. "You set Bellamy up, you set Elle Anderson up, and you set me up. I wouldn't have done any of this if you hadn't put the ideas in my head."

"Beckett." I'm saying his name before I realize it. "Enough."

"No, it isn't!" he screams, the sound echoing off the tops of the trees, scaring a few birds.

I shift forward, the sensation of being watched settling on my shoulders. Quickly scanning the tree line, I don't note anything out of the ordinary, but that doesn't necessarily mean anything. At Avernia, someone is always watching—even if that someone is the forest itself, waiting for the moment it's able to reclaim you.

"Beckett," I repeat, more forcefully this time, reaching for his arm. If he continues, he'll kill Jean-Louis, and while I'm not opposed to that at the moment, I don't think Beckett will be able to live it down. Especially not in his current state.

He jerks against me, frustration tearing from his chest in the form of a deep, agitated groan.

"It will never end," he says, the blood spatter across his face being diluted with his tears. "The founding families will never be happy, and you'll never look at me the same after this."

"You don't know that."

"She was waiting for you," he replies, sawing my heart in two.

I'm not sure which she he means.

"Stop." I yank on his arm. "Stop fucking talking about her and just get up. We can—"

Sudden movement, a shadow dancing in my peripheral vision, cuts off my sentence. Or maybe it's the horrified look glinting in Beckett's blue eyes, the scent of fresh blood permeating the air, or the grunt of effort exerted by Jean-Louis as he drives a dagger into my brother's stomach.

My own scream echoes off the tops of the trees, shaking the mountains. Fear and adrenaline speed through my veins, sending me forward; I grab Beckett's shoulder, dragging him off Jean-Louis, and drive my fist into the older man's face.

He grips my shirt, chuckling, blood spraying from his nose. His head tips backward, like he's falling.

Falling.

No, not just him.

My knees separate from the ground, losing purchase.

We're falling.

Beckett's guttural cry is the last thing I hear as we're catapulted over the quarry edge, plunging into the deep, dark waters below.

Chapter 57

Elle

MOM CALLS THE SECOND I FINISH EXPLAINING EVERYTHING TO Dad. I probably left out a good number of details—like the fact that I'm sleeping with my professor after promising to lie low—but all the stuff about LA, the truth about my acting roles, and a rundown of the student organizations gets pushed out into the open, where I guess Sutton wanted me to put it.

Irritation lights up my spine at the fact that my dad was called at all. Like I'm some little girl incapable of handling things on her own.

Which…maybe has *some* merit to it right now, all things considered.

My face burns as Dad gets to his feet, my gaze falling to the ice pack resting on my knee. Point taken.

Still, I focus on the anger and annoyance because it's easier than dealing with the reality of my situation.

Percy is dead. I'm officially a Death's Teeth member, I guess. One bound to Incarnate, the man I slept beside all night.

Percy is dead. I close my eyes for a moment, sadness filling my chest.

I killed someone. In self-defense, sure, but no matter how many times I scrubbed my hands after Sutton's departure, the blood still seemed embedded into my fingerprints—a part of me, the way it was always destined to be.

Dad sighs and heads into the foyer, as if that might dilute any part of her emotional breakdown when he answers Mom's video request.

"Little one," is the only thing he says in lieu of a greeting.

"Don't little one me," she spits. I swear he adjusts the volume on his phone, but I can hear her plain as day. "First, you don't even tell me you're leaving, and I wake up to an empty house this morning—"

"There were three canines in the bed when I left it."

"—and then I get texts from Quincy about Noelle being in some sort of trouble and her sending pictures of bruises and blood? What the fuck is going on in Fury Hill, Kallum?"

"I'm not sure," he answers, his voice so level compared to the unevenness of hers. "That's what I came to find out."

"You told me this wouldn't happen again," she whispers harshly. "After last semester, you said you'd keep them safe."

He doesn't reply.

My stomach twists, guilt and shame mixing into volatile little knots.

"It's on us if anything…" She trails off, sucking in a deep breath.

"She is fine, Elena." His use of her first name makes me cringe; it's so rare. "No signs of broken bones or internal bleeding. A mild concussion, skin abrasions… Honestly, all things considered, I anticipated much worse."

"Can I talk to her?"

"Let me interrogate her first, and we'll call you back."

She sniffles. "You don't think I can get answers out of our child?"

"I think you need a drink."

"Already on it." Aunt Cora's voice joins the fray, and I can imagine her slinging a tattooed arm over Mom's shoulder, squeezing in close for the camera.

"Isn't it a little early for that?" Mom mutters.

"Keep your hands to yourself, Astor," Dad warns, referring to Cora by her maiden name, even though he and her husband are the closest of all the adults in their social circle. Too close, if you ask me. Same with their wives.

"I always do when you're away," Cora replies, her smirk audible. "It's way less fun when there's no audience."

Horror settles on my face as he hangs up and strolls back into the room, arms at his sides.

Dad settles on the arm of the sofa, staring at me with those unreadable, almost black eyes. Impassive on the surface, but I'm sure he's just as upset with me as Mom is. "Your mother sends her—"

"Emotional instability?"

His eyes crease a little, the crow's-feet at the corners deepening. "One of my favorite things about her."

"You like that she's volatile?"

"Immensely. I struggled to show emotion due to environmental and psychological factors. Your mother was raised in a similar fashion, but she rejected the sentiment and did whatever she wanted anyway. I've always admired how readily she wears her heart on her sleeve."

Glancing down at my hands, I interlace my fingers and pull, discomfort settling in the pit of my stomach.

"You're just like her, you know." Dad lifts his chin, looking out the front windows where he pulled open the curtains. Probably the first time Sutton's living room has seen light during his residency. "Ever since you were little, anyone within a mile radius could tell what you were thinking or feeling just by reading your face. Even when you were onstage or rehearsing for a part, whatever that character needed to convey, it all shone so brightly in your expressions. The honesty was refreshing."

Which is what makes the admittance of lies more unsettling. He doesn't say it—doesn't have to. But I hear the unspoken words anyway and feel the disappointment swelling up alongside them.

"Asher wasn't an open book, but he'd tell us anything if we asked. Getting information out of your sister was never an easy task. I guess I wrongly believed your honesty would carry over no matter what situation you were in."

I chew on my lip, swallowing hard.

"So where is this Jean-Louis Dupont? When was the last time you had contact with him?"

Confused, I meet his gaze. "I didn't tell you his name."

A long, weighted pause ensues. He gives me a look. "Noelle. Did you honestly think I wouldn't have done any homework after being summoned to my injured child's side?"

Scoffing, I cross my arms over my chest. "So why'd you make me tell you about it all?"

"Well, there had to be some sort of recompense. I think you're getting off fairly easy, but I can't speak for what your mother will do when you're home."

"Home?" I blink, frowning. "I don't want to go home."

His features strain. "Noelle, the deal was—"

"I know, but I've made a life for myself at Avernia. You didn't make Asher and Lucy go home when they got into trouble. Why do I have to?"

"You don't have to. You're a twenty-five-year-old woman. Despite how I may want to on occasion, I can't force you to do anything… Though I do want you to consider the consequences of staying."

"If I leave, Sutton has to deal with it all alone."

"Sutton?" Dad's eyes narrow. "The professor?"

"Yes, the one whose apartment we're currently sitting in."

Dad glances around the living room, his gaze lingering on the stack of Shakespearean tragedies sitting atop an old record player. "I don't like him."

I snort. "You don't know him."

"A father doesn't need to know a man to see whether he's good enough for his child. Clearly, he's not up to the task of protecting you."

"This wasn't his fault."

He cocks an eyebrow. "Anything that happens to your mother or you kids is indirectly attributed to me. That's the lot you pick when you start a family."

"Jesus," I say, cringing. "Who said anything about starting a family with the guy? I just like him is all."

"Like?"

"Yeah, it's this feeling you get when someone makes your heart race and—"

"No," he replies, huffing. "I mean, is that all?"

"Why wouldn't it be?"

He shrugs. "Not every guy would stare down the barrel of a

gun with no reaction because he knew you were inside and wanted to keep you safe."

Behind my rib cage, my heart skips a beat, fluttering. "You just said he wouldn't be able to protect me."

"I said I wasn't certain he could, not that he wouldn't try." Exhaling, he looks at the screen of his phone, and I glare down at my hands.

How does Sutton feel about me, and do I feel the same?

Last night at my absolute worst, there was only one person I trusted to care for me. To hold me close and provide comfort.

My Incarnate.

I think I already know the answer.

"In any case," Dad continues, "while I can't force you to leave this godforsaken school, I will advise you to be smart about your decision to stay. Don't do it because you wish to keep making googly eyes at your professor or to spite anyone. Both of those reasons are dangerous, and I will intervene if you put yourself in harm's way again."

Nodding, I squeeze my fingers together. "I know you and Mom kind of forced me to come, but I was looking forward to being around Quincy and Asher again. Los Angeles was fine, but making deep connections was hard." I look at him, my bottom lip wobbling. "No one gets you like your siblings."

The corner of his mouth lifts, and I wonder if he's thinking about his sister, Violet, or the de facto siblings he acquired over the years. Either way, he just wraps his hand around the back of my neck and pulls me into his side, where I wish, deep down, I could just stay forever.

We leave Sutton's a while later, with me limping on a set of crutches that keep getting stuck in the fucking cobblestone pathways. Dad decides to have an impromptu meeting with Dean Bauer about the state of his school, which appears to be in jeopardy by the harsh set of his jaw when he leaves me in Asher's care.

A part of me wonders if there will be a Dean Bauer when Dad leaves Fury Hill.

"You know, I never really thought we looked all that much alike," Asher muses, kicking a rock down the path. "But I guess all you needed was a little bruising to highlight my features—your best ones, by the way."

I shoot him a dirty look. "I wish Dad would've asked Q to come watch me."

"He did. She declined."

Ouch. I swallow, staring at my feet. "Why?"

"Probably felt bad for calling him in the first place. Who fucking knows what goes on in her head?"

Pausing in the middle of the walk, I frown at the ground, replaying Sutton's words from earlier over and over in my head.

I called your sister.

Why had he done that when there's an open investigation into his behavior going on? Why run the risk of telling another faculty member?

Unless she'd already known.

"Hey, Ash?"

He stops ahead, twisting around to look at me. "Yeah?"

"Do you…" Trailing off, I consider the end of that question. What exactly do I want him to say? That he thinks Quincy was the one to rat out my relationship to the dean or that no, he doesn't, which means there's someone else who knows and wanted us to suffer.

Shaking my head, I hobble forward, catching up as Asher begins walking again. Campus is practically silent, which I've come to recognize is pretty standard at Avernia, but somehow it feels more eerie than usual. The sensation of being watched is elevated, and I wonder if that's because of what happened last night or if there are actual eyes lurking between statues and hedges, peering around the corners of buildings, that I just can't see.

The clock tower in front of the Obeliskos chimes, signaling noon. I glance around the empty quad, suspicion still clogging my arteries.

"Does Avernia feel empty to you?" Asher asks, flopping down on a bench in front of the statue of Artemis outside the Lyceum. "Like… It's afternoon. Prime time for students to be peddling their extracurriculars or scurrying to class, yet I've hardly seen anyone out and about."

"Well, someone did die last night, so maybe—"

"What?" His brown eyes widen slightly. "Who?"

"One of my classmates… You didn't hear about it?"

"It's hilarious you think I'm important enough to warrant first-hand knowledge of shit, but also…no? Lucy hasn't said anything about it either. You're sure someone died?"

I glare at him. "I watched him get stabbed repeatedly."

Asher makes a face. "Jesus, just what the hell did you do last night?"

Shaking my head, I pull out my phone and shoot Sutton a text.

Where are you?

He doesn't answer, and my chest tightens, making me dizzy as heavy dread mounts higher and higher in my stomach. A couple of students pass by, giggling to themselves, and then skid to a stop.

"Holy—" Lexington's voice fills the air across the courtyard. "*Elle?* What the fuck happened to you?"

My head snaps up as he, Meg, and Sabrina—her head bandage-free, holding a bouquet of flowers—approach. I grab Lexington's shirt, yanking him closer.

He holds his hands up, blue eyes widening. "Whoa there, killer. I don't have any fruit snacks. I'm about to go visit Percy, though, if you want me to grab some on the way?"

"Percy?" I repeat, tightening my hold on his shirt. "What do you mean you're going to visit him?"

Lexington grunts, trying to pry me off. "He got mugged last night. Dude's been in the ICU ever since."

"They're finally moving him to a room," Sabrina adds, jostling the flowers. "We figured we'd visit since he's always doing that stuff for us."

"Only one person allowed in the room at a time though," Meg says, squinting at me as my breathing grows haggard, my mind racing. "Hey, you kind of look like you should be admitted too. Are you okay, Elle?"

Tears spring to my eyes, and I release Lexington. "So he's all right?"

"He's fine. Most of his injuries were superficial." Meg pokes my bicep. "But you're not fine. Why don't you come with us and get checked out?"

I shake my head, looking at my phone again. *Still nothing.* "No, really, I don't need it. Shouldn't you all be at rehearsal though? *Othello* goes on really soon. Or are you planning to practice in Percy's hospital room?"

Lexington casts me a sidelong glance. "Rehearsal was canceled for the week. No one's seen or heard from Professor Dupont since classes yesterday. We figured he was lying low because of the investigation."

"The what?" Asher mutters.

"Did something happen?" Sabrina asks in a low voice. "You and Percy both looking beat up doesn't seem like a coincidence."

"I heard Beckett Dupont in the Obeliskos earlier this morning talking about the quarry," Lexington adds. "Said he had something to do there today, but I couldn't make out what. He mentioned an attack to someone, but I figured he was just talking about the one last semester."

Asher drifts closer to me, stiffening.

Beckett.

It was Beckett who abducted me.

Something tells me I know who he did it for too.

"What's going on?" Meg asks as I turn in the direction of the Primordial Forest.

If he's out there, I'd bet good money there's a reason. Things he doesn't want the rest of campus to overhear.

Sutton's lack of response indicates they're there, together, and I wonder if he knows.

I'm not going to wait to find out.

"Hold up," Lexington says as I hand my crutches to my brother. "I'll come with."

"Wait! Me too. Moral support," Sabrina says, giving the flowers to Meg and skipping to us.

"Fine," Meg shouts. "I wanted to be Percy's best friend anyway."

I glance back to see Asher frowning.

"Dad's gonna be pissed," he calls out.

"So don't tattle!"

We pick up the pace, my entire body blazing like an inferno as my limbs protest the movement. As we round the corner of the Lyceum, I run right into my sister, whose glasses nearly careen off her face from the impact.

Her jaw is tense as she sizes me up. "Where are you going?"

"None of your business." I start to push past her, shoulder checking her as I move, but she grabs my hand.

"Where's Dad? Asher? How come they let you leave when you're in such bad shape?"

I ignore her.

"Hey," she says, her eyebrows knitting behind her glasses. "I know you're a bad patient, but you should be *resting*."

Her touch burns. I grit my teeth, jerking out of her hold. "You told the dean, didn't you?"

She blinks, eyes widening. "What?"

"You told the dean about me and Sutton…that something was going on between us." I inhale, betrayal weaving through my muscles when she doesn't deny it.

A blush crawls over her cheeks. She looks at Lexington and Sabrina, who take a step back, giving us a little space. "I was looking out for your safety, Noelle."

"Nobody asked you to do that."

"Asked? Of course no one did. It's been my goddamn responsibility since you were born, you idiot." Her nostrils flare. "Idealism was practically your middle name, and you just leaned into it without a care in the world. So long as people liked you and you got their attention, you didn't care what it was doing to your soul, but *I* did. I'm the one who had to watch you get taken advantage of time and time again, and yeah, maybe when you got here, I decided I was sick of just standing by and letting it happen."

"Sutton isn't taking advantage of me," I say, my throat on fire.

"You never see it when you're in it," she replies.

Shaking my head, I give her a long, sad look. Tears well up in her eyes—tears I've never seen her shed. Not once in my life. Something haunted lives in her irises, and a part of me feels bad for not having noticed until now.

Though I suppose we all have our masks. Some look different, and some, like hers and Sutton's, are all too similar.

"He loves me," I tell her. "And you're projecting. I don't know what's going on with you, but… You told Dean Bauer, and Pythia found out."

"So? Pythia finds out everything anyway. You guys—I saw you that day in the Obeliskos. It was only a matter of time."

"Pythia found out, and while I was trying to figure out how to deal with that mess, I learned I was responsible for killing the sister of the man I love. He sent me away so he could process that, and in the meantime, I was abducted. Beaten nearly to death and threatened with worse. The only reason I came out of that cave alive was because of *him*."

She snaps her mouth shut.

"I don't know if I can forgive you," I tell her. "I never would've done this to you. Not in a million years."

"Noelle, I'm—"

If she's going to apologize, she seems to think better of it at the last second. My heart shatters when she turns away and starts back in the direction she was originally heading, leaving me to be swallowed by uncertainty and heartbreak.

She really never believed in me at all.

Chapter 58

Sutton

DROWNING, IT TURNS OUT, IS NOT AS PAINLESS AND SERENE AS you'd think.

It's lonely, waiting for your lungs to fill up. Despite being surrounded by water, cradled in its icy, liquid embrace, the knowledge that everything is slowly ending makes you feel further away from humanity than ever before.

There's no time to act when you're dying. When your efforts have been exhausted, fear and determination take a back seat to acceptance.

The longer I float, descending in a sea of pitch-black toward my demise, I wonder if this is what Bellamy felt. It seems fitting that I'd reach the same fate as my twin—nature balancing itself out.

Of course, I don't get a happily ever after. No chance to see my mother's face or check on my brother or tell the woman I left in my apartment this morning exactly how I feel about her.

Hazel eyes and long, dark brown hair appear before me, just

out of reach. I lift my arms, aware that making it out isn't an option but desperate to touch her one last time.

She slips from my grasp just as my fingers graze her locks, like seaweed being swept away with the current.

One last touch would have been nice, but I suppose I don't deserve even that.

I wonder if she'll cry—no, I know she will. She'll be sad and perhaps even a little angry. Confused.

Alone.

She'll be alone again.

I can't tell if it's the water infiltrating my lungs or if sadness and guilt weigh me down instead. It doesn't matter, I suppose. They have the same effect either way.

Down, down I sink.

Hand outstretched toward the surface, where a tiny sliver of light shines through. That light wraps around my wrist, pulling against my descent.

A fitting metaphor.

Chapter 59

Elle

THE FOREST IS DEFINITELY WATCHING ME SUFFER.

As the sky darkens with rain clouds, it feels like the trees might even be laughing.

"Sutton!" My scream bounces off the leaves and dirt, carrying across the mountain air. Still, we're met with silence, ascending to the quarry as the stillness of the forest fills me with dread.

Where is he?

The sensation intensifies as we crest the hill, the ground turning to rock from soft grass and moss under our feet.

A lone shadow lies near the quarry's edge—so close to tumbling into Lake Lerna below that breathing too hard might knock them over.

We freeze, staring from several yards away. My stomach cramps, disbelief coloring my entire being.

No.

This isn't possible.

It can't be fucking real, but no matter how long we stare,

nothing evaporates into thin air. A part of me is hesitant still, considering Percy's apparent survival, but neither Lexington nor Sabrina seem shocked by this revelation.

"Is that—"

I don't wait for Lexington to finish his question before I'm limping over, my heart pounding, vomit teasing the back of my throat. My skull feels like it's about to implode, and the closer I get, the louder the white noise rushing between my ears sounds.

"Sutton," I sob, tears blurring my vision as I launch myself at the figure's side, barely noting before I'm on my knees that he's not wearing the sweater and slacks he left the house in. Blood pools around the prone body, and from this vantage point, I can see black hair, but my body doesn't believe it yet.

With shaky hands, I grab the person's shoulders and pull, rolling them onto their back.

Blue eyes, cold and unseeing, stare up at the sky.

Similar to Sutton's—but not his.

It's not him.

Relief washes over me, followed very quickly by the realization of who this is.

Beckett Dupont.

I glance at his stomach, where several holes have been shredded through his shirt and skin beneath. Pulling my hands back, I settle them in my lap, unable to look away from his eyes.

Sabrina lets out a strangled noise as she gets closer, covering her mouth with her fingers. Lexington crouches down, feeling Beckett's neck for a pulse.

He sighs. As if there was any doubt.

"What do we do?" Sabrina chokes out.

But my focus shifts. A gun lies close to Beckett's body.

Beckett wasn't shot though.

I lean forward over the edge of the quarry. The lake water is still below, calm and unmoving but as dark and opaque as ever.

If someone fell in, you'd never know. Lake Lerna consumes its victims. She doesn't reveal them or give them back.

Except once.

Panic surges in my chest, and I abandon the three of them, starting back down the side of the quarry. All I can think about is the water—and the green eyes that might have disappeared inside it.

Bile burns my esophagus as I begin shucking off my sweater and tights, breathing hard. Lexington wraps his arms around me at the exact moment I aim to enter the lake, squeezing so tight I can barely breathe.

"Let go!" I scream, thrashing against him. "He could be in there!"

"What are you going to do, Elle? You're injured yourself. Diving in after him when you can't even swim properly will just ensure you die too."

"I don't fucking care," I sob, the tears falling, soaking my face. I punch at his chest, my rage boiling over, making me see red. "I can't—this cannot be how things end. I didn't even get to tell him I love him or have a real relationship, and this isn't…it's not fair! He thinks I saved him, but that's not *true*. He saved me, and I have to tell him. I–I—"

Lexington goes down with me when I crumple, the weight of my fear and anger shoving me to the ground. I cling to his shirt, my cries incinerating my throat as they rip through the lining, obliterating any other noise in the forest.

It's all my fault.

Everything. From eight years ago to this.

I really am the problem. The common denominator. The fuckup.

Maybe Quincy was right not to have any faith when all I do is destroy anything I touch.

"We'll get the police," Lexington offers softly. "They'll be able to bring in search and rescue, and—"

"He's not in the water."

The two of us freeze at the sound of that voice.

A *painfully* familiar voice—one we've spent the entire semester listening to three times a week, minimum.

My heart skips a beat. I open my eyes, peering over Lexington's shoulder as Sutton stumbles forward. He's soaked from head to toe but not enough that it feels like he just got out of the lake. More like he's been out, but God only knows where he's been.

His gaze—dark green, alive but distant—falls to Lexington's back. I shove at my friend, staggering to my feet, and ignore the blistering agony that shoots up my spine as I sprint to him.

He doesn't open his arms, but I wrap mine around him anyway. His stiff, rigid posture and wet clothes send a prick of unease through my heart, but I press my head into his chest and try to pretend I don't notice.

His pulse is there, and that's all that matters.

"Beckett's dead," he announces in a monotone voice.

Easing back, I glance up at him. "I know. I'm sorry."

He shakes his head. "Not your fault…none of this was. I wanted to save him, but we went over before I could. The fall knocked me out briefly. I'm not sure how I got ashore, in truth."

Tears well up in my eyes again, and I bury my face against him. Red stains the collar of his sweater, disappearing beneath the material. I pull back, my stomach twisting.

"You're bleeding," I say, moving my hands up to inspect the damage.

Slowly, he grabs my wrists, removing me. He stares into my eyes, swallowing hard, and shakes his head again. "That's not mine."

"Sutton? You said *we*. Who else was out here?"

"Jean-Louis."

Terror seizes my heart. "Where did he go?"

Maintaining eye contact, he brings my knuckles to his lips. His hands on me are as cold as ever, and the temperature of his mouth matches. As he kisses me there, he lets his gaze float up above my head, toward the lake.

"Your guess is as good as mine."

Chapter 60

Sutton

CARRYING MY DEAD BROTHER OUT OF THE PRIMORDIAL Forest feels somehow like a full-circle moment.

I didn't get to do this for Bellamy, though, so I make sure Elle's friends don't call campus police before I can grab him.

Maybe, somewhere deep inside me, the hope still remains that he'll magically wake. Or that the doctors can do something if we get him to the hospital fast enough.

Regardless, even with the numbness racking my body, I want to hold my baby brother one last time. I want to cry over his body in peace.

Tears stain my face when they declare him deceased just down the hall from the ICU where his father remains comatose.

I have no idea how Jean-Louis got here. Everything after we tumbled into the lake is a blur, just as it was the first time I fell in. I don't know how I got out or how much time passed before Elle found me.

All I know is that I awoke on the embankment with one less

sibling and no Jean-Louis. Instead, when we arrived at the hospital, I'd run into Mother, who told me they'd found him collapsed somewhere on campus, and he was now in a medically induced coma.

Elle waits outside the door for me as I enter the room. Mother sits next to Jean-Louis's bed, holding the shirt they cut off Beckett before taking him away for an autopsy.

She doesn't cry. Barely reacts when she notices I'm in the room. Just keeps staring at the clothing like it might be enough to conjure up her lost son.

The room is eerily silent. I glance around, noting that Jean-Louis isn't hooked up to any monitors. His IV has been detached. The oxygen machine switched off.

I look at her again, willing myself to feel something—anything—when she holds up a tiny clear vial.

"When I was a young girl," she begins, her voice raspy, "I loved a man I was not supposed to. Founding family members weren't to become romantically involved with each other, but we were all so close back then that it seemed almost impossible for there not to be some overlap. At least for me. My father had other plans, wanting to merge our family with Jean-Louis's who weren't founders. All I wanted was to be true to my heart."

I don't say a word.

"Turns out you can be too true if you're not careful. I wound up pregnant with twins—you and Bellamy. A double penance for my indiscretion. That should've been the first clue that we were the cursed ones, not the Andersons."

She sighs, tucking the vial beneath Beckett's shirt.

Silent, I take a seat on the pullout couch behind her.

"It was obvious to anyone who cared that you had none of

Jean-Louis's blood in you. I used to think it was a good thing, until he started plotting in secret. I think he was threatened by the fact that you had double the founding family blood in you when he had none. He didn't want his position in Fury Hill to ever be questioned, since he was only the head of our family because he married in and took my last name. Back then, the city council wouldn't even give me a second thought as the family head. That's why Jean-Louis worked with Death's Teeth to orchestrate taking Bellamy's life…and the attempt on yours. To eliminate obstructions."

I squeeze my hands together in my lap.

"For a long time, I wasn't sure, but the fact that he refused to retrieve Bellamy's body never sat well with me. So eventually, I decided I'd give him a similar fate."

The vial. His mysterious illness. "You've been poisoning him."

"I had hoped the effects would take a toll on him much quicker. Especially after seeing the influence he had over Beckett…" Her voice cracks, and she brings his shirt up, inhaling its scent. "I tried to get him out of the hole Jean-Louis had dug for him, but all the new information he learned only seemed to make him spiral more. Still, I thought maybe you'd be able to reach him. I don't suppose that was fair of me."

My chest burns. "None of it would've mattered. He was too far gone."

"They convinced him that you being both a Blackwater and Dupont meant you'd try to edge him out or something. I don't know what nonsense they spewed… I should have sent him abroad with Gigi." Sighing, she lowers the shirt. "Good Lord. I'll have to tell your sister about this."

"Do you want me to stay?"

She swallows, nodding just once. "I'm not sure how long it'll be before someone comes in here to check on your—on Jean-Louis. It'd be nice to have an alibi."

I'm not sure my word is going to matter all that much when our last name will shut down questions anyway, but I don't say that. I wouldn't want to be alone in a tomb of my own making either.

I get to my feet, watching as she stares at him with a finality I can't quite place. A coldness I've experienced in very specific settings and never paid enough attention to.

You didn't recognize her last night?

Bending down, I hold out my arms as though I'm going in for a hug. Mother meets my gaze and tentatively lifts hers to reciprocate; as she leans in, I drop my hand, pressing against her abdomen.

She hisses, wincing and pulling away, but not before I can feel the thick gauze hidden beneath her shirt.

In the exact spot where I stabbed the Director.

A part of me expects sadness or even disappointment, but I feel nothing.

"It isn't what you think, Sutton."

I brush my hands off on my thighs. "It never is."

Walking back out into the hallway, I'm greeted by Elle as she shoots up out of the plastic waiting room chair. Sabrina sits cross-legged, watching, but I don't give her a second glance.

"Everything okay?" Elle asks, approaching slowly, still limping. Still bruised as fuck, covered in dirt and sweat. She cringes, a blush staining her cheeks. "Well, I know *okay* probably isn't the right word, but—"

"You should go back to your dorm," I interrupt. "Get some rest."

She blinks, frowning. God, that gesture stirs an ache in my chest, but I'm too exhausted—too fucking numb—to acknowledge it.

"Oh, it's no problem," she says, fidgeting. "I figured I'd just wait for you—"

"I'm not sure when I'll be leaving, so you don't need to wait."

"Ah." Her entire face falls, and she retreats a little, her throat bobbing on a swallow. "I see. Um, okay then, I'll just head back to campus."

Pain splits my head in half, meandering its way down to my heart. My hand twitches, itching to reach for her.

Instead, I turn toward the room, allowing the defeat to settle heavily on my shoulders. God, what a fucking disaster everything wound up being—

A hand on my bicep tugs me back in the opposite direction, and before I have a chance to even blink, Elle's leaning up on tiptoe and pressing a rough kiss to my mouth.

My hand comes up, cradling the back of her head, but she doesn't give me time to fall into anything before she withdraws, despair written all over her face even as she gives me a little smile.

"I love you," she says. "Take as much time as you need. I'll be around."

When she walks away, meeting up with Sabrina and heading down the hall, I watch until she's turning the corner, disappearing without looking back. Once she's gone, I head back inside, touching my fingertips to my lips as I settle in beside my mother, letting her put her head on my shoulder.

It'll be the last time we're in a room together anyway.

And when Jean-Louis takes his last breath, I think maybe it wasn't all a disaster.

Epilogue

Elle

OPENING NIGHT FOR *OTHELLO* SOMEHOW GOES OFF WITHOUT a hitch despite all the lost rehearsal time, the injuries, and the fact that our director doesn't show.

We consider waiting, but as the amphitheater on the far edge of campus begins filling up with all the people who bought tickets, it becomes clear that a delay will only make us look bad. The Visio Aternae students step up, guiding everyone through the scene and costume changes, tossing lines as needed, and running around to make sure the production is a massive success.

Which it is, surprisingly. Still, when the curtain's brought down after the final act, it's hard not to feel a little disappointed when Sutton doesn't join the cast onstage.

In the week and a half since his brother's death—and his father's, interestingly enough—I've barely seen him at all. At the hospital, I said I'd wait, but I had no idea at the time that it meant he'd withdraw from me completely.

I mean, I get it. But that doesn't mean it doesn't totally suck.

I'm sulking when my parents come up to congratulate me on the show. Mom's long, dark brown hair spills elegantly over her shoulders, even as she's glued to Dad's massive side. Behind them are my aunt Violet and uncle Grayson, his hand around her waist at all times, and Foxe trails the pair with his hands in his pockets.

"You were fabulous, as usual," Mom says, throwing her arms around me. Luckily, I've mostly healed up from the night in Tartarus, so her overcompensation doesn't hurt anymore. "How in the world did we get so lucky with our talented kids, Kallum?"

Dad smiles softly at her. "All you, my little Persephone."

She blushes, and my heart aches a bit.

"Actually," Grayson says, shoving them aside, "I'd say it's all me. We know where the performing genes come from."

"You're not even a blood relative," Dad replies glibly.

"James genes are that powerful," Grayson says, waggling his brows at Dad.

Violet groans, tucking her black hair behind her ears and pulling me in for a hug. "Save yourself and make up an excuse, or else you'll hear this all night if you agree to dinner."

I laugh. "Thanks for the heads-up."

She smiles, smoothing her fingers over my cheek. "You look good, you know? When you came home last summer, something seemed off, but now…"

Dad rolls his eyes, pushing her and her husband out of the way. "All right, enough hogging my child. Why don't you two go find the others? I know Kieran and Juliet were around here somewhere."

"Why do we have to find your guests?" Grayson snaps, but he drags Violet off to do so anyway.

"Can't stand that man," Dad grumbles.

Foxe steps up, snorting. "You love him and you know it."

"Debatable." Dad places his hand on Foxe's head, giving him a little shake. "You're all right though."

"Gee, thanks."

Mom pulls Dad away to go talk to a few of the other actors, and Foxe rocks back on his heels, giving me a once-over. "Well," he says, nodding, "my mom was right. You do look better than when I saw you last."

"You too," I note, jutting my chin at his arm. "No more cast."

"Ah, no. Been off a while." He sighs, scrubbing the back of his neck with one hand, looking around. "You seen Aurora today?"

"She's my roommate," I tell him. "But not since this morning."

"Yeah, figures. I'm sure she's hiding from me still." After a moment, he shrugs, dropping his arm. "But enough of that. What's next on the agenda for Miss Noelle Anderson?"

Shaking my head, I cross my arms over my chest. "I'm just looking forward to the summer, I think. This semester was fucking insane, and I don't think I've been all that lucky in love, so maybe lying low is—"

"You haven't?"

My back goes rigid at the sudden intrusion, goose bumps scattering along my skin. I spin around, instantly meeting moss-green eyes.

Behind my ribs, my heart thunders.

Sutton blows out a breath, pushing some of the brown hair off his forehead, and pulls his hand around from his back, presenting me with a bouquet of bright red roses. He holds them out but then seems to think better of it, bringing them to his nose to inhale instead.

"See, I brought these for my girlfriend," he says, sighing. "But then I hear her telling some guy I've never met before that she's not actually been lucky in love, and now I'm rethinking the gift. Perhaps I should have gone with yellow for friendship instead?"

"For the record, I'm a cousin." Foxe holds his hands up in surrender.

I swallow, smirking. "I didn't think you'd show up."

Sutton's brow furrows, and he steps closer, pressing the flowers into my arms. "And miss your performance on opening night? How terrible of a director would I have to be to do that?"

My trembling fingers close around the bouquet. "Well, it's just at the hospital, you made it seem like you weren't—"

Cupping my jaw, Sutton swoops in and seals his lips to mine, stealing the words from my mouth and the air from my lungs. I grunt in surprise, the flowers sharp where their thorns press between us, but lean into it anyway.

"Didn't I already tell you that you're stuck with me, *Maiden*?" he asks when he pulls away.

Ugh, yeah. I don't know what's going to happen with that organization or the roles now, but something tells me it isn't over.

He releases me, heading for the stage, and I stand there like all the thoughts have been zapped from my entire being.

Foxe snorts. "I don't think I've ever seen your face get that red."

A speaker crackles somewhere overhead, and suddenly Sutton's standing in the center of the stage, holding a microphone in hand.

"Can we get a round of applause for the cast of our spring final production?"

The crowd obeys, erupting in cheers and whistles.

Sutton beams with pride, something I'm realizing I haven't seen him do before. Not to this extent at least and certainly not since the quarry.

"I was nervous with this lot, I have to say, but they worked hard, and they blew everything out of the water. It's truly been a privilege watching them learn, grow, and work together to make this the best play it could be."

The crowd bursts into applause again, agreement murmuring through the room.

"Which is why I'm sad to say this will be my last production at Avernia."

A hush falls over us. My eyes widen, and I glance at Sabrina and the others where they're mingling across the floor. She shrugs, leaning into Percy, who wraps an arm around her, pressing a kiss to the top of her head.

Though he's not fully recovered, he definitely looks better than when I last saw him. And I'm glad to see them finally giving in to each other.

When they break off to find Lexington in the crowd, congregating together like they're the only three in the world, I hide a smirk to myself, incredibly happy to see it working out for all of them.

"See, this semester, I was lucky in a lot of ways. Teaching has been a great passion of mine for many years, and I've always enjoyed getting to share my love for the theater with others." Sutton's eyes find mine, and I think my heart stops beating. "But it turns out there's something I love a bit more than the theater, and her name is Elle Anderson. So… This is my official resignation. Thank you all for coming out."

Foxe and I blink at each other as he dismounts the stage.

"Did he just…"

I nod, unable to speak, even as Sutton rejoins us.

"Well?" he prompts, grinning as he removes the flowers from my hands, shoves them into Foxe's arms, and laces our fingers together. "You wanted public. It doesn't get much more public than that."

Disbelief colors my thoughts. "You didn't have to *resign*."

"They were going to fire me anyway. Or make my life hell here. Until Dean Bauer is out, I'm not sure this is a safe place for me anyway, so…it's fine." He reaches for my chin, tilting my face up. "I just hope you're still attracted to me even when we don't have the whole student-professor thing going for us."

Snorting, I slide my arms around his neck, nuzzling his nose with my own. "That's what role-play is for, right? Besides, you're the one who said you wanted to keep me forever. No takebacks. No returns."

He shakes his head, kissing me again. And again. And again, until Foxe gets uncomfortable and goes to find my brother.

"God, I love you." Sutton presses his forehead to mine. "I'm sorry I made you wait so long to hear it back."

"I would've waited forever for you," I say, tangling my fingers in his hair.

Because fate, though chaotic and cruel, has no expiration date.

My throat is tight as I knock on Quincy's office door. I think the number of plants in her office has doubled since the start of the semester.

She glances up from a book on classical sculpture when I step inside, marking her place with a highlighter.

"Have a seat," she says, gesturing to the suede armchair across from her.

I obey, even though this is the last thing I'd like to be doing. Still, our parents insisted we work things out, so here I am.

She sighs, long and hard. Adjusts her glasses. Fidgets with the gold rings adorning her slender fingers.

I tap my foot on the ground, waiting. "Well? You summoned me here. Talk."

"Yes, I did." She leans back in her oversize leather desk chair. "Apologies don't come easily to me, you know."

"Well, we're not starting off super strong."

Her nose wrinkles up. "I am...sorry. For meddling, for not trusting you, for saying you didn't have talent. I'm sorry for it all. You were right. I was projecting, and I let my own feelings and problems interfere when I shouldn't have. You're an adult. You should be able to make your own decisions and live your own life."

Pausing, I wait to see if there's more. When she doesn't continue, I nod and stand up. "Okay then. Thanks."

"But there's something you need to understand," she adds quickly, reaching over her desk for my hand. "It's that to me, you're always going to be the tiny, helpless baby Mom and Dad brought home from the hospital. I can't help but picture you that way anytime you're hurting or hiding things or making mistakes, and all I want is for you to be okay. I know you don't need me to, but I can't just turn it off. Believe me, it'd be amazing if I could."

"I'm not helpless though," I point out. "In fact, I've done a pretty good job of getting myself through a lot of bullshit, so maybe...scale it back a little? I appreciate your looking out, but I'm still sad about what you did to Sutton."

"Yeah." She nods, shaking her head. "You're right. Tattling was always your and Foxe's job anyway."

I smirk. "Exactly. I would like to have my big sister back though."

It's not fixed, but it's a start.

This is only the beginning of our stories after all.

She smiles, squeezing my fingers once before releasing me. I head for the door, pausing to admire the collection of books—the ones I gifted to her all those years ago that she displays where anyone can see them.

Everyone has their own way of expressing affection. I can't fault her this one.

Hand on the doorknob, I twist, something shiny catching my eye as I wrench open the door. My heart stops, trepidation filling its chambers.

It's a postcard tucked between the books, the handwriting a neat cursive I've seen before. In a specific journal with everyone's secrets no less.

Picking it up, I look at Quincy. "Where'd you get this?"

She barely looks at it, clicking her tongue with an eye roll. "I think a student gave it to me at some point?"

I stare at her for several beats even as she goes back to reading, wondering why she's lying. Because the moment I picked it up, I knew exactly where it'd come from.

Or rather…who.

Quincy's childhood friend, Eden Ivers, whom I haven't actually seen since they enrolled at Avernia together a decade prior.

Clearly I'm not the only one with secrets.

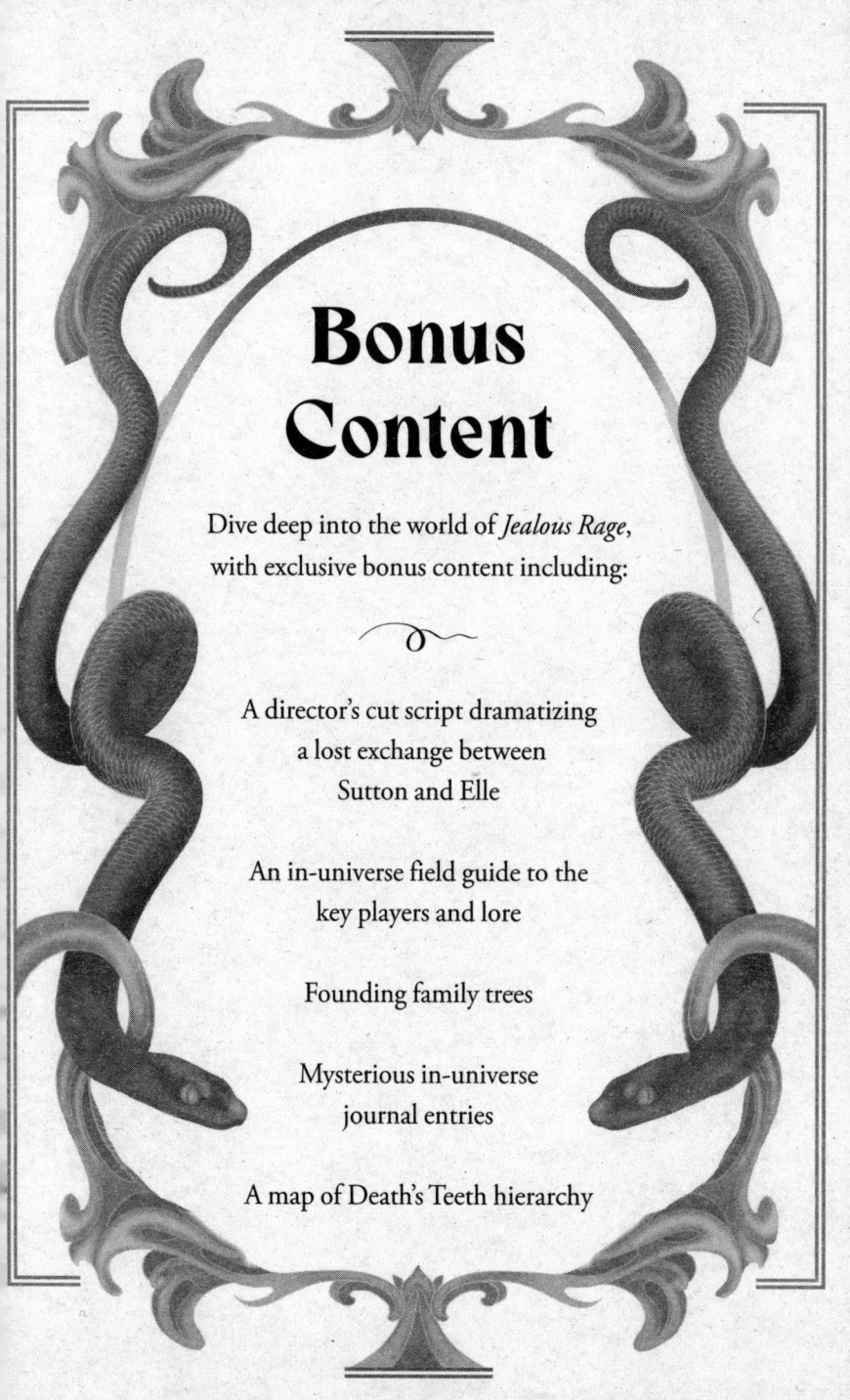

Bonus Content

Dive deep into the world of *Jealous Rage*,
with exclusive bonus content including:

A director's cut script dramatizing
a lost exchange between
Sutton and Elle

An in-universe field guide to the
key players and lore

Founding family trees

Mysterious in-universe
journal entries

A map of Death's Teeth hierarchy

Bonus Scene

Director's Cut

Author's Note: The original version of this story had Elle interacting a bit more directly with Death's Teeth prior to her relationship with Sutton developing more. There was a scene where she attends one of the sex parties thrown by Death's Teeth before she really knows anything about the organization, and Sutton—thinking she's participating in their fuckery—loses it a little. The following scene was found stapled to a handwritten playbill seeming to detail the intricacies of Sutton and Elle's story unbeknownst to either of them…because at Avernia, someone's *always* watching.

ACT 2, SCENE 4
Scene omitted from complete text
Avernia College, Fury Hill, NH. The Apollodorus Library.

[*Enter SUTTON DUPONT, in typical dark slacks and a brown sweater, and ELLE ANDERSON in sheer tights, an overcoat, and short dress. A Death's Teeth party rages in the basement below,*

which SUTTON has just come out of. SUTTON takes ELLE to a
back room and herds her against a bookcase, dropping his head to
her shoulder. The air is rife with tension and confusion and lust.]

ELLE
(speaking softly)
Sutton? Are you okay?

SUTTON
(shaking his head and pulling away)
What are you doing here?

ELLE
(frowning)
Um…Lexington and Percy invited me to a party,
so I figured I'd go. I haven't really been doing
the whole *college* thing since starting.

SUTTON
Don't go back down there.

ELLE
Excuse me?

SUTTON
To that party. You have no idea what you just escaped.

ELLE
Escaped? My friends are still down there. I was
planning to go back before you accosted me.

SUTTON
You're welcome, by the way.

ELLE
(Her face contorts, and she shoves him backward.)
No, you don't get to take credit for something
without explaining what's going on.

SUTTON
Do you have any fucking idea what sort of party that was?

ELLE
It *looked* like a sex party that you're trying to judge
me for attending, but clearly you were there, too.

SUTTON
Where I go should be none of your concern.

ELLE
(visibly hurt by this statement)
Well, then, *ditto.* Now, if we've established
that much, I'd like to go find my—

SUTTON
Fuck, no, that's not what I meant.
(slamming his hands on the shelf behind her, as if bracketing her in)
I just…there are places I'm obligated to be at, and I don't
want you to worry. It's not the same as you going to them.

ELLE

What's the big deal? If it's fine for you, why is it not for me?

SUTTON

(throwing his arms wide as his chest heaves, voice rising)
Because I don't give a fuck about me.

*[ELLE pauses. Her eyes take on a glassy sheen, almost twinkling
in the overhead lighting. SUTTON presses his palms to his
thighs as if to restrain himself from reaching for her again.]*

*[ELLE inches forward, flattening her palms
against his chest. Hesitation flickers in the space
between them, but neither move away.]*

ELLE

I'll bet you use that line on all the girls.

SUTTON

What?

ELLE

*(pushing him until his back connects with
a bookcase across from them)*
Was that not a line just now?

SUTTON

A line? No. That was the truth. You have no idea what
shit opens up when you attend a party like that one.

ELLE

You were there.

SUTTON

Which means I know what I'm talking about.

ELLE

*(scoffing and moving her thumb and index
finger to outline the base of his throat)*

Or you're just like everyone else around here, wanting to use me for your own twisted games. You don't have to lie, Boy Scout. I'd give myself to you willingly. Didn't we already talk about that?

*[ELLE's hands continue their ascent, her nails scraping against
the tender skin of his neck until she can thread her fingers in
the hair at his nape. She shifts, her pelvis brushing his.]*

ELLE

(moving one hand to his stomach, teasingly)

It's okay if that's all you want.

SUTTON

(grabbing her wrist)

What the hell is that supposed to mean? You think I've been resisting all this time because I want a one and done with you?

ELLE

Well, that time in your car, you seemed—

*[SUTTON spins so her back is against the bookcase
and wedges his thigh between hers. She chokes on a
sudden gasp as he presses his knee to her cunt.]*

*[The air shifts viciously, as if invisible flames surround them. Heat
drifts through the corridor, reaching places hidden by the darkest,
coolest shadows. Nothing else exists except the two of them.]*

SUTTON
(in a low, gravelly voice)
I told you that day, I don't *do* hookups. I've resisted because
I want *more*. And I want you to stop selling yourself
short. You deserve more than you're offering me, Elle.

*[SUTTON grinds his knee, grabbing her hip to keep her in
place. She clutches his biceps, her lips parting on a soft gasp.]*

SUTTON
How many goddamn times do I have to say it before
you believe me? How many times do I need to kiss
you before you realize I'm not fucking lying?

*[ELLE's palm slides down to cup his dick, fingers stretching
along the length. SUTTON releases a violent shudder,
almost pinning her as he leans into her touch.]*

ELLE
(murmuring, her lips touching the base of his throat)
I want to touch you, too.

SUTTON

Just touch me?

ELLE

No, not...*just* that.

*[She continues stroking him outside his pants. His
breaths grow more labored, shoulders tensing.]*

ELLE

(whispering)

That feels good, doesn't it, baby?

*[The corridor is nearly silent except for the quiet exchange of
breaths and soft whimpers, almost indistinguishable between
the two. They move in an erotic rhythm, their bodies undulating
against one another in the partially-hidden space, unaware
of—or perhaps unbothered by—the other presence.]*

ELLE

(squeezing, coaching, encouraging)

That's it. My hand now, but maybe my mouth next time.
You'd like me on my knees, I bet. You could wrap my
hair around your fist and bury yourself in my throat.

*[ELLE twists her restrained hand from his grasp, taking
his fingers and collaring her own throat with them.]*

ELLE
(low, seductive crooning)
I'd swallow every last drop.

*[Her movements grow frenzied, stroking faster and harder.
She moves his hand to her breast, pushing his fingers inside
the neckline and curling them around the heavy swell.]*

*[A thread seems to snap. SUTTON grunts and groans,
shoving himself into her as he shudders his release.]*

ELLE
(shakily)
What a good boy.

*[His hand is still on her breast. She continues grinding
on his knee, seeming to chase her own release.]*

SUTTON
(rolling his thumb over her exposed nipple)
I—

ELLE
(covering his mouth with her hand)
Shh. Don't talk. Just kiss me and make me come, please.

SUTTON
(removing her hand)
So demanding.

*[Enter STUDENT ONE and STUDENT TWO, wearing
nondescript casual clothing. They remain separated from
SUTTON and ELLE by a single corridor, staying out front.]*

*[SUTTON leans down, nearly kissing ELLE
when they hear the intruders. They freeze.]*

STUDENT ONE
Come on, man, I don't want to be in here
long. This place gives me the creeps.

STUDENT TWO
Better than the Obeliskos. You know I saw a fucking
ghost on the thirteenth floor last week, right?

STUDENT ONE
(snorting)
What the hell were you doing on the thirteenth floor?

STUDENT TWO
Looking for some old ass book Professor Dupont
suggested to help my performance anxiety. Someone at
the circulation desk told me it was here, though…

ELLE
(pushing at his chest as he remains plastered against her)
Sutton, there are people coming.

SUTTON
Let them.

ELLE

You can't be serious.

SUTTON

(shifting, grinding against her cunt even more as she bites off a moan and he doesn't let up)

I'm very serious.

ELLE

(hissing)

Do you *want* to get caught?

SUTTON

Maybe.

ELLE

(panting, close to her own orgasm)

This is a terrible idea.

[STUDENT ONE and STUDENT TWO exit the same way they entered without stumbling across the pair, and silence blankets the floor once more.]

[SUTTON and ELLE look at each other in panting, charged silence, but something is changing in SUTTON's face. His shoulders tighten.]

SUTTON

(pulling away)

You're probably right. We should stop now.

ELLE
(glaring)
You've got to be fucking kidding.

SUTTON
(shaking his head, voice gone cold)
Consider this a preemptive punishment should
you return to that party downstairs.

[Exit SUTTON.]

*[ELLE stays in place for several beats, staring into the darkness
as if trying to make sense of what just happened. Eventually,
she fixes her clothing and seems to shake herself off.]*

[Exit ELLE.]

*[Enter shadowy figure who walks to the area the couple was just
in. They stand there for a long moment, turning in a circle, before
plucking a book from a shelf and disappearing—as if into thin air.]*

Pawns

Noelle Rose Anderson

KEY DETAILS:
Born August 9th. Leo. Middle cursed Anderson child. Theater major. Flirty, outgoing, passionate.

ADDITIONAL NOTES:
Likes testing boundaries. Afraid of blood. Too trusting. Her past seems determined to haunt her. Wonder how that might play out in a certain relationship...

Sutton Aleksander Dupont

KEY DETAILS:
Born November 30th. Sagittarius. Oldest Dupont child. Theater professor. Outgoing, knowledgeable...haunted. Definitely haunted.

ADDITIONAL NOTES:
Dead twin sister—no visual affects of her in any of his personal spaces. Visio Aternae faculty sponsor. Founding family member, current interim figurehead. In the past, not easily swayed by students, but it appears there is one who can get under his skin...

Asher Blake Anderson

KEY DETAILS:
Born March 14th. Pisces. Youngest cursed Anderson child. Art major.

ADDITIONAL NOTES:
Volatile, violent, protective. Has a cat in dorm. No longer lives on campus. DO NOT APPROACH UNARMED.

Lucy Aberdeen Wolfe

KEY DETAILS:
Born September 13th. Virgo. Oldest Wolfe child. Ecosystem major, political science minor.

ADDITIONAL NOTES:
Kind, naive, prickly. Animals and Asher Anderson are greatest weakness—no longer lives on campus. Few friends, spends a lot of time alone in forest doing cleanups.

Quincy Jane Anderson

KEY DETAILS:
Born April 15th. Aries. Oldest cursed Anderson child. Classics professor—for now.

ADDITIONAL NOTES:
Founded Daughters of Persephone. Loner. Do NOT trust her.

Beckett Viktor Dupont

KEY DETAILS:
Born February 1st. Aquarius. Second to last Dupont child. Former Curator president.

ADDITIONAL NOTES:
Overly attached to his father. Malleable.

Lexington Theodore Abbott

KEY DETAILS:
Born May 19th. Founding family member. Helpful, resourceful, outgoing. Distances himself from founding issues.
ADDITIONAL NOTES:
Seems interested in Elle and Percy...

Perciville Maxwell Whitmore

KEY DETAILS:
Born November 7th. Non-founder bloodline. Dramatic, magnetic.
ADDITIONAL NOTES:
Easy target.

Meghan Simone Valdez

KEY DETAILS:
Born January 30th. Non-founder bloodline. Rule-follower, sarcastic, always prepared. Seems more future-focused than friends.
ADDITIONAL NOTES:
Uncertain if she subscribes to general Avernia superstitions, but is a Pythia subscriber.

Sabrina JoAnn Taylor

KEY DETAILS:
Born July 15th. Blackwater family outcast—born from an affair, mostly ignored by founding families. Theater major. Responsible to a fault...usually.
ADDITIONAL NOTES:
She knows of her relation to Sutton and Bellamy Dupont while he is unaware...

Foxeglove Micah James

KEY DETAILS:

Born April 20th. Taurus. Anderson kids' cousin. Uses humor as a coping mechanism.

ADDITIONAL NOTES:

Spends most of his time moping around campus, waiting like a puppy for someone to give him attention. Seems unstable. Easy target. Not currently on campus.

Aurora Lilith Primrose-Wolfe

KEY DETAILS:

Born May 30th. Gemini. Lucy's cousin. Fashion major. Dislikes liars, men, and scary buildings.

ADDITIONAL NOTES:

Friendly with all Anderson kids. Potential problem.

Justin Bauer

KEY DETAILS:

Mostly unknown despite Fury Hill upbringing and background. Spineless and controlled by higher ups.

ADDITIONAL NOTES:

House was set on fire at semester's start. Inside job, or is someone finally out to get him?

Jean-Louis Dupont

KEY DETAILS:
Born February 1st. Slimy. Suffering from some unknown illness since the death of Bellamy Dupont.

ADDITIONAL NOTES:
CEO of Grandeur Playhouse in LA. Makes kids do his dirty work. Not from the Dupont family bloodline—he married in, changed his last name, and became the patriarch.

Claire Elodie Dupont

KEY DETAILS:
Born March 9th. Stuffy, proper. Self-medicates. Founding family bloodline. Former pianist.

ADDITIONAL NOTES:
Seems to come and go from the Dupont Manor frequently. Rarely talks about her husband. Easily embarrassed. Suspicious...

Avernia College

(uh-VER-nee-uh)

Noun

1. Cursed hunting grounds for vulnerable students, unwelcome to outsiders. An elite, private arts college established ? by the Dupont, Ouellette, Westwood, Blackwater, Anderson, and Abbott families.

2. Named after Avernus, volcanic crater in Italy once believed to be entrance to the Underworld.

Lake Lerna

(lern-uh)

Noun

1. Large body of water between the White Mountains and the Primordial Forest's quarry.

2. Haunted. What goes in does not come back out...usually.

The Primordial Forest

(pry-MOR-dee-uhl)

Noun

1. Expansive wooded area surrounding Avernia College—stretches across a majority of Fury Hill and over White Mountains.

2. Some archives swear the trees have minds of their own...

The Obeliskos

(ah-buh-lisk-uhs)

Noun

1. Biggest of three campus libraries.

2. Likely haunted. No ghost sightings reported, but students avoid the thirteenth floor for some reason. .

The Lyceum

(lye-SEE-um)

Noun

1. Main academic building for Avernia students.

Lethe's

(lee-thees)

Noun

1. Bar frequented by Avernia students.

2. Those who go in can expect to forget their time spent.

Tenarus Cave

(ten-AJR-uhs)

Noun

1. Cave system etched into the White Mountains bordering campus. Accessible, supposedly, through the Apollodorus basement.

2. Sacrificial site. Steer clear.

The Apollodorus

(uh-pahl-oh-DOOR-uhs)

1. Second largest library on campus. ~~Hosts overflow archives.~~ Winding, endless basement.

2. Debauchery awaits beneath the ground floor.

~~Tartarus~~

~~The Quarry~~

~~Elysian Dorms~~

Limbs of Fury Hill

Westwood

David
|
Baron —— Cate
|
Zachary

Blackwater

William
|
Henry Elijah II —— Christine
| |
Henry Elijah III   Sabrina

Dupont

Jean
|
Claire ——————— Jean-Louis

Sutton   Bellamy   Beckett   Giselle

Ouellette

Gabriel
|
Julie

Anderson

Cronus
|
Kal ————————— Elena
|
Quincy   Noelle   Asher

Abbott

Charles
|
Angelica ————————— Zane
|
Lexington   Shelby

Lost & Found

Journal Entry #13

Something has gone wrong at tonight's instauratio. Or perhaps right, depending on who you ask. It seems the intended three were swapped—through no fault of the Director's own, of course.

God forbid they be held accountable.

Another pawn has unintentionally entered the scope of this group's vision...yet they seem to have no idea they're being watched. I wonder how much of this town curse would be null and void if people had a modicum of self-awareness.

Ah well.

Doesn't matter anymore, I suppose.

Death will do what it wants regardless.

> —found on a scrap of paper outside
> Professor Anderson's ancient civ lecture

Journal Entry #201

The air on campus is...off. Malice seems afoot, but the administration continues to pretend otherwise. Are they in on it?

Do they know things we don't?

I find that a little hard to believe given how I came to this position, but it's not unthinkable. Things have been amiss since Death's Teeth didn't get the sacrifice they wanted.

A part of me wonders how long it'll take for them to seek a replacement.

Is Incarnate really safe as long as he doesn't accept?

—found scribbled on a bookmark,
tucked between the shelves in
the Apollodorus archives

Journal Entry #4000

Quincy. Noelle. Asher.

The three Anderson descendants of the newest generation. They all share this detachment and ambivalence that must have been passed down from Cronus.

Did he care at all when he stole Manon Dupont from the arms of her late husband, or when he buried the men he called friends? Would any of his descendants care about the carnage left in their wake just by being on campus?

I can feel Death's presence lurking in their shadows. One in particular has a heavier link.

Almost as if Cronus himself is walking these grounds again.

How long will it take for the curse to manifest—and what will be left of us once it does?

—found on a torn, crimson-
stained envelope in Tartarus

Journal Entry #?

I'm not sure why I was asked to start journaling about my time at Avernia, but in the interest of preserving history, I accepted.

That was a mistake. I've seen too much...and said far too little.

This will be my last entry.

If you find this, don't trust the

—found under a rock near Lake Lerna,
water-damaged and mostly illegible

Death's Teeth Hierarchy

Center: Death

Layer 1: Incarnate, the Maiden, the Sacrifice

Layer 2: The Director

Layer 3: Elders & Founding Family Members

Layer 4: Veteran Members

Layer 5: Fledglings—Abecedarians

Layer 6: Sacrifices

Acknowledgments

I don't know what it is about the second book in a series that's such a challenge, but my struggle streak continued as I drafted *Jealous Rage*. We don't need to talk about how many months late I turned it in to my editor, nor how many drafts sit in my computer's graveyard hard drive. (Just know there were at *least* fifteen, and that was before the two major rewrites.)

Growing pains. That's what I call the problem books. Elle and Sutton were the hardest couple I've written *because* my craft was improving, and I was constantly challenging myself with them. They're both extroverts with a lot of emotional baggage they hide behind their hobbies and masks, and making them open up even to me was difficult.

However, I like to think it paid off in the end, because they have some of my absolute *favorite* moments out of every book I've written so far. I truly adored them and the outlandish cult-y stuff happening in this book, so I hope you did too.

Plus, as a former theater kid, diving into the technical and academic aspects of theater made me very happy.

None of this could have been possible, though, without my own supporting cast of characters.

As always, to my readers: I'd have no career without you, and no one to share my imaginary friends with. So thank you for being here.

To my best friend, Emily McIntire: I really hoped Sutton would dethrone Kieran for you, and I'm glad I got close. Thank you for being my soul sister a million times over.

To my PAs Jackie and Debra: Thank you for keeping my life afloat when I disappear into my writing/editing caves and for never getting truly offended when I ignore your messages. I couldn't function without you.

To my agent, Savannah: Thank you for championing me as your client and for all the advice and support you give without fail.

To Mary, Brittany, and the rest of the Sourcebooks Casablanca team: Thank you for *everything*. Seriously. You guys have made my dreams come true.

To Becca: Thank you for driving me around when I flew to California and not judging me when I left early, and for always being around to lend an ear. You talked me off multiple (metaphorical) ledges with this series, and I am forever grateful.

To my therapist: Thank you for trying to keep me sane and being my gossip doctor. Don't read these books, though, because then I won't be able to tell you my secrets anymore.

Lastly, to Lord Byron, Poe, and Arrow: I really write these books so I can afford top-tier veterinary care for you three. I hope you appreciate my efforts and reward me with long, healthy lives.

About the Author

Sav R. Miller is a *USA Today* bestselling author of adult romance with varying levels of darkness and steam.

In 2018, Sav put her lifelong love of reading and writing to use and graduated with a BA in creative writing and a minor in cultural anthropology. Nowadays, she spends her time giving morally gray characters their happily-ever-afters.

Currently, Sav lives in Kentucky with her dogs Lord Byron, Poe, and Arrow. She loves sitcoms, silence, and sardonic humor.

Website: savrmiller.com
Facebook: srmauthor
Instagram: @srmauthor
TikTok: @authorsavrmiller

MONSTERS
& MUSES

Welcome to the Monsters & Muses, a series of dark and twisted modern-day romances inspired by classic Greek myths by Sav R. Miller, *USA Today* bestselling author

PROMISES & POMEGRANATES

Kal Anderson may be cold, but he's burned with an obsessive need for Elena since he first saw her…enough to steal her away to his secret island where she can be his and his alone.

VIPERS & VIRTUOSOS

Aiden is a tortured musician who carefully guards his heart…until he meets Riley and loses it, and himself, in her hypnotic blue eyes.

OATHS & OMISSIONS

Lenny Primrose will do anything to be free of her controlling mob boss father…including fake a romance with the assassin who almost killed him.

ARROWS & APOLOGIES

Mayor Alistair Wolfe wasn't supposed to blackmail his one-night stand into working for him…or find himself falling for her more with every forbidden touch.

SOULS & SORROWS

When an ex-ballerina gets herself into a bind at an underground auction, Cash Primrose becomes so enamored that he ends up placing a bid…

LIARS & LIAISONS

Violet Artinos never would've made a move if she'd known the stranger she kissed was her ex's younger brother…or how darkly complicated things could get.